It's a Vet's Life

Cathy Woodman was a small animal vet before turning to writing fiction. She won the Harry Bowling First Novel Award in 2002 and is a member of the Romantic Novelists' Association. She is also a lecturer in Animal Management at a local college. *It's a Vet's Life* is the fourth book set in the fictional market town of Talyton St George in East Devon, where Cathy lived as a child. Cathy now lives with her husband, two children, two ponies, three exuberant Border terriers and a cat in a village near Winchester, Hampshire.

Other books by Cathy Woodman

Trust Me, I'm a Vet
Must Be Love
The Sweetest Thing

It's a Vet's Life

CATHY WOODMAN

arrow books

Published by Arrow Books 2011

4 6 8 10 9 7 5 3

First published in Great Britain in 2011 by
Arrow Books
Random House, 20 Vauxhall Bridge Road,
London SW1V 2SA

www.randomhouse.co.uk

Addresses for companies within The Random House Group Limited can be
found at: www.randomhouse.co.uk/offices.htm

The Random House Group Limited Reg. No. 954009

A CIP catalogue record for this book
is available from the British Library

ISBN 9780099551621

The Random House Group Limited supports The Forest Stewardship
Council (FSC®), the leading international forest certification organisation.
Our books carrying the FSC label are printed on FSC® certified paper. FSC is
the only forest certification scheme endorsed by the leading environmental
organisations, including Greenpeace. Our paper procurement policy can be
found at www.randomhouse.co.uk/environment

Typeset by SX Composing DTP, Rayleigh, Essex, SS6 7XF
Printed and bound by CPI Group (UK) Ltd, Croydon, CR0 4YY

To Jess, with love

Chapter One

Horses for Courses

'Maz? Maz, we're in business.' The figure of Alex, my fiancé, appears in the doorway, bright sunlight glancing past him, casting his shadow across the stone floor inside the Barn. 'Hurry,' he goes on.

'Sh,' I whisper from the sofa, as George stirs in my arms at the sound of his father's voice. 'Not so loud. He's only just gone off.' I press my lips to the top of George's head. He doesn't seem to have got the hang of napping even after twenty-one months. In fact, I reckon the gene for sleeping, if there is such a thing, has bypassed him entirely.

'But, Maz, it's on its way.' Alex lowers his voice as he moves closer.

'That's what you said before.' I smile. Alex has been on tenterhooks for at least a week. 'Are you sure this isn't another false alarm?'

'Absolutely. One hundred per cent.' Alex's fiercely blue eyes flash with impatience. His short, dark hair is flecked with grey, which he claims is a consequence of being with me, rather than his advancing years, something I enjoy teasing him about since I'm younger than him. At the moment, it's also adorned with curls of wood shavings.

We've been together for three years, through both happy and testing times, and he's still as attractive as ever, dressed today in a check shirt and snug-fitting jeans that hug the contours of his lean, yet muscular thighs. Almost every day I thank my lucky stars that I accepted my best friend Emma's request to look after her practice to give her a break. If I'd turned down that opportunity to come and work in Talyton St George, I'd probably still be working as a city vet somewhere in London, and Alex and I would never have met.

'Come on, or you'll miss it, and it isn't something you see every day,' Alex says. 'Bring George with you.'

I wake our son with the slightest touch on one cheek. He lifts his head, blinks and stares at me, frowning.

'Hiya, are you coming outside to help your daddy?'

'No,' George mumbles.

'I think you mean yes,' I say.

'No.' George's mouth curves into a dribbly smile. His hair, dark and glossy like a flat-coated retriever's, sticks up damp from his forehead, and tiny beads of sweat bubble up across the bridge of his nose.

Picking him up, I pad across the cool floor and slip into a pair of flower-power clogs which are lying where I left them, behind the front door and alongside George's toys and a rack of magazines, ranging from *Horse & Hound* and *Veterinary Times* to *Mother & Baby*. I'm not sure why we have them – we don't have much opportunity to sit down and read.

'Alex, wait for us,' I call, but he's already striding ahead and disappearing into one of the stables in the double-storey block to the left-hand side of the yard.

2

The ground floor consists of a row of loose boxes, while steps lead up to the old hayloft that's now the Talyton Manor Vets' office and surgery.

Opposite the Barn where we live, there is an assortment of vehicles parked on the gravel: four-by-fours, an ancient Bentley and a horsebox in purple livery. Beyond these is the rear of the Manor House where Alex's parents live with their dogs, and a Shetland pony which is often to be found in the drawing room. That makes it sound incredibly grand, but the place is falling down around their ears. Its windows are cracked, its roof tiles slipping and its walls crumbling. If it were an animal, the RSPCA would have been in to rescue it by now.

To the right-hand side of the yard, there are green fields, subdivided into paddocks with electric tape, where several horses are grazing, flicking their ears and swishing their tails at the flies which are out in force, strangely energised by the June heat.

I reach the stable and look over the half door. Alex stands at the head of his beautiful chestnut mare, holding on to her by a rope attached to a leather head collar with brass buckles, as she lies on rubber matting scattered with fresh shavings.

Gradually, the scent of horse and disinfectant replaces the sweet smell of baby bubblebath and fabric conditioner in my nostrils. The mare's flanks grow dark with sweat and Alex's forehead shines. George seems to be getting hotter too – and heavier. I shift him onto one hip.

'No!' George wriggles to get down, as the mare strains and groans, taking me back to a painful and not-so-distant past when the River Taly burst its banks, and I went into labour prematurely with George. I shudder even now to think of the icy black water, the ever-diminishing patch of ground on which I stood, and the waves of pain that racked my body. I remember the relief I felt when Alex turned up, emerging from the darkness to rescue me, and the panic when the baby was born all blotchy and lifeless, and I thought we'd lost him. I can also recall the angst I went through, wondering if I could ever bond with a child. I can smile about it now. I never intended to be a mother, let alone endure a water birth like that one.

'Shall we leave you to it, Alex?' I don't want George's toddler noises to upset Liberty and stop her in the middle of giving birth. I have every sympathy with what she's going through.

'Stay,' Alex says. 'You and George missed the last one.'

This is Liberty's second foal – Hero was born last May. Alex's mare was a promising showjumper until an attack of colic and the ensuing emergency surgery to save her life brought her career to a premature end, along with Alex's ambition to be selected for the British Showjumping team.

'I hope you're not planning on brainwashing our son into following in our footsteps. Aren't three vets in the family enough?' I say lightly.

'I'm thinking of the future of the practice.' Alex grins.

'Don't you mean practices?' Alex runs Talyton Manor Vets, a farm animal practice with a few small animal clients, alongside his father, while Emma and I are partners in Otter House. 'Anyway, I thought Seb was being groomed to take over from you when you're too old and decrepit to do the James Herriot thing any more.'

4

'It's a little more sophisticated than that nowadays.'

'You still spend a lot of time with your arm inside a cow,' I point out. 'Your offspring might not appreciate the outdoor lifestyle.' Alex has two children, other than George, from a previous relationship, a failed marriage. Seb is only five. Lucie is almost nine, and I would guess that of the three, she is the most likely to follow in her father's footsteps. 'How's she doing?'

'Liberty's doing fine. Aren't you, my girl?' Alex squats on his haunches beside her, his eyes on her tail end where the water bag appears and bursts, spilling fluid across the floor, before Liberty strains once, twice and three times more. 'Ah, I can see feet. It's on its way.'

'Is everything all right?' I ask, anxious for both the mare and foal, and Alex, when nothing more happens for a while.

'She's resting.' Alex checks his watch. 'It's quite normal.' However, he moves in closer, examining the foal's feet which are clearly visible now. I see Alex's body tense as the mare strains again.

Something is wrong.

Alex swears out loud, making George jump and grab a handful of my blouse to steady himself.

My mind races ahead. It's too late to get Liberty to the nearest equine hospital with surgical facilities, and there's no way we can use the operating theatres in either practice because they're designed for small animals, not horses. The biggest patient we've had in for surgery is a Great Dane and we had to extend the table with a trolley for him.

'It's coming backwards.' Alex's voice is flat and matter-of-fact.

'Shall I run and fetch your father?'

5

'It's too late for that. Hang on to her for me.'

I wonder what to do with George and decide to hold on to him. If there isn't time to fetch help, there isn't time to go and grab George's buggy. I open the stable door and take hold of Liberty's head collar, hanging on while George tries to lean down and touch her ears, and Alex tips most of a bottle of obstetrical lubricant over his hands and tries to work out how to deliver the foal.

'I wish it was coming any way other than this. It needs to come out right now.'

I know what he means. I can vaguely recall the notes I wrote at vet school about managing a foaling. When the foal is coming out backwards, hind feet first, the umbilical cord gets squeezed against the mare's pelvis, cutting the oxygen supply and triggering the foal's first breath. If it breathes with its head inside its mother's womb, it will take in fluid and drown.

'Is it the right way up?' I ask.

'It is,' Alex confirms.

That's a start, I think, as Alex takes hold of the foal's back legs and hauls at it with all his weight behind him, his feet pressed against Liberty's buttocks, the muscles in his arms taut and corded, his skin glistening with sweat and effort. It looks brutal, but there is no other way.

'Push, Libs,' he growls through gritted teeth. 'You've got to bloody well help me out here. Can you give me a time check, Maz? In five minutes. If it hasn't budged by then, I'm going to have to . . .' His voice trails off as he takes another pull, but I know what he was going to say, that he'll have to cut it up.

I feel sick at the thought of the foal coming out in

6

pieces, but if that's the only way to save the mare . . . I glance around at the cobwebs and dust in the rafters above, wondering if we could drag the mobile anaesthetic machine in and attempt a Caesarean, but the potential for infection is just too high. Mare or foal? It's Hobson's choice and I'm glad I'm not the one having to make it.

It seems however that it's too late to be thinking about making choices. I have no need to hang on to Liberty any longer. She's giving up, her eyes dull, her body trembling as she rests her head on the floor. I check my watch, aware of my heart beating in my ears as Liberty strains weakly yet again and Alex curses, and the time ticks by.

'Alex, we're on the countdown now, four minutes gone. I'll go and get the kit,' I say, afraid that if he doesn't make a decision soon, he'll lose both of them.

'One last go,' Alex mutters. He slaps Liberty on the flank. 'Come on, girl. You can do it.' He takes another grip on the foal's hind legs, Liberty gives one last heave and the foal slides out along with a gush of bloody fluid. With a grunt of relief, Alex drags the foal right out so it's lying on the mat alongside the mare. It's wet and shiny, and still. And the mare is struggling to get up, so I move back worried about George's safety with three-quarters of a tonne of distressed horse throwing herself around.

George, now quiet, seems struck by the significance of this moment. He watches Liberty stand up, steady herself then look for her baby. She sniffs its back as Alex clears the membranes from the foal's nostrils. He grabs it around the hindquarters and lifts it with superhuman strength, so its head hangs down and fluid drips out of its nose and mouth. He lies it back down again and twists its ear, trying to get it to take its first breath.

'Please . . .' I murmur, remembering to breathe myself. 'Please be okay.'

Alex rubs and bangs the foal's chest, but nothing happens. While Liberty licks at the foal's dark, wet coat, Alex stretches its head and neck out straight, closes its mouth and one nostril with his hands, then bends down and blows into the other. I watch the foal's chest rise and fall, rise and fall again, but it's no good if it isn't breathing for itself.

'Alex.' I move around and touch his shoulder. 'Alex, I think it's time to stop.' A lump like a tumour forms in my throat at the thought of losing something we've looked forward to for so long, eleven months to be precise. 'It's been too long. It isn't going to make it . . .' I tug roughly at his shirt. 'Alex, you can't perform miracles.'

He mutters something. I can't hear the words exactly, but I think he's suggesting that he can.

Suddenly, the foal coughs. Alex pauses and, keeping watch on its chest, puts his cheek close to the foal's muzzle. He glances up and a small smile crosses his face. The foal coughs once more, then lifts its head and gazes shakily around the loose box.

Tears of relief prick my eyes. I know my Alex. He can do almost anything he puts his mind to. I should have had more faith.

Immediately, Alex turns his attention to the mare, checking the pulse at her cheek and the colour of her gums. He gives her neck a quick rub, and moves around to look under her tail. Apparently satisfied that there's no sign of bleeding that might indicate a tear from the rather traumatic birth, he returns to the foal.

'That was a bit of luck,' he says, glancing up at me. 'When they're coming backwards, I usually give them a fifty-fifty chance, if that. I thought she'd had it.'

'She?'

Alex lifts one back leg and nods.

'Yep. It's a lovely filly this time. Beautiful.'

She's dark brown, almost black, with bright, intelligent eyes with a white star between them. I'm not sure how Alex can possibly judge her qualities so soon, although I recall he was the same with George, very much the proud father.

'What now?' I ask.

'We'll let mum and baby get to know each other. The foal should get up and start sucking within the next half-hour or so. We'll leave the cord to break naturally, and then I'll treat the navel.' Alex hesitates as he stands up, rubbing his back. 'I'm sorry, Maz, I'm talking to you like you're one of my clients.'

'I don't mind. You've always done that.' Chuckling, I step towards him and kiss his cheek. 'I love it when you come over all masterful . . .' Liberty is reaching round to lick at her foal's coat. 'What are you going to call her?'

'Any ideas?' says Alex.

'I don't know – she's your baby. You decide.' At least it isn't like naming a child. An animal isn't going to have to worry about being teased at school, or being classed as posh or chavvy because of their name.

'I thought Scheherazade, after the Persian queen.' Alex reaches out one rather sticky and bloodstained hand as if to take mine.

'That's a bit of a mouthful, isn't it? Just imagine standing in the field and calling for her. It's a pretty name though . . .'

'It will give the commentators something to think about.'

'When you're jumping her, you mean? Alex, you're such a pushy dad.' It won't be for ages yet. He won't start breaking her in to ride until she's three or four.

'I'll call her Shezza for short.'

'Oh, your mother won't like that. She'll say it lowers the tone. Hey, go and get washed first,' I say, pushing him away. 'You're filthy.'

'You didn't used to mind,' he says, grinning.

'It's George,' I say lightly. 'I don't want him getting any nasty bugs, do I? I've got to go to work tomorrow and the nursery won't have him if he's unwell.'

Liberty stands up, leaving the afterbirth behind her. Her foal lifts her head, stretches her front legs out and tries to get up, lunging forwards and nosediving back onto the mat. On her second attempt, she makes it and stands with her legs splayed out, wobbling for a moment before taking her first tentative steps straight for her mother, where she nuzzles at her flank. George chuckles at the sight of the foal falling over. He has a wicked sense of humour.

'Why couldn't you have stood on your own two feet that quickly?' I say to George. He was a lazy baby.

'He doesn't have to run away from predators,' Alex observes. 'He's got two parents to watch out for him.'

The foal's head disappears up between Liberty's hind legs where she latches on to a teat and starts sucking noisily.

'She sounds like your father drinking his tea out of the saucer, Alex.'

'At least we're not going to have to worry about feeding her. She's just like George in that way. I'll check the afterbirth, and then we'll leave them in

10

peace. I'll pop out again in an hour, or so.'

Alex picks up the afterbirth, the red-grey membrane left of the placenta which supported the foal while it developed in the womb, and lays it out on the floor. It reminds me of one of George's sleepsuits, a little larger and cut off at the waist, with the feet still on.

'It's all here,' Alex says, meaning there's none left inside the mare to make her sick. 'I'm a bit paranoid – I might have seen lots of foalings, but it's different when it's your own.'

I let Alex slide his arm around my shoulders and kiss my cheek.

'I suppose I'd better tell the parents. Mother's been on edge as usual.'

Alex has always said he thought his mother would have loved him more if he'd been born a horse, I muse, as he looks at me expectantly, and I realise he's hoping I'll go, so he can stay with the new mum and foal. He doesn't really want to leave them just yet.

'All right, I'll go,' I sigh.

'You couldn't fetch me a clinical waste bag on the way back, could you?'

'You'd better give me a clue where to find them,' I say, amused. Neither Alex nor his father is exactly tidy.

'They should be in the usual place. There's a box on the shelf beside the radiator.'

Taking George with me, I head outside, up the steps and into the surgery. I don't need a key – the door isn't locked. I hesitate just inside, gazing around the room they call the office which leads on through another door into the consulting room/operating theatre, and a box room which contains a couple of old cages and an awful lot of junk. A fly buzzes frantically from behind the blinds. I open the window and let it out, along with the smell of cow and mothballs. I can find the radiator and the shelf beside it, but there's no box of orange tiger bags. I survey the rest of the chaos.

'It's time your daddy and grandfather had a good clear-out,' I tell George. He wants to get down, but I don't dare let him. Old Fox-Gifford's shotgun is out on the desk, lying across Alex's laptop. The gun's supposed to be locked up in the cabinet in the house when he isn't using it, but he prefers to keep it to hand in case he comes across some poor unsuspecting squirrel or magpie, both of which he classes as vermin.

Giving up on ever finding a bag, I take George across the yard to the back door of the Manor, or what Sophia calls the tradesmen's entrance, from which a pack of dogs come chasing out, whining and barking, as if they've never set eyes on us before. When I first met this motley assortment of Labradors and spaniels, my legs turned to jelly, but I know them better now. They are literally all bark and no bite.

'Oh, don't be silly,' I growl at them, in an imitation of my father-in-law to be, and they calm down, milling around my legs and sniffing at George's feet. I glance down to where one of the spaniels is cocking its leg over a pot of scraggy geraniums. Something white, a letter, among the red blooms catches my eye. I retrieve it very carefully. It's unopened, marked as being from the Royal College of Veterinary Surgeons and addressed to Alex's father.

'The postman must have dropped it,' I tell George as I lower him to the ground so he can walk. Together, we make our way through the rear lobby, stepping over cast-off shoes and green wellies. It's cooler inside the house, almost cold, until you reach the kitchen where a wall of hot air hits you.

12

Alex's mother, dressed in an ice-blue blouse, grubby cream breeches and flat, lace-up shoes, is taking a kettle off the Aga that makes the room snug in winter and far too warm in summer.

There was a time when I couldn't imagine having any kind of relationship with Sophia, but now she's stopped calling me Madge and she looks after George for us one or two days a week, and because we have the Fox-Gifford men in common, we are on warmer terms. I can't say we're friends – we're very different, coming from contrasting backgrounds – but we are both self-reliant and share a love of animals, foxes excepted. Sophia hates foxes with a passion.

I hesitate beside the huge oak table. There are several dog bowls, filled with tripe and biscuits, lined up on it. The stench makes me gag.

'Hi, Sophia.'

She turns to face me, tall and slim, her face lined and her grey hair stiff with hairspray.

'Hello, Maz, and darling George. I'm just putting the sugar beet to soak for the horses.' She tips the water from the kettle into a bucket on the floor. There's a pan of linseed bubbling over on top of the Aga too. She doesn't believe in feeding prepared foods. 'Can't stop. Everything wants feeding.'

'That's a shame. I thought you might like to come and see the new arrival.'

'Liberty's had her foal.' Sophia's tired face lights up. 'Oh, why didn't you say?'

'We had a bit of a crisis – it was presenting backwards. Alex had to pull it out in rather a hurry.' I watch her wipe her hands on a raggedy tea towel and fling it down on the table where it lands in the tripe. She leaves it where it falls, and grabs an old coat from the pegs on the way out through the lobby, as Old Fox-Gifford comes limping along with his stick from the corridor beyond. He's wearing a striped shirt with cord trousers that have faded to a peculiar shade of red, similar in colour to a huntsman's jacket.

'What's this? What's going on here?' he says gruffly.

'Maz says Liberty's had her foal,' Sophia says.

'Good. Good. But why didn't anyone come and tell me?' Old Fox-Gifford dashes his stick against the floor.

'Maz has just explained there was an emergency.'

'All the more reason to have called me,' Old Fox-Gifford mutters, his expression one of annoyance. 'I could have delivered it.'

'There was no time,' I explain again, but Old Fox-Gifford isn't listening, as usual.

'Foalings are my forte,' he goes on, his complexion growing darker and ruddier, his sideburns bristling. 'Alexander knows that. What was he thinking of?'

Emergency or not, I doubt Alex would have called on his father for assistance this time. When Liberty's first foal, Hero, was born last year, Old Fox-Gifford couldn't help interfering and telling Alex he was getting it all wrong.

'It wasn't a personal slight,' Sophia says, somewhat snappily. I've noticed recently how she humours Old Fox-Gifford's opinions far less than she used to. 'Alexander dealt with it.'

'Oh, I found this in the flowerpot outside,' I say, remembering the letter in my hand. 'I don't know how it got there.' 'It's something from the Royal College. What are they hauling you up for?' I add, referring to the fact that this august institution plays a role in policing the veterinary profession.

'Nothing.' Old Fox-Gifford snatches it from me and

14

stuffs it into his trouser pocket without looking at it. 'I'm in no trouble whatsoever, never have been and never will be.'

'Maz isn't implying that you are,' Sophia says, defending me.

'I was joking,' I say, surprised by his reaction.

'Not funny,' he snorts.

Hal, the old black Lab, the one I operated on a couple of summers ago when Old Fox-Gifford shot him in the leg by mistake while cleaning his gun, sticks his nose into my crotch.

'Go away,' I tell him. He's blind and completely deaf, perfectly good excuses for not taking any notice of me, I suppose. 'Go on. Push off.'

'Leave the poor old dog alone.' Old Fox-Gifford smiles as he goes on, 'It's one of the few pleasures he has left,' but he prods him with the end of his stick anyway, and Hal limps away, lame on all four legs now. In fact, I can't believe how he's gone on this long. Like Old Fox-Gifford who's in his seventies, he's pretty well indestructible.

Back outside, we stand admiring the new arrival and it reminds me how we all admired George in very much the same way. George wants to run off around the yard, but I'm nervous to let him go with all those dogs wandering about, and he doesn't want to stand around while we talk horses.

'Let me take George,' Sophia says, holding out her hand. 'Come to Humpy.' The children call her Humpy. I'd prefer George to call her Granny to save him from future embarrassment, but she refuses to countenance it. 'Here, my preciousss . . .'

George takes her hand willingly and accompanies her around the yard, where he shows her the wheels on

Alex's car, patting them, and returning with streaky, black cheeks. I am grateful to Sophia though. Without her, I wouldn't be able to work as many hours as I do. My mother lives too far away to do any babysitting. She has been to visit a couple of times, but her home, her life, is in London, not here. I too used to consider myself a Londoner – I grew up on a council estate there, a world away from Talyton St George.

We did have a nanny – she lasted all of two weeks. She seemed perfect, but Sophia expressed disapproval from the start. According to her, I should have chosen a plain girl so as not to lead Alex into temptation; utterly ridiculous, I hasten to add, and not the reason she left. It was more about the Barn being too small for us all, and the nanny being more like Peyton Flanders in *The Hand that Rocks the Cradle* than the magical Nanny McPhee. I had assumed that being a qualified nanny meant she knew more about looking after a baby than I did, but I was wrong.

'I'd better get on,' Sophia says, as the horse in the stable next to Liberty's starts banging against the door.

'The dogs want their grub too,' Old Fox-Gifford observes.

Smiling at the way that the animals take precedence in the Fox-Gifford household, I reach for George's hot, sticky hand, ready to take him indoors, just as a mobile rings. Old Fox-Gifford struggles, with his stick hooked over one arm, to get at the phone in his pocket. It could be one of the originals, a black brick of a thing that he holds to his ear.

'Fire away. I say, fire away.' He stares at the phone and stabs randomly at a few buttons. 'What's wrong with this bloody thing?'

'I've told you, you need a new one,' Alex says, and

I can only look on, amused at the contrast between the way Alex and his father run their practice, compared with me and Emma, as Old Fox-Gifford barks rather abruptly at the person at the other end of his mobile.

'What's up?' Alex asks when Old Fox-Gifford peers at the mobile to work out how to switch it off. I'm sure he needs glasses, but he'd never wear them.

'It's Jim over at Sandy Down.'

'What does he want this time?' Sophia raises one thin eyebrow. 'You were there only this morning, weren't you?'

'I checked on a couple of calves. He wants me to have another look so he can sleep soundly in his bed tonight.' Old Fox-Gifford smiles. 'I told him to have a warm bath and a whisky – that'll help him sleep. Stupid bugger.'

Sophia glares at him. Not in front of George.

'I'll go,' Alex says.

'What for?' Old Fox-Gifford growls back, his tone immediately defensive.

'To save you going out again.' Alex glances down at his father's feet. I hadn't noticed before, but he's wearing slippers, grey moccasins. 'You look as if you've signed off for the day,' he adds, making light of it.

'I dashed out when your mother told me about the foal. No, Alexander. I'll go.'

'Aren't you going to change out of your slippers first?'

'I keep a pair of boots in the car.'

'We can go together,' Alex suggests.

'I can manage. I'm not –' he opens his mouth to utter a curse, but apparently aware of Sophia's expression, thinks better of it – 'dead yet.'

17

'I wasn't—' Alex begins, but Old Fox-Gifford cuts him off.

'In my day, I didn't have a regular day orf each week to be with my family.'

'Indeed. You were never here when Alexander was a baby,' Sophia says, but he chooses to ignore her.

'You can't do without me, Alexander, so I'll thank you to stop patronising me and let me get on with my work. Jim's my client. He's asked for me, so it won't be much good you turning up there instead, will it?' With that, Old Fox-Gifford turns and shuffles off to his dented old Range Rover, climbs in still in his slippers, turns the engine, then with a roar and scrunch of gravel, reverses out onto the drive at speed. He accelerates forwards, leaving behind a trail of oily smoke.

Later, when George is upstairs asleep in his cot in the nursery, Alex and I are sitting together on the sofa. The old ginger tabby lying perched on the arm of the sofa at my feet, stretches out one paw and digs his claws into the leather. I give him a half-hearted 'look', but he takes no notice. It's too late to salvage the remains of the sofa anyway, and I suppose I should offer to buy a replacement – Ginge is my cat, the furniture belongs to Alex.

'Alex, tell me, why did you offer to go out for your father? It's your weekend off. Time for us.' I reach out and stroke his knee. 'I'm not nagging, I'm worried about you. You'll run yourself ragged.'

'Maz, please, don't fuss.' Alex massages the nape of my neck, undoing the knots of tension that have twisted and tightened there during the past week. 'You know what it's like.' He smiles ruefully. 'It's a vet's life.'

'I don't know what it's like though. We run our practices in different ways. We have support staff. We have another vet, for goodness' sake.'

'But that's expensive, as you've said. And you lose a certain amount of control.'

'It isn't about control, Alex. It's about teamwork. At Otter House, we're a team.' A great team, I think, my chest tightening with affection and pride.

'Clients choose Talyton Manor because they know they'll get the personal touch. They can be sure they'll see either me or my father.'

'How can you function though, if you're permanently knackered because you're always on call?'

'I keep you happy though?' Alex whispers, letting his arm slide around my shoulders and holding me tight.

'Yes, you do . . .' I turn and kiss him on the lips. He makes me very happy, but we're like tightrope walkers, constantly straining to keep our balance. Keeping home and work commitments in equilibrium was difficult enough, but having accidentally thrown a child into the mix, Alex and I have made life more complicated than it might have been.

'It'll get easier, Maz.' Alex gives me an extra squeeze and I find myself melting into his embrace. 'You know, you'll make someone a fantastic wife someday.' His voice is warm and teasing. 'If you ever get around to getting married,' he adds with more edge.

'Is that a hint that I should be getting on with the arrangements?'

'That would be good.'

'We haven't set a date.'

Alex proposed after George was born, after the floods, and we decided to get married as soon as possible. It didn't happen though – life took over. Alex was working all hours, I was tied up with George and returning to work, and then there was the fiasco with the nanny, and – there's no excuse really – we just didn't get round to it. 'What about next summer?' I go on, thinking that that will give me plenty of time to organise a wedding.

'I reckon we should get married at Christmas,' Alex says.

'This Christmas?' I glance at the ring on my finger. It's antique gold set with a sapphire and two diamonds. Alex bought it for me when we had a couple of days in London, visiting my mother with George.

'Why not?'

'Because it's only, what, six months away?' I pause. 'It isn't the best time, is it? Most people – like our guests – are pretty busy in the run-up to Christmas.'

'Well, it's no use waiting for a good time because there never will be one. We're always busy.' Alex nuzzles my hair. 'Maz, I love you . . .'

'Love you too . . .' I murmur, my heart lurching with a yearning desire. We don't tell each other we love each other anywhere nearly enough. 'How about next spring?'

'It's the lambing season, not good for me,' Alex points out. 'And any time in the summer, you're busy.'

He's right. What with people wanting last-minute vaccinations before they put their pets into boarding kennels so they can go away and the extra appointments taken up by holidaymakers travelling with their animals, summer is the busiest time of the year for Otter House.

'So, December it is,' Alex says. 'How about the third

Saturday of the month? I've checked the date in the diary. It would mean we could have Christmas with the three children and go on honeymoon after that. Any more objections?'

'It'll be pretty cold . . .' I say lightly, because I cannot believe that we've set a date at last. I didn't think, until just before Alex proposed, that I was the marrying kind, but my pulse thrills at the idea of being Mrs Fox-Gifford . . .

'You can borrow one of Mother's fur coats.' Alex is joking. He knows I'd never wear natural fur, on principle. 'Go on, Maz. It would make it extra special.'

'Christmassy, you mean,' I say, smiling.

'Well, yes. We can have candles, holly, carols . . . snow.'

'Snow?' I give Alex a nudge in the ribs. 'Does it ever snow in Talyton?'

'Talyton isn't exactly renowned for its white Christmases. In fact, I can't remember a single one.' Alex grins ruefully, pulling me so close I can hardly breathe. 'So, Maz, I'm sorry if it feels as if I'm neglecting you and George, and with Father not being as young and fit as he was, I can't do much about my working hours, but one thing I promise you –' he presses his lips to mine – 'we'll be married by Christmas.'

Chapter Two

Before George

BG, Before George, everything was so . . . orderly. As it is, I feel as if I'm always rushing about like a headless chicken. Fastening my tunic, one of those fun ones with cartoon animals printed on a lilac background, I abandon a half-finished mug of black coffee in the staffroom at Otter House, and head for the consulting room where I switch the computer on and load the waiting list. I was hoping – I glance up at the poster of a flea, and correct myself – itching to catch Emma to tell her my news, but it'll have to wait. She hasn't turned up yet.

According to Frances, our receptionist, she's stuck in traffic which has to be a euphemism meaning she's overslept. There isn't any traffic in Talyton at this time on a Monday morning, unless it's the school holidays when there can be queues of cars and coaches carrying holidaymakers to the coast at any time of day, causing gridlock through the narrow one-way streets.

I notice that I'm still wearing my engagement ring. I slip it off and slide it onto my necklace, a discreet gold chain that I bought for the purpose. Knowing how good I am at losing stethoscopes, I worry about something as small as the ring.

I call the first client of the day in from Reception to join me. It's Clive, who runs the Talymill Inn down by the river with his wife Edie. He's in his late fifties, but is looking older. He places a plastic box on the rubber-topped table, as if it's a box of eggs, opens the front and calls for the cat inside.

'Cassandra, out you come. Cassandra . . . Cassie, love . . .' His voice, that still bears a hint of an East London accent, rises unnaturally high, but no amount of sweet-talking will persuade Cassie to venture out. Clive picks up the carrier and gently tips it to slide the cat out, but she remains resolutely lodged inside. He tries another tack, taking a small tub of cat treats out of his pocket and shaking it, but there's no response. Cassie isn't stupid.

'That's the difference between dogs and cats,' I observe. 'You can tell a dog what to do, but you have to ask a cat.' Clive has always had dogs before: ex-police dog, Robbie, and a rescue called Petra whom Alex and I had to put down a couple of summers ago when she turned on Edie for no obvious reason. 'Shall I get her out for you?' I continue, amused, but Clive is dismantling the carrier.

He lifts the upper section off, exposing the cat who sits on a purple cushion, cowed and wary. As Clive's big hands reach down to make a grab for her, she takes a leap to the edge of the table, but it's too late. Clive sweeps her up and hugs her to his chest.

'That's enough,' he chides.

Client and pet are a mismatched pair: a burly ex-policeman with a friendly smile and a twinkle in his eye, and a fluffy blue and cream Persian cat with a rather cross expression. Clive's scalp is taut and smooth, and his paunch is swollen, straining the buttons on his black shirt. Cassie, who has more than enough hair for both of them, sports a diamanté collar, and looks as if she's been groomed to within an inch of her life.

'What brings you here? I haven't seen you around for a while.'

'Missed me, have you, Maz?' Clive smiles, hanging on to Cassie as she struggles to leap from his grasp. 'You could have come and found me. You know where I am.'

It's light-hearted banter. I've known him for three years now, since I operated on Robbie, and I'm a soon-to-be-married woman and he pretends to be the put-upon husband, but he isn't. He'd do anything for Edie.

'How's Edie?' I ask. 'I thought she might have come along too.'

'Oh, she had a heavy night last night. Busy, behind the bar, I mean.'

'Well, it's good to hear you're still so popular,' I say, filling the rather awkward silence as Clive appears to be deciding whether or not to unburden himself. I like Clive, and have a lot of respect for him and Edie the way they've worked on restoring the Talymill Inn, but I'm a vet, not an agony aunt.

'To be honest, we're too busy,' Clive says. 'Sometimes, I feel like we're victims of our own success. We were supposed to be retiring down here to lead a quieter life, yet it hasn't quite worked out that way. We're working harder than ever, and I'm beginning to think about giving it up.' I raise one eyebrow in question. 'You know what it's like,' he goes on. 'You can't get the staff. Or you can, but they aren't up to the job. What about you and Emma?'

'We're not taking on new clients at the moment. Our assistant starts today, but it'll be a little while until he's up to speed. He's a graduate straight out of vet school. I hope he's going to be happy here.'

'You've made quite a few changes since I was last here.'

'We had to have the whole place redecorated after the flood.' It was chaos, I think, smiling at the memory of how we coped, tripping over each other, seeing our patients in an old mobile home in the car park while the work was done. In the process, we chose a pale lilac and white theme instead of the blue Emma used to favour.

'I was expecting to see Cassie before now,' I say, putting it tactfully in case Clive has taken her to a different vet to be spayed. I can't have seen her for over a year.

'Oh, we haven't had her done yet. Edie doesn't like her going outside. She's afraid she'll wander off and get run over on the main road, so we've had a bit of the garden fenced off to make a run. She can't get out, but we've had the odd tom get in.' Clive chuckles. 'The last one came in a couple of days ago. That's why I'm here. Edie's worried about Cassie's eye. There was a bit of a fight, and we thought she might have scratched it.' Clive thrusts the cat in front of my face. 'Can you see it?'

I can see a pair of big orange eyes, one of them looking a little teary.

'The left one,' I say.

'Edie thought the right.'

'It looks like the left to me. Let's have her down on the table.'

25

Clive lowers her.

'Stay,' he says. Unfortunately, Clive doesn't understand 'cat', and the cat doesn't understand 'dog'. He lets go and Cassie flies off, landing with a soft thud on the worktop and padding across the keyboard, sending the waiting list on the monitor into oblivion.

'Sorry about that.' Clive lifts her back onto the table.

'It's all right. I can get it back.' I move over and click the mouse to call up Cassie's records. 'Hang on this time, Clive.' Briefly, I wonder about calling one of the nurses in to help, but they're busy in Kennels, caring for the inpatients, and Cassie isn't a 'care' cat, as in one to watch out for. I think Clive can manage her – if only he stops treating her like a small dog.

I examine both of Cassie's eyes, and add a drop of orange dye into each one to check for scratches.

'She's fine,' I pronounce as we stand in the dark, in the glow of the UV lamp. 'There's no sign of a scratch.' I switch the light back on. 'Is there anything else?'

'Edie wanted her checked over,' Clive says. 'She's put on a bit of weight.'

'You know, you really should have her spayed if you're not intending to breed from her. If you leave it to chance, you'll end up with hundreds of kittens, and there are more than enough needing homes without adding to the feline population.' I think back to Gloria Brambles and the Sanctuary the first year I was here, how she collected all the waifs and strays, including my cat. I acquired Ginge after the fire in which Gloria succumbed and Alex almost lost his life, going in after me as I tried – and failed – to save her.

'I don't know how many times I've told Edie that, but will she take any notice?'

I pick up my stethoscope – actually, it's Emma's, but

26

I've mislaid mine again – and have a listen to Cassie's chest before I feel along her belly with my fingertips, checking for any abnormalities. There are some: three marble-sized objects floating about inside her.

'Is there a problem?' Clive asks, reading my expression.

'She isn't putting on weight.' I kiss Cassie on the top of her head and a few loose strands of fluff tickle at my nose. 'She's pregnant.'

'I told Edie that's what it was. She'll be over the moon. She's always worrying about the cat.' Clive utters a self-mocking sigh. 'I wish she'd worry about me.'

He doesn't mean it, I think. He and Edie always seem so close, and I wonder if Alex and I will be the same after however many years of marriage. I'd like to think so.

'How pregnant is she? I mean, how many are there? How long until she pops them out, and what should we look for when she's ready?'

'One at a time, Clive,' I say, amused. I can tell he's looking forward to the arrival of Cassie's kittens at least as much as he claims Edie to be. It's quite touching. They haven't got any children. Clive confided once that it wasn't because they didn't want any. It never happened, something he regrets deeply.

I didn't understand before, but now I've got George . . . well, he's taught me a lot, about happiness and what life's really about.

'I can't tell you exactly how many kittens there are. I can feel three, but there may be more. I reckon she's about three to four weeks gone, so she'll give birth in five to six weeks' time.'

'Not long to prepare the nursery then,' Clive

remarks drily. 'If anything goes wrong, we'll be straight here.'

'Call first though. Not that you'll have any problems,' I add. Clive and Edie had more than enough trouble with their dogs. Cassie has to be third time lucky. 'In you go.' I direct her back into her carrier, into which she hastily slinks. 'Who's the dad? Do you know?'

'Edie will know. She's had the water pistol out ready for any tom she disapproves of.'

'Remember to call me if you need to,' I say, as Clive picks up the carrier. I don't know why I'm being so insistent on this when I'm so sure Cassie will be fine. It's odd. Call it a gut feeling, but something about her doesn't seem quite right. Is she a fraction thinner than she should be? Is there something about the look in her eyes? I'm not sure. I can't put my finger on it.

'Thanks, Maz,' Clive says. 'What do I owe you?'

'Oh, nothing today.' It didn't take me long, ten minutes max. Clive isn't having it though, and eventually we agree a fee to cover the eye exam. Clive walks up to Frances at Reception to settle up, at the same time as our new vet, in a striped shirt and cream chinos, comes elbowing his way through the double doors, his arms wrapped around a glass vivarium.

Will is moving into the flat at the top of Otter House. He starts work tomorrow, an event I'm looking forward to with some trepidation. I can't help being apprehensive, considering what happened with our locum a couple of summers ago, but Will has great references from his tutor at vet school, and the principals of the practices where he's gained his hands-on experience so far. He's personable and polite, a bit geeky, maybe. He reminds me of Prince Harry, but with specs, tall, freckled and sandy-haired. I hope he'll fit in.

He stops at Reception, resting the vivarium on the desk in front of our receptionist. Frances takes one look at the tank and screams, at which Will utters a polite apology.

'A scorpion?' Frances exclaims, backing away until she's pressed against the filing cabinet. 'Don't you have to have a licence to keep that?'

'It depends on the species,' Will says, his brow furrowed with concern. 'It won't hurt you.'

'That scorpion is more frightened of you in that top, than you are of him,' I say, joining them. Frances, who is in her sixties, is wearing one of her jazzy tunics that might have come from the 1960s. She's always refused to wear a uniform.

'Of course not, I'm not scared,' she says. 'It's just that it's making the place untidy.'

I smile to myself. Will's going to have to work hard to regain Frances's respect. Planting a scorpion on her desk, her territory, and half scaring her to death is not the best way to get into the receptionist's good books on your first day in a new job.

'At least we know Will likes animals,' I say, when he's picked up the vivarium and carried it off through the door into the corridor on his way to the flat.

'Those creatures are not animals. They're insects,' Frances says, revealing a trademark smear of lippy across her teeth. From where I'm standing, the auburn wig is doing a pretty good impression of natural hair. I decide against arguing the point. If Emma fails to turn up, I'll be seeing the appointments and operating. I can't afford to waste any time.

'Emma's here,' Frances observes, as a silver Saab turns up and takes over Clive's parking space.

'Hello, stranger,' I say, as Emma walks in, looking cool and summery in a red cotton skirt and white top. Her brunette hair is tied back in a sleek chignon.

According to one of the professors at vet school where we met, she is Catherine Zeta-Jones to my Gwyneth Paltrow. In spite of all she's been through in the past few years, she gives the impression of being happy and in control of her life, whereas I feel decidedly mumsy and out of kilter. I made an effort this morning, but didn't get around to straightening my hair that's developed an annoying kink in it since I had George.

'I'm not that late,' Emma smiles. 'I overslept.'

'What came in?' I ask, knowing Emma was on call with Izzy last night.

'Nothing in the end. I fielded a couple of phone calls – one was a wrong number. It turned out they wanted Talyton Manor Vets, not us. It was something about a cow, and I told them we don't do animals larger than a Great Dane, unless it's the direst of emergencies.'

'That must be the call that woke me up,' I say ruefully. 'They rang Alex after they'd called you.' I hesitate. 'You said there were two calls. What was the other one?'

'One of ours. Aurora was worried that Saba was going to make herself bald from scratching, and it was keeping her and her boyfriend awake. It kept me awake too,' Emma says ruefully. 'Which is probably why I overslept this morning.'

'I thought we'd got our clients better trained.'

'Oh, I couldn't be too cross with her. She's a good customer. Has she been in? I told her she could turn up first thing and we'd fit her in.'

'She hasn't been in yet,' I say, glancing around the waiting room, even though I know there's no one here.

'I expect she's having a lie-in,' Emma sighs. 'She doesn't open up until eleven.' Emma's referring to Aurora's shop, a fashion boutique that's a little avant-garde for Talyton St George. Many might assume that there isn't much demand for luxury lingerie here before eleven o'clock in the morning, some that there is no demand at all, but, having found a pair of Aurora's skimpy briefs inside a dog before, I know differently. Behind the facade of scones, jam and clotted cream, and tight-knit community, Talyton St George is a hotbed of lust and desire. At least, that's what the local gossips would like everyone to believe. They thrive on intrigue, both real and imaginary.

'It's all right for some not having to get up in the morning,' Emma goes on. 'I'm shattered.' She picks up the post from the desk in Reception and tidies the stand of collars, leads and toys. 'What did Clive want?'

'Oh, he brought Cassie for a check-up. She's . . . pregnant.' As soon as I utter the word, I want to take it back. I look away, fiddling with the end of Emma's stethoscope which is still around my neck. I guess I'm always going to find it awkward talking about pregnancy and babies of any kind, with Emma.

'That's nice.' Emma hesitates, raising one eyebrow. 'I'm assuming it was planned.'

'I don't think so. She had a one-night stand with some feral tomcat. Allegedly.'

'Did you have a good weekend off?' Emma says, changing the subject.

It's my turn to hesitate now. 'The foal arrived safely, thanks to Alex. It was a close-run thing.'

'And?'

'Nothing much.'

'There's something else. I can tell from the way you're smirking, Maz.'

'Actually, I'm really excited,' I admit. 'Alex and I have set the date for the wedding.'

'Oh, that's fantastic news.' Emma throws her arms around me and gives me a hug. 'At last.'

'When is it? What's the date?' Frances joins in. I'd forgotten she was listening.

'The third Saturday in December. This December,' I add, aware that both Emma and Frances are staring at me, Frances open-mouthed, Emma with a frown.

'December?' they say at the same time.

'We'll have to check with the vicar first, of course.'

'It isn't the best time of year for photos,' Emma says. 'Have you thought about that?'

'I'm sure you can have goose bumps airbrushed out,' I say lightly.

'What if it rains?'

'It's just as likely to rain in June or July as it is in December. We can do the photos indoors if necessary.'

'Well, you and Alex mustn't keep putting it off,' Frances sighs. 'I'll just have to get hold of a decent coat for the occasion.'

'A set of thermals will do. Oh, it's lovely, Maz. I can't wait.' Smiling, Emma opens the door into the corridor for me, and we walk through to Kennels, or the Ward as we sometimes refer to it. 'By Christmas, you'll be a married woman.'

'I shan't feel any different.'

'I did.'

'But you'd been with Ben for ages.' They were together for most of our time at vet school. Ben was studying medicine. Now he's one of Talyton's GPs.

32

'You were like an old married couple before you ever walked down the aisle.'

'I didn't feel any differently about Ben. It was more about celebrating our love for each other in front of family and friends.' Emma smiles. 'Oh, that sounds a bit . . .'

A dog throws up in Kennels.

'Sick?' I finish for her. I can hear Izzy, our head nurse, moving around, clearing up. I think it must be the English setter who's in to have a wart removed from his eyelid. The pre-med must have disagreed with him.

'Maz, you are so cynical sometimes,' Emma says.

I know what she means and I feel a twinge of guilt at not being able to express how I really feel, because it sounds soft and silly. I go on, 'No, that's really sweet, Em. Romantic . . .'

'We could call ourselves Mr and Mrs at last. And the whole event was beautiful. It was truly the happiest day of my life, and, when the going gets tough, I cherish those memories and remind myself of what we promised each other.'

I admire Emma's conviction of the existence of everlasting love, but she's always known where she's going: husband, her own practice and children. It's all happened, except for the last part, the family.

I would have been content with what Emma has. Having children was never on my agenda, and yet, with all my training and the fact that a considerable part of my job involves advising owners on different forms of contraception, Alex and I still managed to have a happy little accident in George.

'What about the dress, Maz? Have you thought about the dress?'

'I can't say that it's been uppermost in my mind,' I say drily. 'George was giving me the runaround this morning.'

'You have to have the most amazing dress. It's your big day.'

'That sounds expensive to me. I'd like a nice dress, but I can't see the point of spending a fortune on something you wear only once.'

'You can't skimp on it. You're beginning to sound like a Fox-Gifford already, if you don't mind me saying,' Emma teases. 'If you think you're walking down that aisle in sacking tied up with baling twine, you're very much mistaken. I'm coming shopping with you. We can park in the city centre, shop and stop for lunch.'

'A day out? It's tempting but, what about—'

'George will be at nursery, and Will can cover. That's what he's here for.'

'Will he cope?'

'Of course. We'll give him some time to acclimatise first. Izzy will be here to supervise.' Emma lowers her voice. 'It'll do him good. That, or he'll have a nervous breakdown.'

'Or Izzy will.'

'You only get married once, so you have to make the most of it,' Emma rushes on. 'What about brides-maids? You have to have bridesmaids.'

'I'm not sure I want all this fuss,' I confess. This is all about me being with Alex for the rest of our lives, side by side, hand in hand.

Unexpected tears prick my eyes and my heart aches with yearning.

Before I met Alex, I didn't want to get married. Finding a husband, and having a big fat wedding, wasn't on my 'to do' list, probably because of the way my own father abandoned me, my brother and my mother when I was twelve years old. It's why I've worked so hard to escape my roots in the city estate where I was brought up, to have an amazing career doing something I love, and now to provide my son with everything I never had.

'Don't be upset, Maz,' Emma says.

'I was thinking about my mother.' I picture her in her flat in Battersea, dressed in one of her revealing outfits, her nails varnished and chipped, and her skin like a dried-out tangerine.

'You are going to invite her?'

'Yes, of course.' My heart shrinks with regret though that she won't be involved in the preparations for the wedding. She's visited us a couple of times to see George, but we've never been close, not like Emma was with her mum. 'I'm not sure how this wedding is ever going to happen. Alex and I are both so busy,' I continue.

'Well, it is happening,' Emma says adamantly. 'I'll help you organise everything. You'll need a planner. I can probably print one off the Internet.'

'Thanks, Em.'

'That's what friends are for.' She grins. 'Now I'm here, I'd better make a start on the ops. I didn't even have time to pick up doughnuts on the way in.'

'I'll get them later.' It's the least I can do. Emma's always helping me out and I do what I can for her.

'Actually, could you buy iced buns instead?'

'Are you okay?' I reach out and touch her forehead. 'You aren't sickening for something?'

'No, I fancy a change, that's all.' She takes a step

35

away. 'Don't worry about me, Maz. You have more than enough to keep you occupied.'

I'm still thinking about Emma's offer of help when I get home later, having collected George from nursery. He's been having too much of a good time. He toddles about in the Barn, trying to run away from me and tripping over his own feet, when I'm wanting to lift him into the highchair for pasta.

'George, come and have your tea,' I say as sternly as I can.

'No,' he says, cruising around the sofa.

'Please, George.'

'No.'

'Okay then, don't come here for tea.'

'No.'

'So, you mean yes,' I say, and although he doesn't understand the concept of double negatives just yet, he falls down onto his bottom, laughing. I can't help laughing too. It doesn't matter what kind of day I've had, George always cheers me up, and I wish Emma could have that too. My dearest wish is that I could make her dream of having a baby, a family of her own, come true.

Chapter Three

To Have and to Hold

It's Will's first day. He's pink-skinned as if he's been scrubbing his face, and he bears a throat-tingling scent of aftershave and mint toothpaste. He has a price tag dangling from the collar of his shirt, and he's even shined his shoes.

'Morning, Will,' I say, when I find him hanging around in Kennels, squatting down and stroking Tripod, the practice's three-legged black and white cat, who's purring and rubbing around Will's legs in ecstasy at having some one-to-one attention. 'How are you?'

'I'm fine. I'm looking forward to getting started. I think,' he adds.

I can remember how tense I felt just before I walked into the first paid consultation of my career. I was so nervous, I forgot to charge the client.

'Um, Will, you've left the label in your new shirt.' I pick up a pair of curved scissors from the prep bench – clean ones, I hasten to add. 'Would you like me to . . .?' I hope Will doesn't mind, but I feel as though I'm talking to George.

'Thanks,' he says, rubbing the back of his neck as he stands up to let me snip the tag off.

'Good luck for today,' I say. 'Remember that Emma and I have every faith in you.'

Will glances at the clock. 'I'd better go and see if anyone's waiting.'

'All right.' I smile to myself – there are twenty minutes to go until the first appointment.

As he leaves, Will holds the door open for Izzy who's turned up with a basket of clean drapes ready to be folded and sterilised later on.

'Of course,' Izzy says, when I ask her to keep an eye on our new vet. Her complexion is freckled and her hair grizzled like a Border terrier's. She's in her early forties, but looks younger, being slim and fit from dog training and helping out on the farm at home. 'I'm up for a bit of handholding.'

'And you a married woman,' I tease. When I first met Izzy, I wasn't sure I would get along with her, but she's a dedicated nurse and loves the animals. She can also be very funny and deeply sarcastic at times.

'You don't mind?' I add.

'I can show him how I like things done around here,' Izzy smiles. 'My way.'

Will's first patient is a cockatiel, called . . . You've guessed it, Cocky.

Emma and I hover in the corridor outside the consulting room, Emma looking somewhat pale-faced.

'I don't think we should worry so much, do you?' I say apprehensively. 'He has Izzy with him. He'll be fine. Won't he?'

'He probably knows far more than we do, than we ever did, but . . .'

38

But, I muse. That's the trouble. Emma and I are both remembering our mistakes, the ones we made when we first went into practice.

'Let's leave him to it,' I say. 'I've got plenty to do until Bridget comes in at ten.' Bridget is Shannon's mother. Shannon is our trainee vet nurse.

'Shannon's really worried about Daisy, so I thought it best for her to see one of us.'

'She'll have to get used to seeing Will,' Emma says. 'I'm planning on him staying here for a long time.'

Will's presence at Otter House Vets is intended to make our lives easier, but I'm not so sure that's going to happen, because there's a sudden fracas on the other side of the door: a yelp of 'Ouch,' and Izzy's voice, alternately strident and apologetic, telling Will to check both doors are locked, and the owner of the cockatiel not to worry, we'll catch him.

I'm not sure whether to laugh or cry. Will's very first patient, and he's let it go.

I wait for a few minutes, listening to the odd thud and clatter, and muffled conversation, then decide I can't wait any longer and head for the office to deal with some paperwork, organising a couple of referrals before taking Will's next couple of clients through to the prep area in Kennels to treat their animals. Soon, Bridget arrives with Daisy, but Will hasn't vacated the consulting room yet, and Emma is operating now, and I don't want to get in her way.

'Have you any idea what's going on in there?' I ask Frances. 'I thought he'd have finished by now.' We booked him every alternate appointment, deliberately leaving the others free to give him plenty of time.

'He's still in there with the cockatiel,' says Frances.

'No?'

'I offered to help, but Izzy won't let anyone in or out of the consulting room.'

'Great,' I sigh. 'What am I going to do now?'

'You'll have to see Daisy in the staffroom.'

'It's too untidy,' I say, 'and Tripod and Miff are sharing the sofa.' Miff, a Border terrier, belongs to Emma. 'I wonder if I can take Daisy into the office.'

'When needs must,' says Frances, but there's no need to find an alternative venue because the consulting room door slides open. The client, Peter the greengrocer, a short, chubby man with a whiskery moustache and a crown of black hair around a shiny bald spot that reminds me of a case of ringworm, emerges from the darkened room with the cockatiel safely in his cage.

'He got him in the end,' he says, beaming. 'You did give that young man the runaround, didn't you, Cocky?'

'I'd call it a fly-around,' says Izzy, smiling ruefully as she walks out with Will following behind her, high colour in his cheeks, hair rumpled and a bashful grin on his face. He has a plaster on one finger too.

'Cocky bit me,' he says.

'He drew blood,' Peter cuts in. He has a broad Devon accent that can be difficult for someone who has not tuned in to it yet to understand. 'I can tell he's a practising vet, not a real one like you, Maz. And he definitely needs more practice. You should have got Cocky's head between your fingers so he couldn't turn on you.'

'I should have asked you to hold on to him for me,' Will says.

'Oh, no way. He'd have my finger off.'

Will glances in my direction. I roll my eyes in sympathy. He'll learn.

I look towards Bridget who's waiting patiently with Daisy, a hefty tan and white British bulldog. They say that dogs look like their owners, and to me, there is some resemblance here in the shape of the jaw and the set of the eyes, and the fact they're both hugely overweight.

'I'm sorry to have kept you waiting,' I say, noting Bridget's frizzy blonde hair and tatty green sweatshirt with the Petals logo on it. 'I hope you've got someone to mind the shop.' She owns the florist's in Market Square, just up the road from Otter House.

'I've put a note on the door.' Bridget drags a reluctant Daisy behind her. Daisy doesn't walk. She waddles, panting and stopping for breath every couple of strides. She reminds me of a table with a leg at each corner, not some delicate Chippendale design, but a solid farmhouse affair.

'Come on through.' I close the consulting room door behind her. 'What can I do for Daisy?'

'She's become so lazy,' Bridget says. 'I have to take her down to the Green in the car to get her out for a walk, and when it's hot like this, all she does is sit down. I told Shannon I was worried about her heart, and she suggested I made the appointment.'

I remember Shannon mentioning it – she said she was ashamed of the state Daisy was in.

'Is she better when the weather's cooler?' I ask.

'I don't know, to be honest. I haven't taken her out at all for a few days now – I didn't think it was fair to keep making her go for walks. She has an allergy to exercise, like me.' Bridget smiles weakly, as if trying to make light of the situation. 'That's my excuse anyway.'

'Let's get her weighed first, then I'll check her over.' It's a struggle, because it means going back out into the waiting area and persuading Daisy to stand on the scales. Her weight flashes up on the display.

'That can't be right,' Bridget says, frowning, and to prove that it is, I move Daisy off and reset the scales, before weighing her again.

'It is right,' I say. 'Look at that.'

I let the figure sink in. Bridget appears shocked. I run my finger down the laminated chart displayed on the wall, and read out what a Bulldog bitch should weigh.

'So Shannon was right,' Bridget says.

'You don't have to weigh her to see she's over-weight. In fact, she's more than that. She's obese,' I point out.

'She can't be . . .' Bridget hesitates. 'She's big-boned.'

'Trust me, her bones aren't exceptional. She has a pretty average frame.'

Bridget glares at me, radiating scepticism, disbelief and denial.

'I can't feel her ribs, let alone see them, and look at these rolls of fat,' I exclaim.

'They're folds of skin,' Bridget insists. 'All Bulldogs have them.'

My heart sinks. This isn't going too well. Obesity in dogs is a growing problem for us vets, even in a country practice, and it's difficult to do anything about it when the client is overweight too. It's a sensitive subject, and I can only guess how Bridget is feeling: guilty for letting her dog get into such a state, embarrassed and painfully aware of her own weight problem.

'Let's check her over,' I say, and, between us, Bridget and I lift her onto the table where I listen to her chest and examine her joints. Her lungs sound crackly – as if someone's inside her chest popping packing bubbles – and I wonder if she has some fluid in there. She growls when I move her left elbow and both hips. She also has a skin infection.

I hang my stethoscope around my neck, and go through Daisy's problems with Bridget.

'There's no point in merely treating the symptoms. We have to address the root cause which is Daisy's weight problem. It's up to you,' I go on. 'I can advise you. I can't make you do anything about it, but, if Daisy carries on as she is, she'll end up crippled with arthritis and hardly able to breathe. It'll shorten her life.'

'You mean, she could die from it?'

'Yes, she could.' We stand in silence for a moment, listening to Daisy's harsh panting as she sits slumped on her haunches, on the table. I would kiss her, but, unlike most of my patients, she's rather offputting with all the scabs around her face and ears.

'Do you do gastric bands for dogs,' Bridget asks eventually, 'or liposuction?'

'It's much simpler than that. Daisy needs fewer calories and more exercise. If the energy going in as food is less than the energy going out through moving around, she'll lose weight. She doesn't need a tread-mill, or hydrotherapy pool, or a doggy gym. All she needs is more walking. Doesn't she go out with Seven?' Seven, Shannon's dog, isn't overweight.

'She can't keep up with him,' Bridget says. 'I told Shannon not to bother to take her.'

'Well, I don't want Daisy to overdo it at first. She should have two fifteen-minute walks a day to begin with. We'll put her on a strict regime of a measured amount of diet food twice a day, nothing else.'

'No gravy?'

'No gravy,' I confirm.

'What about her biscuits at bedtime?' Bridget answers the question herself. 'No . . . What about Seven? Can he have the diet food?'

'It would be better to feed them separately.'

'What about carrots? I read somewhere that you can give carrots as treats to dogs.'

'No carrots,' I say firmly, although I'm rapidly losing the will to live. 'Carrots equal extra calories, not as many as a cream cake, but enough.'

'I'll start her on the diet on Monday then, and give her the weekend to get used to the idea.'

You mean, to let you get used to the idea, I muse.

'She can have all her favourite things before she ends up on rabbit food,' Bridget continues.

'It is dog food, I can assure you,' I say. 'Now, is it possible for you to leave Daisy here for a few hours, so I can get an X-ray of her chest, and Shannon can give her a bath?'

'Yes. I don't see why not.'

'Shannon can take her home at the end of her shift.'

'Thanks, Maz. I'm glad I brought her along.'

'No problem,' I say. 'That's what we're here for.'

'Absolutely no extras?' Bridget checks on the way out, having handed Daisy over to me. 'It's all right for her to have her breakfast milk?'

'No extras. No milk. Just the diet, and water to drink. Nothing else is to pass her lips.' I smile. 'Remember, I'll know about it when we weigh her next time. I'd like to see her in a week.' Izzy runs a slimming clinic for our fatties – dogs and cats – every fortnight, but I prefer to monitor Daisy myself until I'm happy that she's on the right track.

I coax Daisy slowly along the corridor to Kennels where I find her a bed for the day, and ask Emma to stick her on the end of the list for X-rays and a bath. Will takes over the consulting room once more, and I find myself at a loose end. I suppose I should make the most of it because it won't last. I end up in the office, searching the Internet for tips on how to plan a wedding and set a budget. As well as the dress, flowers and the reception, there are apparently other essentials to consider: underwear that works with the dress, and possibly the hire of a calligrapher to write the names of your guests on the invitations, and favours for the tables. I hadn't realised how much was involved, or how much it was all going to cost.

As I sit there, wondering how Alex and I are going to fund it, I overhear voices in the staffroom, Frances and a person of the opposite sex. It takes me a moment to realise who it is. It's Lenny, the delivery driver, who brings supplies from the wholesaler to the practice at least once a week, often more. Izzy and, increasingly, Shannon deal with the order, checking it as they unpack. Frances is the member of staff who deals with Lenny himself, inviting him in for coffee or tea before he drives on to the next practice on his round, Talyton Manor. Lenny hasn't been delivering here for long – the last driver was sacked for selling the goods he was supposed to be supplying on eBay.

I confess that in order to hear what they're saying, I abandon the computer and wander into the staffroom on the pretence of grabbing a biscuit from the tin.

'Hello, Lenny,' I say, taking a chocolate biscuit that's already out on a plate on the worktop. 'How's it going?'

He's sixty-four – I know because he told us that his

granddaughter made him a cake with sixty-four on it – but he looks younger.

'Not bad,' he says, glancing towards Frances who is perched on the opposite end of the sofa from him. Like Will, she's wearing new clothes: new shoes, to be precise, red ones with a kitten heel. 'I must be on my way.' He stands up, brushing crumbs from his trousers.

He's well-groomed, like a recently trimmed schnauzer, with black eyebrows, lots of white hair and a salt-and-pepper beard. He always wears grey trousers, a white short-sleeved shirt embroidered with the wholesaler's logo, and a tie. Best of all, he's constantly cheerful, but now I think about it, that could have something to do with Frances . . .

'Thanks for the biscuits,' he says as he heads out through the practice, Frances and I following close behind. We wait in Reception, watching Lenny go, heading back across the car park with his trolley to his van.

'Why do we always have chocolate Hobnobs or Bourbon creams on delivery days?' I ask Frances.

'Lenny has such an early start and a long drive to get here.'

'And?' I smile. 'Doesn't he have breakfast like everyone else before he sets out?'

'Well, yes, I imagine so. It turns out that it's convenient for him to stop here for a tea break.'

'Are you sure that's all he stops for?' I tease. 'I think you're blushing.'

'Me?' Frances touches her throat. 'Oh no, it's high blood pressure – Dr Mackie's given me some pills for it.'

'Well, I hope they start working soon.'

'Who's going to start working soon?' says Izzy, emerging from the consulting room.

'The tablets,' I say. 'Don't worry, Izz. What have you done with Will?'

'I told him, he's going to have to work on his stamina. He's having a lie-down.' Her mouth curves with amusement. 'He's gone up to the flat for a break. He needs it after the incident with the bird.'

'What went wrong?' I ask her. 'Why didn't you catch it for him?'

'Will wouldn't let me. I didn't want to embarrass him any further in front of Peter. He had everything ready, gloves, swabs, and silver nitrate stick.'

Cocky's well-known to us. He comes in regularly to have his beak trimmed. If left, it grows crooked and curls at the end so Cocky can't eat.

Izzy continues, 'If Will hadn't pussyfooted around, he would have got Cocky back within minutes. I can't believe I've wasted so much time.'

'It'll get better. We're bound to have a few teething problems.'

'He isn't a baby, Maz. He's a grown man with professional qualifications, but it's like he's one of those people who's incredibly clever in theory, but practically useless.'

'Oh, I hope not,' I sigh. 'Izzy, let's not rush into making judgements just yet. Let's give him a chance.'

'How long for? Remember the trouble we had with Drew?'

How can I forget? Drew was our locum a couple of summers ago now and he really messed up, amputating the wrong leg – one of the healthy ones, not the one with cancer in the bone – which meant the dog, a Great Dane called Harley, had no chance of survival. I could have forgiven him if he'd faced up to what he'd done, but he disappeared, flying off back to Australia where he came from.

'Drew was a one-off. He didn't care. Will does.'

'How do you know that?' Izzy says sceptically.

'He likes the animals. You should have seen him with Tripod earlier on.' I pause. 'Izzy, it's the poor guy's first day . . .'

'Well, I'll be watching him,' she says, and I smile to myself. Everyone will be to start with. Frances has already reported a couple of requests coming from clients asking to see the new assistant with their pets. They want to check him out. In fact, I'm surprised that a representative of Talyton's Meet and Greet Committee hasn't made an appearance yet. Fifi Green, Chair of Talyton Animal Rescue, local councillor, and well-meaning busybody, takes her role very seriously.

I go and help Emma in Kennels. We X-ray Daisy's chest before Shannon bathes her, and soon, the room is steaming up with the scent of medicated shampoo and wet dog. The smell clings to my clothes, and is still there when I get home at the end of a long day.

I pick George up from the Manor where Sophia is trying to unblock a pipe at the base of the washing machine. George is 'helping'.

'This happens every time I put the horses' numnahs in,' she grumbles, referring to the cloths that go under their saddles. 'Would you like a cup of tea, Maz?'

'No, thank you. I'd better go and put dinner on.'

'George has had a huge helping of cottage pie for lunch.'

I thank Sophia again. 'I'll see you later,' I add before making my escape, holding on to George's hand so he can't rush back to continue sticking his fingers in the slow flow of grey water that's coming out of the machine.

When we go inside the Barn, George wanders off to find his favourite car to play with. I find Ginge lying crashed out in the sun. I touch him, he lifts his head and hisses before realising it's me. He blinks and stretches out one paw in apology, claws sheathed now.

'If I were you I'd go and sleep upstairs on the bed, if you don't want your tail pulled,' I whisper to him. I'm proud of Ginge's restraint. In spite of starting out half wild, he's settled down, and it seems as if he knows how precious George is to me, because, when George did pull his tail the other day – not out of malice, but more as an experiment to see what would happen – Ginge leapt up, yowling. He didn't lash out or bite. I felt really guilty because I hadn't been there to protect him. He's an old boy now. He doesn't deserve any hassle at his age.

George and I eat pasta (again), and I'm putting him to bed when Alex arrives home. Alex opens a bottle of wine and we sit down later, once our son is asleep, just the two of us, and I think, this is how life should be.

'We need to talk about the wedding,' I say eventually. 'We have to decide on a budget. I've been Googling. I didn't realise how much everything was going to cost.'

'Don't worry about that, Maz.' Alex leans back into the sofa. 'It costs what it costs, and I think I can rely on you not to go too mad.'

'Alex, I hope you're going to take on some responsibility for this wedding.'

'Mother's keen to help,' he says, with a cheeky wink.

'You've told her then?'

'Of course. I'd let her take some of the strain, if I were you. It would make her very happy.'

'I doubt it would have the same effect on me.'

'She's already dug out her hat.'

'Not a riding one, I hope.'

'Her wedding hat. She's worn the same one for years.'

'As long as she doesn't wear that hideous fox fur with the glass eyes and moth-eaten tail . . . I couldn't have that in the photos.'

Alex chuckles, yet I feel a little guilty for not wanting to involve the future mother-in-law, or my mother, in the planning of the wedding.

'What about the reception?' I say.

'I thought here, at the Manor.'

'I'm not sure about that.'

'It won't be the same as my first one,' Alex says, reminding me with a jolt that this will be his second marriage. It's history and, although he has contact with his ex-wife through their two children, I don't feel that she's a threat to our relationship in any way. However, I am still seized with irrational jealousy at the thought that Alex has done this before.

'It was summer for a start,' he goes on. 'We had a marquee on the lawn. It'll be too cold for that in December.'

'No,' I say. 'I'd be quite happy if we held it in a pub like Izzy and Chris did, at the Talymill Inn.'

'I'd prefer somewhere a bit more upmarket like the Barnscote,' Alex says. 'It will be cosy there at Christmas with the open fires. Elsa will do me a good deal – I treat her pigs, the happy ones.' They're called happy pigs because they're free-range, not because they don't get eaten. 'It's local, and not too far from the church,' Alex continues. 'All we need is good food, somewhere everyone can warm up, have a few drinks and catch up, especially for those of our guests who meet only for hatching, matching and dispatching. It needs to have good acoustics for the speeches.' Alex cocks his head. 'Or poor acoustics, maybe, so no one can hear what the best man's saying.'

'Have you asked Stewart yet?'

'He offered as soon as I told him we'd set the date. I dread to think what he's going to drag up, what secrets he's going to reveal. Have you decided who's going to give you away?'

'I shall do it myself.' I giggle. 'I'm not some chattel to be handed from one man to another. It's a ridiculous tradition and I'm not going along with it.'

Alex grins. 'You'll be the talk of the town, Maz. You rebel.'

I rest my head against Alex's chest and listen to his heartbeat. He smells of antibiotic, the outdoors and musk. I can see a few dark curls of hair on his chest where the top buttons of his faded blue chambray shirt are unfastened.

'So, are we any further forward?' I ask.

'I'll get in touch with Elsa and arrange for us to go and have lunch or dinner there to refresh your memory of what the Barnscote's like, if we can find a babysitter.'

'Your mother spends enough time with George already, and Shannon's too busy revising for her exams to babysit at the moment.'

'What about that friend of hers who came with her the last time?'

'She gave me the impression she wouldn't do it again, not because of George, but because your father freaked her out, shooting at a rat in the yard.' I pause.

'You know, Alex, I wonder if we could just book the register office and go and get married on the quiet. You, me, George and a couple of witnesses.'

'You can't do that, Maz. I thought you wanted the big white wedding. Anyway, everyone would be so disappointed.'

'We could still have a party.' Do I want the big white wedding? I didn't think so, but I realise that the pictures in my future wedding album include me in the fairy-tale dress and Alex in top hat and tails, surrounded by family and friends. I feel almost sick with anticipation. With a bit of organisation and planning, it will be a wonderful day. I glance towards my gorgeous husband-to-be. I'm not sure how I'm going to wait until Christmas.

Chapter Four

From this Day Forward

A week goes by, and the wedding plans fall by the wayside for a while, but I console myself with the thought that there's plenty of time . . . It's summer. There are months until December.

On the Tuesday, when I go in to work in the morning, George is grizzly because he's overtired.

'I'm sorry, George,' I say, because he really doesn't want to go to nursery today. I don't know what Sophia was doing with him yesterday, and I resent that. It should be me looking after him, but I need to work too.

Fleetingly, I yearn for the days when all I had to look after was my patients and myself. I used to think how tough it was. Now I know it's a doddle compared with parenthood, especially when your partner has deserted you. That sounds dramatic, but that's how it feels, with Alex working late most days now that the light evenings are here. I have no right to expect anything else, because I know very well what his job entails, but I'm sure he didn't put in quite so many hours when I first met him.

I leave George with Flick, the manager at the nursery, trying to restrain myself from running back to him, and feeling like the worst mum in the world. I walk along to Otter House, catching up with Shannon who's bringing Daisy in for her check-up. Shannon's mother has always worked, and she brought Shannon up alone from when her dad died, and she's turned out fine. I tell myself to take comfort in that and not fret so much.

'Mum's busy making up orders, otherwise she'd have brought Daisy along herself,' Shannon explains.

I can't help wondering if she's just too embarrassed after the last time.

In the practice, I spend the morning consulting while Emma guides Will through his fourth list of ops. He's doing as well as can be expected, but we're not completely confident that he can cope alone. Emma and I decided who was to do the honours this time by tossing a coin. I won.

I help Shannon coax Daisy onto the scales in Reception, watched by a cat that looks on from its carrier with a supercilious expression, as if to say, you'll never catch me on one of those.

Shannon checks the display. 'She's lost loads. That's unbelievable.'

'Yes, and I don't believe it either.' I move closer. 'It's impossible.' Then I laugh out loud. Daisy's on the scales, but she's also leaning against the wall. The wall is taking the strain. Daisy rolls her bulgy eyes and growls when we ask her to move, but eventually she settles in the right place.

'She hates people going on about her weight,' Shannon says.

'She does appear to be developing a complex.' I stroke

Daisy's coat. I still don't kiss her. Her skin is greasy, her hair rough and bristly. She isn't in great condition.

'What should we do next? Cut her food down even more?'

'How much walking is she doing?'

'Not a lot, to be honest. Mum's been feeling under the weather, and it's a pain walking Daisy with Seven, because Seven wants to run around playing, while Daisy drags along behind. I take them out separately after work, but I'm not usually up in time in the mornings . . .'

'You'll just have to get up earlier then.' I'm teasing. 'Shannon, you've got enough to deal with. Let's reduce her food by another quarter for the next two weeks and see if that makes any difference. Has she had any extras?'

'Not that I know of,' Shannon says. 'She'd love to get hold of Seven's food, but I stand over them so she can't. Oh, one thing – I found her drinking out of a bucket that had flower food in it – it's sugary, but there can't be all that many calories in it, can there?'

'Does she drink very much – water, I mean?'

Shannon thinks for a moment. 'I don't know. She isn't drinking any more than normal.'

'It might be worth measuring her fluid intake over twenty-four hours. It would be a useful practical task to link with the theory you're studying at college.' Shannon is doing her second year of a vet nursing diploma on a day-release basis.

'I'll try. It won't be easy with Seven and the flower buckets all over the place.'

'I'll leave the logistics with you. Let me know how you get on. Otherwise, we'll book Daisy in for another appointment in two weeks' time.'

'Will do,' Shannon says brightly.

Next, there are seven Springador puppies, Labrador-springer spaniel crosses, to check and give their first vaccinations. The owner has enlisted the help of several family members to bring them to the practice.

'Hello, Jan,' I say, letting the trail of people and pups in arms into the consulting room. Jan is a longstanding client who is married to the local oyster farmer. She's slim, blonde and freckled, and in her late twenties, quite cool in a surfer-style printed cotton dress and flat sandals. Whether I'm imagining it or not, she always seems to bring the scent of the sea with her.

'I've brought everyone with me,' she smiles. 'I don't want my boys and girls padding around on the floor until they've had all their jabs.'

'They're very cute,' I say, having tried and failed to shut the door with so many people crammed into what is really a very small room. 'How do you tell which one is which?' To me, they are all very similar: black with wavy coats, ears and paws that are too big for their bodies, and soulful brown eyes.

'They're colour-coded with nail varnish. Look.' Jan shows me the paw of the puppy she's holding. It has one claw painted pink. 'This is Bonnie. She's the naughtiest of the bunch.'

'So we know which one is which,' I say. 'That makes it easier. I'll check them all over first, then inject them. That way they'll be less likely to upset each other.'

I examine each puppy, one at a time. Shannon takes notes for me on the computer.

'They're great, Jan. All fit and healthy,' I pronounce, before looking towards Shannon who's squatting down, almost inside the fridge under the workbench, pulling out box after box of vaccine. 'Shannon, is there some problem?' I ask, with a growing sense of unease.

'Um, I'm not sure. Let me go and look in the fridge in Kennels.' Shannon stands up and straightens her uniform. Her cheeks are red, her expression anxious.

'I'm sorry for the delay,' I say, when she disappears through the door into the rest of the practice. 'There must have been a mix-up when they unpacked the delivery.' It would be a first though, I think to myself. I know Shannon's been allowed to check the deliveries, but I can't imagine Izzy allowing any mistake to slip through.

Suddenly, I hear Izzy's voice and the sound of feet pounding back along the corridor towards the consulting room.

'It's no good, Shannon. There's no excuse for this. How many times have I told you to check and double-check? You'll have to apologise. Maz . . .' Izzy hesitates as she comes in. 'I didn't realise you wanted the vaccine right now, this minute.'

'So there's no puppy vaccine in the practice?' I surmise. I turn to Jan. 'I'm so sorry about this, especially as you've all been inconvenienced.' I think quickly. 'I'm afraid I'll have to rebook you. Naturally, there'll be a discount.'

'I should hope so. It's a real pain,' Jan says. 'I wanted to get this lot vaccinated, and out and about as soon as possible.'

Jan and her entourage return to make another ultra-long appointment with Frances, while I head for the staffroom where Izzy is continuing her rather one-sided discussion with Shannon. Izzy is understand-ably furious because it reflects on her as head nurse. Steam rises from a cup of coffee beside the kettle. Metaphorical steam is coming out of Izzy's ears.

'You're lucky,' Izzy says. 'Frances says Old Fox-Gifford used to throw his mug at her, if anything went wrong.' Frances used to work for Talyton Manor Vets – Old Fox-Gifford accused Otter House of poaching her, and I don't think he's really ever forgiven us. 'What did go wrong, Shannon?'

'There'll be time for the inquest later,' I cut in. 'Shannon made a mistake. Everyone makes mistakes.' It's a shame it had to be this one because we need that vaccine. I've rechecked the list of clients booked in for the rest of the day, and there are three, if not four, more dogs for their annual jabs. We need to get hold of some dog vaccine, otherwise I'll have to cancel, and that is going to be expensive, and have a knock-on effect on bookings for the rest of the week. We're lucky in that we're always fully booked, fitting in extra patients when they need to be seen, often at the end of routine consultations. BG, Before George, I used not to mind, but it gets difficult when I have to pick him up from nursery before they close.

'What are we going to do?' says Izzy. 'I can order more now, but it won't come until lunchtime tomorrow.'

'I'll check with Alex first, but I expect he'll have some we can borrow.'

Having contacted Alex, and seen the last patient before lunchtime, a cat well on the road to recovery after a bout of flu, I drive back to the Manor. I could have asked Shannon to go as penance, but the Fox-Giffords' practice is in such a mess, it's almost impossible to find the fridge, let alone any vaccine.

I clear a pathway through the Talyton Manor

surgery, moving a box of dental equipment, gags and files for rasping horses' teeth, and a stack of business journals that neither Alex nor his father can have ever read, to reach the doddery old fridge. Inside, I find three boxes of dog vaccine, one of which is way out of date. I also discover a Creme egg from Easter, half a ham roll squashed in cling film, and a couple of blood samples, congealed in their tubes and of no use now.

'Will you really use all that today?' Alex says, coming into the surgery.

'Under normal circumstances, I'd say no, but we've got three or four booked in already, and Will's got a habit of using two vials when one should do.'

'How does he manage that?'

'He's been squirting the vaccine right through from one side of the scruff to the other.'

Alex grins. 'Perhaps you'd be better off employing George as your assistant.'

'We might have to get rid of Shannon too, if this happens too often,' I say, but I'm joking. Shannon is working really hard for her exams, it's no wonder she's forgetting the on-the-job routine. I wonder if she should have some time off to study. I change the subject. 'Alex, you really need to take your father in hand. Look how much you've wasted. You'll never use all that. How many dogs do you see in a week?'

'A couple.'

'Exactly.'

'I expect it was on offer – he can't resist a bargain.'

'You should have gone in with us and we could have split the order,' I suggest.

'It's a great idea, Maz, but you know Father wouldn't have it.'

'Even if it saved him money?'

'You know what he's like. My boss doesn't like getting into bed with the competition, whereas . . . Let's say, I find it a lot of fun.'

'Alex! I don't know what you mean,' I go on archly. I put one of the in-date boxes into a cool-bag that I've brought with me, thanks to Izzy, and head back towards the exit, towards Alex who's waiting for me in a rumpled shirt and grass-stained trousers, his lightly tanned arms held out to catch and embrace me.

'Kiss?' he says, pressing me gently against the wall.

I look into his eyes.

'It's very tempting . . .' I murmur, 'but I've got to get back.'

'Maz . . .' My name seems to catch in his throat. 'Five minutes . . .'

'No, Alex.' Fighting my instinct to say, oh, what the hell, I press my palms against his chest. 'I really have to go.'

I can feel Alex's reluctance as he slowly releases me.

'I'm sorry,' I say, reading a touch of resentment in his expression. 'Don't blame me. Believe me, I'd stay if I could.'

'Perhaps we should amalgamate the two practices as well as the vaccines, then we could spend more time together,' Alex says, his tone lightening slightly.

I smile. 'There's no way. Look at the state of this place. Seriously, Alex, don't you ever worry about health and safety?'

'It isn't all that bad, Maz.'

'That's because you've grown used to it. Alex, it's appalling.' I think of the walls in Otter House, cleaned meticulously every week by Izzy and Shannon. 'I couldn't work here.'

60

'It's lucky you don't have to then. I'll see you later,' Alex says gruffly.

'Later,' I agree. It's no use asking when. Neither of us will know. 'It would be good to catch up. We need to book the reception. For the wedding,' I add, when Alex stands there, frowning.

His face cracks into a smile. 'Gotcha, Maz,' he chuckles.

I give him a dig in the ribs. 'This is serious. The Barnscote might be booked up for Christmas. We've left it a bit late.'

'Oh, don't worry. The Dog and Duck will have room for us.'

'The Dog and Duck. I hadn't thought of that one. Yes, that could be perfect.'

'But it's such a dive,' Alex says, incredulous.

'Gotcha back,' I say, laughing. The Dog and Duck is one of the local pubs where the clientele is as old and faded as the flocked wallpaper. 'We'll talk about it later.'

'One last kiss then,' Alex says.

'One . . .' I say, but when I get back to Otter House and check the time, I realise that it may have been four, or five. I see the next few appointments before catching up with Emma in the staffroom. Will is upstairs in the flat with his creepy-crawlies, Izzy is clearing up after the ops and Shannon has gone out to do some shopping. Frances remains on duty at Reception.

Emma sits perched on a stool, sipping at some kind of herbal tea.

'I couldn't find anywhere else to sit,' she says, grinning.

Although Emma once decided that we wouldn't have any practice animals, Tripod still lives here, keeping Emma's Border terrier, Miff, who comes to work with her, in order. Miff belonged to Emma's mum before she died. She's middle-aged now, with a grizzled coat and growing grey at the muzzle. Emma treats her like a baby, buying her new collars and raincoats. She's wearing a pink collar today, printed with red love hearts.

As Emma anticipated, the animals have rather taken over. In fact, they're lying on the sofa together.

'Shuffle up,' I tell them, but Tripod rolls over, showing his belly, and Miff opens one brown eye, giving me one of her looks that means, I'm not here. Really . . .

I pick her up and shift her along so I can sit down. She wriggles up against my side, asking to be stroked.

'You are so smarmy,' I tell her, at which she wags her tail. We're good friends now. I look after her when Emma and Ben go away. 'How was your day?' I ask Emma.

'All right, once I'd got Will under way with his first bitch spay. I was going to leave him to it, but I stayed in the end. Izzy asked me to, on the quiet.'

'She worries too much. She complained about the first few ops he did. The holes were too big, he put in too many stitches and used too many swabs.'

'I think she described the first one as a chainsaw massacre,' Emma chuckles.

'I hope she was exaggerating.'

'I asked Frances if the clients like him.'

'What did she say?'

'She said there's been a mixed response. The older ladies think he's charming. Aurora didn't seem overly impressed, but you know what she's like . . .'

I recall catching her in the consulting room in a compromising position with Drew, the locum, examining a rash on her chest, or so he said.

'I've had a look at the takings and they've gone up which is great now we have an extra member of staff to pay for.' She pauses. 'Talking of money, have you and Alex come up with a budget for the wedding yet? I want to know how much we have for the dress – I thought we'd hit the shops at the end of the week, if that's all right with you. Will says he's happy to hold the fort.' Emma's face lights up. 'Do you realise that's the first time since Drew left that we've been able to go out together?'

I know what she means – we've met for dinner at each other's houses, but we haven't been able to go out and about as such because one or other of us has always had to be available for emergencies.

'I could get used to this,' Emma goes on. 'I like having staff.'

The following day, Lenny the delivery driver turns up with emergency supplies of vaccine while I am getting ready to operate with Shannon.

'I'm going out with Emma to try on wedding dresses on Friday,' I say, pulling on a rather fetching theatre cap before I scrub up and slip into a gown and gloves. A surgical mask completes the ensemble.

'That's cool,' Shannon says.

'How do I look?' I say, giving a twirl. Shannon smiles. It's a small smile, but a smile all the same. She's seemed down recently. What I mean by that is that, although she hasn't got the bubbliest personality, she's usually quietly cheerful, or has been since Drew, the locum who broke her heart, left us.

We continue with the job in hand, spaying Aurora's dog, Saba. Saba, a black standard poodle, is one of our regulars. She had a litter of Labradoodle puppies eighteen months ago, and Aurora has decided that she can't cope with any more litters. Shannon's dog is one of Saba's puppies. He's called Seven because he was the seventh to be born. He has a harelip that meant he couldn't feed from his mum, so Shannon took him on and hand reared him.

'Did you manage to work out how much Daisy's drinking?' I ask Shannon while I start the surgery.

'I did. I meant to let you know. It was . . .' She frowns, then gives me the figure in total.

'So, is that excessive?' I ask. 'Is it more than the average daily intake for a dog the size of Daisy?'

'It seems quite a lot.'

'Can you remember from your lectures at college what it should be per kilogram of dog?'

Shannon sighs. 'I can't do calculations, Maz.'

'Of course you can.' Shannon had good grades in her exams at school. 'I'm not doing it for you,' I add. 'Divide what you've measured by Daisy's weight in kilos and what do you have?'

She does some workings on the back of Saba's anaesthetic record card, and announces the result.

'So it's way over,' she says, sounding surprised. 'Could it be the weather though? It's been hot and Daisy's always panting.'

'I'd say it was more than that. We'll have her back in for blood and urine tests.'

'Shall I book her in for tomorrow?'

'Make it today. The sooner we find out what's wrong, the better.'

'You don't think she's diabetic?' Shannon asks.

'There are lots of things it could be, but diabetes would be top of my list.'

'You can treat it though?'

'It's quite a commitment, but we can get it under control.' I continue operating. 'Let's not worry about that though until we're sure of the diagnosis. Could you open a spare instrument pack and get me another set of Allis forceps, please? They seem to have gone AWOL.'

Shannon fetches a pack of instruments and opens it onto the tray so the contents slide out with a clatter.

'Shannon, I said Allis forceps. Those are mosquitoes.'

'I'm sorry,' she says, red-faced and flustered. She scurries away and returns with yet another pack. 'Maz, I can't do this.'

'Of course you can.' I'm sharp with her, but halfway through a bitch spay is not the time to suffer a crisis of confidence. 'You're doing really well.' Shannon hasn't fainted since the first time she watched a major op, but I don't like to remind her of that.

'I don't mean this.' Shannon checks Saba's pulse and breathing, keeping half an eye on the watch attached to her scrub top before writing her observations onto the anaesthetic record. 'I mean my exams. I've been trying to learn the instruments, but I keep getting them all mixed up. I don't know anything. I'm going to fail.'

'Shannon, you won't fail. Why don't we run through some of the stuff together?'

'Because it won't make any difference.'

'You don't know that. Come on, it'll be good for me to exercise my brain.'

'All right,' she says reluctantly. 'That would be good, Maz. If you have time . . .'

'I can make time.' Actually, I wish I could create

more time, an extra couple of hours here and there, so I could teach Shannon, and sit down and chat with Alex over a glass of wine more often than the odd occasion we've managed in the last few months. We used to do that, spend time together. Admittedly one or other of us was just as likely to fall asleep, but at least we had the opportunity, whereas now, with George acting like the passion police, any romance is wishful thinking.

I glance towards the patient's head. Even under anaesthetic, Saba still manages to look glamorous, with her neatly trimmed fur and her perfectly manicured paws, filed and possibly polished, that stick out from under the drapes.

'How is Seven?' I ask. In the background, on low volume, the radio is playing 'Who Let the Dogs Out'.

'He's fine,' Shannon says. 'He hasn't quietened down like you said he would though.' I feel a little chastened at Shannon's scepticism about whether or not I really know what I'm talking about, as she goes on, 'He's still molesting Daisy, even though he's had his nuts off. Are you sure you removed all the right bits, Maz?'

'Quite sure,' I say, amused. 'You were there when I did it.'

'I couldn't actually watch, not because I'm squeamish, but because it was Seven.'

'It's different when it's your own,' I agree. I notice Shannon's wearing more eyeliner than usual. Black doesn't really suit her complexion. She's so pale that I sometimes wonder if I should suggest running some bloods to check for anaemia. 'Are you okay?'

'It's the exam thing, that's all.'

'Are you sure there's nothing else bothering you?

66

Shannon, if you don't want to talk to me, you can always try Izzy, or Emma, or Frances—'

'Not Frances,' Shannon cuts in. 'She'd tell everyone.'

'You could speak to your tutor at college.'

'Maz, it's nothing. Nothing much,' she qualifies. 'Actually, I'm worried about Mum . . . She's been really down recently and she won't go to the doctor, even though I've asked her to over and over.'

That seems unreasonable of Bridget, I think, considering how Shannon's already lost her father. 'Would you like me to mention it – in passing, I mean?'

'I'll deal with it, Maz. I've had an idea.'

Shannon says no more on the matter, so I change the subject.

'What do you think of Will? Are you getting on all right?'

'He seems . . . reasonable enough.' She brightens. 'He's a bit of a geek. And all he talks about are his scorpions and tree frogs.'

'Not really your type then?' I say, grinning.

'Definitely not. Maz, I haven't got time for a boyfriend. I couldn't anyway, not after Drew. Men are soooo not worth it.'

Shannon sighs and I smile to myself. I don't suppose it will be long until she changes her mind.

Bridget brings Daisy in the same afternoon at Shannon's request. Shannon and I take some blood and do a quick test for glucose before running some through the lab to check Daisy's liver and kidney function.

'Daisy, you look as if you've lost a bit of condition.' I run my hands along her chest, where her ribs should be. 'Shannon, we should try to get a urine sample.' I give her a collection dish and pot, and send her out to the garden, wishing her every success.

'You'll be lucky,' Bridget smiles. 'Daisy's very shy about that sort of thing.'

'How is it going with the diet?' I ask while we wait. 'I mean, with Daisy's diet . . .' Talk about putting my foot in it. Bridget's cheeks acquire a deeper hue. I wonder about her blood pressure – she's far more likely to have a problem than Frances whose occasional high colour seems to have more to do with an affair of the heart than a problem with the arteries.

'She's always starving.' Bridget shrugs. 'Daisy's like me. Neither of us are any good at sticking to a diet. Maz, if this is diabetes, what are we talking about, treatment-wise?'

'It will mean daily insulin injections, and a strict diet and exercise regime, but you have a vet nurse to do all of that for you, and we're just around the corner if you need any help or advice.'

'Thanks, Maz.' Bridget pauses. 'Shannon's been telling me that you're getting married. I'm sorry if I'm speaking out of turn, but I'd be more than happy to talk flowers with you – even if you don't choose to order them from me. I can advise you about winter blooms and foliage, and give you an idea of whether or not you're getting a good deal. You've been so kind to Shannon . . . and Daisy. It would be a pleasure.'

'Actually, I haven't thought about flowers yet,' I admit. 'I'm not terribly organised. Emma and Frances have already decided what I should have, but I'd prefer to make my own choices. Do I have to book an appointment, or just drop in?'

'Why don't you drop in one night after work when I'm not busy in the shop. Come in for a glass of wine and nibbles.'

'Thanks. That would be great.' That will be something else to tick off the list.

'Tonight then?'

'A day next week would suit me better, if that's all right.'

'We're back,' Shannon interrupts, Daisy's claws tapping along the floor behind her. 'Success!' She waves a pot of dog wee at me – with the lid on, I hasten to add. I test it quickly for glucose. It's positive.

'So, Daisy has diabetes,' says Shannon.

'We'll run the blood through the lab to check there's nothing else going on,' I say. 'You can get that done before you go home, can't you, Shannon? Then I suggest we book Daisy in for a twenty-minute appointment first thing tomorrow morning. If my nine o'clock is booked already, come in for twenty to.' I hesitate. 'I'm not planning to give Daisy anything now – we need to get her into a routine. She's going to have to come in every day until we get her condition stabilised.'

'What about Sunday?' says Shannon. 'We don't have a surgery on a Sunday?'

'Will can see her. He'll arrange a mutually convenient time.'

'But . . .' Shannon hesitates. I know what she's thinking. Does Will know what he's doing?

'I'll have a word with him and let him know where we're at.'

'Thanks, Maz,' Shannon says, apparently reassured.

'Um, what are the signs of diabetes?' says Bridget.

'Polydipsia – that's drinking lots,' says Shannon, 'along with weeing lots and eating lots.' She smiles. 'You see, I have been revising. I do know something.'

'So, it's the same in dogs as it is in humans?' says Bridget.

'Pretty much so,' I say.

'It sounds . . . What happens if you don't do anything about it?'

'You die,' I say, putting it bluntly. 'Eventually, the blood sugar level goes up so high that the body can no longer cope. The uncontrolled diabetic collapses, has fits, then goes into a coma, and that's it.'

'You are going to let Maz treat her, aren't you, Mum?' Shannon says, wide-eyed with concern. 'You aren't going to let her die?'

'I shan't let her die,' Bridget sighs. 'I'd better make that appointment.'

'I wish you'd look after yourself like you do the dogs,' Shannon says quietly. 'I can bring Daisy in tomorrow morning so you can see the doctor before you open the shop.'

Bridget doesn't respond. From her expression, I don't think she's being difficult. I think she's scared.

'Please, Mum,' Shannon says. 'For me?'

'Oh, all right. For you,' Bridget says eventually. 'Yes, I'll have a chat with Dr Mackie.' Shannon glances at me, her face etched with relief.

Bridget has the last word though. 'I'm sure there's nothing wrong with me.'

When I picture the fairy-tale dress, it is a blurry silhouette of off-white silk. I really don't know what I'm looking for. I hope Emma has a better idea than I do. She gave me some magazines to inspire me. There were some beautiful dresses, too many to choose from.

'Where do we start?' I ask as we leave the multi-storey car park in Exeter, Devon's historic cathedral city, and head into the shopping centre.

'In this vast metropolis . . .'

'You are joking, right.'

'Well, yes, although I'm comparing it with Talyton St George. Anyway, we can try the charity shops if you want the vintage look. We've got the department stores, if you want something ready-made and straight off the hanger, so to speak. It might be advisable because you haven't got much time to order a dress that needs making up from scratch, and have it altered if needs be.' Emma pauses. 'You're bound to lose a few pounds before the wedding day.'

'That won't be such a bad thing.' I'm still carrying a couple of kilos of baby weight.

'Does Sophia know you're out shopping for the dress?'

'I haven't mentioned it. I don't want her taking over, Em. I expect her to be offended that I didn't ask her opinion, but she's completely out of touch.'

We make a start in a bridal shop where we are welcomed by an assistant called Cara who appears to have been Botoxed, burnished with fake tan and basted with foundation that doesn't match the shade of her skin.

'So which of you young ladies is the blushing bride?' she says, having introduced herself. She wears a navy jacket and skirt, and a diamanté hairclip in the shape of a starfish in her sleek mahogany hair. 'It's Maz here,' says Emma, and if I wasn't blushing before, I am now.

'Emma's my wedding planner and matron of honour, if she'll accept the position.' I've rather sprung it on her, although I can't imagine her turning it down. 'Please, Em, I need you to keep Lucie, Seb and George in order.'

'How can I resist? Oh, I'd love to,' she says, hugging me. 'I'm so excited. How are we going to choose this dress?'

'I don't know.' I don't know where to start.

Cara steps in.

'Have you a theme for the wedding?' she asks.

'Not really.'

'Of course you have,' says Emma. 'It's a country wedding . . . A Christmas wedding.'

'A Christmas wedding,' I echo.

'So as well as the dress, you're going to have to think about how you'll avoid those blue arms and goose bumps in the photos and video. Of course, these things can be airbrushed out nowadays, but it's always better not to start with them in the first place. You can still choose quite a revealing dress, if you add a coat or cloak. We have a lovely hooded cape lined with faux fur for the winter season.' Cara pauses. 'Take a seat. I'll fetch some coffee and we can talk through some preliminary ideas.'

'You did remember to wear decent underwear?' whispers Emma when Cara is on her way back with a cafetière, cups and saucers on a tray.

'Yes, thanks to you.' I smile.

'What time of day is the actual wedding ceremony?' Cara asks.

'Late morning, I hope. We still have to agree a time with the vicar.'

'That's ideal. You know what they say – always get married in the morning. That way, if it all goes pear-shaped, you haven't wasted the whole day,' Cara says brightly. 'Anyway, according to the law of the land, you have to marry in daylight so the groom can see he's marrying the person he thinks he is.'

There's nothing I can say to that, and even Emma appears lost for words.

'Have you thought about your silhouette?' Cara says. 'The shape of the dress?'

'I know I don't want to look like a meringue.'

'Think about highlighting your best bits,' says Emma. 'You have a neat bust, slim hips and a flattish stomach. I am so jealous.'

I'm beginning to feel like an exhibit in a show for best pet.

'A column dress might suit you, Maz, or a fishtail shape which hugs the figure then flares out below the knee. We'll start with those,' Cara says. 'How about a train? Are you getting married in a church, registry office or somewhere more exotic?'

'The local church,' says Emma.

'That's wonderful. It gives you so much more flexibility when it comes to choosing the train. A cathedral-length would make quite a statement.' Cara appraises me once more. 'Let's try the column dress first. Come through to the changing room and take your clothes off. Have you got your shoes with you?'

I glance down at my flat pumps.

'They won't do. You need something with a decent heel. I have a pair you can try for now.'

I strip down to my underwear and wait, surrounded by mirrors that make me feel completely exposed. I half expect Gok Wan to walk in, but it's Cara who turns up, laden with dresses. She helps me into the first one, a plain ivory gown with a cowl neck. She zips and buttons me up at the back before tweaking the sides and sticking a few pins into the fabric, making me wince.

'That is gorgeous. You do have a lovely figure.' She pulls the curtain across to show Emma. 'Doesn't she look fabulous?'

Emma looks me up and down. 'I'm not sure.'

'I feel a bit like a nun.'

'We can't have that,' Cara says. 'That won't put you in the mood for your wedding night, will it. Take it off. I have plenty more.'

Five dresses later and we are no nearer finding the One.

'This is more difficult than finding a husband,' I say.

'Well, in both cases, you have to be sure of your choice,' says Cara. 'Ah, here's the one I was looking for. Try this.'

'Go on, Maz,' Emma says, sensing that I'm already running out of enthusiasm. 'I tried over a hundred when I was looking for mine.'

'Is that all?' says Cara. 'I've had brides in here who've tried on more than two hundred and fifty before they could make up their minds.' She pulls the curtains back across, helps me into the next dress and laces it up tightly.

'It's a smaller size,' she explains. 'We can order the next size up,' but I can see as she steps back and wrinkles her nose that she already knows I'm not going to like it. 'Personally,' she goes on, one hand on her hip, 'I think it's wrong for you. It's too bouffant over the hips and it's making a shelf of your bosom.'

'Would you unlace me, please?' I can hardly breathe and it's a relief to discover my ribs are intact, only bruised, as the dress comes off again.

'Don't worry, Maz,' Emma calls out. 'There's always eBay.'

'I have two more,' Cara says, unappreciative of Emma's teasing. 'There's the one I describe as being after the Duchess of Cambridge's style, but it's white which won't suit your colouring, although we can obtain one in ivory. Then there's the mermaid gown –

74

that's in ivory, with a sequinned bodice and scalloped sleeves. I'll find that one for you.'

The mermaid gown is a perfect fit. It's stunning. I feel several inches taller, very much the princess and definitely not a mermaid.

'I reckon that could be the one,' says Emma.

'You don't sound terribly convinced,' I say.

'It isn't that . . . I'm disappointed we've found it so soon.'

'Oh, but you still have to choose the shoes, headdress, cape, and bridesmaids' dresses,' Cara says quickly. 'You've hardly started yet.'

'It is the one though,' I agree, smoothing the silk at the front and the back. 'It fits perfectly.' A thought occurs to me though and I turn to examine my rear in the mirrors.

'Does my—?' I begin.

'Absolutely not,' Emma cuts in. 'There's nothing wrong with your bum.'

'You have a most shapely derrière,' says Cara, and I find that the bride is blushing again.

'Whatever you do, don't let the groom have a sneak preview,' says Cara. 'Remember it's unlucky if he sees the bride in her dress before the wedding.' She tips her head to one side and smiles, flashing her fiercely white teeth. 'I'm sure most grooms take advantage of that superstition to avoid long shopping trips with their brides-to-be.'

'Mine does,' I smile back. 'Alex hates shopping.' I turn to Emma. 'Do you think he'll like it?'

'Alex won't be able to keep his eyes – or his hands – off you.'

Chapter Five

Pets Win Prizes

It's the day of the Country Show, one of Talyton St George's annual social events and highlight of the year for many. The weather doesn't disappoint by breaking with tradition. We've had heavy rain overnight and the forecast is for sunshine and showers.

Recalling my very first experience of the event when I wrecked my coolest pair of pumps in ankle-deep red Devon mud, I choose to wear a practical down-to-earth pair of green wellies. Having gradually morphed from a city girl to a country vet, my transformation is complete with a waxed coat. Do I regret it? I don't need to express myself through fashion any more, but – call me shallow – I do miss it sometimes. Perhaps I'll make up for it by choosing something special for the honeymoon.

Lucie and Seb are staying with us for the weekend and, although we agreed that Alex wouldn't be on duty, leaving me with the three children when he's out on a call, guess what – he is.

Alex and I travel to the showground with George.

Sophia drives the horsebox, taking Lucie, Seb and Lucie's pony who's entered for the Mounted Games as a member of the Pony Club team.

Alex parks the four-by-four in the 'Officials' section of the field that's roped off from the other parking, and close to the entrance of the show where we are allowed to bypass the turnstiles for the general public of Talyton St George and from miles around. Once we're in, Alex pushing George through the wet grass in the buggy, Fifi Green greets us with a balloon on a stick for George. My maternal feelings kick in and I start worrying about George poking his eye out.

As I bend forward to remove it from his grasp, Alex says, 'Leave it, Maz. I'm watching.'

'He might hurt himself.'

'He'll soon learn,' Alex says.

I turn back to Fifi, resisting the urge to comment that I don't want George learning by experience, not yet anyway.

Fifi's hair is copper and blonde, with a fixed wave. Her eyelashes have to be false, as are her nails, and probably her teeth. She's wearing a canary yellow blouse and a navy and yellow spotted A-line skirt, wedge-heeled wellies and a blue beret set at a jaunty angle.

'I hope you appreciate the hat, Maz,' she says, noticing me looking at it. It isn't her usual style. 'We have guests from our twin town here today. It's my contribution to the entente cordiale.'

I catch sight of Alex winking at me and try not to giggle. Fifi means well, but she can be over the top sometimes.

Fifi tweaks the scarf at her neck. She's getting on a

little bit now, in her sixties, but she's determined not to show it. I don't blame her. I hope I'm half as energetic at her age.

'Where's your father?' she says. 'I told him to be here half an hour earlier than I wanted him, so he'd be on time. Isn't he with you?'

'You'll have to make do with me today,' Alex says. 'Father is sick.'

'Sick? Are you sure?' Fifi says, her voice rising in surprise.

'Quite certain,' says Alex. 'I heard it from the horse's mouth this morning!'

'Oh, dear.' Fifi sounds somewhat deflated.

'You can tell he's feeling rough if he isn't here. He wouldn't normally miss this for anything.'

'Is there anything I can do? I'm sure I can rally the troops to take some chicken soup or crab apple jelly up to the Manor.'

By the troops, Fifi means the good ladies of the WI, of which she is Chairperson.

'That won't be necessary, Fifi.' Alex flashes me a glance, rolling his eyes. 'I expect Mother's thrown a bit of bute into his breakfast.'

'Bute?' Fifi frowns, wrinkling her brow and I think, Botox can't have reached Talyton St George just yet, because, if it had, Fifi would have been first in the queue.

'Bute – it's an anti-inflammatory drug for horses,' Alex explains. 'I was joking, Fifi.'

It takes her a second or two to realise what he's said, but when it sinks in, she takes Alex's hand and gives it a tap.

'Naughty boy. You're just like your father.'

Not too much like him, I think, amused. I would

never have agreed to marry someone like Old Fox-Gifford.

'It's such a shame he couldn't be here,' Fifi says wistfully. I've always thought she has a soft spot for Alex's father. 'He's so good at these things.'

Alex is listening, his expression impassive and I wonder what he's thinking, if he resents being in his father's shadow.

'When's he going to make you a senior partner then?' Fifi goes on. 'I'd say you were old enough by now.'

'Ah, but he'd have to pay me more, Fifi, and you know how tight he is,' Alex says lightly.

'Come along then. We'll have to make do with you,' Fifi continues. 'At least we have a representative from each practice.'

Three years ago, I had the dubious honour of judging the class for the Best Pet with Old Fox-Gifford. The next time we sent Drew, the locum. Last year, Emma did it, under sufferance.

'We'd better make a start. You should have these.' Fifi hands out 'Judge' badges. George takes a fancy to mine and, for the sake of peace and quiet, I let him have it. It isn't a pin-on one. It's supposed to thread through a buttonhole. Fifi purses her lips in disapproval, and disappears into the ticket booth to find another one.

'There you go, Maz. Please don't let it fall into the wrong hands. The free lunch is exclusively for our show officials. But it's all right to bring George along, if you need to,' she adds.

'Thanks, Fifi,' I say, not wishing to upset her by letting her know I'm not all that keen on the idea of lunch.

'I remembered, Maz,' she says, as if she can read my mind. 'I've asked Elsa to provide a vegetarian option this year. There's a hog roast for the carnivores.' She glances from me to Alex and back. 'It's a happy pig, Maz.'

'Was a happy pig,' I correct her gently.

We follow Fifi along the main avenue, walking between the marquees and stalls with their rails of waxed coats, deerstalkers and boots, and everything you could possibly need for your horse and dog – because most people here are accompanied by either a spaniel, a Labrador or a terrier of some or other variety. There are sober-looking men in country tweeds, selling farm insurance and contracts for maintaining milking machines. There aren't many takers for the Hen Welfare tombola which is right next to Talyton Animal Rescue's, but there's quite a crowd around the next stall, Jennie's Cakes.

'Isss . . .' George waves his balloon and points towards a shining tractor on display. 'Isss. There Iss.'

'George, it's a tractor,' Fifi says. 'Tractor . . .'

'It's Travis,' says Alex. 'Travis the tractor from Bob the Builder.' He smiles ruefully. 'And I should know. I'm the world authority on those stories. Seb loved them, and George does too.'

We round the corner past the WI tent. I stop and take a look inside to give Frances a wave, but she's arranging scones on a plate at one of the long trestle tables and doesn't see me.

'Horsey,' George says, pointing with his balloon as we pass the farriery display. Sophia has taught him well.

'It's going to be a great day,' says Fifi. 'All the organisation will have been worth it.'

The air is sweet with the scent of deep-frying doughnuts and coffee, and the atmosphere electric with the sound of generators and a crackly public address system.

'Hi, Alex. Hello, Maz.' Chris, Izzy's husband, shouts a greeting as he drives a handful of woolly sheep along the next avenue with the help of two collie dogs, only one of whom has its mind on the job. The other comes trotting over to see us.

Chris puts his fingers between his teeth and whistles, but the dog, a striking black, tan and white collie, ignores him. 'Freddie, get back here!' Chris yells.

'Go on, Freddie,' I tell him. 'You'll get the sack, if you're not careful.'

Freddie was one of ours – Otter House Vets', that is. Either his owner was completely heartless, or she really thought she couldn't afford the fees, but she dumped him at the practice soon after I began working there. Freddie was seriously ill, but he pulled through with supportive treatment and Izzy's nursing care. Izzy took him to Chris's farm to see if he had any aptitude as a sheepdog. It turned out that he hadn't, and it doesn't matter because, without Freddie, Chris and Izzy wouldn't have got together.

When we reach the Pet Show ring that's divided off from the main thoroughfare with bales of straw, posts and rope, there are competitors already waiting. My heart sinks a little. There are about thirty of them with all kinds of animals: dogs, cats and rabbits, some on leads, some in carriers. There are rats and hamsters too, a duck, a python and what looks like a tarantula in a box.

There's Raffles who belongs to the Pitts, Stewart and Lynsey. He's being shown off by their eldest boy,

Sam. Raffles is one of ours, but Alex looks after the cows on the family farm. Raffles, though short on legs, is long on character. He would win for being the cutest pet, with his reddish tan coat and fluffy blond knickerbockers.

Saba, the standard poodle, would win for being the most glamorous pet. Her curly black coat is newly trimmed, and her collar and lead studded with what look like Swarovski crystals. Her owner, Aurora, is dressed in black leather trousers, long boots, and a short jacket.

Cheryl from the Copper Kettle, the tea shop, is here too. She used to be one of ours, but moved on to another small animal practice some way away, after an unfortunate misunderstanding. I gave her prize-winning stud cat a closer shave than she thought she'd asked for, when she brought him in to Otter House for a tidy-up.

She's brought the same cat, Blueboy, a blue Persian, along today. He's wearing a harness and sitting on a cushion that's covered with bling. Cheryl wears grey trousers and a waistcoat covered with cat motifs. Cats dangle from her earrings and bracelet. Her hair is short and dark, except at the roots where it's silvery grey.

'This is going to be a bit of a marathon,' Alex says aside to me. 'How on earth are we going to choose?'

'I don't know,' I say, smiling. 'What did you and your father used to do before Emma turned up and opened her practice? You must have had a system of some sort.' When he doesn't respond, I go on, 'The first and last time I did this, we gave points out of ten for each animal, and Fifi added the two judges' scores together to give a final score. The pet with the most points wins.' I pause. 'Or we could decide to go for the cutest, or the most exotic.'

'Or the one in the best condition,' Alex says.

'How do you tell if a tarantula is in good condition?'

'Count its legs? You tell me, you're the small animal specialist,' Alex grins. 'Come on, we'd better hand George over to Mother and make a start, otherwise we'll be here all day.'

Sophia joins us with Seb and Lucie on the other side of the ropes. Lucie has her blonde hair tied back with a purple ribbon, and she's already kitted out in her riding gear: white shirt, Pony Club tie and jodhpurs. Seb, who takes after Alex in appearance, wears a blue checked shirt and slops about in wellies that are at least two sizes too big for him.

'I'll look after George.' Lucie drags the buggy back out of the ring, unclipping the harness and hauling George out. 'You sit there on the bale,' she tells him.

'No,' he says, and sits down anyway.

'Lucie has a real knack with little kids,' I say to Alex.

'It's a pity she doesn't have the same knack with Sebastian,' he says. 'Will you be all right there, Mother?'

'Yes, I've roped a couple of the Pony Club mums in to supervise the ponies for the next hour or so. It's no thanks to your father. He should have been here.' Sophia turns to Fifi. 'He's never had a day off sick, not since he recovered from the bull attack. And that would never have happened, if he hadn't been so stubborn and gone into the pen with it. Everyone knew he was a rogue.' I take it she's referring to the bull, not her husband. 'They called him Lucifer, after the Devil.'

'Did you call the doctor?' Fifi asks.

'Dr Mackie's coming out to the Manor after surgery.'

'He must be dreadfully unwell, if he's allowed you to call the doctor. Are you sure he should be left on his own?' Fifi says. When Sophia answers her with a dark stare, she goes on, 'Well, I'm sure he'll be better soon. Dr Mackie's such a lovely young man. Did I ever mention he's done wonders with my bunions?'

'You have mentioned that before, Fifi,' Sophia says curtly, 'on more than one occasion. Now, shouldn't you be getting on, Alexander? I can't possibly miss the Mounted Games.'

'Come on then, Maz.' Alex takes my hand. 'Into the lion's den, or unto the breach, or whatever the saying is.'

Fifi organises the competitors into a line, asking those with pets of a convenient size to stand them on the straw bales, before Alex and I walk up and down, the picture of unity, the perfect couple in love. I squeeze his fingers. He smiles.

'I like that one,' I say quietly, pointing out a small, scruffy grey-black terrier. 'That's Lucky, one of ours.'

'I know Lucky,' Alex says, reminding me that although the dog is registered with Otter House, the family to whom he belongs have other animals, cattle, ponies and chickens, registered with Alex's practice. 'I've never quite trusted him, and I have to admit that he reminds me of a rat,' Alex goes on in a whisper. 'And you can't choose on the basis that he's one of your clients. That isn't fair. I prefer the tarantula.'

'That isn't one of yours?' I say in disbelief.

'It isn't – I'm not biased.'

It's supposed to be fun, I muse, but every pet owner believes their pet is the best, and I can feel the tension as Alex and I walk up and down the line, unable to make a decision. Sensing the weight of their expectation, I wonder how anyone can make a decision, when each pet is equally precious in the eyes of its owner.

Aurora is posing for Alex's benefit, but I'm reassured at his response. He looks away from her legs, giving me a wink and a look.

Lucky doesn't help his chances of winning by snapping at Alex when he moves to stroke him.

'You know he doesn't like strange men, Alex,' says the lanky teenage boy who's with him. He's about fifteen or sixteen, and wears his jeans down around his thighs, showing off his stripy pants.

'Thanks for that, Adam.' Alex grins.

'I didn't mean strange as in weird or anything,' Adam says hastily. 'If you remember, Lucky was abandoned on the motorway before we adopted him. You can't blame him really.'

'It isn't a particularly endearing quality though, biting first and asking questions afterwards,' Alex says. It's just like a reality show on television. A good sob story can do wonders for your chances.

'Your father never has any difficulty coming to a decision,' Fifi interrupts. 'Come on, Maz.' She touches my elbow. 'You will have to make the casting vote, otherwise we'll miss out on lunch.'

Alex looks at me. 'What were the criteria for Best Pet again?'

'I'm torn between Raffles and Lucky.'

'The scruffy one? It tried to eat me.' Alex rubs his chin. 'I'm inclined towards the spider.'

'That wouldn't be your father's choice,' I say, amused. 'He'd class it as vermin.'

'The girl seems to know a lot about tarantulas, where they come from and how to keep them.'

'I'm not sure, Alex. Picking the spider might cause a bit of a stir.'

He chuckles. 'Let's do it then.'

It wasn't such a good move. The girl with the spider is delighted with her red rosette and the perpetual challenge cup that she keeps for a year, but Cheryl immediately lodges an objection with Fifi who calls me and Alex over to adjudicate.

'Blueboy has won prizes at the National,' Cheryl says. 'He's a champion, yet he's been placed beneath a bug. It's a disgrace.' She's looking at me when she says this. I don't think she'll ever forgive me. 'Look at Blueboy. Look how beautiful he is.'

Beauty is definitely in the eye of the beholder in this instance. Blueboy has squinting orange eyes and a grumpy expression, very much like Cassie's, who happens to be one of his many daughters. His hair is long and lustrous though, bathed and conditioned.

'Cheryl, this show is for the children,' says Fifi.

'Where does it say that in the rules?' says Cheryl.

'It doesn't. It's common sense. We should use this opportunity to let our young people shine. It's supposed to be fun.'

I can tell from Cheryl's expression that it's only fun when you win.

Fifi continues, 'Cheryl, please accept defeat gracefully. Blueboy is no less of a show cat, and this is hardly the National Cat Show, or whatever you call it.'

'That's true.' Cheryl begins to back down. 'It's a pretty tin-pot affair really. And the judges are hardly qualified.'

'Well, I don't know,' Fifi says, defending us. 'They are vets.'

'What do they know?' Cheryl shrugs her bony

shoulders, and turns to me again. 'I thought you'd like to know that Clive dropped by to ask my advice about Cassie. It seems to show a distinct lack of trust in veterinary advice, if you ask me, but that's by the by. They've ruined her, of course. It's such a shame they didn't come to me.'

'What do you mean, they've ruined her?' asks Fifi.

'Mating her with a common moggie. She'll never be able to produce a pedigree litter in future.'

'It won't make any difference,' I say, with restraint.

'Her blood is tainted,' Cheryl insists.

I look to Alex for a second opinion.

'Maz is right,' Alex says firmly. 'There's no reason why she shouldn't breed a pedigree litter next time, so long as she's bred to a pedigree cat. The rest, well, it's an old wives' tale.'

Cheryl's cheeks flush deep scarlet. 'You vets know absolutely nothing about Persian cats. I despair of the profession today. Persians are a special breed.'

'I despair too,' Alex says quietly into my ear, as Cheryl retreats. 'Cat breeders aren't merely a special breed, they're a different species.'

'Oh, Alex, you are a one,' Fifi giggles, overhearing. She organises the competitors into making a lap of honour around the ring to the applause of the audience that has gathered and I take a moment to speak to Alex.

'Do we have to go for lunch? Your mother wants us to have the children back so she can run the Mounted Games team.'

'I feel as if we should put in an appearance,' Alex says seriously.

I rest my hand on his arm. 'We've done our bit. I'd rather spend the rest of the day with George, and watch Lucie compete.'

'We are pillars of the community. We are obliged to schmooze.' The corners of his eyes begin to crease and his mouth curves into a boyish grin.

'You're winding me up,' I say, laughing.

'You bet I am.' He grabs my hand and links his fingers through mine. 'I fancy stout and oysters –' he lowers his voice and whispers in my ear – 'and you.'

'Careful,' I warn. 'I hope you're not going to get overexcited.'

'What's going on here then?' Fifi rejoins us. 'Oh, young love,' she sighs. 'I can't wait for the wedding. It's December now, isn't it?'

I think she knows very well when it is, and somehow, even though Alex and I haven't got around to writing the guest list yet, she's made the assumption that she's invited.

'Just a word of advice for you, Maz,' she goes on. 'Don't forget to use your contacts. We have an excellent variety of potted trees at the garden centre, if you should choose to follow the royal couple's example of bringing nature into the church.'

'It's a kind thought, but I don't think so, Fifi. The church is spacious, but it's hardly Westminster Abbey.'

'I do hope you're going to choose some special touches to make the day your own. You have to consider the wedding photos.'

Photos? The photographer. I haven't booked a photographer yet. I start to panic. There is so much to do. I feel as I did just before my finals at vet school, that shaky, sick sensation that I haven't done nearly enough work to pass the exams.

'We'd better be off, Fifi,' Alex says. 'We have to rescue Mother – she has all three of her grandchildren on her hands.'

'You aren't joining the Show Committee for lunch then? That's a shame – Old Fox-Gifford always makes a point of joining us.'

'You know what he's like – he'll never turn down a free lunch,' Alex says.

We join Sophia and the children. George refuses to go back in the buggy, so Alex gives in and carries him on his shoulders, prompting Seb to play up in the most spectacular fashion, even though Alex promises him a turn later.

'Everyone's watching. That naughty little boy,' says Sophia, 'that's what they're thinking.'

'I not little,' Seb protests in baby language, something he reverts to frequently, even though he's nearly six. 'I not naughty either.'

'Well, you are,' Sophia insists sternly. 'Humpy says so.'

'Humpy says so,' Lucie echoes. She adores her grandmother.

'Alexander, can you manage here? Lucie and I need to get the pony warmed up. The Games are in the arena at one sharp.'

'Don't forget, Daddy,' Lucie says, her eyes gleaming with anticipation.

'I'll be there. I promise. See you later.'

Alex and I take the boys around the showground, letting them explore the cab of one of the shiny new tractors. Alex has half a stout and several oysters at the oyster bar, and I taste so many local cheeses that I can't tell the difference between them any more. Seb and George have ice creams and I indulge in a guilty pleasure of mine: melt-in-the-mouth candyfloss freshly spun. We all end up with sticky faces and sticky fingers – thank goodness for baby wipes.

'I wanna drink,' says Seb, as we pass the beer tent on our way to the main arena for the Mounted Games.

'Please . . .' says Alex.

'Please . . .'

'I'll get you one,' I offer. Anything for a moment's peace. I can see why parents pander to their kids. I thought I'd be a strict mother, but sometimes it's easier to follow the path of least resistance. 'You stay out here with the buggy, Alex. You don't want a drink, I take it?'

'I'd love a beer, but I'd better not, not that I expect to get called out today. Everyone's here at the show.'

'I'll be back in a mo'.' I give George a wave before I head inside the beer tent where the air is thick with the scent of wet clothes, malt and mothballs. I'm not sure why. Maybe the older generations of farmers have pulled their best tweeds out of storage for the occasion. I head past the tables to the bar beyond, where Clive is serving.

'Hi, Clive. How are you?'

'Well, thanks, Maz. Edie's looking after the pub, and the cat, of course. What can I get you?'

'Just a coke to take out, thank you. Last of the big spenders, that's me.'

He pours a coke and hands it over.

'What's this I hear about a vasectomy gone wrong?'

'A what?' My neck grows hot with embarrassment. It seems a strange subject for Clive to raise even though we're on good terms.

'You know. You're a vet,' he says awkwardly.

'You must have got the wrong person. My Alex hasn't had the snip.'

'No, no, it's not that.' Clive blushes furiously. 'I wasn't thinking about anyone in particular. I'm sorry.

No, I'd heard a rumour about some sheep, a ram.'

'Oh? It's the first I've heard.'

'I must have got hold of the wrong end of the stick. Ignore me. I'm always putting my great big foot in it. What's it called? The practice of dontopedalogy?'

'Something like that.' I say goodbye and go out to meet up with Alex, by which time Seb doesn't want a drink, but is demanding a go on the bouncy castle further along the walkway. While he's having a quick bounce, I ask Alex about the vasectomy rumour.

'It was an odd thing to say,' I point out.

'You know what this place is like. You've lived here long enough.' Alex gives me an affectionate dig in the ribs, making me slosh the coke. 'There is some truth in the rumour though. Robert over at Headlands Farm booked a couple of rams in for the snip. Father missed one of the teaser rams.' Alex means one of the rams that the farmer uses to see if the ewes are ready for breeding. 'Anyway, it didn't become apparent until the lambing season back in March when, instead of all being black-faced lambs, there were a large proportion of white ones. It caused a few laughs, I can tell you.'

'You didn't tell me,' I say, a little hurt. 'It can't have been all that funny. Wasn't Robert annoyed? He must have lost quite a lot of money,' I add, but Alex diverts, grabbing a hat from a stall and sticking it on my head.

'Suits you, Maz.' Alex chuckles. 'What do you think of Mummy in a hat, George?'

George holds out his hands for a hat too. Alex drops one onto his head, but it's far too big, slipping down over his eyes and making him cry. Alex whips it off and puts both hats back while I console George with some of Seb's coke, and I'm thinking, sugar rush, he's never going to sleep tonight. Seb comes off the bouncy castle, his hair stuck up with static, and then he wants the drink and we take ten minutes to find his wellies, by which time the commentator is announcing the start of the Mounted Games in the main arena so we have to fly.

There are five teams representing different branches of the Pony Club. Each team consists of four children on ponies with a reserve. Lucie's team wear purple vests over white shirts and shiny boots. It's starting to look as though Lucie is getting too big for her pony, the bay, Tinky Winky, but the other members of her team have their legs down around their ponies' knees.

There are several races, all relays: the flag race; walk, trot and run; mug race; Farmer's Market; bending poles. The sun is shining now and I can feel my nose beginning to burn. I plaster George with sunblock, but he won't keep his hat on for more than two seconds at a time.

The ponies gallop up and down, the riders with their reins up short, and legs flapping. Lucie's expression is one of intense concentration. She's taking it very seriously.

For the last race, she is the final member of the Talyton team to set off. She sets off at a trot as the member with the baton comes galloping in from the course, and my heart is in my mouth at the changeover, but it's perfect and Lucie is away, weaving in and out of the poles. She turns the pony on a sixpence at the end of the course, and weaves back at full gallop, just pipping the team who comes in second at the finishing post, and belting on out of the arena altogether into the collecting ring.

'Another win for the local team, Talyton St George Pony Club,' the commentator announces over the tannoy as the crowd cheers.

'Wow, they're good,' I say. 'You'll be doing that in a couple of years, Seb.'

'And George will be,' Alex says proudly. 'You know, I think they've won.'

They have, and there's more applause when all the teams regroup to collect their rosettes. Lucie can't stop smiling when her team collects the trophy from Sophia, District Commissioner of the branch. I watch how Lucie sticks the rosette into the bridle below her pony's ear, just as her teammates do, and then they're off for their lap of honour, galloping around the ring, arms in the air and ponies completely out of control.

'It's a shame my father couldn't be here to see that,' Alex says. 'He'll be gutted he missed it. Mother's been trying to win that trophy back for years. We won it way back when I was fifteen, the last year I was eligible to compete.'

'A very long time ago,' I say teasingly.

'Thanks for that, Maz.' He smiles as he watches his mother speaking on her mobile as she walks out towards the collecting ring in the distance. 'I expect she's giving Father the news – and reading him the riot act for not being here to see it.'

'It's been a great day so far.' I check my watch. 'It must be time to go home soon though. I've got so much to do.'

'Like what?'

'Washing. You know, the boring stuff that has to be done.'

'Oh, Maz.' Alex slides one arm around my waist and

rests his chin into my shoulder. 'It can wait. It'll have to wait because Mother's invited us for dinner.'

'Oh, Alex.' I'm disappointed. 'Do we have to?'

'I said yes.'

'You could have run it past me first.'

'Mother had already arranged it. Mrs P has put a meal together.'

'Thrown one together, more likely. I wonder what it is this time,' I say, my appetite completely disappearing. Mrs P cooks, cleans and irons for the Old Fox-Giffords in return for accommodation in one of the tied cottages on the estate. I've heard her described as 'the woman who does', but you only have to see the state of the Manor to know that she doesn't do what she's supposed to terribly well.

'Maz, Mother's only trying to help. We've all been out for the day, we've got the three children . . . It's her way of lightening the load.'

'Oh, I know.' It's sweet of her, but the idea of having dinner with Alex's father, listening to him air his opinions, is not appealing. 'It's meat and two veg, I guess.'

'No, actually. Mrs P has prepared roast pork and a nut rissole.'

'That'll be interesting. Do you think I should grab a sandwich first?'

'Mother will expect you to set a good example to the children – you'll have to clear your plate.' Alex kisses me on the cheek, and I realise I can't possibly back out, even if I could engineer a minor ailment for George and an excuse to stay at home with him. When I marry Alex, I shall be marrying into the Fox-Gifford family. They have expectations, and although I'm sure I'll never be able to meet them – because I don't ride, shoot or fish, and in their eyes, I'm still a townie – I shall do my best for my husband. My husband? I wonder if, after the wedding, I will ever get used to saying that. I kiss Alex back. My husband and I . . .

Chapter Six

Catch-22

When we eventually return to the Manor ready for dinner, Sophia is on the warpath. There is a note from the doctor stuck on the door, saying, 'Sorry I missed you,' and Old Fox-Gifford is out with the dogs. He comes back soon after, his gun slung over one shoulder, joining us in the drawing room where Seb is sitting on one of the sofas taking the battery out of a remote-controlled car, and George is playing with his toy tractor, following the pattern on the Axminster. Having given him a mint from the tin on the side table, Lucie and Alex are shooing Skye, the Shetland pony, who ambled in through from the garden, back outside.

'So you thought fit to join us at last, Fox-Gifford,' Sophia says sarcastically. 'Where have you been? I've been trying to get hold of you.'

'Granpa, we won!' Lucie interrupts, running over to Old Fox-Gifford, as Alex closes the French windows before the pony can push his way back in. 'We won the Mounted Games.'

'Congratulations, Lucie,' Old Fox-Gifford says,

patting her on the shoulder when she throws her arms around his waist.

'I wish you'd been there,' she says. 'We won almost every race, our handovers were perfect, and I didn't drop the mug in the mug race this time.'

'Oh, well done. I wish I'd been there too.'

'It seems to me that you could have been,' Sophia cuts in. 'You tell me you're dying and I come home to find you out with the dogs. You could have at least been here when the doctor came.'

'The old dogs needed their afternoon constitutional,' says Old Fox-Gifford. 'They like their routine.'

'Granpa, did you tell a lie?' says Lucie, stepping back, her eyes wide with astonishment.

'I felt a bit peculiar this morning. By this afternoon, I felt much better. It must have been something I ate.'

'I doubt it,' Alex says. 'You have a cast-iron stomach.'

'All you had to do was call the doctor to let him know not to waste his time, then you could have come along to the show for the rest of the afternoon. You've missed Lucie's moment of triumph, and Talyton Pony Club's finest hour,' says Sophia, gloating. 'You will be there for the championship.'

'Will you, Granpa?' Lucie says.

'I hope I'll be around to see it . . .' Old Fox-Gifford utters a long, drawn-out sigh.

'One minute you're saying you're fine. Now you're making it sound as if you're about to . . .' Sophia glances towards the children.

'Go on, say it,' says Old Fox-Gifford. 'Pop orf. Yes, I'm feeling better than I did this morning, but I could pop orf at any moment. I've had my time – I don't want to hang about, useful to neither man nor beast.'

'Don't be ridiculous,' says Sophia. 'Granpa's being very silly.' She addresses this particularly to Lucie who's looking worried. 'He isn't going to die. He isn't even sick, because, if he was, he would have been here waiting for Dr Mackie, not rampaging through the countryside with the dogs.'

'Granpa isn't sick,' Seb agrees. 'If he was sick, he'd be like this.' He coughs and retches and puts his hands around his own neck as if he's trying to strangle himself.

'No, Seb,' says Sophia.

George has already picked up on it though, and he's coughing and spluttering like Seb.

'Boys, let's have some decorum,' Sophia goes on.

'What's decorum?' asks Lucie.

'Self-control, darling,' she says.

Shortly afterwards, we settle in the dining room, seven of us at one end of the magnificent table that stands in the centre on a brightly patterned Persian rug. George is strapped into the highchair, the one Alex had as a baby that's been kept up in the loft for the grandchildren. I have thrown a jumper over my shoulders because it's cold in this room. The fire is never lit in here, and there's an all-pervading smell of damp and school dinners.

Mrs P stays on late to serve roast pork and nut rissole. There's watery soup of indeterminate origin to start with.

'What do you think this is?' I whisper to Alex, when Mrs P has disappeared, rattling out through the door with her trolley and soup tureen.

'We could send some off to the lab to find out –' Alex trickles the soup from his spoon back into the bowl – 'but your fancy analyser machine probably won't be able to pick anything up. Whichever substances are in there are in too low a concentration to be detected.'

'Daddy, stop playing with your food,' Lucie interrupts sternly. 'He must shut up and eat up, mustn't he, Humpy?'

'Don't be cheeky, Lucie,' says Sophia. 'Mind you don't splash that lovely rosette.'

Lucie has her Mounted Games rosette on the table in front of her. It's red, white and blue with long ribbons. She keeps touching them and laying them straight.

'There's potential for a clash with the wedding,' says Sophia happily, apparently unable to let the subject of the Mounted Games drop. I'm not sure who is most excited about it, Lucie or Sophia. 'Of course, the team has to come first. You can't let the other members down.'

'Mother, this is my wedding you're talking about,' Alex says. 'Lucie will be bridesmaid.'

I can see that Lucie's torn now. We wanted to ask her on her own, not in front of everyone. Bridesmaid or Mounted Games at the National Horse Show in December? It's a difficult call.

'I did go to your last one,' says Sophia.

'I didn't,' says Lucie. 'I wasn't born then.'

'You might not get another chance at the championship,' says Sophia. 'I'm *chef d'équipe* and I'll be needed. What time is the wedding?'

'I don't know yet, Mother. Maz and I need to see the vicar.'

'If you make it early in the day, we can follow the ponies on,' says Sophia.

She can't be serious, I think, but she is. I abandon the soup and break off a piece of bread roll for George.

The nut rissole is chewy and the potatoes cold, but it's food and we're hungry. Alex makes much of Mrs P who beams with pride at his praise for her culinary talents. He isn't being patronising. Secretly, he adores her. She's been part of his life since he can remember.

'I want ketchup,' says Seb.

'I'll get it,' says Mrs P.

'Real ketchup. Not healthy stuff like Mummy buys,' Seb continues.

'What do you say, Seb?' says Sophia.

'Thank you, please,' he says, giggling, at which George grins and throws the piece of bread roll I gave him over the edge of the highchair, where it's pounced upon and snarled over by Old Fox-Gifford's dogs.

'Off that!' Old Fox-Gifford grabs his stick from where it's leaning against the table and pokes at the horde of hounds. 'Leave it.'

'It's too late, Father,' Alex says, looking on amused. 'Hal will have digested it by now.'

'The old boy got it then?' Old Fox-Gifford's eyes sparkle with glee. 'He's still top dog.'

'Here, top dog,' Seb says, dropping half a potato and creating a second skirmish.

'Not at the dinner table,' says Sophia as the dogs go quiet, and the dust and hairs settle once more. 'Manners maketh man.'

'He's just a boy, Humpy,' says Lucie. 'A stupid little boy.'

'Lucie, please don't start,' Alex says.

'Is there ice cream for dessert?' Seb asks, his mind on food rather than retaliating against his sister.

'Ice cream and peaches from a tin,' says Sophia.

'Hurrah,' says Lucie. 'My favourite.'

'Mine too,' Old Fox-Gifford says gruffly.

'You're an old fraud,' Sophia tells him. 'Last week, you said it was apple pie and custard.'

'Perhaps my tastes have changed, dear Sophia,' he says.

'You do it to be difficult, giving poor Mrs P the runaround over her desserts. No sooner does she get the recipe right than you order something else.'

With a sigh of annoyance at his wife's nagging, Old Fox-Gifford picks up his glass and drains the brownish claret, straining the bits between his teeth and wiping his mouth with a stained white napkin. This is the only place where I've seen napkin rings of monogrammed silver in daily use.

Seb is collecting the rings and stacking them up into a tower in front of George who, with one swipe of his arm, knocks it back down again. I make to take them away, but Sophia stops me.

'It's all right, Maz. The boys can have them to play with.'

'They're precious though, aren't they?'

'Yes.' She smiles. 'There was an occasion when we thought one of our guests had walked orf with one as a keepsake, but we found it in Hal's bed. It was when he was a pup. He chewed it to pieces, left some in his bed and swallowed the rest.'

'It's no wonder his teeth are in such a state,' Alex comments. 'In fact, I've been wondering about offering him up as a guinea pig for Maz and Emma's new vet to practise on.'

'Hal's a dog,' says Seb, raising his eyebrows.

'I wasn't talking literally,' says Alex.

Seb looks at him quizzically.

'It's a metaphor,' says Lucie. 'We've been doing them at school.'

'It doesn't matter. It was a flippant comment.' Alex looks at me, eyes sparking with humour.

'Are you casting aspersions on our assistant?' I say archly.

'Well, you were the one who told me he needed more experience in handling birds, for example. Apparently, everyone got into a bit of a flap when he let go of a cockatiel and couldn't catch it again,' he goes on in explanation.

'Will's all right,' I say. 'It was a case of first-day nerves, that's all. It could have happened to anyone.'

'It wouldn't have happened to me,' Old Fox-Gifford says smugly. 'When I qualified, we were omnicompetent from day one. These young vets have been force-fed a diet of scientific facts. They haven't a clue about the art of veterinary medicine.'

'I think we can learn from each other,' I point out. 'Will's like a walking textbook – he knows about the current treatments for various conditions.' I refrain from adding that he isn't sure how to apply them, but I'm sure that will come with time.

I'd like Alex to tackle his father about taking on an assistant like Emma and I have, but I know he won't, so I decide to raise the subject for him. Old Fox-Gifford is on his second or third glass of claret now and seems quite mellow.

'Have you thought about what would happen to the practice if you were ill for more than a couple of days?' I ask him.

'It was a couple of hours,' Old Fox-Gifford says defensively. 'And I know what you're going to say. Alexander and I are self-sufficient. We don't need more staff.'

'If you won't take on an assistant, you could employ a receptionist. You used to have Frances here.'

'And why did she leave?' Old Fox-Gifford says.

'Because you hit her in the face with a pen,' says Alex.

'I wasn't aiming directly at her.'

'I'd appreciate you having someone else to take the phones.' I can laugh about it – I'm still in possession of a sense of humour. There are days when I'm with George at home, and I'm left to answer the phone, providing advice if Alex is tied up on a call. Several times, I've told clients with sick cats or dogs to come to the Manor, and seen them myself on Alex's behalf.

Sophia points out that, as his wife, or almost his wife, it's part of my role to share the phone duties with him.

'Actually, Sophia, it isn't. I have a career. I work long hours. The last thing I should have to do is spend the free time I do have answering the competition's phones.'

'You can't pay someone to take calls overnight,' Sophia says.

'There are answering services.'

'What about the personal touch?' says Alex. 'That's so important. We haven't got wonderful premises, and we're a bit rough and ready. The personal touch is our USP.'

'You could make some improvements to the surgery, just by giving it a good decluttering and a clean,' I say. 'I don't understand how you can work effectively in that muddle.'

'We're used to it,' Old Fox-Gifford says stubbornly. 'I have a system. I know exactly where to find things. We don't need a cleaner either. Alexander gives the place a mop-down now and again.'

'That isn't a vet's role,' I say. 'Isn't it more cost-effective to employ your vets to treat your patients, and other people to clean and answer the phones?'

'Alexander won't have to clean when he's senior partner – that's something for him to look forward to when I'm gone.'

'Oh, let's not talk about business tonight,' says Sophia.

'What else is there?' says Old Fox-Gifford. 'Apart from dogs, of course.'

'And horses, Granpa,' Lucie joins in cheerfully.

Later, after we've finished dinner and we're collecting the children together to take back to the Barn for a bath and bed, Old Fox-Gifford corners me in the drawing room where we have been sitting drinking coffee. Sometimes, I wonder if he has a list of items to tick off in his head, like my wedding planner. Today, he wants to give me the benefit of his opinions on schooling.

'You do have George's name down for school.' He mentions the name of the boarding school Alex attended from the age of eight.

'He'll be going to the local primary school in town,' I say firmly.

'Much as that's suitable for ordinary boys, it's no good for those with brains or sporting aptitude.' Old Fox-Gifford's face seems to swell and redden. He tucks one finger in the collar of his shirt and tugs at it as though giving himself room to breathe.

'It's changed since then.'

'Its reputation is worse,' Old Fox-Gifford insists. 'They don't do sport any more. It's softball, frisbee and dance. Dance?' he snorts. 'That isn't a sport. It's for pansies.'

There is no point in arguing with his non-PC views. They have been entrenched in his psyche and vocabulary for over seventy years. He isn't going to change now.

'There are no losers any more,' he goes on. 'Fifi says everyone is a winner at sports day. How can you run a wheelbarrow race without a winner?'

I fold my arms. I am not going to pack George off to boarding school.

'Education is the most important thing you can give a boy,' says Old Fox-Gifford. 'The right school gives him access to the best universities, the most influential contacts, and appropriate social circles, including girls of one's class.'

'It didn't work for Alex then, did it?' I say, hardly disguising the triumph in my voice.

'You are an incredibly stubborn woman, Maz. This is about George's future. If you are worried about the fees, Sophia has funds set aside in trust for the grandchildren.'

'Look, it's very kind of you to offer, but if I wanted him to go to a private school, I would find the money myself.'

Old Fox-Gifford stares at me, unblinking.

'When you marry my son, I'm guessing you'll skip the part in the vows that says to honour and obey.'

For once, I don't feel the urge to disagree with my future father-in-law.

'How is she?' I ask, watching Daisy wander into the consulting room on Monday morning with Bridget and Shannon. Daisy looks better already, more sprightly, her eyes brighter and her attitude one of mild interest rather than apathy.

'She's doing well,' says Shannon, 'but guess what, Mum's been to the doctor and it's really weird – she's diabetic, like Daisy.'

'That's a coincidence,' I say.

'I've got an appointment at the hospital later,' says Bridget. 'I told Dr Mackie I'd rather come here . . .'

'What was his response to that?'

'He laughed.'

'Are you still all right about me dropping in to Petals after work tonight?' I ask.

'Oh, yes, of course. I'll be back in plenty of time,' she says. 'Just turn up whenever you're free.'

'How did you get on with Will over the weekend?' I ask, checking the computer. 'You saw him on Friday, Saturday and Sunday.'

'Fine. I've got Daisy's diabetic record here.' Shannon pulls out a chart from her bag, and reads off the number of units of insulin Will gave Daisy the previous morning.

'Did Will show you what to do, Bridget?'

'I watched him, so I've got a vague idea.'

'Good, because that means you can have a go today.' I supervise as Bridget tests for sugar, or glucose, in Daisy's sample, and writes it onto the chart. I decide on a dose of insulin and show Bridget how to draw up the required dose without getting air bubbles in the syringe, and inject it under Daisy's skin at the scruff of her neck. Luckily, being a bulldog, she has lots of loose skin.

'I'll let you have a bottle of sterile water, so you can practise injecting something like an orange at home, before I let you loose on Daisy tomorrow.' I'm hoping both Daisy and her owner have plenty of that indomitable bulldog spirit.

'I don't mind injecting an orange. Oranges don't have feelings,' says Bridget. 'Can't you do it, Shannon? You know I'm not good with needles. I'm afraid I'll hurt her.'

'You have to do it, Mum. I can't do it at the same time every day when I'm working shifts here. Besides, you'll have to learn how to inject yourself. Daisy can be your guinea pig.'

'Thanks for reminding me of that, Shan.'

'At least you won't necessarily have to have injections for ever.' Shannon scratches Daisy's cheek.

'Why is that?' I ask Shannon.

'Because Mum and Daisy have different types of diabetes,' she says smoothly.

'Great. Shannon, you say you don't know anything, but you do. It's all up there –' I tap my head – 'already.'

'I suppose so. It's just that when I'm in an exam, it all disappears, like a computer that's been wiped.'

I inject Daisy in the scruff of the neck.

'You see, she didn't notice.' I resist the impulse to give Daisy a treat because that would upset her strict routine of diet and exercise. 'Well done.'

'What if I make a mistake?' says Bridget. 'What if some of it shoots out the other side?'

'It's unlikely – the needle's tiny – but if it does just leave it.'

'Should I give her some more to make up for it?'

'Never top up the dose. It's better to underdose than give her too much, because what happens if we give her too much insulin, Shannon?'

'Her blood glucose level will fall and she'll go into a hypoglycaemic coma.'

'And the treatment for that is?'

'Sugar. Give her glucose tablets, or a Mars Bar.'

'Mars Bars are for people, not dogs,' I say. 'Why shouldn't you give a dog a Mars Bar?'

'Oh, I remember,' she says after a moment's thought. 'Chocolate is poisonous to dogs.'

'I'd hate to be a dog,' Bridget smiles.

'You won't be eating any more chocolate anyway, Mum.'

'Ah, I've checked that already. You can buy diabetic chocolate, so I'll still be able to have my daily fix.'

Shannon glances at me, rolling her eyes in mock despair. I reckon Daisy will find it easier to stick to her diet than Bridget will.

Bridget takes Daisy back home, and Shannon helps me with the appointments for the rest of the morning. Partway through though, Izzy turns up in the consulting room in her lilac scrubs, white clogs and plastic apron.

'Maz, Will's having a spot of bother in theatre. He says he's fine, but I'd be much happier if you came to give him some support for a few minutes in between consults.'

'Oh dear,' I say, fearing the worst, but Izzy smiles, eyes flashing with humour.

'He's spaying a cat, and he can't find the uterus,' she explains.

'Maybe she's been spayed already.' I rub my chin and discover a small spot, a sign of stress, perhaps. 'It does happen.'

'This cat had kittens not so long ago, so it seems unlikely.'

'He is looking in the right place?' I say lightly.

'Thereabouts,' Izzy says, apparently unconvinced.

'Well, he hasn't had much experience yet.' It's Catch-22 – without experience, Will isn't going to become fully competent, but it's a worry, letting him loose on our patients so he can have a go.

Izzy and I head into theatre where Will stands over the operating table. He's dressed in a mask, gown and gloves; the exposed skin of his neck and forehead glisten with perspiration. The theatre light shines down on the patient who is lying on her side, invisible under the drapes, apart from an expanse of shaven flank.

Izzy perches herself on the stool at the cat's head and checks the anaesthetic. She clears her throat.

'I hope you're not going to regret shaving so much hair off, Will.'

'The area has to be sterile,' Will says, flushing.

'Clients don't like it though,' Izzy points out.

'There's a balance to be struck,' I say gently. 'Now, would you like me to scrub?'

'Ummm . . . I'm . . .' Using forceps, Will is concentrating on trying to trace the uterus through a small cut in the cat's flank.

'Have you thought that it might be a good move to make a bigger hole?' I suggest.

'I don't want to make it too big,' he mutters.

'There isn't any point in minimising the size of the hole through the skin if you can't get your forceps in there.' I'm trying to be tactful, especially with Izzy present, but Will isn't really listening. 'Will, stop fishing and make that hole bigger.'

He lays the forceps down on the instrument tray, picks up the scalpel and starts gingerly extending the hole.

'A bit more,' I say. 'Don't be scared. You can make the incision as long as you need it to be.'

When Will's finished and Izzy is grinning at me, and

I'm frowning at her to say, stop it, Will picks up his forceps again, and lo and behold . . . As he withdraws them from the hole, there's a tiny pale pink tube, like a strawberry lace, in their grip.

'I've found it,' he says, both relieved and triumphant. 'Thanks for the advice, Maz.'

'It's nothing.'

'I'll be all right now.'

'Good. I'll leave you to it.' I retreat to the staffroom, worrying about Will. He's only been here two or three weeks, yet he looks shattered and his confidence seems to be fading. I hope he isn't going to burn out a couple of months down the line.

I make a cold drink and take my sandwiches out of the fridge, and just as I'm about to sit down, Frances appears in the doorway.

'Maz, please can you have a word with Mr Brown. He's trying to pay his bill in apple crumbles.'

'That's a new one on me,' I say, leaving my lunch on the worktop.

I join Frances and Mr Brown in Reception. Mr Brown, who's dressed in his usual brown cardigan and nylon trousers, stands at the desk with his dog's lead looped around his arm. Pippin is a grey and white shih-tzu. He reminds me of a muppet when he sits with his head to one side and peers through his fringe.

'What's this about apple crumbles?' I ask.

Mr Brown gestures towards three foil-topped casserole dishes on the desk.

'I didn't have enough money on me when I brought Pippin to see your assistant on Friday. We don't have a lot going spare at home,' he says ponderously, and I recall that he cares for his disabled wife. He doesn't work.

'Really, this isn't necessary,' I say.

'I'm a pretty sound cook,' he says. 'It's a WI recipe – they gave me cookery lessons. Soused mackerel with mashed potatoes is my speciality dish, but my apple crumble comes a close second. That's according to my wife. I am not one for blowing my own trumpet.'

'I've no doubt that they are delicious,' I say, 'but you needn't have worried. There must have been an error. I'll alter the bill.'

'I expect it's the new boy,' Mr Brown smiles. 'He was very nice. He was kind to Pippin and he paid attention to what I was saying. Some people don't, you know.'

Sadly, some of them don't have the patience, I muse. 'How is Pippin?'

'He's quite well at the moment, thank you,' Mr Brown says. 'However, he did have a touch of his usual tummy problem this morning.' He proceeds to detail the riot of colour that Pippin created on the lawn, and how he couldn't pick it all up . . .

'Mr Brown,' I say, as tactfully as I can, 'you're putting me off my lunch.'

'Oh dear, Maz. Am I holding you up? I'm holding you up.' Mr Brown pauses. 'Keep the apple crumbles as a gift. I'll be in to collect the dishes at the end of the week.'

'That's very generous of you,' I say. 'Thank you.'

'It's a pleasure,' says Mr Brown. 'Come on, Pippin. Let's allow the lady doctor to have her lunch in peace.'

As he walks out with Pippin, Frances lifts one corner of the foil on one of the dishes. 'That would pass muster with the WI.'

'I'll go then,' I say.

'Oh, before you do,' Frances says, 'I wanted to tell you, and no one else. Emma's pregnant.'

111

'No?' My heart starts to beat faster. Could she be? Could Emma's luck have changed at last?

'I know these things.'

'Frances, has Emma told you this, or is this to do with your sixth sense and psychic powers?' I can't believe she would have told Frances before me, but maybe she hasn't . . .

'She's pale and tired and she has that "look" about her. It's difficult to describe, but it's like a . . . translucence.'

'I admit she looks weary, and –' it occurs to me that I've been a bit slow on the uptake here – 'she's gone off doughnuts. Oh-mi-God.' I clasp my hands together with joy.

'There you go,' Frances says, eyes gleaming with excitement. 'There's the proof.'

'Have you asked her?'

'I don't need to. She'll tell us when she's ready.'

I shan't ask her either. I'd hate to upset her, asking if she's pregnant, if she isn't. The signs are all there, but I can't see how she can be – she hasn't had time off for IVF, the route she's had to go down before in her quest to have a baby. However, even this slight doubt can't suppress the excitement that is bubbling up inside me. If Emma really is pregnant, it's the best news ever.

Much later, I leave Will starting evening surgery. I scan through the list of appointments and, reassured that there isn't anything too challenging for him, I say farewell to Izzy who's staying on to work with him, before I walk along to Petals to talk flowers with Bridget.

Seven is delighted to see me, rushing across the shop floor and jumping up. Daisy is more circumspect,

112

wandering up for a sniff and returning to the dog bed under the counter.

'Hi, Bridget,' I say.

'Hello, Maz. Would you like a glass of wine?'

I hesitate.

'It's all right. It's low-alcohol, low-calorie . . .' She laughs. 'How can you call that wine? I've got a bottle of the real thing somewhere if you prefer.'

'No, thank you, but I wouldn't mind a cup of tea, if there's one going.' I'm suddenly reminded of the state of Bridget's kitchen. Tea made from boiled water sounds safer from a microbiological point of view than wine in one of those grubby glasses.

We settle down with tea and crisps, sitting at a fretwork table, on chairs with floral cushions, at the back of the shop. There's a price list propped up like a menu at a pub, and the air is filled with the scent of crushed dahlias, cut stems and perfumed sweet peas. Seven plants his bottom on my feet.

'They're pretty,' I say, pointing out the clouds of pink, white and purple blooms.

'Unfortunately, they'd be difficult to get hold of for your wedding in December,' Bridget says. 'What theme have you opted for? You have chosen the dress?'

'Oh, yes, I have the dress. It's quite simple, a mermaid shape in ivory with a few sequins.' The more I think about it, the more I love it. I've tried it on several times on the quiet, and I can't wait to wear it on the big day.

'That's a good start. What colour are the brides-maids' dresses?'

'I haven't really decided yet. At least, Emma hasn't.' I smile. 'She seems to be making all the decisions.'

113

'So you haven't brought a swatch of material along with you?' Bridget shakes her head in disapproval. 'Aren't you leaving it all to the last minute?'

'I've still got over five months,' I say, counting down to December in my head.

'That isn't long in the scheme of things.'

I don't understand why time should pass so much more quickly when you're planning a wedding than normal.

'Most brides are ready a year before,' Bridget goes on. 'Do you want to go down the traditional route, or the modern?' She grins. 'Here, have a flick through the photos.' She hauls a huge file of pictures onto the table. 'Let's see if any of these bridal bouquets inspire you.'

I feel like a fish out of water. I haven't been to all that many weddings, which is surprising because I do have friends who are married, not just Emma, and Izzy who got hitched two years ago now. However, I was often working weekends, and for various reasons, when I asked to swap duties, I was made to feel indispensable.

'There will be flowers in the church because it's close to Christmas,' says Bridget. 'You could tie it in with the Christmassy theme: holly and ivy.'

'Holly? Won't that be prickly?' I'm concerned for the person catching the bride's bouquet, the one who, by tradition, will be the next woman to be married.

'I can see it now, Maz. A bouquet of evergreens interspersed with scarlet and cream. Depending on the colour of the bridesmaids' dresses, of course. It will look stunning.' Bridget passes me the bowl of crisps. I decline, and, flicking through the files, she takes a handful for herself. I want to tell her to look after her health – for Shannon's sake, if not for her own – but I bite my tongue. 'What do you think?' She shows me a photo of an evergreen bouquet.

'I'm not sure,' I say, realising that I should have been paying more attention to the bridal flowers at the weddings I have been to. 'It's . . . Bridget, to be honest, I haven't got a clue what I'm doing.'

'Let's start at the beginning, shall we?' she says, amused. 'And I won't let you leave until you've made a decision. We don't want you falling behind on your "to do" list.'

Bridget is right, I think, when I'm driving home. I can't afford to fall behind on the dreaded list that's beginning to take control of my life. My head is filled with flowers and foliage. Anemones, calla lilies or amaryllis? Eucalyptus, ivy or twisted willow? Bridget took me through every combination, and more. At least, that's what it feels like. I've made my decision on the bouquet and the bridesmaids' flowers, and the arrangements for the church and the tables at the reception . . . I'm exhausted. I can't imagine how I can possibly make any more decisions when I have so much else going on.

Chapter Seven

A Higher Love

Three weeks later, and I'm in the staffroom at work, confirming the booking for the photographer on my mobile.

'I'll send a cheque for the deposit,' I say.

'That's great,' the photographer says. 'I'll be in touch nearer the time to go through any special requests you might have. Bye, Maz.'

When she cuts the call, I want to cheer. Another job I can cross off the list.

'Maz. Maz.' Frances is in the staffroom right beside me, waving the practice phone. 'It's Saba.'

'I've heard everything now,' I say drily. 'A poodle that's learned to talk.'

'You know what I mean,' Frances says. 'It's Aurora about Saba. She's fallen forty metres down a cliff. Tom, the coastguard, is there. Saba's in a bad way, but not so bad that she'll let him near her to rescue her. She isn't keen on men.' Frances hands me the phone and Aurora takes over, her voice laced with panic.

'Maz, I don't know what to do. I'd go down myself,

but I'm afraid to move her. Can you come straight out? Saba needs you.'

'What about the RSPCA inspector? She's more qualified to abseil down a cliff than I am.' I've had a go once before, supposedly for fun, but my vertigo kicked in, and all I could do was close my eyes and hang on.

'She's on holiday,' Aurora says. 'Tom's tried her.'

'I'll be with you asap,' I say, realising that without me, Saba won't be going anywhere. 'Where are you?'

'On the cliffs at Talymouth. If you stop in the car park, we're about five minutes from there on foot. Keep to the path.'

I pack the visit case, muzzle, sedatives – for the dog, although I just might need them – and blankets before I hit the winding road to Talymouth. On my way through the seaside town, past the pastel-coloured Regency hotels and B&Bs, to the seafront, I try not to think about what I might be letting myself in for. Forty metres down doesn't sound too bad, but when you realise that the cliffs are about one hundred metres from top to toe – I try not to think about it – it's a long way to the rocks at the bottom.

I park in the car park, ignoring the ticket machine. There's a warm breeze, whisking up dust and ice-cream wrappers. Seagulls call and white horses dance on a blue-green sea. As I walk down the sandy path along the top of the cliffs, Aurora runs towards me in a sequinned vest and tiny shorts.

'Maz, she's this way,' she calls, pointing back to the coastguard's Land Rover that's parked behind some scrubby gorse bushes. 'Thanks for coming. I didn't have her on the lead. She ran after a rabbit and went over the edge.'

Tom, the coastguard, greets me with a handshake and a smile. He's well-built with prematurely grey hair, and, in spite of the July heat, dressed in orange waterproof clothing. I'd describe him as rugged.

'Believe me, I'd rescue that dog if she'd let me, but I'd rather keep my face,' he says in a strong Devon accent. 'She won't let me near her.'

'Is she hurt?' I ask.

'She's lying down, so I'm assuming she's injured herself.'

'Oh, Saba,' Aurora wails, at which there's an answering whine.

'Let's get you kitted out then,' Tom says.

Soon, in a helmet, harness and boots, and, having been given a crash refresher course in abseiling, I'm dangling from a rope above the rocks at Talymouth. Tom is alongside me with a pack containing a safety bag, splints, tape and shots of painkiller and sedative, in case Saba needs them. I feel a rush of excitement followed quickly by fear. I'm a mum. I can see danger in eating a grape whole, the jeopardy in an inch of rainwater and the peril of the hot tap, but these are nothing compared with the risks of hanging one hundred metres up by what looks more and more like a thread to me.

'Hang on there, Maz,' Tom says. 'Take it slowly.'

'Slowly? I want it to be over with as quickly as possible. I am not good with heights.'

'Now is not the time to tell me that,' Tom smiles. 'I think the dog's paralysed, and I don't want you getting stuck halfway down because you're paralysed with fear. I'll have to rescue the two of you.' He pauses for a moment. 'I could ask that Aurora to help, but I think she's afraid she'll break a nail.'

'That's rather sexist of you,' I say lightly, trying to ignore the rapid knocking of my heart.

'Silly woman,' Tom says. 'Aurora, I mean. Not you. How many times do we tell people through the press, and down on the beach, to keep their dogs on leads when they're up on the cliff path? This is the third dog in three weeks.'

'Did you have to rescue them?'

'One made its own way back up. The other fell onto the rocks. It didn't make it.'

'Thanks, Tom. You're so reassuring,' I say, unsure if he's winding me up deliberately, or if it's his naturally blunt manner. He seemed reassuring at first, but I'm not so sure I'd choose him as an abseiling partner in the future.

I can taste salt on my lips, and feel my hair sticky and damp across my face. The sandy cliff crumbles away under my feet, and if I look down – I mustn't look down – I can see the water rolling off the red rocks below.

Gradually, we make our way down to the ledge where Saba is lying on her side, facing out towards us. She takes one look at Tom and snarls.

'Hey, Saba. What's got into you?' I say soothingly, at which she turns her eyes to me, appraising me as if to say, do I know you? She does. I hope she doesn't remember the operations I've performed on her otherwise I'll get the same reception as Tom. I'm not sure she's that much danger to us though, because she doesn't seem to be able to lift her head.

I edge towards her, and slip the muzzle over her face, fastening it carefully behind her ears, at which she yelps in pain. I'm not sure what to do. Tom was right. She's paralysed, which suggests either a neck or back injury, and in an ideal world I'd strap her to a stretcher, but this isn't ideal, sixty metres up on a narrow ledge. I give her shots of sedative and painkiller, and strap her neck instead, using splints and tape to immobilise it as far as I can, before Tom helps me get her into the safety bag ready to lift.

Saba snarls the whole way up, in spite of the sedation, so at first, I miss the fact that Tom is gesticulating and yelling at someone above our heads.

'Get back, you –' he curses.

I look up, catching the flash from a camera.

Tom glances towards me. 'Some people!'

We continue our ascent, arriving safely at the top where I crawl through the rough grass well away from the cliff edge and throw up – with relief. I'm shaking. I did it. I actually did it. I've been over the edge.

'Maz, I'm so grateful,' Aurora says, coming over to me as I return to help Tom extract Saba from the bag. 'You've saved Saba's life.'

'Don't raise your hopes,' I say, as I hold Saba's head. 'She's safely off the cliff, but she's critically injured. She's damaged her spine and that means she may never be able to walk again.'

Aurora's hand flies to her mouth.

'I'm going to get her back to the surgery, X-ray her neck and operate if I can,' I go on. 'If not, I can refer her to the nearest specialist orthopaedic practice.'

'I feel so guilty.' Aurora is crying. 'I've often walked her up here without a lead. She hasn't done that before. You know, I hate that rabbit.'

I wonder about the rabbit's fate. Did it manage to duck into a burrow and escape, or did it meet with a sticky end? Tom expresses his sentiments for the fate of the mystery photographer who has disappeared off in a small white van.

'Do you have any idea who that was?' Tom asks Aurora.

'I think he said he was from the paper,' she says nonchalantly.

'How did he know we were here?'

'There's quite a crowd.' Aurora points to the people who are dispersing now.

'What a prat. There's no way I'd have picked him up, if he'd fallen,' Tom observes.

'There's a good case for having cliffs banned,' Aurora says vacantly.

'Thanks, my lover,' Tom says, using the Devonian term of endearment which, when I first heard it, rather surprised me. Lots of people around here call each other my lover, when clearly they are not, but perhaps Tom has aspirations. He appears to have had a change of heart where Aurora, the thoughtless dog-walker is concerned, and I suspect it has much to do with her legs. 'I'd be out of a job,' he goes on.

Tom and I get Saba into the back of my car, and I drive her to Otter House where I park as close as I can to the entrance of the practice.

Shannon rushes out. 'Shall I fetch more help?'

'Please . . . and the stretcher would be useful.'

Shannon returns with Will, and Frances who doesn't want to miss out on the action.

'Shouldn't you be looking after the phone?'

'Don't worry, Maz. I have it with me.' Frances holds it up to show me. 'I would never desert my post, except in the case of fire or flood.' She smiles, remembering, I suspect, the occasion when we did have to vacate Otter

House in a hurry during the Great Flood of Talyton nearly two years ago.

Will unrolls the stretcher in readiness for transferring Saba from the back of the car into the practice.

'Will and I will lift the patient onto the stretcher,' I say. 'Shannon, you are in charge of keeping Saba as calm and as still as possible. It's imperative we keep her head steady so she can't move her neck. Will, I reckon she's snapped her cervical spine in the fall, so this exercise could be purely academic. If she's completely severed her spinal cord, there won't be anything we can do.'

'Poor Saba,' says Frances. 'Aurora must be distraught.'

'She could turn up at the practice at any time.' She wasn't in a fit state to drive, and I think Tom and his team were keen to give her a lift back into Talyton. 'If she does, can you make her one of your legendary cups of tea and supply some biscuits? She can wait for news if she likes, but it could be some time before we have any answers.'

We move Saba carefully, treating her like eggs loose on a tray, carrying her through to the prep bench.

'There's a good girl,' Shannon coos. 'What can I do, Maz?'

'Stay with Saba. Will, can you do a full neuro exam, assess her reflexes and see if you can localise the site of the injury? I'm going to set up for some plain X-rays and a myelogram.'

'Are you planning to refer her?' Will asks.

'If her condition stabilises enough to be able to transport her somewhere. Come on, Will. Get started.'

I try to infuse the team with a sense of urgency, and within half an hour, we have plenty of useful pictures.

As I feared, Saba has broken her neck, chipping off the peg on the second bone that allows the head to turn, as if you're shaking your head. If I don't fix it, the bones will move relative to each other and damage the spinal cord irreparably. Saba will be paralysed from the neck down. If I do fix it, it may already be too late, or the surgery itself may cause further injury, and Saba might still be paralysed from the neck down. Either way, the odds aren't great.

Will and I stand in the darkened X-ray room, looking at the films on the viewer.

'I'm going to have to get the Meccano out. I'd like you to assist, Will.'

'Have you done many of these before?'

'One. A long time ago.' I smile wryly. 'It's a bit of a risk, but it's kill or cure. It's all right – I'm pretty handy with a drill.'

I might think I'm handy with the drill, but I'm out of practice and pretty slow, and I'm apprehensive about operating so close to the nerves that supply the whole of Saba's body from her neck down. This means that three hours later I'm still operating, tightening the screws in the plates that I've set across the bones in Saba's neck to immobilise them. We X-ray again to check everything is in the right place using the X-ray machine that Will has dragged into theatre.

'It's all looking good,' I say. 'Let's get her closed up, then we can get her into the big kennel and keep a twenty-four-hour watch on her.'

'I'm up for that,' says Shannon. 'I'll take first shift.'

'I'll take second,' offers Will.

'Great. I'll do the third.'

'Isn't it your day off tomorrow?' Shannon says.

'I don't mind,' I say.

'I'll finish off for you now then,' Will says. 'You could do with a break, Maz, after your daring cliff-top rescue.'

'Do you think it'll be in the *Chronicle*?' asks Shannon.

'There's every chance,' I say with a sigh. 'Someone took a photo over the edge of the cliff. Aurora said he was from the paper.' I smile. 'I didn't have a chance to do my make-up, but it'll be good publicity for Otter House.' I pull off my gloves and call Aurora – Frances sent her home when she turned up earlier.

Finally, I head for home myself, and let myself into the Barn. Alex is in the kitchen area, wearing a red apron, and stirring something in a pan.

'Hi, there,' I call.

'Hello, darling,' he says, looking up.

'Where's George?'

'In bed.' Alex holds his finger to his lips. 'Sh!'

'Is he all right?'

'Mother's had him toddling around the stables all day. He's exhausted.' Alex walks round to join me. He gives me a hug and a kiss on the cheek.

'That's nice,' I say, turning to press my mouth against his.

'I've cooked us some of that fresh pasta, and there's a bottle of Rioja open on the side.'

'Are we celebrating, or something?'

'I suppose we are in a way. Your daring cliff-top rescue? I hear you've had an exciting day. I've health-checked some sheep, treated a horse with low-grade colic and diagnosed pregnancy in endless cows. There's been nothing to raise my pulse today, apart from seeing you,' he adds with a grin.

I smile back, reassured that he loves me, even if he doesn't say it anywhere nearly often enough.

'How did you find out?'

'It's all over town – I stopped to pick up some fruit and veg from the greengrocer's. Peter told me. Bridget told him, and Aurora told Bridget.' Alex pinches my bottom. 'If I'd known in time, I'd have been there. I know how much you hate heights. In fact, I can't believe you agreed to do it.'

'I had no choice. Saba wouldn't let the coastguard near her.'

'How is the dog?'

'Heavily sedated. Shannon and Will are watching her.' I check the time. 'I'm on the early shift from five.'

'It sounds as though I'll have to get you to bed early then,' Alex says, his breath warm against my face.

'That sounds like an excellent plan to me,' I murmur.

'How is she?' I ask Will the next morning. Like me, he appears to have been up all night, his glasses smudged, his eyes dark with exhaustion and a bottle of some caffeine-containing power drink in his hand. He's wearing the same shirt as the day before and has a tiny spattering of blood across his cheek where he must have nicked a patient's artery when he was last operating, but hasn't washed.

'Will, you can't have that in here,' Izzy says, taking the bottle off him. 'You know the rules.'

'I'm sorry. I forgot. Anyway, back to the patient. Saba's conscious, comfortable on painkillers, she has sensation in all four limbs, but she can't support her weight. She wags her tail when you say her name.'

'There are some positive signs then.' I bend down to stroke her silky curls. She's remarkably clean and bears a perfume that's more Coco by Chanel than Eau de Chien. 'Has she passed urine?'

'She has a catheter. I put it in last night,' Will says.

'It's early days yet, but I wonder whether she should be referred to a specialist for rehab.'

'We could set up a pool for hydrotherapy in the garden,' says Izzy. 'Couldn't we borrow a paddling pool from somewhere?'

'It wouldn't be deep enough, and it doesn't sound terribly hygienic.'

'What about the bath in the flat? We've used that for rehab before.'

'I remember. The dachshund with the slipped disc. What was his name?'

'Daffy.'

'He pooped in what was my bath at the time,' I point out. 'We can't use that.'

'There must be a way,' says Izzy. 'Leave it with me. I'll think of something.'

She finds me the number of a local hydrotherapist.

'I don't care how much it costs,' Aurora says magnanimously, as I ask her about it when she comes in to see Saba later. She's lucky – we've allowed her visiting rights as she is the only person Saba will take food from. 'Saba has comprehensive health insurance that will cover it, and even if she didn't, I'd find the money. My dog means everything to me. She's more loving, more appreciative and more loyal than any man.' She sighs. 'I'm single, yet again.'

'I'm sorry . . .'

'Don't be. He was good-looking, had money, but the sex wasn't up to much.' She smiles. 'Oh, Maz, don't be embarrassed. I thought you vets would have heard it all. Aren't you marrying the delicious Alex very soon?' I don't want to talk about it, but she continues, 'It was a smart thing to do, snagging him with an unplanned pregnancy.'

'It wasn't like that,' I say, hurt.

'I'm very grateful for what you and Will have done,' says Aurora. Watch out, Will, I think, amused at the thought of Will and Aurora getting together. He's so meek and mild that Aurora would have him for dinner, like a black widow spider. An eligible bachelor, professional with good prospects, a few years younger than her. I'm not sure how she'd take finding those exotic creatures in his flat though.

'Oh,' she goes on, 'I've left a copy of the *Chronicle* with Frances. You and Saba are headline news. And there's a nice mention of my shop.'

'Was it you who rang the paper?' I have to ask.

'You have to make the most of these opportunities, Maz.' I watch her expression, cool and calculating. 'When can I come back and see Saba?'

'Tomorrow. Same time.'

I check the front page of the *Chronicle* – I'm there in full colour, staring up towards the top of the cliff, the sea behind me. I'm grimacing with fear and effort. My hair sticks out from under my helmet like straw from a scarecrow's head.

Local Vet Rescues Dog reads the headline.

'It's good, isn't it,' Frances comments. 'It's a great likeness.'

'So it should be,' I say. 'It is me, after all.'

'Have you booked Maria to do your hair for the wedding? Maz, you really should get on and do that. It wouldn't take five minutes.'

Chapter Eight

To Love and to Cherish

It's a hot, dry summer and, although it's only the middle of July, the grass in the paddocks at Talyton Manor is scorched, and much of the ground almost bare, apart from a few clumps of nettles and crowns of dock leaves. The weather might be bad for farmers and their livestock, but it has one great benefit. You don't have to put your wellies on every time you step outside the front door.

'Come on then, George.' I pick him up, along with a carrier bag of shopping, and carry him inside the Barn. 'I need to get the tea on.' I'm looking forward to Alex coming home tonight because he's on daddy duty, as I call it. I've had George to myself all day, and although I've loved it, I'm shattered.

He's been so busy 'helping' that I haven't managed to get anything done apart from some shopping at the Co-op. When I got back to the car, I found George had inadvertently shoplifted three grapes and two fudge bars, slipping them into the front pocket of his dungarees. Did I as a pillar of the community and a professional person go back to the shop and 'fess up? No, I dropped a donation into a charity box on the quiet.

I pick up the post from the floor and stick the oven on, and I'm just dragging the washing out of the machine, a load of Alex's shirts and trousers, when Alex turns up.

'Hi,' he says, on his way through to the open-plan kitchen area.

'You're early for once,' I say, pleased to see him.

'I thought I'd spend some quality time with my fiancée, and my son,' he adds, kissing me.

'After you've been in the shower. You stink of cow,' I say, laughing as I push him away. 'I'll put the dinner on. Does pizza, garlic bread and green salad suit you?'

'Sounds great.' Then he says ironically, 'You shouldn't have spent all day slaving over a hot stove.'

'You know I didn't.'

'Where's the boy?'

'Dada.' George toddles across the floor to his dad, who sweeps him into the air and rubs noses with him. George giggles. 'Dada.'

'Perhaps you could take him upstairs and give him a shower as well,' I suggest, 'or a bath.'

'Maz, I've only just walked through the door.'

'I know, I'm sorry . . .'

'Give me five, and I'll come and help you with George and dinner.'

'Thanks, Alex.' My chest tightens with love and desire. Sometimes I wonder if I deserve him. Not only is he the most attractive man I've ever met, he's kind and generous with it.

I find some plates, listening to one of George's CDs, Favourite Nursery Rhymes, and the sound of water running in the shower. Alex is as good as his word, returning downstairs a few minutes later in a pair of jeans, and towelling his hair dry. I can't help noticing the angry weal down his arm.

'What have you done there?'

Alex looks at me as if to say, it's nothing, but as he drops the towel onto the clean washing in the basket beside the machine, he winces.

'One of Stewart's cattle caught my arm in the crush, gave me a bit of a squeeze.' He swears lightly then apologises. 'It was one of those things.' He tips his head to one side. 'I was thinking about something else, some fiancée or other of mine.'

'Do you want some ice on that?'

'It's fine.' Alex flexes his fingers. 'I'll be a bit sore for a couple of days, but it'll soon wear off. I've had worse.'

He finds himself a shirt before we sit down at the table. George is strapped into his high chair with a finger of pizza and some cucumber in front of him. He isn't a great fan of lettuce – of anything green, in fact – but I keep trying.

'So, Maz,' Alex says, 'have you thought any more about the honeymoon? Where would you like to go?'

'Surprise me.'

Alex ruffles his hair in mock frustration.

'You have to give me some idea, a clue. Somewhere hot and sunny? Somewhere cold and crisp in the mountains?' He takes my hand. 'I don't want to make a mistake.'

I want to say, I don't care where we go as long as I'm with you, but that would sound soft, so I don't. 'Somewhere warm, but not too hot for George.'

Alex frowns and I realise I've said the wrong thing.

'What's George got to do with it? He isn't coming with us, Maz. This is our honeymoon. That's why I thought we'd compromise and spend Christmas with the children before we went away.'

'I assumed . . .' My voice trails off. I can't imagine leaving George behind for two weeks. I don't think I can do it.

'It's traditional for newlyweds to make a baby on honeymoon, not take one with them,' Alex says, smiling.

'We aren't a traditional couple. We already have a baby on board. Oh, I don't know what to do . . . Somehow, I pictured George coming along with us.'

'Yeah,' Alex says ruefully, 'and George ending up in the bed with us, which means we'll have lots of sleepless nights, and for all the wrong reasons.'

We both look at George who is quiet for a moment, squishing pizza between his fingers.

'I'll talk to Mother. I'm sure she'll be more than happy to have him.' Alex pauses, while I'm thinking, two weeks is too long, too much time for Sophia to brainwash our son with the Fox-Gifford family values. 'She's always trying to get George to herself –' Alex strokes my fingers, his skin snagging against mine – 'just like I'm working on getting you to myself. Call me selfish, darling, but that's what I want.' Alex's voice is like shards of brittle toffee. 'It's up to you though.'

'I don't know, Alex.'

'How can I convince you?' He raises my hand and presses his lips to the inside of my wrist, thrilling my skin, my whole being, until I'm melting inside.

'I'm torn,' I mutter.

'Two weeks. Just you and me . . .?'

It's difficult to resist. Impossible.

'Oh, Alex . . .'

'So, that's a yes then.' He leans closer and presses his lips to my cheek. 'George stays at home with Mother. I'd better start doing some research on the best places to go. It isn't very long until Christmas, and I don't want to risk going for a last-minute deal.'

'Don't remind me – I've got so much more to do,' I say, sitting back.

'Is there any of that pizza left? I'll get it,' Alex goes on, as I make to get up, but before he can pick up his plate, his mobile rings from the sofa where he must have dropped it on his way indoors.

I raise one eyebrow, waiting as Alex paces up and down. It's gone six and Alex isn't on call tonight so I can only assume it's a routine enquiry. Don't people around here realise that it's polite to keep calls to office hours? I smile to myself, because our clients are exactly the same.

'I'm sorry, Maz,' Alex says, cutting the call. 'I've got to go. It's one of the Pony Club. Their horse has injured itself in the field. It's non-weight-bearing so I can't leave it.'

'You aren't on call tonight.' Neither of us is. That's the whole point, to spend some quality time together. I am in turns disappointed and annoyed, as well as being sorry for the horse.

'It's one of those things. They're one of my specials.'

'You mean they won't see your father?'

'Something like that.' Alex starts hunting around for his keys. 'George, have you picked them up?' he says, impatiently.

'No,' says George.

'Are you sure?' Alex is trying to sound stern, but I can hear the humour bubbling up in his voice.

'No,' George says, shaking his head, and laughing.

'Does that mean yes?' Alex looks to me for help.

I shrug. 'Try upstairs. You've probably chucked them in the laundry. It wouldn't be the first time.'

'Okay, I'll have a look. I'll take the X-ray machine with me rather than have to come back for it. Hopefully, I won't be long.'

'See you later then,' I say, resigned. By the time he's back downstairs with his keys rescued from the laundry basket, a thought has occurred to me. 'Alex, if I get called out, what am I supposed to do with George?'

'You aren't on call.'

'Yes, but if Will wants me . . .'

'You'll have to ask Mother, or take him with you.' Alex pulls on a sweater. 'Don't wait up tonight, George. Go to sleep for Mummy.' He kisses me as he leaves me, pondering one of a vet's life's bigger questions: Why do animals always seem to injure themselves in the middle of dinner or a great film? That's why I don't watch films any more. I've seen far more beginnings than I have ends.

Half an hour later, Alex texts me. He's going to be a while, so I get on with bathing George and putting him to bed, reading the story of the dog, Hairy Maclary from Donaldson's Dairy, who reminds me of Lucky, one of my patients and the dog who snapped at Alex at the show. Sophia bought the book for George, another example of Fox-Gifford indoctrination. That boy will love horses and dogs, or they will have failed in their duty as grandparents.

At ten, I retire to bed. At ten thirty, I'm lying awake, unable to sleep for wondering when Alex will return. After midnight, the light on my mobile pierces the curtain of darkness that has fallen across my eyes. The tune of 'I'm Getting Married in the Morning' tickles my eardrums. I really must change the ringtone, Izzy's idea of a joke.

'Hi?' I say, fumbling for the phone. I recognise the familiar number of Otter House Vets.

'Hello, is that you, Maz? Good evening.'

'I'm pretty sure you'll find it's morning, Will,' I say, suppressing a wry smile. 'What's up?'

'I'm sorry to bother you, but I've got a cat in labour here, and I realise this sounds pathetic, but I don't know what to do. It's a Persian cat, Cassie. I've checked her over, but I can't decide what to do for the best.'

'I'll be right there,' I decide. 'Is Shannon with you?'

I can hear the relief in Will's voice. 'She's getting theatre ready in case.'

I pull on a sweatshirt and joggers, run my fingers through my hair and tie it back with a couple of turns of a hairband. George? I'll have to take George with me. I can't bother Sophia at this time of night. And Emma will be in bed asleep, and I don't want to do anything to disturb her, if by any happy chance she is pregnant, as Frances has suggested.

I pick George up out of his cot. (I haven't moved him into a bed just yet because he'll never stay there.) He opens his eyes and smiles, and my heart skips a tiny beat that he's in a good mood and willing to cooperate with being strapped into his car seat.

I listen for a moment, hoping Alex will turn up, but he doesn't and there's no time to waste.

'Let's go, George. And remember, this is why you don't want to be a vet when you're older.'

George is wide awake and ready to go when we arrive at the practice. Because I've forgotten to bring the buggy to trap him in, Shannon takes him for me. Her expression suggests she's about to tell me she's a nurse, not a babysitter, which is perfectly reasonable, but she keeps quiet. She holds his hand as George potters about in his striped pyjamas, tipping squash out of one of those leakproof toddler drinking cups and scattering biscuit crumbs as he goes.

We all go into the prep area where Cassie is on the bench, straining feebly with fluid leaking from her rear end. She's panting like mad and really upset. I can sympathise now, as I did with Liberty, having given birth to George.

Clive and Edie stand with her. Will leans against the cupboards beyond, flicking through a textbook, a picture of indecision.

'Hi,' I say, as cheerfully as I can. 'Fancy meeting you here.'

'I've said before, we should have shares in this place, Maz,' Clive jokes, but I can tell he is worried. 'We could have a ward named after us.'

'Okay, Will, tell me what you think,' I say.

Will, the diligent, newly qualified vet, runs through Cassie's vital signs.

'When did she start pushing?' I ask.

'About – oh, I don't know.' Clive looks at Edie for guidance, but she is vague. 'About two hours ago? Not all that long before last orders.'

'What can you feel, Will?'

'There's a kitten in the pelvic canal coming head first. I wasn't sure if I should deliver it or go straight for a Caesar.'

I wash my hands, slip on a pair of gloves and have a quick feel to check.

'We'll go with the Caesar,' I decide. Shannon picks

136

up a consent form – Izzy's trained her well – and Clive signs Cassie's life temporarily into my hands.

'Would you and Edie like to make yourselves a drink in the staffroom?' I ask Clive. Edie looks as if she could do with a strong coffee.

'What about George?' says Shannon. 'I can't look after him and the anaesthetic at the same time.'

'I'll look after him,' Edie offers.

'I'll be there, Maz,' Clive says, his expression one of reassurance. He's aware, as we all are, that Edie's under the influence, but he'll supervise, making sure that George comes to no harm.

'I wish he was as happy to go to nursery,' I say, smiling as George toddles off with Clive and Edie without protest.

'Is that normal, letting clients loose in the practice?' asks Will. 'I mean, is that wise?'

'They're lovely people, and I know them pretty well.' I change the subject. 'Now, do you want to operate or assist?'

'Um –' Will pushes his glasses up his nose – 'I'll assist.'

'In that case, you can do the next one.'

'I hope you don't mind me calling you out, only I wasn't sure . . .'

'It's fine. It's better to be safe than sorry.' I smile encouragingly. Will needs to work on his confidence. 'I can remember what it's like. You think you've got it, that you understand the rules you learned at vet school, but then the patients come along, real patients, and they don't behave as they do in the textbooks.'

'I didn't like to call Emma.'

'No, always call me first,' I say. 'Come on then, let's get this party started.'

Will and I anaesthetise the cat. Shannon monitors Cassie's pulse and breathing, while I shave the cat's belly, sending clusters of fluff floating off into the air. Will cleans Cassie's skin, and I scrub up at the sink and slip into a gown and gloves.

'Is she asleep?' I ask, having arranged the drapes to isolate the surgical site under the cool gleam of the theatre light.

Shannon pinches Cassie's paw. There's no response.

'Ready to go,' she says, waiting for me to make the first cut through the skin and muscle into Cassie's swollen belly, before she disappears briefly to return with a white wire cage containing a heated pad and towels, ready for the kittens.

I hope they're okay and we haven't left it too late, what with Clive and Edie in no great hurry to get down here, having to lock up the pub first, and Will dithering about what to do.

'How many are we expecting?' Shannon unfolds a towel and places beside it a dropper bottle of a drug to stimulate breathing if necessary.

'Two or three.' I thought I could feel three. As I cut through into the cat's womb, I mop up the fluid that comes flooding out and make a grab for the first kitten. I hand it to Will, who hands it to Shannon. It's a dark, wet, seemingly lifeless mass, like a toy that's been left out in the rain.

'Go ahead.' I remove a second kitten and hand it to Will. 'Clear the mouth and nostrils and give it a rub.' I check the rest of the womb. There are no more kittens. If there was a third, it's been re-absorbed and disappeared without trace. 'How are we doing?'

'Mum's fine. This one isn't breathing.' Shannon

raises the kitten to her eye level and peers at its chest. 'Oh? Cool. It is.'

The kitten gasps, mews and twitches. It doesn't look very strong, but I heave a sigh of relief. It is alive.

'It's a little boy,' Shannon coos, before putting it very gently into the cage, with a drape over the top to keep it snug while we're bringing Cassie round.

'This one's alive,' says Will, 'but it has a hernia. Look.'

I can only glance briefly away from my task of closing up the womb and the body wall, but it is enough. Where the kitten's umbilical cord should have been, there is a tear, and I can see the kitten's insides.

'Will, you'll have to mask it down on the other machine and see if you can close it up.' Is it worth it? I decide we have to try. It would be a shame to give up now.

'Shannon, can you grab Will a spay kit? Thanks. I'm almost done here.'

While Will is operating to repair the kitten's hernia, very slowly but surely, Shannon watches over Cassie who's coming round, and I keep a close eye on the kitten's anaesthetic. Shannon asks me to help her revise for her exams that are coming up in a couple of days' time.

'Maz, what's the difference between smooth, skeletal and heart muscle?' she says.

'Now you're asking.' It's been a long time since I studied muscles, apart from Alex's . . . 'Skeletal muscle is voluntary and looks stripy under the microscope.'

'So does heart muscle, doesn't it?'

'Yes, but heart muscle is involuntary. It beats spontaneously, the rate and strength of the beat controlled by the nervous system.' I don't like splitting everything into chunks. It's all part of the whole, like the team at Otter House.

'MNEC,' sighs Shannon. 'Mum Never Eats Cake.'

I'd be surprised, I muse, considering Bridget's physique, although I suspect she won't be eating as much as she used to now she's been diagnosed with diabetes.

'Muscle, Nervous, Epithelial and Connective. I spent three hours trying to make sense of my notes and only got as far as muscle. I'm never going to get through it all.' Shannon shakes her head mournfully. She looks tired, her eyes shadowed.

'You aren't overdoing the revision, are you? Remember, you have a full-time job as well. It isn't like you're at school and have all the time in the world.' I wonder if she's out partying too. She used to be a party animal.

'I'll be fine as soon as I've got the exams over and done with.'

'Do you remember your first Caesar?' I say, smiling.

'How could I ever forget? That's how I ended up with Seven.'

Soon, Cassie and her kittens are awake and back in their carrier, and we are standing around the prep bench.

'How are my babies?' slurs Edie.

'And Cassie too, love,' Clive adds. He's holding on to George who is tipping forwards trying to poke his fingers into the carrier.

'Cat,' he says.

'No, George,' I say.

'Cat!' he exclaims.

'You're right, it is a cat. I mean, no, don't put your fingers in there. Cats can bite. Ouch!'

140

'Bad cat,' says George happily.

He's wrong. They're lovely cats. Cassie is more relaxed now, making noises in her throat as her kittens burrow underneath her.

'She's going to be a great mum,' I say.

'Thank you for looking after her,' says Clive. 'We're very grateful.'

'What colour are they?' Edie asks. 'It was difficult to see.'

'There's a black and white boy, and a cream girl,' says Shannon.

'That's a strange combination,' Clive observes.

'Who's the dad?' I say. 'I reckon Cassie entertained two visiting tomcats.'

'Really?' says Edie.

'That's what cats do. They put themselves about a bit.'

'There, I thought you were such a nice girl, Cassie.' Edie smiles.

Once Clive and Edie have headed for home, Shannon cleans up with Will helping, or getting in the way, and I write up the case notes. Cassie is on the slim side, unusual for our patients nowadays with all the quality pet food available, and I make a comment on her record to check this out when she returns for a check-up. After that, I have a chat with Will.

'Do you feel happy about doing the next one?' I ask.

'I think so. Thank you, Maz.'

'What for?'

'For being so bloody nice about it, and not making me feel like a complete idiot.'

'I can tell you, I'd much prefer you to ask when you aren't sure than blunder on regardless as our locum did.'

'I heard about your troubles – Frances told me.'

'Drew was hopeless. Selfish. He didn't care about the patients at all.' I pause. 'Will, don't worry. You're doing really well.'

'Thanks again,' he says.

'You'd better go and have a break.' I check the clock on the wall. 'We have less than six hours until it's time to do the ward round.'

Will groans. 'It's much harder than I thought it would be.'

'You'll feel better after some sleep.' I watch him go out through the door into the corridor, hands in his pockets and head bowed, and I wonder if he would have managed without me, if I hadn't been available. Would I trust him with sole charge? I don't think he's ready for that, and I can't help questioning if he ever will be.

I realise as I'm driving home with George now fast asleep in the back, that my work–life balance is precariously balanced, and it would not take much to tip me over the edge, one way or the other. I'm lucky. I have it all; child, fiancé, career, money. I am loved and cherished, but I have no time to myself. There is no slack and it makes me wonder how I'm going to find the opportunity to plan this wedding. It's been a month or so since Alex and I set the date, and apart from the dress, photographer and flowers, preparations have not really advanced any further. I begin to panic. What I thought was a long time, is not very long at all.

Chapter Nine

Something New

It's going to be one of those days. It's eight thirty in the morning a few days later, and I'm standing in the tiny play area outside nursery with Flick, the nursery manager who's dressed in a white blouse, black trousers and an apron covered with brightly coloured butterflies. She's about the same age as me, in her early thirties, petite, blonde and determined. For once, it isn't George who is saying no to nursery. It is nursery saying no to George.

I should have anticipated this problem. I remember how Frances had to look after her granddaughter at the practice when she had a rash that turned out to be flea bites from the pet cat. These aren't flea bites.

'I have to be at work –' I check my watch to prove a point – 'now.'

'You'll have to find someone else to look after him today. You must understand, as someone with a medical qualification, that we can't have him here unless you can prove he isn't infectious to the other children.'

'I can't do that. I have to go to work. I'm fully booked all day.'

Flick draws herself up to her full five feet, and a little more, tall.

'Take some time off. It would be irresponsible of me to accept him.'

I show her the rash on George's arm. It isn't much, and I'm desperately hoping she'll make an exception.

'They not fleas,' George pipes up cheerfully, and I wish he was a little behind rather than ahead with his talking. 'Not fleas, Mummy.' I can see the other mums recoiling in horror as if they think I've coached him in what to say.

'All right,' I say, backing down. Outside, at the nursery gates, I call Alex on my mobile. He's unobtainable. I might have guessed. Who else can I try?

'Who would like to have a spotty boy all day, George?' I say with a sigh. He smiles up at me from the buggy. 'I can't ask Emma because she's working too. It's Will's day off and I can't see him being all that keen on babysitting. There's Lynsey – she's offered before, but if that rash is infectious, she won't thank me if any of her brood go down with it. There's only one thing for it, George. You'll have to come to work with me.'

When I reach Otter House, I have a word with Frances.

'It's a complete disaster,' I say. 'Sophia and Old Fox-Gifford have gone to London for a couple of days to visit some old friends – Alex says it's to relive their lost youth – so I can't ask them to have George. Flick at the nursery won't have him because of this rash on his arm.' I had wondered about covering it up, but they would have found out when he washed his hands before healthy snack time.

'I'll have him, Maz,' says Frances. 'Bring him around here. Oh, doesn't he look like his daddy now.'

I push the buggy behind the desk, but George isn't keen on not being able to see what's going on at the other side. He stretches and leans against the straps of the harness, squealing to get out. The patient who's waiting, an ancient basset hound, looks even more mournful than before.

'Is it serious?' Frances says. 'It isn't meningitis? I saw a programme about how you check the rash by pressing a glass against the spots.'

'Thank you, Frances. I am a vet.'

'And better than any doctor, so you know what I'm talking about.'

'I'll take him in to Kennels. George, come and see the animals.'

I know George isn't unwell, but I check with a glass in the staffroom en route to Kennels anyway. The spots disappear with pressure from the glass which means they're superficial not deep, as I knew anyway. It's fine. I rub my temple. Sometimes, I think I'm going mad.

George isn't impressed by the sight of the inpatients. There's a sick, fluffed-up pigeon that's due to meet its maker. It's been in for three days, showing no sign of improvement. There's also a black cat with a collar injury that hisses at us when we approach.

Izzy isn't all that impressed to see George either. I explain the situation and she isn't overly sympathetic, but then she doesn't have any children. She has dogs.

'I can't look after him, Maz. I haven't a clue when it comes to under-eighteens.'

'Pretend he's a puppy,' I suggest lightly. 'It's cheeky, I know, but I wondered if I could ask Shannon to spend some time with him and make do without a consulting nurse today.'

'You're going to have to do without one anyway, I'm afraid. She's called in sick.'

'Are you sure? That isn't like her. What's wrong?'

'A sore throat. A virus. She was pretty vague.'

'I can't remember her having a day off in all the time she's been here.'

'No, she's had off days, from too much partying the night before, but she's been reliable. It's probably exam stress, but she's finished them now, so hopefully, she'll be back tomorrow,' says Izzy.

My heart sinks. What am I going to do with George?

It's no use. He'll have to watch from his buggy in the consulting room for some of the time and sit with Frances for the rest. I hope the clients don't mind too much. I wish either Alex or I had a normal job, something nine to five in an office where you could catch up with your work the next day if you needed to.

At lunchtime, I play ball with George in the garden outside – we use one of Miff's tennis balls that I found in the long grass under the apple tree – and feed him on sandwiches from the Co-op. While we're enjoying the sunshine together, I call Jennie of Jennie's Cakes.

'Hi. It's Maz here. Can I talk to you about wedding cakes?'

'Are you planning more than one wedding?' she says, sounding amused.

'I was thinking about cupcakes, like the ones you did for Penny.'

'There's a story behind those . . .'

'I know. The dog – Lucky – ate the original cake the day before the wedding, and you saved the day by making cupcakes. Jennie, no one – apart from Penny,

146

of course – would have known any different.' I pause. 'Oh, I'm not sure. Alex's father has offered to pay for the cake and champagne, and I can't help thinking that he'd prefer me to choose something more traditional.'

'I can drop in to the practice sometime,' Jennie says. 'I'll bring some cake samples and piccies.'

'That would be great. Thank you.' I return George to Frances's care before the afternoon's consulting begins. Frances survives the rest of the day, although not before George has dislodged her wig and spilled juice on the post. Emma catches me after Frances has left for home, and has a look at George's rash. George is delighted to show her every spot on his skin, pointing at each one as if he's drawing a dot-to-dot.

'I reckon that he needs some antibiotics,' Emma says, getting up from where she's been kneeling on the floor in the staffroom. 'Why don't you call in on us on the way back to the Manor? Ben can write you a prescription.'

'I'll get him up to the surgery tomorrow.'

'Ah, tomorrow. That's what I wanted to talk to you about . . .' Emma hesitates before going on. 'I have a hospital appointment for a scan late afternoon. Maz, you must have guessed!'

Emma is positively glowing. She beams with joy, and I have no doubt now.

'You're pregnant . . .'

She nods. 'I reckon I'm about twelve weeks gone.'

'Emma, how exciting.' I throw my arms around her as tears of joy prick my eyes. Frances was right. 'That's wonderful. I'm so pleased for you and Ben. But how? How can that be?'

'The usual way, Maz. And yes, you're right, I didn't have any IVF this time.' Emma has had pregnancies resulting both naturally and through fertility treatment before. 'It's happened all on its own – with Ben's input, of course.'

'Too much information,' I smile, stepping back.

'Sorry,' Emma giggles.

'I thought you were . . . but I didn't like to ask.' I shade my eyes, looking at Emma as if her happiness is dazzling. 'Frances was pretty certain you were. It was the doughnuts that gave it away.'

'I hoped no one had noticed.'

'You can't keep anything secret here.'

'The jam in the middle started to taste like iron filings.'

'I can't say I've ever tried them,' I say, laughing with her.

'How I imagine they might taste then,' she amends.

'You will come in to show us the photos tomorrow?'

'Of course.'

'Oh, Emma, I can't wait.'

Her expression grows serious. 'I'm trying to keep it real,' she says. 'I want it so much . . .'

I reach out and touch her hand.

'You're bound to worry,' I say gently, 'but I'm sure everything will turn out fine this time.'

'Thanks, Maz.' Emma sighs. 'I don't know what I'd do without you.'

'Same here.'

I hope the results of the scan are favourable. Emma wants this baby more than anything in the world. It's selfish of me, I know, but I wonder if Emma will be able to make the wedding, let alone be maid of honour any more. On a quick calculation, it's just a few weeks before this baby is due.

The next morning's ops seem to go very slowly with

a cat castration, a bitch spay and two lump removals. Will sees the appointments with Izzy, while I operate with Shannon.

'You are feeling better today?' I ask her, when we're working on Sally, a golden retriever who has a lump on her flank. 'Yeah,' Shannon says non-committally, as I remove the growth and surrounding skin, and send it off for histology to find out whether it's anything to worry about. I'm probably just as concerned as Penny, Sally's owner. Sally is one of my specials. Penny is a warm, vibrant person, an artist who moved down here to Devon after she was disabled in a car crash. Sally is both her companion and assistance dog.

I begin stitching up. When I stick the needle through Sally's skin, Sally flinches and lifts her head, which isn't great timing.

'Turn her up,' I say urgently, stopping to help Shannon soothe the dog and keep her still while she breathes in more anaesthetic.

'I'm sorry. I let her get too light too quickly.'

'Yes, now I'll have to scrub up again,' I say wryly. 'Perhaps you shouldn't have rushed back to work so soon after having that virus, or whatever it was.'

Eventually, we move Sally back to the big kennel and I watch her come round, take her tube out and check she's warm enough.

'Good girl, Sally,' I tell her, and even though she's still half asleep, she wags her tail in response to my voice. 'Okay, Shannon,' I call. 'Sally's tube's out. Shannon?'

I get up stiffly – must be getting old – and look for her. She's nowhere to be seen, which is not good, considering she's supposed to be responsible for the inpatients and her break isn't for another half an hour. I find her in the corridor on her mobile.

'Shannon –' I hold the door for her to come back into Kennels –'we agreed, no mobiles except at break times.'

'I'm sorry, Maz. I had to phone home. Mum's not answering.'

'I'm sure she has a good reason. She's probably serving a customer.'

'I have to go out for a few minutes. I need to make sure she's all right.'

'Shannon, you're on ops. You can't just leave.'

'She could be on the floor. Anything.' I can hear the panic rising in Shannon's voice. 'She's been having trouble with her insulin. Her blood sugar levels are all over the place. I've left her with Seven and Daisy.' She holds out her hands, palms upwards. 'Who knows what might have happened?'

'Okay, Shannon, I'm coming with you. Let me get Izzy to take over here. Have you got your house keys, in case your mum's gone out?' I knock and walk into the consulting room. There is a cat on the table, a powerful stench of pus and Will is cleaning his glasses. Apologising for the interruption, I call Izzy out.

'If you could just take over in Kennels,' I say, 'I'll explain later.'

'Maz, could you come here for a minute?' Frances says as Shannon and I head out through Reception. 'Clive's on the phone wanting a quick word.'

'Tell him I'll call back by one.' I can't stop. Part of me is saying Bridget's fine and another is fearing the worst.

We pace briskly through the car park, and left along to Market Square to Petals, receiving a few odd looks from people in the cars that are stuck behind a slow-moving tractor and muck spreader in the one-way system, because we're still dressed in our scrubs. It takes a glimpse of my reflection in the window of the Copper Kettle to make me realise that I'm still wearing my theatre cap too. It isn't a good look.

I whip it off and stuff it into my pocket as we reach Petals. It has a green awning and a stand of flowers outside on the pavement. The sign on the door reads OPEN, and Seven is on the other side, whining and making nose-prints on the glass.

Shannon pushes the door open, ringing the bell on the way into the shop.

'Mum,' she calls, 'Mum!' while Seven trots back and forth, as if he's showing us the way. Daisy snuffles about unperturbed, lapping from the buckets on the floor.

I follow Shannon and Seven past the counter, through to the back of the shop where Bridget is sitting slumped on the step that leads into the living accommodation beyond.

'Mum?' Shannon's voice catches. 'Oh, Mum.' She falls to her knees beside her, and takes her hand. 'When did you last eat? Where is your bag?'

Bridget is pale, her frizzy curls stuck to her forehead, and her body trembling. She's tried to pull her polo top off, but managed to get only one arm out of the sleeves.

'I d-d-don't know,' she stammers.

'When did you have your insulin?'

'Don't remember.'

'Sugar,' I say. 'She needs sugar.'

'She has a bag. Her glucose tablets will be in there. Mum –' Shannon shakes her roughly by the shoulder – 'where's the bag?'

I check in the shop. There's a cloth bag on the counter. I open it, find a packet of glucose tablets and hand them to Shannon, who gives two to Bridget, guiding her hand to her mouth.

'Water,' she mumbles.

'I'll get it.' I move past them to find my way to the kitchen where I rinse out a glass and fill it from the tap. Glancing around at the cutlery and plates stacked up in the washing-up bowl, and the overflowing pedal bin, I wonder how much time Shannon has had to devote to looking after her mother recently.

'How long does it take to work? When will she feel better?' Shannon asks.

'Not long,' I say, wondering whether to call an ambulance. 'Why don't I ring Dr Mackie. Your mum needs to see a doctor. Shannon, has this happened before? Is this why you were off sick yesterday, because you were worried about your mum?'

'I didn't know what else to do. It's been so hard recently.' She sniffs. 'I'm the only one, you see.' She's still holding her mum's hand.

'I know I shouldn't,' Bridget says more clearly now, 'but I depend on Shannon.' She looks up through a glitter of tears. 'I'm sorry, love. I'm useless.'

'Don't be silly, Mum.'

'I wish you'd said, Shannon. It's no wonder you had such a struggle with your exams and everything.' I pull my mobile out of my bag and call Ben. It takes a few minutes to arrange an appointment – he's too busy to visit and it isn't far to the surgery. 'He'll see you in half an hour,' I tell Shannon. 'You must take the rest of the day off.'

'But, Maz—' she protests.

'You can't be in two places at once, and your

152

mum needs you now. And I need to get back to the practice.'

Shannon walks back through the shop with me.

'What am I going to do? In the long term, I mean?'

'Shannon, this isn't insurmountable. We'll talk to Ben later – I mean, Dr Mackie. It might be that we can negotiate with Izzy so you do all the late shifts for a while, until your mum's diabetes is stabilised. She might be able to have one of those diabetic alert dogs, the ones that can detect low blood sugar levels from a change in body odour.'

'We can't have three dogs,' says Shannon.

'Seven appears to show some aptitude for the role. Cheer up. You can't possibly give up vet nursing to look after your mum. I won't let you. You're talented and caring, and after a few weeks, your mum won't need you watching over her like this.' I pause. 'If the doctor sends you to the hospital, I can give you a lift.'

'I can drive, Maz.' Shannon smiles weakly. 'You're busy enough already. You've done the ops, and you're booked up all afternoon, and you're fitting Jennie in in between, so you can order your wedding cake. I don't know how you do it.'

I smile back. 'Neither do I, Shannon. Neither do I.'

When I return to Otter House a couple of minutes later, there is no let-up.

'Maz,' says Frances, 'can you have a word with Will, once you've spoken to Clive? I've had a client complaining about the amount he charged for lancing an abscess this morning. It was the tiniest abscess – although the pus apparently spurted everywhere – and the cat's had one before and it cost about a third of the amount when you dealt with it.'

'How much was it?'

153

Frances gives me a figure.

'Will must have made a mistake,' I say. 'It's all right, Frances. I'll have a word.'

'That isn't all,' she says, stalling me. 'A couple of our regulars have gone over to the other side.'

'What do you mean? They've died?'

'They've registered with Talyton Manor Vets because they reckon Will overcharged them.'

'I see . . .' I phone Clive to delay having to broach what might be a delicate subject with Will. The practice is mine and Emma's, but Will is a fellow professional and he's entitled to some respect.

I wouldn't be too happy if my boss had told me, in my first job, what I could and couldn't do, although, in retrospect, he did tell me off for not giving enough injections. At the time, his clients were accustomed to expect a shot of long-acting antibiotic with a touch of an anti-inflammatory – my boss's euphemism for steroids – or a shot of vitamin B, or a tonic to boost appetite and the immune system. He had quite a way with words, and he made his living, and acquired a couple of sports cars, on the back of those shots.

Clive answers the phone.

'Is everything all right?' I ask.

'I wanted to check whether or not I should bring Cassie to the surgery,' he says. 'The kittens have been pulling her stitches out. Edie tried making her a boob tube to cover them, but it hasn't worked. She made holes in strategic positions so the kittens could feed.'

'Is the wound closed, or open?' I ask, amused at the thought of Cassie in clothes.

'It looks closed and there's a dry scab on it.'

'Is Cassie well in herself?'

154

'She's the same as ever.'

'In that case, we can leave it for now. If the wound starts weeping, or there's any redness or swelling, bring her straight down.'

'Thanks, Maz. I'll see you for the appointment to have the rest of the stitches out.'

'Okay, Clive. I'll see you then.'

I decide to go upstairs to the flat to talk to Will; he has a corn snake curled around his fingers when he opens the door.

'Hi, I hope you don't mind me interrupting your lunch break.'

'No problem,' he says. 'Do you want to come in?'

'Yes, please. If that's okay,' I add, when he hesitates.

'I'm sorry, I haven't tidied up,' he says, letting me through.

I look around at the tanks filled with exotic creatures – there seem to be more than ever.

'It looks pretty tidy to me,' I say, comparing it with the state of the Barn.

'Would you like a drink? Squash or coffee?'

'A cold drink would be good, thanks.' I move towards the window, as Will fetches a glass from the open-plan kitchen area. There are photos on the shelf alongside me, Will and his parents, I guess, standing outside the door of a house, wisteria falling around Will's shoulders.

'Where do your family come from?' I ask when he hands me the drink.

'Berkshire. My father's a banker. I decided I didn't want to end up commuting into the City every day. That's why I chose to be a vet.' He sighs. 'Now, I can almost see the appeal of sitting idle on a train for a couple of hours, morning and evening.'

'Girlfriend? Significant other?' I say tentatively.

'Not at the moment. My last girlfriend found a snake under the duvet on her side of the bed.' Will blushes. 'It bit her leg, and that was the end of it. It was a case of giving up her, or the snakes, and the snakes won out.' He grins ruefully. 'I thought it would be simple enough finding a girl who appreciates snakes, but it turns out I was wrong.'

'She wasn't a vet student then?'

'She was studying for a degree in mediaeval history. She gave it up after a year when she found that pole dancing was a far more lucrative career.'

Will's a dark horse, I muse. I can't imagine him frequenting night clubs, let alone dating a pole dancer, although I remind myself she was probably a perfectly respectable woman. Just because she discovered a somewhat questionable route to financial independence doesn't mean she's a slapper.

'What was it you wanted to see me about?' he asks.

'It's about the cat with the abscess. The owners have complained to Frances about the cost and I wondered if there could have been some mistake.'

'I charged a consultation fee, time for lancing an abscess, antibiotics, a shot of painkiller, and the lab fee.'

'Lab fee?'

'I sent off a sample for culture and sensitivity.'

'Why?' I notice a heap of dead chicks defrosting on the draining board and shudder. 'Is that your lunch over there?'

'It's for the pythons,' Will says, frowning. 'I sent a sample to the lab because it's the correct approach, the right thing to do.'

'Will, I hate to dampen your enthusiasm, but

sending off a sample isn't going to make any difference to the cat's welfare. This is a first-opinion, not a referral, practice. We don't do the bionic vet here.'

'What do you suggest?' he says coolly.

'We'll drop the lab charge. I'll adjust the rest so it's closer to what I charged the first time. It seems as if I'm interfering and undermining you, but unfortunately, I set a precedent when I treated the cat the first time. Is that okay?'

'I suppose it'll have to be.' Will shrugs. 'Don't people want the best for their pets?'

'On the whole. It's just that they can't always afford to pay for it.' I smile. 'Thanks for the drink and the chat. I must get back downstairs. No rest for the wicked and all that.'

'I'll be down later,' Will says.

Much later, the inpatients are all up and ready to go home, and I'm on tenterhooks, waiting for Emma to return from the hospital.

She turns up in Kennels as I'm typing up the last of the notes and Izzy's washing the instruments in the sink. The autoclave is on, emitting the familiar and reassuring scent of steaming cotton.

'Well?' I ask.

'Come with me,' she says in a conspiratorial whisper. 'I have something to show you.'

I follow her into the corridor and beyond to the office where we're less likely to be disturbed. It's difficult to keep anything private. At Otter House, the walls have ears, so to speak, and those ears usually belong to Frances. Once we're inside, Emma closes the door behind us.

'I wanted to show you first. Well, Ben's seen them. Obviously.' She's grinning, touching her stomach with

157

one hand, and holding out a series of scan photos in the other.

'All's well, I take it,' I say tentatively. I feel as if I can breathe now. The baby's healthy.

'It's early days – 13 weeks, according to the measurements – but so far, so good.'

'Let me see.'

'They'll make you go all broody,' Emma teases, snatching the photos to her chest. 'You'll want another one.'

'I don't think so.' I recall the sleepless nights, the anxious moments when George did go quiet and I'd wonder if he was still breathing, and the endless steaming and mashing of fresh fruit and veg to give him the best possible start. 'No, definitely not.' I watch Emma's expression, and smile to myself. Little does she know. 'I'm so pleased for you and Ben,' I add, taking the photos from her.

'Oh, it's sucking its thumb in that one,' I say, my heart melting. It reminds me of George and he seems so grown up now. 'It's cute.' I don't want another baby. Aah, maybe I do . . . But not while Emma's on maternity leave. 'Do you have any idea if it's a boy or girl, or is it too early to say?'

'I've said I don't want to know,' Emma says, and I wonder if there's something she isn't telling me.

'Are you sure everything's okay?' I ask quietly.

'It's fine, but there is a minor complication. If you look at the pictures, there's one baby sucking its thumb.'

'Yeah, I got that.'

'Look at that one again, and count the heads.' She pauses as I take this in. There are two heads, which means . . .

158

'There are two babies,' Emma goes on. 'I'm carrying twins.'

'Oh, that's amazing. Fantastic,' I say, hugging her. 'Wow, there aren't any twins in your family, are there?'

'I don't know quite where they came from, Maz. Oh, I'm so happy.'

'How will you cope?' I say, recalling how much time and energy one single baby can consume.

'I don't mind. I've wanted to be a mum for so long that, if the doctor had said there were eight babies in there, I wouldn't have cared.' Emma smiles. 'I'll have a nanny. No, maybe after your experience, I won't. Ben and I can afford to get some help in, someone to do the garden and the housework, if we need it.'

'You really must take care of yourself. You must say if you want to cut your hours. Don't push it.'

'Thanks, Maz. I appreciate it,' she says, and I feel a twinge of shame at how I reacted when she told me she was pregnant with Heather, the baby she lost. It wasn't until I had George that I understood. It was a slow realisation. I was a reluctant mum at first, with George turning up out of the blue because I missed a single contraceptive pill.

'If there's anything I can do . . .' I go on.

'You can tell me exactly what I'll need to buy, what you found useful, what you needn't have bothered with. Oh, I'm so excited . . .' Emma's voice trails off. 'And nervous. No, not nervous. Petrified.'

'Oh, Em –' I reach out and touch her back – 'I've said it before and I'll say it again – it'll be all right this time.'

'I hope so, but I can see that when I should be enjoying this pregnancy, I'm going to worry the whole time.'

'Are you going to tell everyone now you've had

your scan?' I ask. 'I mean, I don't have to mention it to anyone, not even Alex, if you don't want me to, although I'll find it hard to keep it a secret.'

'I'm going to tell the staff here and you can tell Alex, of course, and I don't mind if other people know, but I want to keep it all very low key.'

Frances comes bursting into the office.

'Maz, Mrs Tarbarrels is here for her appointment.' She stops abruptly. 'Oh, Emma, are those what I think they are?' Emma holds the scan photos behind her back, but it is too late. Frances is on the case. 'That's wonderful news, dear. Congratulations.' Frances moves across and gives Emma a hug.

'I'll leave you to it,' I say. Frances is right. It's wonderful news, but it's going to seem like a very long six months.

Chapter Ten

In Sickness and in Health

It's almost the end of July and Alex is working longer than ever, reinforcing my concerns that we will never be ready for the wedding. It's also the school holidays and Lucie and Seb are here for two weeks while Alex's ex-wife travels off to Mauritius, or St Lucia, somewhere exotic. I don't understand why she doesn't want to take her children on holiday with her. I still can't imagine leaving George behind while Alex and I go on honeymoon.

Their stay has been planned to coincide with Pony Club camp, an annual event at the Manor, thanks to the Fox-Giffords' hospitality. By tonight, the place will be overrun with children and their ponies for five days of chaos, fun and water fights. It all kicks off this afternoon.

I gaze out of the window onto the street at Otter House, glad to be at work. Sophia has all three children today, and I worry about how she's coping. Frances is arranging flowers in a vase at Reception, practising her techniques for the WI meeting tonight.

She looks up from the sweet peas and foliage. The scent combines oddly with the fragrance of dog wee that emanates from the direction of the glass doors where some pesky patient of ours must have cocked his leg.

'Maz, no news is good news,' Frances says, when I check my mobile for messages for the umpteenth time. 'Sophia is very capable. If she can break the spirit of some of those wild horses she's had over the years, she can manage three children.'

'I don't want her breaking their spirits though.'

Frances smiles. 'I expect she's locked them all in a stable.'

I hope she's joking. She is joking, of course. I can't help grinning back.

'That's better. I'm sure they're all fine.' Frances answers the phone.

'It's for you, Maz,' she says. 'It's the photographer. Are you free to speak to her now?'

My heart sinks a little. What can she want? I thought I'd sent the deposit, confirming the booking, and it's too soon to be running through exactly which photos I want for the wedding. I take the phone and the woman on the other end gives me a longwinded excuse for why she is no longer available for the third Saturday in December.

'I'm so sorry,' she says, promising to send the deposit straight back. 'I wish you all the best for your special day. Goodbye.'

'Bad news?' Frances says sympathetically.

'Yes, the photographer's cancelled. She's emigrating. Frances, what am I going to do?'

'Find another one? There'll be others.'

'But I chose this one. She was highly recommended.'

I feel slightly panicky. 'I rang a couple of others when I first contacted her, and they were already booked up for the date of our wedding.'

'They can't all be booked up,' Frances says.

'I bet the good ones are.' I scratch at a niggling spot on my chin. 'I wish we'd started planning sooner.'

'I can help. When I get five minutes, I'll phone around and give you a list of photographers who are available to save you wasting your time.'

'Thank you, Frances. That would be great.' Frances glances towards the car park.

'Here's Clive. No Edie again.' I notice Frances's sharp intake of breath and the slow, disapproving shake of the head. 'Poor man.'

'What do you mean, poor man?'

'Having a wife who's a drinker.'

'Oh, Frances . . .' I sigh.

'She's an alcoholic,' Frances goes on.

'You really shouldn't listen to gossip.'

'Edie has her ankle in plaster at the moment.'

'And?' I say. 'That doesn't prove anything.'

'She'd had a few too many and tripped over the cat. Fifi told me. She has a friend who works at the Minor Injuries Unit, and she said that Edie came in reeking of drink at ten in the morning.'

'Sh,' I say, as Clive pushes the door open. I'm not sure how our clients would take it, finding out how we gossip about them behind their backs.

'Hello, Clive. How's Cassie?'

'She's here to have her stitches out – the one that's left. The kittens have taken the rest out for you.' He smiles. 'Does that mean I get a discount?'

'Come on through.' I usher him into the consulting room. 'Let's have a look at her.'

'She seems well, but she's lost more weight,' Clive says, as Cassie shoots out of the box and runs up his chest where she clings with her claws stuck into his T-shirt.

I help him, unpicking her claws from the material, so he can lower her onto the table, turn her over and show me her belly. Cassie stares at me, eyes wide as if she's assessing me. Friend or foe? She blinks. Friend.

The wound has healed reasonably well, considering the kittens have been sucking at the stitches. All that is left is a thread without a knot. I pull it out with tweezers. Cassie starts purring.

'She's relieved to have a break from her babies,' says Clive. 'They don't give her a chance to sleep.'

'How are the kittens?'

'They're growing like mad.'

'Cassie's eating well?' I ask.

'I think so. Edie would have said . . . although she doesn't always notice these things.' He looks away from me, towards the corner of the table. 'She isn't always in a fit state.'

I don't know what to say.

'Oh, Maz, I don't know what to do about it,' Clive goes on quietly. 'She's addicted to drink and can't, or won't, see what it's doing to her. To us. To the business.'

'I'm so sorry.' I pause. 'If there's anything I can do . . .'

'Thank you. I thought she might come round when Cassie had her kittens, when she had something depending on her, something else to focus on.' Clive shakes his head. 'I think she's getting worse.'

'Has she seen the doctor, or a counsellor?' I'm

floundering. 'Clive, I know what it's like to live with a heavy drinker. My father was an alcoholic.'

'Did he get better?' Clive asks.

'I don't know. It isn't a story with a happy ending. He left us, walked out on his family and we never heard from him again.' I shrug resignedly.

'I didn't know . . .'

'It isn't something I talk about.' I swallow back the lump in my throat. I haven't cried for my dad for years. This is ridiculous. 'I do wish I'd found him. I'd have loved him to have met George, for George's sake, not his. I could never forgive him for what he put us through – my mum, brother and me.'

'It was the drink though?' Clive gazes at me, challenge in his eyes.

'I don't believe that. My father was ill – it's an illness, isn't it?' I pause. 'It can't help with you running a pub, being behind the bar . . .'

'It's very hard,' he admits. 'Have you finished with Cassie?' he adds, abruptly changing the subject.

'Not yet. I'd like to check her over again.' Cassie stands on the table, purring away and letting me kiss the top of her head. Her gums are pale and she has a murmur I can hear with the stethoscope, a breathy sound of extra turbulence as the blood flows through her heart.

'Is she all right?'

'I'm not sure.' It's better to admit it than pretend. 'She's obviously a good mum, but I wonder if there's something else going on here.' I wonder if I'm being paranoid because Clive's had such bad luck with his dogs before.

'I'd like to take some blood – just to put my mind at rest.'

'Go ahead, if you think it's necessary.'

165

I call Shannon through to help. Cassie doesn't like it, but it doesn't take long.

'Shannon, if you can run this through the machine this afternoon, I can give you a call at about six, Clive.'

'Great,' he says, but I know it might not be, and when I get the results later, they are not good. I call Clive at the pub.

'I'm afraid there are some changes in the blood,' I say. 'Cassie's anaemic and her kidneys aren't working properly. Does she drink more than she used to?'

'Not that I've noticed, but she'll drink out of anything, taps, the birdbath, the toilet.' Clive hesitates. 'How serious is this?'

'Pretty serious. Kidney damage is irreversible. All we can do is support her with drugs and a targeted diet, and retest her in a couple of weeks. If anything changes in the meantime, let me know and I'll see her before.'

'What's caused it? Cassie's a young cat.'

'We may never know, but there is a genetic condition that runs in Persian cats, where cysts develop in the kidneys so they don't function normally.'

'Can you operate?'

'No. There's nothing that can be done.'

'So . . .? Does it get worse?'

'Yes, eventually.' I can tell from Clive's tone of voice that he's upset. I steel myself. 'Some live longer than others.'

'If it's genetic, will the kittens have it too?'

'I'll need to take another blood sample to send off to a specialist lab to see if Cassie is carrying the gene for polycystic kidney disease. If she isn't, the kittens are in the clear. If she is, we can test the kittens, or wait and see. People don't always want to know the whole picture.'

'Oh no, that is the worst news. I'm gutted . . . How am I going to tell Edie? It's just our luck, isn't it? Sometimes it feels as if life's just one long bloody slog.' His voice fades then returns, sounding brighter. 'It's finally happened,' he chuckles blackly. 'I've become a grumpy old man.'

'Let me know if you need to talk . . . about anything. Tell me if or when you want to book Cassie in for the blood test, and keep in touch.'

'Will do. Thanks, Maz.'

I don't feel as though I deserve any thanks for delivering bad news. It puts the problem with the wedding photographer into perspective. The fact that ours has cancelled, and Frances has failed to find another local professional with availability for the date in December, is a bit of a nightmare but hardly a matter of life and death.

As I turn into the drive up to the Manor later the same day, I take a deep breath. I'm not expecting peace and quiet. Partway along, where the drive curves through an area of parkland, I find a black pony in a head collar and dangling rope on the loose, tearing towards me at full gallop.

Sophia is running up behind it, followed like the Pied Piper of Hamelin by a charge of children in jodhpurs and Pony Club polo shirts. A woman and another girl chase along, taking up the rear.

I jump out of the car.

'Block it orf, Maz,' Sophia yells.

I have no choice. As the pony approaches, I can see

the sheer panic in its eyes, and the sound of its thundering hooves fills my ears. It's petrified, and I can't say that I'm too calm either, wondering which way to jump, because if it maintains its line, it will mow me down, or end up on the road, which doesn't bear thinking about.

Shouting and screaming at it to stop, I wave my arms, at which, to my short-lived relief, it veers away. But it smashes straight into the fence, crashing through the post and rails and cantering towards the pond where it stops and stands under one of the trees, head down, shivering and shaking.

As I approach, slowing down as I reach it so as not to send it galloping off again, I can see blood and sweat dripping from its chest.

'Steady there, pony,' I say as soothingly as I can, having run at speed across the field. The pony rolls his eyes at me, showing the whites. He's hurt and scared, and I wonder what's happened to upset him like that. Also, I think how lucky it is that he didn't have a child on his back when he bolted. I walk up to him slowly and make myself small – apparently, ponies like this because it makes you look less of a threat. I reach out and grasp the rope, then move in and rub the pony's neck at which the gaggle of children that have gathered with Sophia a few metres away utter a collective sigh of relief.

'Maz, is he all right?' Sophia comes striding up, takes one look and says, 'Have you got your mobile? Call Alexander.' She turns to beckon the woman and girl who have caught up with us. 'I should wait there, Jennie. It isn't a pretty sight.'

It's too late though. Jennie – of Jennie's Cakes, from whom I ordered the wedding cake – arrives at the pony's head with her daughter, Georgia, who is a year or two older than Lucie.

'I don't care,' says Georgia. 'I'm going to be a vet like Alex one day.'

Georgia is very much like her mum, petite and brunette. Of the two though, she is the most upset, bursting into tears at the sight of the blood on the ground. She takes the rope from me, and throws her arms around the pony's neck.

'Poor Guinness,' she cries.

'We've had him three weeks,' says Jennie.

I'm on the mobile to Alex who turns up with George – luckily, they were at home. Alex hands George over to me, takes one look at the pony and decides we'll have to box him back to the yard.

'I'll sedate him when we get there and have a proper look at that wound. If it isn't too deep, I can flush it out and stitch it up here. If it's full of splinters, I might have to refer him to the equine hospital.' He raises one eyebrow as he talks to Jennie. 'You don't have much luck with your ponies, do you?'

'I can't quite believe it. This one is insured for vets' fees though. I learned my lesson after what happened to Bracken.'

'Perhaps we could negotiate on the wedding cake,' Alex says, to lighten the mood. After all, his father is paying for it, not us.

'That sounds good to me,' Jennie says. 'I'll go and get the truck.'

'Mother's on the case.' Alex looks up the drive. Sophia is on her way at the wheel of the Fox-Giffords' lorry, rattling over the gravel, then bumping off-road across the grass. She stops, jumps out and opens the ramp. Alex loads the pony, and then we all pile in to

169

the front, and Sophia drives us the short distance back to the yard.

Although Jennie and Georgia want to stay with Guinness, Sophia has other plans for them. Jennie is on duty in the kitchen, cooking up dinner for thirty Pony Clubbers, and Georgia is to continue setting up her camp bed.

'I'll find you another pony for camp,' says Sophia. 'We always have a few spares. You can borrow my horse, Jumbo. He's big, but he's a good boy. He'll look after you.'

'It's a shame,' says Jennie. 'We bought Guinness to jump this summer. Will he still be able to do that after this?'

'I don't see why not,' Alex says. 'There'll be a few other hurdles for him to clear beforehand, so to speak, but he should make a complete recovery.' He pauses. 'Mother, is there any chance of you taking George? I could do with having Maz here as my assistant.'

'If that's all right with her,' I say lightly.

'If you're worried about Guinness being a horse, pretend he's something smaller, like a dog,' Alex teases.

'George can join in with the other younger brothers and sisters – Fox-Gifford and a couple of the Pony Club dads are going to play croquet before dinner,' Sophia says.

'Thanks, Mother.'

Alex leaves me in one of the stables with the pony while he fetches some kit from the surgery. When he returns, he sedates Guinness.

'So you're the vet, and I'm the nurse,' I observe.

'You can be a vet too, if you like,' he says.

170

'Not tonight.' I'm not on duty, and I don't want the responsibility.

I help Alex as he examines the pony's wound, and pulls out splinters of wood from the flesh with tweezers.

'How's it looking?' I ask.

'It isn't that bad. I'm going to give it a good clean, and leave a drain in so the fluid doesn't build up. There'll be less likelihood of an abscess forming that way.'

'I assume he'll have antibiotics and anti-inflammatories for a few days.'

'And stable rest. I guess Mother will let Guinness stay here so Georgia can look after him.' Alex smiles. 'It'll make it easy for me to check up on him.'

When he's finished, we wait for the pony to recover from the sedation, watching him from a straw bale that Alex dragged into the stable earlier to act as a table for his kit.

'If you had an assistant . . .' I begin, reaching up behind his neck and letting his hair curl and uncurl around my fingers.

'We wouldn't have been doing this together,' Alex finishes for me.

'Alex, why don't we go on a date tonight? George is occupied, studying the gentlemanly pursuit of croquet ready for when he goes off to Cambridge.' I'm being ironic. 'We don't have to go out for long.'

'I can't make it, Maz. Stewart called me just before Guinness ran through the fence. I said I'd pop up to the farm. It's one of the cows. It isn't urgent, but he doesn't think it'll wait until the morning, and, to be honest, I'd rather visit tonight because I'm booked up all day tomorrow.'

'So, I'm second to a cow, yet again,' I say, more annoyed than I should be. I'm bitterly disappointed. It shouldn't matter. We live together. We sleep together. The problem is that I'm beginning to feel as if Alex is using work as an excuse to avoid me. Each time he says he can't spend time – quality time – with me, it's like a rejection. When I tackle him about it, he becomes defensive. The more it goes on, the worse it gets.

The pony takes a step forwards and nuzzles at the shavings on the floor.

'Guinness is looking brighter,' says Alex, squeezing my thigh. 'Another ten minutes or so, and we can leave him to sleep it off.'

When we finally leave the stable, Alex kisses my cheek, and I watch him go off to his car, torn between acceptance and regret. With Alex's attention, the pony will recover. Without it, sometimes I'm scared that our relationship will sicken and die.

If I could capture a single moment, stopper it inside a vial and keep it for ever, I might well choose this one. On the last day of camp, I'm at home with George, lying on the sofa in the Barn. The doors are open to the yard at the front and bright sunshine glances in past a pot of scarlet geraniums. I can hear the soft caw and cluck of a hen as she stalks around the stone floor in her feathery bloomers, searching for crumbs. The peace doesn't last though.

Lucie comes flying in with three other Pony Clubbers on a scavenger hunt.

George, who's been snoozing in the travel cot I set up as a trap for him – he's almost too big for it now – wakes up.

'Thanks for that, Lucie.'

172

'Sorry, Maz. We're looking for a piece of string. It's on the list of things to collect.'

'Isn't it cheating, coming in here?'

'No,' she says, and I smile to myself. In the eyes of the Fox-Giffords, there is no such concept as cheating. Winning is everything, by fair means or foul.

'There's probably some string in the kitchen,' I begin, but Lucie's ahead of me, scrabbling around in the drawer by the sink.

'Found it,' she says, snipping a piece off the ball. 'Maz, don't let anyone else have it. We want to win the prize.'

'It's a good one then?'

'Humpy's bought purple tail bandages from Hack 'n' Tack.'

Lucie and her team rush out again, leaving George looking perturbed. I sweep him up and find him a drink in his special cup before I stand with him, looking out onto the yard. It's a good day. Guinness the pony is well on the road to recovery, and Sophia has enlisted me to do a Pony Club badge with the children.

'A test on dogs – working and hunting breeds – would be marvellous, Maz,' she said, and when I protested that I didn't really approve of hunting, she went on to say that I was lucky she hadn't asked me to do the after-lunch talk on worms. Alex did that one earlier today.

An hour later, I take George out to the yard in his buggy, where he's surrounded by Pony Clubbers, mainly girls. I have a handful of 'volunteers' press-ganged by Sophia to bring their dogs along for the purpose of the badge. Old Fox-Gifford is here too, with Hal as an example of a working Labrador. Once the girls have mauled George, who loves them, they turn their attention to the dogs. Sophia calls them back.

'You can see the dogs in a minute,' she says. 'Maz, the vet from Otter House, will talk to you and explain the different kinds of hunting dog.'

'Hunting? I thought we agreed on working breeds.'

'Those as well, but we'd like to concentrate on hunting dogs, real dogs. Then I have a little test for you so you can identify the breeds here. If you pass the test, you will receive a badge.'

'Hello, everyone,' I begin, but no one appears to be taking any notice.

'Girls and boys, sit down on the bales and listen to Maz,' Sophia says, and they all sit down. To my consternation, Sophia does too.

'I'm expecting to learn something new,' she says.

No pressure then, I think to myself, amused.

I decide to introduce the subject, ask the audience what they already know about working dog breeds, and then ask the owners to parade their dogs, one at a time.

There's a brace of tricolour foxhounds that howl almost incessantly. The beagle and the Jack Russell terriers join in, followed by Old Fox-Gifford's Labs and spaniels. It's a riot.

In the end, I award all the children badges before they run away to find their ponies for one last ride. Sophia organises them getting tacked up.

As Old Fox-Gifford prepares to head back to the Manor, I join him, pushing George in the buggy. I've been meaning to talk to him for a while.

'I wanted to check how you were getting on with finding someone to help you out while Alex and I are away,' I say. 'I'd like Alex to have a practice to come back to.'

Old Fox-Gifford hesitates, Hal and a young Labrador bitch at his side, the bitch taken on as an eventual replacement for Hal, and for breeding. She's called Poppy, which is a shame because, if we ever did have another baby, it's a nice name for a girl.

Old Fox-Gifford walks towards the paddock where Liberty and her foal are grazing, their excitement at seeing the other horses over. He rubs his back. He looks like a very old man, but I find it hard to feel sorry for him. He isn't the kind of man I can get close to. We've come to a civil agreement – since I operated on Hal to save his life, Old Fox-Gifford stopped the sexist remarks about female vets and he appears to have come to terms with the idea of me and Alex getting married. He loves George too, in his own way.

'What makes you think I can't look after the practice? I've not been put out to grass yet.'

'I don't want Alex to have to worry about what's going on back here at home.'

'While you're enjoying your honeymoon,' he says. Do I detect a note of lasciviousness, I wonder, rather repelled? 'He doesn't have to worry. I'm well able to work. For many years, before Alexander came back from university, I worked day and night, seven days a week, fifty-two weeks of the year. I was never sick or sorry.'

'Until the bull got you,' I point out. If I was talking to anyone else, I'd be more tactful, but Old Fox-Gifford doesn't do what he calls pussyfooting around. 'Life has changed, hasn't it?'

'What are you suggesting? That I'm past it?' His eyes flash with anger, but no one can stay angry for long in the presence of a long-legged filly like Scheherazade who's cantering around the paddock again, playing and snorting at the dogs, feigning a buck and a kick.

'I wasn't—'

'You were.'

'All right. I was suggesting that it would make your life easier if you had someone in to give you a hand, some back-up. Alex was called out three times the other night.'

'I'd have gone on one or other of the calls if he'd asked me, but he didn't.'

'It would be better for your clients not to have to wait for a vet, if you were tied up.'

'They understand. They're farmers and stockmen, loyal and bonded to the practice, not the fanciful, fickle and ignorant pet-owning general public.'

'That isn't the impression Alex gave me.' Immediately, I wonder if I should have said anything.

'What has he said?' Old Fox-Gifford says sharply.

'Nothing. Not really. I think Guy Barnes was upset when Alex took two hours to get to him the other night because he was busy elsewhere on another call.'

'That's up to Guy,' says Old Fox-Gifford. 'I was ready to go, but he insisted on waiting for Alex.'

'Oh?'

'Don't you go reading anything particular into that,' he says. 'Guy can be whimsical.'

I don't know Guy well, but people around here describe him as a steady sort, straightforward and loyal.

'So what happens if Alex is away and Guy won't see you?' I ask, determined not to give up until I have a satisfactory answer.

Old Fox-Gifford doesn't respond. He has his eyes on

the foal, and I wonder if he's comparing his failing body with her agility and youth.

'You know,' he says eventually, 'a good wife doesn't interfere with her husband's business.'

'I'm not married yet and I'm not going to be a wife who's seen and not heard.'

Old Fox-Gifford smiles.

'I wouldn't describe my wife as a shrinking violet,' he says, as Sophia's voice rings out across the fields, giving instructions to a ride of six small children and their ponies. 'A country vet needs a capable and supportive wife, and –' I almost miss the slight catch in his voice as he goes on – 'I couldn't have chosen better.'

Old Fox-Gifford disappears inside the Manor, leaving me standing in the yard, touched that he feels that way, and wondering if he's ever expressed that sentiment to Sophia.

'What shall we do now, George?' I say.

'Come and have tea and cake with the rest of us,' Jennie calls across from the gazebo that's been set up on the lawn, and we end up joining the party to celebrate the end of camp. Afterwards, I help wash up.

'George, it must be time to find Lucie and Seb,' I say eventually.

'I'm here, Maz,' Lucie says, running up to me. Her eyes glitter with exhaustion, but she's still smiling. She shakes her head, water arcing from her hair.

'What happened to you?' I ask.

She's covered in dust and muck, and smells of hot horse. Her jodhpurs are filthy. They were probably – I'm hazarding a guess here – cream at the beginning of the week. Her shirt is wet, her Pony Club tie caught around her ear.

'You look a wreck,' I chide. 'When did you last have a wash?'

'Just now. Josh threw a bucket of water at me. And I threw a wet sponge back. And then Georgia turned on the tap for the hose and everyone joined in. Even Humpy got wet.' Lucie giggles. 'She isn't very happy. She's given us all a black mark and gone inside to get changed. We're supposed to be packing up now.'

'Go on then,' I say. 'Do you need some help?'

'Yes, please, Maz.'

I take George along and assist Lucie and some of her friends in sorting their clothes and packing their bags in their tent. I'm not sure how much help we are, but George loves it.

'So what's the best thing about Pony Club camp?' I ask.

There is some debate.

'The friends, the food and being able to ride all day.'

'The "funnest" thing is the water fights.'

'No, it was Sam fainting when Daddy showed us the jar of pickled worms,' says Lucie.

I chuckle to myself. It happens every year.

The children might be sorry that camp is over, but you can almost see the relief in the ponies' faces as they're loaded back into the horseboxes and trailers. They have worked twice a day, jumping and turning endless circles, spiralling in and out again. They've galloped cross-country, been on a picnic ride, and had a go at dressage to music and gymkhana games.

The smell of cold baked beans and burnt sausages lingers in the air. A trailer of dirty straw is waiting to be towed away. While helping tidy up, I find a couple of broken buckets and some lost property. There's a bridle and three brushes – I'm not sure if the latter are for children or ponies. I've found Lucie brushing her hair with a dandy brush before.

The children have loved it, but what is Sophia's verdict? I ask her later, when the last of the horseboxes rattles away down the drive, and Old Fox-Gifford is out on the lawn bemoaning the hoof prints.

'It was a great success,' she says. 'This year's tally was one staked pony, one lame one, a sprained wrist and a broken arm. Some years, it's been so much worse!'

Chapter Eleven

Alas, Poor Harry

I've learned to read that when the clients' eyes glaze over, it's time to stop. Clive and Edie don't want a lecture on the pathology of polycystic kidneys, no matter how fascinating the subject is to me. What they're looking for is reassurance, practical advice and medication.

Sometimes I feel I might need medication myself, I think, as I hear the sound of a woman wailing outside. I know that cry. It's Allie Jackson, roving reporter for Talyton's local newspaper, the *Chronicle*, and I don't know how many times I've heard her upset.

Frances pokes her head around the door.

'I'm sorry to disturb you in the middle of some-thing.' She smiles apologetically towards Clive and Edie. 'Maz, it's Harry. It's bad.'

'We'll go now,' Clive says. 'We've taken up enough of your time already. An appointment to see you again, you said?'

'Yes, I'll have the blood test results by then, and I'll have another look at Cassie to see if she needs to come in to go on a drip for a while.' I've taken blood today to test for the rogue gene. If she doesn't eat or drink overnight, she's going to need fluids.

As Clive and Edie leave with Cassie, Frances ushers Allie inside. Accompanied by the smell of floral perfume mixed with body odour, she's wearing a cheap trouser suit with a yellow blouse, and carrying a shoebox filled with hamster bedding. There is no lid, an ominous sign that Harry, formerly known as Harriet, who had a narrow escape from the practice's waste compressor over a year ago, really is not well this time. He must be at least three years old now, a good age for a golden hamster. Mind you, he's been well pampered.

'I know he's on his way out, Maz, but I wanted to be absolutely sure . . .' Allie puts the shoebox on the table and crushes a tissue to her nose. 'He's suffering terribly.' I thought she might be here expecting me to find a cure, but she's resigned to Harry's fate. 'Is there any way you can put him out of his misery?'

'Let's take a look at him,' I say, almost in tears myself. I don't normally cry for hamsters, but I'll probably have to make an exception for Harry. He's been quite a character. Very tentatively, I lift the bedding to reveal the hamster beneath. He's comatose, but I can't help imagining that there's a hint of malice remaining in his expression. His beady black eyes are open and unresponsive, and his mouth wide, gasping for breath.

'He's been drinking more recently.' Allie makes an attempt at black humour, continuing, 'Mind you, so have I, a bottle of wine a night to help me through what I know is coming.'

'He's in a bad way,' I agree. 'I think it would be kindest to help him along.'

'Into the next world, hamster heaven,' Allie sighs.

181

'Yes.' I toy with the idea of asking her to sign a consent form, but decide I've known Allie long enough for there to be no confusion.

'I'll take him through and let him have some anaesthetic.'

'You aren't going to hurt him, are you, only he's sooooo small.'

'We have a small plastic box, he can go in just as he is, in his bed, so there's no need to disturb him. He'll breathe in the gas that sends him to sleep so he isn't aware of the final injection.' I'm not sure he's going to need much. He's pretty well gone already.

'Can I see him after to say goodbye?'

'Of course.'

Harry is dead. With a sense of finality and secure in the knowledge that he'll never try to bite me again, I do what I never dared do in life, run my finger along his back, touching the tiny bones of his spine through the orange-brown fluff. I bring him back to Allie, wrapped in paper towel. He does look peaceful, although I can't get his eyes to close. Allie strokes him, tears rolling down her cheeks.

'Thank you, Maz,' she says eventually. 'I'm so grateful for how you've looked after Harry these past couple of years. I know people don't understand – it seems as if you are the only person who does – well, he's more than a hamster to me . . . he's my best . . .' she utters a strangled wail, '. . . friend. I could tell him everything, and know he'd never tell anyone else. Not because he couldn't talk, but because he was so loyal, he just wouldn't have.'

I offer Allie tea and a biscuit before she goes on her way, but she declines. 'What do I owe you for today?' she asks.

182

'Oh, nothing today.' I always find it difficult to charge for a dead small furry, or small fury as they're often called around here, especially as far as Harry is concerned. It seems wrong to break a habit of a lifetime, of Harry's lifetime anyway. 'Are you going to take him home?'

'Oh. Oh? I don't know. I haven't had a chance to think about it.' Allie pauses. 'Is it possible to have him cremated and take his ashes home?'

'Possible, but expensive.'

'I don't mind how much it costs.'

Allie might believe that now, but I'd hate her to rush into a decision she might regret because she's in shock. She has a family, and I can't think she earns all that much.

'Why don't I hold on to Harry here while you have that cup of tea. You can sit in the staffroom to give you time to collect your thoughts.'

'I must look a wreck,' she says.

I gaze at her. 'You're in no fit state to drive. Take some time out.'

'Are you sure, Maz?'

'It isn't anything to be embarrassed about. It's really upsetting losing a pet.' I think of Ginge – I'm afraid I'll have to make a decision for him very soon.

'Even a hamster.' A flicker of humour crosses Allie's face. 'It's all right. I know you lot think I'm mad.'

There's nothing I can say to that, so I show Allie to the staffroom, calling for Shannon to make tea if she's free, and apologising for the untidy state, chasing Tripod off the sofa. It's odd, but the more staff we have, the less work we seem to get done.

I return to the consulting room to see my next patient, Saba, who is walking again, albeit moving like a drunken ballerina. It's a miracle to me. She's going to need swimming sessions at the hydrotherapy pool for some months yet, but I'm pleased with her progress. It could have been so much worse. When I've sent her and Aurora on their way, I head back to the staffroom where I find Allie still chatting with Shannon.

'Next time, I'll have something I can't get so fond of, like a spider or stick insect.' Allie cracks a small smile through the tears.

'Have a chat with Will, our new vet, if you need advice on choosing an exotic,' Shannon says. 'He keeps snakes, geckos and tree frogs. They aren't very cuddly though.'

'Thanks for the tea, Shannon,' Allie says. 'The talk has really helped. Maz, I'm going to plant a rose in the garden to remember Harry by.'

I wonder if we should send Shannon on a bereavement counselling course. She seems to be good at it.

A few days later and Cassie's result comes through. It's positive. Clive brings her back because he's worried about her. I admit her, take blood, hand it over to Izzy and set up a drip. Cassie purrs the whole time. It isn't a healthy, happy purr, but the desperate purr of a sick cat.

'It isn't fair, is it,' I say, stroking her head.

'What about the kittens? They still have those, or . . .' Izzy hesitates.

'There's a fifty-fifty chance the kittens will have it too.' I pause. 'Where do you want her?'

'I thought she might be happier in Isolation under the stairs. It's quiet there. Do you want me to feed her later?'

'You can try her with a little convalescent diet if she doesn't throw up again beforehand.'

'Will do.'

We settle Cassie in, and later I call Clive to update him on her condition and give him the latest blood results.

'Her kidneys aren't working so well.'

'She's worse then? Oh, I knew she was worse. I didn't need the blood test to tell me that.'

'I know. It gives us a guide though. It means we can compare any future deterioration . . .' My voice trails off. What's the point? I'm not so different from Will. I did the blood test because I wanted to be seen to be doing something, but couldn't think of what else to do.

'She's feeling rough, isn't she?'

'She's feeling sick because of the toxins building up in her body.'

'Cheryl didn't say anything when we bought her, Maz,' Clive begins. 'It isn't the money, it's the principle of the thing. Breeding sick cats and selling them to people like us. It isn't right.' He pauses. 'She would have known about this condition, wouldn't she?'

'I'm sure she's heard of it. She might not have thought about the possibility of it affecting her cats though. There are lots of responsible breeders who are already eliminating it from their breed-lines.'

'I wish we'd done more research, but we thought, she's local, and we hadn't heard of anyone who'd had a problem with her cats. The cattery was nice, clean and tidy, and she had the kittens in the house. We should have spoken to you first, shouldn't we, but Edie saw the ad, and we went to have a look and then we couldn't resist . . . So, what are her chances of coming home?' Clive asks eventually.

'I don't know. If she doesn't pick up on the drip, we'll have to think about how long it's fair to prolong her life. If she was a human, she'd be having regular dialysis and be on a waiting list for a transplant. Listen, Clive, I'll call you if there's any change in her condition tonight. If not, call tomorrow after we've done the ward round at about nine.'

The next morning, I join Will in Kennels to check on the inpatients.

'This is the renal failure cat?' Will checks Cassie's ID, as he carries her through from Isolation.

'No.' Izzy glares at him. 'She isn't. And don't say, righty-oh, it's a good job I checked then, because I don't mean it like that. She is called Cassie, and she's a patient with renal failure, not a disease as such.'

'I'm sorry.' Will stares, his forehead like a ruckled drape. 'It's what we did at vet school.'

'It's disrespectful,' Izzy continues, then, noticing me glaring at her, she softens her attitude. She wants the best for the animals. 'I'm not saying you have to kiss them, like Maz does, but our patients respond to kindness. It's about holistic nursing, looking at the whole patient.' She shrugs. 'You're a vet though. It's different for nurses.'

Will puts Cassie on the prep bench and we look at her together.

She looks brighter and hasn't been sick, so I suggest we try her with some liquid food. 'If she keeps it down, we could see how she does without the drip now she's rehydrated.'

'Shouldn't we leave her on fluids for longer?' Will asks, hinting that he would.

'We could, but if she can't maintain her fluid intake by herself, she isn't going to survive at home. I'm reluctant to prolong everyone's suffering – Cassie's and her owners'. Cassie's a stressy cat anyway – it's better she's in her own environment than here. In fact, if we can, I'd like to get her back to them by tonight.' According to Clive, the kittens are taking a little solid food mixed with cat milk replacement formula, but I'd prefer them to have their mother back as soon as possible so she can continue nursing them.

'Shouldn't we run more bloods this morning?' Will says.

'How much will that cost the client, and will it tell us anything useful that means we'll alter the management of Cassie's case? In a perfect world, we would, but, as you know, this is far from a perfect world.' I go on, when Will doesn't respond. 'Clive and Edie aren't made of money, and Emma and I aren't into profiteering from other people's misfortunes.'

'It's their choice,' Will argues. 'I give them the information. They decide how far they want to go. I expect you're going to have a go at me now for referring that spaniel – I mean, Jack – for an MRI.'

'That's expensive,' I say. 'Is it going to help the patient?'

'Yes, because if he does have a brain tumour, he can have surgery. He'll have a chance.'

'This is all hypothetical, but what's the point in putting the dog through that, only to find it's a malignant tumour and it's already spread?'

'Have you always been such a pessimist?'

Will's question makes me stop and think. I suppose I did used to expect positive outcomes for the majority of my patients. Am I becoming overly cynical, or am I feeling this way because I'm overtired and over-wrought?

'We'll see what happens to Jack, shall we?' I try to think of something to cheer Will up after Izzy's criticism and my reality check, and recall seeing him spattered with liquid barium not long ago. He managed to get more over himself than inside the patient.

'So, how's that Labradoodle you saw the other week, the one that ate the corn on the cob?'

'It –' Will turns to Izzy – 'I mean, Toby, is doing well. He's back to his normal self after the operation, although he's not allowed to eat everything he comes across now. He has a muzzle to stop him scavenging when he's out and about.' Will smiles. 'They call him the Dyson at home.'

That's better, I think. Will seems happier. In this job, you have to laugh as much as you can, otherwise – I glance at poor Cassie, at the haunted expression on her face – you'd break down and cry.

'Maz, Cheryl Thorne is in Reception,' Frances interrupts. 'I've asked her to come back after morning surgery yet she won't budge. You know I'm not easily defeated, but she insists on seeing you now.'

'Thanks for trying, Frances.' I sigh out loud. 'That's all I need.'

'Cheryl runs the Copper Kettle,' Izzy explains to Will. 'She breeds Persians, and Cassie's one of hers.'

'I really don't want to have anything to do with her,' I say, but I'm guessing that this confrontation is inevitable. Clive must have spoken to her. 'Is there anyone else waiting?'

'Mrs Dyer with Nero to see Izzy for a weigh-in, and Mr Brown with Pippin to see Will.'

'All right then. Show Cheryl into the consulting room and I'll see her first. Izzy, I'd like you in with us.'

'What, like a witness?' says Izzy.

'Yes, otherwise it's her word against mine.'

In the consulting room, Izzy stands beside me. Cheryl stands opposite, at the other side of the table. Her earrings, black cats, tremble at the sides of her neck. Her ultra-short fringe stands upright like the fur on a cat's back. She's quivering, ready to pounce.

She slaps the palm of her hand onto the table.

'You!' she snaps. 'You listen to me.'

'Good morning, Cheryl,' I say, as calmly as I can when inside, my heart is hammering faster than a hyperthyroid cat's. 'You can have five minutes.'

'You know how I feel about you, Ms Harwood,' she says. 'In my opinion you are incompetent and utterly unprofessional, which is why I'm no longer a client of your practice.'

That's fine by me, I think, biting my tongue.

'It has come to my attention that you've been spreading vicious and unsubstantiated rumours about my babies.' I remember she always refers to her cats as her babies.

'Hardly unsubstantiated,' I point out. 'I've blood-tested a cat bought from you, and she's positive for the PKD gene which she has to have inherited from one of her parents, both cats belonging to you. She didn't get her DNA from any other source.'

'What do you know about genetics in Persians?' Cheryl says, suddenly defensive. 'They're a special case, you know. They don't follow the rules.'

'Oh, Cheryl, they aren't that special. The gene has come from one, or both, of the parents. My question for you is, do you test your cats routinely before you breed them? Only I've checked the disease-free register and your breeding concern isn't listed.' I pause. 'It seems to me that you are the irresponsible person here, selling cats who are going to die prematurely, to members of the public who know no better.'

'What do you know about it? I knew you wouldn't listen. I'm going to speak to my own vet – they'll back me up when I go to the Royal College with my complaint.'

She means the Royal College of Veterinary Surgeons. I've done nothing wrong, so her complaint won't go far. However irrational it is though, I can't dispel the sense of apprehension that Cheryl's presence has triggered. Time has not altered how I feel about her. She stresses me out.

'Holy kidneys, she was mad,' says Izzy, once Cheryl's left the practice.

'She doesn't change,' I say, and I try to dismiss the incident from my mind, although I do mention it to Clive when I send Cassie home to see if she can cope again for a while, however long that will be.

'Cheryl's been in,' I tell him.

'I'm sorry. I had to say something. I asked her to keep it between us.' He smiles ruefully. 'I should have expected this. I hope it wasn't too awkward. Is she going to have her cats tested?'

'I don't think she has any intention. She's in denial of the whole situation.'

'What else can I do to stop her sending more cats like Cassie into the world, apart from naming and shaming her? Oh, and putting a claim through the small claims court for our money back on the purchase price and vet's bills.' He hesitates. 'Let's get Cassie home. We didn't think she was coming back, Maz.'

'It is a small miracle,' I say, 'but unfortunately, all I

190

can guarantee is that she will be back here at some stage.'

'We're going to have the kittens tested eventually, just not right now. I'll call you to book them in.'

'Special delivery for Frances,' says Bridget, coming into Reception with a bouquet of flowers at the end of the afternoon, as Clive is leaving.

'Who are they from?' Izzy and I try to look over Frances's shoulder as she slips her specs onto the end of her nose to read the card that comes with them, but she turns away. 'Is it your birthday?'

'Izzy, you know very well that it isn't. My birthday was last month.'

'Don't keep us in suspense.'

'They could be for an apology,' Frances points out, poker-faced. 'Or a thank-you. Why do you assume that they're a romantic gesture? I'm too old for all those shenanigans.'

'Twelve red roses?' I say. 'That rather gives it away, I think.'

'Who is it?' says Izzy.

'Oh, leave her alone, Izzy.' I look at Frances. 'You don't want to spill all about your private life, do you?' I turn away to hide a smile, knowing that Frances will be unable to resist.

'I admit there are certain details one should keep to oneself, but suffice to say Lenny and I are—'

'An item?' I say at the same time as Izzy says, 'In love.'

'Seeing each other. He's taking me out for dinner.'

'That's great,' I say, 'but you will be careful. Don't go rushing in. You don't know him all that well.'

'He's a gentleman,' says Frances. 'He's always polite and charming, and he has a cat.'

'So does Cheryl,' I point out, amused. 'She has several cats and it makes her neither polite nor charming.'

'Ah, but there's something about a man who admits to owning a cat,' Frances says. 'It shows a caring side.'

'Well, I hope he's going to care for you in the way you deserve.' I'm genuinely pleased – and a little apprehensive for her. Frances was widowed many years ago when her husband's trawler went down in a storm off the coast at Talymouth. As far as I know, apart from what I suspect was a minor flirtation or attraction on her side to Old Fox-Gifford when she was first working at Talyton Manor Vets, there hasn't been anyone else.

Although Frances is quite fixed in her opinions, and can act like a hellhound at the gate of the underworld with clients like Cheryl, she is kind and thoughtful. She is the person who notices I am only just holding it together at the end of a fraught day.

'Maz, dear – note I am speaking to you now as your friend, not your receptionist, when I say, go and fetch your son from the nursery before it shuts. You have to stop this.'

'Stop what?'

'All this bombing around, playing the perfect vet, fiancée and mother. You don't have to run yourself ragged. Don't worry about people like Cheryl. Try to stop stressing out about poor Cassie because you can't change it.'

'Anything else?' I say, forcing a smile.

'Accept all the help you're offered, especially where the wedding plans are concerned, and give yourself a break.'

'But everyone else at Toddler Group copes.'

'All these yummy mummies – they're all front. They don't have jobs like yours,' says Frances sternly, 'and, although I'm not a betting woman, I'd bet if you scratch the surface, you'll find they feel the same as you. You're clever and successful. What are you trying to prove?'

'I don't know.' I shrug miserably.

Frances pats my hand as I dissolve in front of her, like a pillar of salt.

'You, dear, need to take a breath and lower your expectations. Let things slide a little.'

I wish I could, I think, but I can't. If I did, I'd lose the plot. For example, when I get home the same evening and Alex turns up an hour later, striding into the Barn, and leaving his kit in the kitchen sink and muddy boots in the middle of the floor where George is toddling about, I have to say something.

'Can't you dump all of that in the surgery?'

'Not now, Maz.' Alex sighs wearily. 'I'll pack it up later.'

The dirty cotton drapes from the day's operations go in our washing machine because the one in the surgery broke down weeks ago, and Alex hasn't called in the repair man, or ordered a replacement. I don't think he's always been this inefficient, and he can't blame George any more, because he's sleeping through the night. Alex is run ragged so things like household maintenance have slipped. One of us has to keep it together, and it looks like it will have to be me. At least I have help at work. But it doesn't stop me feeling furious with him. 'What's for dinner?' he says.

'It's cold.'

'What, not rabbit food again?'

'No, it isn't salad. It was hot, and it's gone cold because you're so bloody late.' There are tiny explosions of frustration and disappointment in my belly. I know he's on call every other night, but he's always late for dinner.

'I'm not doing it to avoid you. I'm doing it for us – you, George and me,' Alex says when I tackle him about the hours he spends at the practice. 'I've got to keep a roof over our heads.'

'It isn't entirely your responsibility,' I point out more gently. 'I contribute too.'

'Yes, and I appreciate that, but you're down to a four-day week with George, and you're still paying the mortgage on your share of the partnership at Otter House.'

'So, you're saying I don't do my fair share?' I can't believe we're beginning to argue about money. A gulf of noisy confusion exists between us, our relationship like a radio out of tune. 'What do you mean? I thought you wanted me to spend time with George.'

'I do, but . . . What the hell. I'm having a few financial problems at the moment, clients not paying their bills on time, some not settling them at all.'

I've never really talked finance with Alex. We slipped into an agreement where we shared the bills. It didn't occur to us to have a joint bank account. We carried on as we had always done when I moved in. It made sense. We're both earning, and I was under the impression that Alex was well off.

'I thought . . .' I begin.

'You thought?' says Alex, a hint of challenge in his voice, a shadow across his eyes.

'The very first time I met you . . .'

'When you spooked my horse, crawling out of a ditch like a Swamp Thing.' A brief smile crosses Alex's lips, making me think I'd rather be kissing than discussing money.

'You said you owned the place – that's how you put it. You have the Manor, the Barn, the estate.' I falter at the expression on Alex's face.

'The bank has them,' he says slowly.

'The bank?'

'They've been mortgaged for some time. Father made some dodgy business decisions in the nineties, thanks to his friends on the local Council. We've been paying for them ever since.' He hesitates before plunging on, 'Then there's Astra and the children . . .'

'Why didn't you tell me before?' It's a shock to me.

'You never asked. Maz, I don't like talking about money. It seems rather—'

'Vulgar? That's what you were going to say, Alex. I can't believe you've withheld this info for so long. Didn't you trust me to handle it?'

'Of course I trust you, Maz.' Alex tries to make light of it, moving round and ruffling my hair, which I hate. 'I didn't want to worry you.'

'You're the vet. You'd better give me the prognosis,' I say, my forehead tight.

'We're keeping up with the payments. The debts should be repaid in the next ten years or so, if everything pays its way, the horses, the cattle and the practice, which is why –' he prods me playfully – 'I have to keep working all these hours.'

'I know we've talked about this before, but shouldn't you take on another vet?'

'Can't afford to. Simple as that.'

'If you took on an assistant, you could take on more clients,' I say hopefully, although it's pretty unlikely because the number of farmers keeping animals is ever decreasing, meaning less work for vets like Alex. I gaze at him. It's meant to be good to keep some mystery in a relationship, but not this. He doesn't respond. 'Alex, how bad is it?'

'As I've said, it's nothing to worry about,' he says sharply.

'Alex, we're getting married soon. We shouldn't have secrets. No more secrets. Promise?'

'Promise.'

Do I believe him? I suppress a twinge of doubt. I have to, otherwise what else is there left?

I offer to put his dinner in the microwave, but he says he isn't hungry. I drop it in the bin to make a point and let him make himself a sandwich.

'I might be able to help.' I move behind him and slide my hands over his shoulders, feeling for the muscle and collarbones diving under his open-necked shirt. Alex turns his head, scouring his stubbly chin against my wrist. 'I could take out an extra loan as a top-up on my mortgage.' Wrong thing to say. I feel his body stiffen.

'Absolutely not.' Alex wrenches himself from my embrace. 'I'm not taking money from you.'

'You wouldn't be taking it. You can pay me back with interest if that makes you feel better about it.' I speak lightly, but inside, I'm hurting that he's rejecting what is a well-meant offer of assistance. 'What's the problem? Your male pride?'

'You're so bloody condescending sometimes.' Alex glares at me, his eyes flashing with sudden anger.

196

His words are like ice injected into my spine. He doesn't easily lose his temper, and he's never directed it towards me before.

'I was only trying to help,' I say, faltering as tears spring to my eyes.

'I feel bad enough about the situation without you rubbing my nose in it,' Alex goes on. 'I'm managing it. It's under control, so for goodness' sake, shut up. I don't want to hear any more about it.'

A tear rolls hot and wet down my cheek. Seeing it, Alex softens slightly.

'Maz, I've made you cry. I'm sorry . . . I didn't mean it. What I said. I lost my rag. I shouldn't have done.' Alex steps towards me and I step back until I'm pressing myself against the freezer. I try to push him away, my palms against his chest, but the look in his eyes is gentle and apologetic, and I find myself melting into his arms.

'Let's have no more talk of money, Maz,' he says.

'Alex, I'm beginning to wonder if you've forgotten that we're getting married soon. All that I have I share with you . . .' Toying with one of the buttons on his shirt, I quote from the traditional wedding vows as he presses his lips to my forehead. 'That includes any debts, you know.'

'Maz,' he says in a tone that means, back off. 'Forget it.' Releasing me, he turns his attention to making his dinner, taking the bread out of the bread-bin. 'Tell me what you and George have been up to today.'

'Alex,' I say, feeling bruised by the row we've just had. 'Have you forgotten? I've been at work all day too.' I gaze at him as he picks up a knife to spread butter on a couple of slices of bread. Why do I feel as if he's shutting me out? What is biting him to make him lose his temper like that? What will life be like when we are married? My gut knots up like tangled string. Is it possible that he is having second thoughts?

Chapter Twelve

Something Old

This morning, I'm listening in on the other side of the consulting room door, the one into the corridor, so I'm not too conspicuous. I know I shouldn't be spying on Will, but I can hear the sound of raised voices. He's supposed to be admitting a dog for a routine castration, but he's taking ages.

'Mrs Taylor, there are always risks involved with anaesthesia and surgery,' he confirms.

'What kind of risks?'

'Of a fatality,' he says matter-of-factly.

'So what you're saying is that he could have his little op and never come home?'

'Yes, but it's a remote possibility.'

'How remote?'

'It depends on which journals you read for the published figures.'

'But it isn't so remote that you can ignore it? Frances didn't mention this when I booked him in.'

'That's because she's a receptionist, not a vet,' I hear Will say.

And I think, tone it down . . . but I can't do anything. It wouldn't look good, me going in there to give him a talking-to. I bite my lip.

'What exactly are the chances of me getting him back home alive tonight, and not in a box?' She's upset. I can tell from her voice. 'No, I've changed my mind. I'd rather put up with him shagging everything in sight, thank you.'

'I can give him an injection instead to bring down his levels of testosterone, the male hormone. It's a temporary measure.'

'I'm going to leave him as Nature intended. My other half was right. This is cruel. It's a mutilation. Simon will be so relieved. He's spent the past week with his legs crossed.'

After Mrs Taylor and her dog have left the practice, and Will's admitted the last op for the day, I have a quiet word.

'I, um, heard Mrs Taylor cancelled the op today.'

'It was her decision.' Will frowns.

'Yes, but she'd decided to have the dog neutered and you worried her so much with the risks that she changed her mind. We have to be straight with clients, but not over the top. It isn't good for business,' I say lightly. 'Emma and I have to pay your wages.'

'Point taken, Maz,' he says. 'I'll plan what I say more carefully next time.'

'Good. I'll catch up with you later, after morning surgery.'

'I'll go and scrub up.'

'How many ops have you actually admitted today?'

'Three: a cat for X-ray, a dental, and a debride and suture wound, one of Emma's.'

'You're cool with that?'

200

Will nods. 'I reckon I know what I'm doing.'

He doesn't sound convinced, so later I duck out of the consulting room between patients to check up on him. I glance through the porthole in the door to Kennels to make sure it's safe to go in, and catch sight of Izzy hanging on to a cat I know rather too well. Cleo has striking green eyes, tortoiseshell and white fur, and a ferocious temper.

Will slides a needle into Cleo's front leg to inject some anaesthetic. I can see her body begin to relax, but before she slips into unconsciousness, she utters one last yowl and sinks her teeth into Will's thumb.

I go in as Will's gasping and telling Izzy he's fine, and she's apologising at the same time.

'I told you she was a "care" cat,' she says.

'She got me once,' I observe, while Will, with blood dripping from his thumb, sprays the back of Cleo's throat with local anaesthetic to relax her vocal cords, so he can slide a tube down her windpipe and connect her up to the anaesthetic machine. 'I'll keep an eye on her. Go and wash your hands. Are you okay?'

Will rinses the blood under the tap, and dabs his thumb tentatively with paper towel.

'It's just a flesh wound, no harm done,' he says nobly. 'Righty-oh, let's get this wound tidied up.'

'Yours, or Cleo's?' Izzy says lightly, disconnecting Cleo from the anaesthetic and carrying her into theatre to reconnect her there.

'Will, you should get some antibiotics for that.' I recall the agony I went through because I tried to ignore it. 'We have a tame medic in town – Emma's husband, Ben.'

'I'll see how I feel later on.'

I open my mouth to argue that he has to go, but

change my mind. I spend too much time with George. I really must stop talking to Will as if he's a child.

As it turns out, it's rather convenient that one of the ops was cancelled because, not long after I've seen my last appointment, Frances turns up in the staffroom.

'Maz, I have a young man in Reception.'

'Lucky you, Frances,' I tease. 'What does he want?'

'I thought I'd ask you rather than Will. I'm not sure he'll cope.' I can see a strip of white skin between Frances's mask of orange foundation and her wig, the ash-blonde one that's been set into unmovable waves. 'It's about a goat.'

'A goat? Tell him to call Talyton Manor.'

'He has the goat with him,' says Frances.

'Well, he can take it straight up there.'

'He won't do that,' Frances says. 'I've explained that we don't do goats, but he refuses to have anything to do with Talyton Manor Vets. Your Alex is out on a call, and Old Fox-Gifford is at the surgery, but he won't see him because he lost the last goat he took up there.'

'Lost it?'

'It escaped, Maz. They never found it. In fact, they reckon someone probably shot and ate it, because it disappeared without a trace.'

'I didn't hear about that,' I say, frowning. Alex and his father are getting rather good at keeping things quiet. 'What can I do though? I don't know anything about goats, and if I did, I can't remember.'

'I imagine you know more than you think.'

'That doesn't mean I should rush in and look at it,' I counter. 'Perhaps Will should see it – he's keen on exotics, and a goat is pretty exotic for us.' I decide to have a chat with the young man in question, heading out to Reception where I find him standing there, with a black and white pygmy goat on a harness and lead.

'Hi, I'm Maz. How can I help, Mr – er?'

'Russ Jackson from Oakmore Farm. This is Ella. She's kidding. The water bag burst half an hour ago and she's no further forward.'

Russ looks at me hopefully. He's in his late twenties, and about six foot three. He has white-blond hair and a light fuzz on his chin. His eyes are the palest blue, the pupils dark and expanded, as if he's slightly stoned. He's dressed in jeans and a tweed jacket, a silver chain around his neck. The goat strains and drops a few pellets on the floor.

'She needs a Caesarean,' he says.

'All I can do here, Russ, is give first aid, emergency treatment to relieve pain, while you make arrangements to get Ella to a large animal vet. This is a small animal practice. We specialise in cats and dogs.'

'Ella is a small goat,' he insists, 'and now we're here, you have to see her.'

'I'll call Talyton Manor for you.' I move around the desk and grab the phone. 'Excuse me for a minute.' I take it outside to the car park and call Alex. 'I have one of your clients on the doorstep.' I relay the message through Stewart because Alex has his arm inside one of the cows at Barton Farm. 'Russ Jackson.'

'Oh, the odd chap, the singer-songwriter from which band was it, Alex?' says Stewart. 'Some Indie group. We can't remember the name, but he made a shed-load of cash and moved here to play the farmer.' Stewart chuckles. 'He hasn't got a bloody clue.'

'Stewart, can we cut the chat, please? He has a goat with him that needs a Caesarean, urgently. Tell Alex to get himself back to the Manor asap to deal with it. Or, at a push, he can get down here and do it at Otter House.'

'Alex, your fiancée wants you,' I hear Stewart say, then his voice cuts out.

I dial again.

'Alex says you'll have to do it,' Stewart tells me. 'He says that Russ, more often than not, has his goat on a lead, so strictly it's more of a pet than farm livestock.'

I'm angry that they are not taking it seriously.

'Tell my fiancé that I'm not happy about being dropped into this situation like this, and if I get sued, I'll make sure he suffers for it.'

'I'm sure you will, Maz,' Stewart says, laughing. 'I'll let him know.'

'One more thing, get him to text me with details of what he uses to knock out a goat.'

'Will do. Good luck.'

I return inside. Although I'm apprehensive, my heart beats faster, anticipating this fresh challenge.

'Please,' says Russ. 'She's in real trouble.' The goat bleats plaintively, as if to say, do something, making up my mind. If the water bag ruptured half an hour ago, there's a risk she's already lost her kid, or kids, and she's in danger too.

'I'm telling you that I have never done a Caesar on a goat, so this decision is yours, and it's at your own risk.' I give him a rough estimate of the cost.

'I don't want to pay any silly small animal prices,' he says, but I stick to my guns. 'It's strange how you're so much more expensive than Talyton Manor Vets. It's a bit of a rip-off in my opinion.'

'Talyton Manor don't have much in the way of overheads,' I point out, 'and they don't have support staff.'

Having asked Russ to complete a consent form, and sent him on his way, leaving the goat with me, I call Izzy through and ask her to set up for a goat Caesar, at which she says, 'Do you need anything special for that?'

'The bitch spay kit? Some extra artery forceps? Retractors?'

'I'll throw a couple of kits together,' she says, smiling. 'A goat. How exciting.' She holds the doors open for me as, having weighed Ella on the scales, I lead her through to Kennels. 'When Frances said there was a goat in Reception, I thought she was kidding. Get it, Maz!'

'Ha, ha. Very funny, Izzy. You ought to go for a new career in stand-up. You could offer an evening's entertainment at the Talymill Inn.' I check my mobile and draw up a dose of sedative, according to Alex's texted instructions: sedation, epidural and a local nerve block for a left flank approach. 'Where's Will? He might be able to help with this.'

'He's upstairs in the flat. I'll buzz him,' says Izzy. 'Do you think we'll need more back-up?'

'Shannon's having a late lunch – she's gone home to play with Seven. It's Emma's afternoon off. I don't think she'll want to see it, but it would be good for Shannon.'

'I'll get Frances to call her then.'

Within ten minutes, the goat is in theatre, surrounded by vets and nurses. Frances hovers at the door. Will and I assure each other that the principles are the same as dealing with a cat or dog, but Izzy stresses about sterility, so we cover Ella's feet with theatre caps.

'I don't know why you're making such a fuss,' says

Will. 'The goat's cleaner than some of the dogs that come in wet and muddy after a walk.'

Will and I operate together, while Izzy monitors the goat with Shannon in support.

'You know I went home to let the dogs out,' Shannon begins. 'Well, I picked up my exam results at the same time.'

'And?' I glance up from the goat. 'Don't keep us in suspense. I don't think I can take much more.'

'I passed,' she says with a squeal of delight. 'I can't believe it.'

'I can,' I say. 'I had every faith in you.'

'One more year to go before I qualify,' she says, as Frances, Will and Izzy join with me in offering Shannon our congratulations.

It isn't long before Shannon is rubbing down a single black and white kid that was simply too large to emerge from its mother by the natural route. It is very cute.

'It's a girl,' Shannon says. 'This is great. I can't wait to tell the others at college.' She pauses as the kid utters a bleat. 'Should I get the large kennel ready for them?'

'I'm going to send them home as soon as mum is up and about,' I say. 'We haven't got the facilities to keep them.'

'We could set up a pen on the lawn out the back,' Izzy suggests.

'I don't think so . . .'

'You're probably right, Maz,' she says. 'The smell's getting on my goat.'

'And your jokes are getting on mine.' I chuckle aloud behind my surgical mask. 'That's enough of the goat jokes now.'

'All right, I'll butt out.'

'Izzy!' I turn to Will. 'Should we sew or staple?'

'It's no use asking Will,' Izzy sighs. 'By the time he makes up his mind, that kid will be someone's dinner.'

'I'll sew,' Will says quickly. 'That's if you don't mind, Maz. I could do with the practice.'

'Go ahead. I'll give Russ a call.'

Russ returns shortly after with a bale of straw and a bed of old towels in the back of his four-by-four. The goat and her kid go home, and Shannon gets Russ's autograph on the practice's headed notepaper. It's a good outcome, but I wouldn't want to make a habit of it.

'I draw the line at a cow,' I tell Alex later, 'and I don't want a repeat of what happened today.'

'I hear you handled the goat brilliantly though, as I'd expect.' He smiles.

'Alex, this is serious. It put me in an awkward situation. I'm not confident dealing with farm animals. Russ's your client. Promise me it won't happen again.'

'I can't promise, can I? How do you suggest I keep clients like him under control?' He puts down the journal he's reading in order to avoid tidying up, I suspect. He hasn't got very far, I notice. It's open at page two. 'Yours aren't much better. The other day, Father saw the people who own those two Bernese mountain dogs you sometimes see on the Green.'

'Why? They're ours.'

'Because they turned up on a whim and they used to be clients of ours before they came to you, if you remember, and Father says he'd forgotten about it. We still had their records on file.'

'Why doesn't that surprise me? You know you can't just take on our clients without contacting us first. We've been through all this before.'

'And you know I have no influence on my father,' Alex says, amused. He puts his arms out to me. 'I'm sorry, Maz.'

I sit down with him on the sofa.

'Guess what else I've done today?' I say more cheerfully.

'I don't know. Surprise me.'

'I picked up the wedding invitations from Penny.' As I've mentioned before, Sally's owner is an artist, and I commissioned her to do a sketch of the church. Her husband, Declan, had them printed up. 'Don't you want to see them? They look great.'

'I'll have a look later,' Alex says.

'I thought we might write the invites together,' I say, a little disappointed that he doesn't share my enthusiasm.

'Not tonight. I'm shattered.'

'Alex, I'm worried about you . . .'

'Me? I can look after myself.'

'I know that. Perhaps it's your age—'

'Maz, I'm not that old,' he cuts in.

'It's just that you're always so tired.'

'Never too tired,' he says huskily into my ear.

'Alex, please listen to me for once – without dismissing it, or making a joke of it. This isn't the first time someone's refused to see your father with a patient, which suggests that you do, in fact, have a problem. It's pretty clear to me that you're taking on the extra work on his behalf without considering the consequences.'

'Maz, you're making a fuss over nothing.' Alex kisses my hair.

'Stop trying to distract me.' Half laughing, half annoyed, I push him away. 'This is important. You really must get some extra help, hire a locum, or take on an assistant.'

'I've always been tired. Don't you remember how I'd come round to the flat at Otter House with dinner from Mr Rock's, and fall asleep on the sofa, much as I do now? Maz, it doesn't mean I don't . . . love you.' He slides his hand onto my thigh, but I can't be diverted. I want this situation sorted, so I can concentrate on the rest of the arrangements for the wedding.

'If you had another full-time vet, you could have a couple of days off each week and you wouldn't spend virtually every night on call. I'd get to see you while you were awake, not semi-conscious, and George – he'd get to see more of his dad.'

'George does get to see me,' Alex says, his voice suddenly hard. 'I make sure of that. You know I do.'

'What about the others then?'

'Seb and Lucie, you mean. Why do you call them "the others" as if they're aliens? You said you were cool about them being here.'

'I make them welcome.' I didn't intend to come across as resenting them. 'What I'm not happy with, is you agreeing to have them here on your weekends off, when it's me who ends up looking after them because you're covering for your father.'

'It's one of those things,' Alex sighs.

'It's hard work looking after someone else's children, especially Seb. He's a nightmare.'

'He's a boy,' Alex says. 'George will be just the same.'

I hope not.

'You can always hand over to Mother,' Alex goes on. 'She loves having her grandchildren around.'

'It doesn't seem fair to impose on her either. Alex,

both your parents are getting on. They should be enjoying their retirement by now.'

'They're happy. They like to keep busy.'

'Well, you'll end up like your father. You won't get to retire either,' I point out. 'At this rate, you'll die of some stress-related illness by the time you're sixty-five.'

'It's great to see you're looking on the bright side, Maz,' Alex says sarcastically. He pulls away from me, picks up the journal again, and sits staring at the same page.

My chest feels hollow, my heart knocks in an empty space, like the chasm of misunderstanding and difference that is opening up between us. When we first got together, I thought, this is it. Alex is the One. My soulmate. But it doesn't seem like it now. I thought I could talk to him about anything.

Hot and prickling with anger, I bite my lip. Men! I have a better relationship with Ginge than Alex at the moment. I suppose I've always got on better with animals than the male species. Animals listen, catch on to how you're feeling, and don't answer back.

I gaze at Alex. I want to be close to him. I don't care if he doesn't share my point of view, but I'd like him to respect mine. I'd like to be happy and at ease with him again, not treading on eggshells, wondering what mood he's going to be in when, and if, he gets home in the evenings. I'm not asking too much, am I?

The next day, I catch up with Emma over coffee and cream slices in the staffroom.

'I've heard all about the goat.' Emma sits down on the sofa and touches her bump which has already expanded to surprising proportions for someone who is only seventeen or eighteen weeks' pregnant, even if she is having twins. 'That was brave of you, considering the last time I remember you anywhere near a goat was in the dissection room at vet school.'

'Actually, the last time was when I took George on the Toddler Group outing to the petting farm at Talysands over Easter,' I say. 'He wanted to stroke a kid, but it nudged him and made him cry.'

'Not an auspicious start for a budding vet expected to inherit the family practice.' Emma grins.

'Alex wasn't impressed when I told him.'

Emma is wearing a cream belly band with a navy cotton blouse over the top. She has her hair loose around her shoulders. 'Apparently, there's some goat's cheese for you in the fridge. Frances said Russ Jackson dropped it in this morning.'

'That was kind of him. I think he realised I wasn't best pleased about having to operate on a goat.'

'Did you have a word with Alex about it?'

'I did, but you know what he can be like. He didn't take it seriously.' My heart sinks a little at the memory of our conversation. 'I talked to him about taking on another vet at Talyton Manor because he's working virtually single-handed.'

'And?' Emma bites into a cream slice.

'He's in denial, just like his father.'

'He'll have to get either a locum or an assistant by Christmas,' Emma says, aghast. 'He's got a wedding to go to, and a honeymoon.'

'Tell me about it. Occasionally, I wonder if Alex is hoping the whole wedding thing will go away.'

'No? You've got that wrong, Maz. He adores you.' Emma tries to reassure me. 'There's no way he'd change his mind. He'd have me to deal with, if he did.'

'That's enough about me, Em. How about you?'

'I felt the babies move for the first time the other day,' she says happily. 'Properly, I mean. I wasn't sure before. It could have been wind, but this is definitely them, like butterflies.'

I think back to George, remembering how, as he grew bigger, he ended up booting me under the ribs like a footballer.

'It's going so quickly now,' Emma goes on. 'Another three weeks and I'll be having another scan. Although they have said I can ask to be checked at any time if I'm worried.'

'You're bound to worry.'

'What with the consultant, midwife and Ben, I feel like a medical case study. Would you like to check my blood pressure, Maz, only Ben hasn't checked it since breakfast?' Emma's being ironic. 'I can tell you without using any gadgets, that it's pretty high right now. I'm not sick. I'm pregnant.'

I laugh. 'Would you like a cup of tea?'

'No, thanks. I'm here to work, not put my feet up. Really, Maz.'

'Do you need to cut down your hours at all yet?'

She smiles wryly, her upper lip dotted with cream. 'I wouldn't mind having another afternoon off in the week – that's if you and Will can cope. I don't want to put any pressure on you, Maz. It's important you and George have plenty of time together.'

'There are occasions when I think we have too much time,' I say, smiling back. 'His favourite word is still no, and he has some spectacular tantrums.'

'Will is coping, isn't he? He could manage another afternoon a week sole charge, as long as we made sure he had Izzy on duty with him?'

'I hope so. He's going to have to do more without one of us holding his hand when you go on maternity leave.'

'He isn't a terribly practical person, is he?' Emma sighs.

'He has moments when he shines, but not many. Though he was good with the goat.'

'What can we do, though? We can't sack him.'

We gaze at each other, and say simultaneously, 'Can we?' as Izzy comes into the staffroom, hands on hips.

'I'm sorry to interrupt your break,' she says, 'but I've told Will he can't carry on. One of you will have to finish off.'

'What's wrong?' asks Emma.

'He didn't go and get any antibiotics for that cat bite injury, and now his thumb is twice the size it should be. All he's managed in the last hour and a half is to take a couple of skin biopsies. He's fumbling about, dropping instruments all over theatre. In fact, he isn't all fingers and thumbs, he's all thumb. Literally.'

'I'll take over,' I offer, getting up from the sofa, at which Tripod jumps onto the cushion I've vacated and sits there, blinking at me as if to say, how dare you take my place. At least I have some sympathy for Will, having been in a similar position myself before. 'What's left?'

'A couple of particularly smelly dentals,' Izzy smiles.

'Are you sure you don't want me to do them?' says Emma.

'If you carry on consulting, I'll send Will to the doctor. Who's next?'

'It's one of the Labradoodles.'

213

'Do you need a hand?' I'm thinking pregnant vet, biggish dog, manual handling . . .

'Shannon can help.'

'She isn't exactly cut out to be a weightlifter either.'

'Maz, don't fuss. I'll be fine.'

'If you're sure.' Leaving Emma to it, I head into Kennels where I find Will running his thumb under the cold tap. 'You really have to see Ben.'

'Maz, I'm busy.' He grimaces with pain.

'I don't want to lose you because you've lost your thumb. Go on. Get yourself to the surgery.'

'I haven't got an appointment,' he stammers.

'You don't need one. Just turn up.' I frown at him, aware of his scent of aftershave and anal gland. 'Say that Emma sent you.'

'Thanks,' he says eventually. 'I feel such an idiot. I thought I could work through it.'

'Will, always remember you have to look after yourself as well as your patients.'

After lunch, I see the afternoon appointments, the ones booked for Will. They're fairly straightforward. There's Cocky, the cockatiel, who's started plucking his feathers out, making him look a sorry sight. I catch him to check for parasites and his general state of health, making sure the lights are down and the fan is off. He's easy to get hold of, and I keep a gentle but secure grip on his head so he can't turn and peck me.

'That other vet doesn't have much of a way with birds,' says Peter, Cocky's owner. 'I can tell.'

I smile to myself, then, having put the bird back in his cage and checked a feather under the microscope in the lab, give my verdict.

'Cocky is stressed out. That's why he's plucking his feathers.'

'How can he be stressed?' Peter is laughing. 'He's living in luxury.'

'He could be lonely,' I suggest.

'I leave the Skybox on for him all day.'

'I expect it's the endless repeats driving him mad,' I say, joking.

'Perhaps I should swap channels. I could find him some wildlife documentaries.'

'That won't make the slightest difference. Cocky's idea of a happy, stress-free and fulfilling life isn't the same as ours. Ideally, he needs food, water, warmth and the company of his own kind.'

'I couldn't have another bird,' Peter says. 'He'd be jealous.'

Before he goes, I talk to him about improving Cocky's diet and environment, but I'm not sure he's going to make the recommended changes. Like many of our clients, Peter is a law unto himself. He'll do what he thinks is right, follow some tips he's found on the Internet about parrots and extrapolate, and then complain that the bird is no better. We'll see.

'Maz, Cheryl's here,' Izzy says. She's covering for Frances while she has her break. I wouldn't be at all surprised if she is on the phone to Lenny.

My heart sinks. 'What can she want now? Can't you send her away?'

'I'd like to – with a flea in her ear, literally, but she seems contrite, for once. She says she can come back if it isn't convenient.'

'No, let's get it over with,' I sigh. 'You'll be present as witness again, Izzy?'

'No problem. Come through,' she calls. 'Maz will see you now.'

215

Cheryl walks in, looking pale and anxious, more like a cat in a trap than one on the hunt this time.

'Hi,' I say, as she stands there, fiddling with the cat on her keyring. Her nails are painted with paw prints.

'I wanted to ask how Cassie is, Edie's cat?'

'I can't say. It's confidential.'

'Oh? Only I've tried contacting her and she won't talk about it.' Cheryl shakes her head. 'I know I've treated her badly, but I still care for that cat. I care for all my babies. I cry every time I send one out into the big wide world.'

'It's a pity you didn't care enough about them to test their parents before you bred from them.' I am in no mood to be conciliatory even if Cheryl is. I don't trust her motives.

'I've offered to refund the purchase price and pay half the vet's bills, but Edie hasn't come back to me yet.' Cheryl purses her lips before going on, 'I'm here to apologise to you too, Maz. I'm very sorry I misjudged you.'

I glance towards Izzy who rolls her eyes, unconvinced, as I am, of Cheryl's change of heart.

'I'm asking you to help me clear my colony of this hideous genetic disorder so I can start anew.'

I touch my throat. I'm not sure. It seems like I'd be walking into the lion's den.

'I'm not prepared to do that. You'll have to deal with it with your current vet.'

'I can't. I've left the practice because they didn't know anything about cats, let alone Persians.' She pulls an envelope from her bag and pulls out a letter. 'Here are the notes from my previous vet. As you can see, I've paid my bills.'

I read through reluctantly. There's no statement saying that Cheryl's been the client from hell, but reading between the lines, she's been her usual demanding self, complaining that she had to drive thirty-five miles to their out-of-hours emergency service, and refusing to have a kitten tested for ringworm because she doesn't have, has never had, and never will have ringworm in her breeding colony. Here, whoever typed the notes has inserted a grumpy-faced emoticon.

I gaze back at Cheryl. I want a peaceful life. I don't want her back as a client at Otter House. I can't forgive her for putting up posters of her cat Blueboy for all of Talyton to see after I gave him that close shave. Frankly, I don't like her and I don't trust her.

'I promise I won't cause any more trouble, Maz. I know I can be annoying and difficult, but I love my babies, and I want the best attention for them.'

'You haven't exactly been supportive of Clive and Edie. They're very upset. Not only is their beloved cat dying of an avoidable genetic disease, you claimed it had nothing to do with you.'

'I was frightened. Now this has got out, I'm persona non grata in the showing world. Everyone's rather –' Cheryl pauses – 'well, catty. It's supposed to be a hobby, and I like the social side and the buzz of the competition, but, having gone through something like this, well, you know who your friends are.'

I am aware how Izzy's body stiffens. I'm sure she's biting her tongue. I can imagine her comment. I can't believe that woman has any friends.

'Please, can I come back? I want the best for my cats. I don't want to be seen as some monster selling sick kittens.'

I'm not sure what to do. If I don't take her on, will she continue breeding from the same lines?

'I can't take you on at the moment. I'm going to meet with my partner and the staff here at Otter House and talk it through with them, to see if we can come to any kind of arrangement. I'm not promising anything though.'

'Can I pop in tomorrow to find out what your decision is?'

'I'll call you,' I say firmly. I will not be manipulated or coerced.

'What did you do that for?' Izzy says once she's gone.

'What else could I do? I had to find some way of getting rid of her.'

'I suppose so. We'll have to call a practice meeting. We haven't had one for a while.' Izzy cheers up. 'Can we order sandwiches?'

'It's always a good incentive to make up for losing a lunch hour,' I say. 'You can draw up a list of what everyone wants.'

'I thought lists were your thing,' Izzy says, amused. 'How are you getting on with the wedding plans?'

'I'm getting there. I'd like to to get on with sending out the invitations, but I really want Alex to help, and he's always too busy, or so he says.'

'Oh, Chris was no use either. He couldn't see the point of having invites when everyone knew when the wedding was anyway. He thought we could do it by text, until I reminded him that some of the maiden aunts hadn't got mobiles. The funny thing was that, when they turned up at the wedding, most of them had.'

'How many maiden aunts do you have between you?'

'Nine,' says Izzy. 'I had a close shave.'

After Cheryl, I see one more, the Cave family of mum, dad, two teenage children and one of those late, last-minute babies. They are grockles – tourists – passing through on their way home from a camping holiday in Cornwall. They're wearing hiking boots, khaki shorts and T-shirts.

They bring their dog, a giant mastiff, with a tan coat, wrinkled brow and saggy jowls. His head is tilted to one side.

'This is Monty,' says Mr Cave. 'He's got something down his ear. I've looked as far down as I can with a torch, but I can't see anything much.'

'That's because he's got no brain,' says Mrs Cave and I wonder from her weary manner if she's referring to the dog or her husband.

'Does he mind people touching his ears?' I ask.

'He isn't overly keen,' says Mrs Cave.

I decide to slip a muzzle on anyway, the biggest one we have. I fasten it behind Monty's head, my hands becoming laced with slobber, then take the otoscope and extra long forceps. I have a look down with the light while Mr Cave kneels on the floor, restraining him. As soon as I touch Monty's ear, he shakes his head. He's obviously very uncomfortable.

'How long's he been like this?' I ask.

'Since the beginning of the week,' says Mrs Cave. 'We stopped here because we didn't want him to have to wait until we got to our vet at home. We rang them but they didn't have an appointment until next Tuesday, whereas you fitted him in straight away.'

I can see clearly now. The dog keeps still. There's a grass seed stuck down the ear canal close to his eardrum.

'Hold on tight.' I grab the end with the forceps and slowly pull it out.

'Is that all it was?' says Mr Cave, seeming disappointed as I check that the seed hasn't damaged the eardrum itself. Luckily, it's intact, so I send them on their way with ear drops to calm the inflammation down.

'Thank you,' says Mrs Cave. 'We'll go and have tea now. We love Talyton St George. It's such a sleepy place.'

Sleepy? I smile to myself. If only they knew . . .

I get ready to leave work, planning to collect my engagement ring from the safe where I've left it for the day, having mislaid my necklace. On the way home, I notice the pale band of untanned skin around my ring finger, and realise I've forgotten to pick it up.

Chapter Thirteen

A Horse in the House

It's the first weekend in September, I'm not on call, and the children – George, Lucie and Seb – are with Sophia and Old Fox-Gifford for a couple of hours. I confess I'm loving the peace and quiet. I stroll down the stairs in the Barn, my hair still damp from the shower. I hesitate partway down, aware of another presence in the house. Ginge? He's lying in the sunshine that streaks in through the long windows at the back, stretched out. I pause, watching his chest from a distance, and for a moment, I wonder if he's still with us.

'No! Stand!' Lucie's voice makes me and the cat start. Ginge apparently decides there's nothing to worry about and lowers his head once more. Relieved, I continue down the stairs to investigate, drawn by the odd shuffling noise and clatter of cutlery.

'Lucie?' All becomes clear. Lucie is in the kitchen area with the foal who is trying to make a grab for the apple she is chopping up on the worktop. 'Lucie, what are you doing?'

She looks up. 'It's okay, Maz,' she says, wide-eyed

and innocent. 'Shezza's allowed to have a tiny bit of apple. Daddy wants to wean her soon.'

'I don't care about the apple. I mean, what is Shezza doing in here?' Sophia, as I predicted, hates the pet name, but in spite of her attempts to change it, Shezza has stuck.

'She wanted to come and have a look inside.' Lucie and the foal gaze at me unabashed, partners in crime. 'It's important to de-spook her while she's young so she's used to absolutely everything she might find scary. She didn't like the washing basket on the floor, but now I've let her snuffle at the clothes, she's fine.'

'Lucie, just because your grandparents think it's acceptable to have a pony in the house doesn't mean I do. In fact, I can't think of anyone else who does.'

'She isn't a pony,' Lucie says witheringly. 'She's a horse.'

'She'll make a mess indoors,' I counter. 'Lucie, you can't housetrain a pony. Get her outside. Now!'

It's difficult, disciplining other people's children, especially your fiancé's. I could shout, but I don't want to spook the foal, as Lucie calls it, and have it careering around the Barn. Lucie stares at me, her mouth pursed mutinously, but I'm used to her black looks. I give her a look back.

'When you're older and you have your own house, you can keep as many animals indoors as you like. I really need you to take Shezza out of the kitchen, because I want to bake George a birthday cake.' I take a quick maternal guilt trip around the kitchen to hold the back door open, wondering exactly how many horsey germs I'll expose everyone to, as Lucie leads Shezza out past me. Shezza dances on her toes and flicks her tail. Liberty whinnies from the stable, calling for her, and I smile to myself because it reminds me of my anxieties whenever I let Lucie take charge of George.

I return to the kitchen to give the floor and worktop a few squirts of antibacterial cleaner and a wipe-down, before I turn to making George's cake.

Frances has advised me to keep it simple, but I want George to have the best cake ever. I have a recipe, one she recommended, for a Victoria sponge mix. You can't go wrong with that, Maz, she reassured me, after I'd convinced her not to make it for me. Anyway, this is not going to be any old cake. It's going to be a tractor for George's second birthday.

Five minutes later and I'm looking at the ingredients I've lined up on the kitchen worktop and at the book Frances lent me, with pencilled notes, an idiot's guide. It's supposed to be like surgery. You have a recipe to follow, the right instruments and there you go.

'Why don't you ask Humpy to bake it?' Lucie says, flying in again without Shezza this time. 'She's good at cakes, except they sometimes come out a bit hairy.'

'A side effect of having a pony and all those dogs in the house,' I point out. 'I don't want to bother Humpy,' I add, although this is more about not wanting Humpy to come and bother us.

'Can I help you?' Lucie asks.

I sigh inwardly. There I was looking forward to an hour with no children . . .

'Haven't you got homework to do, or something? Aren't you going out riding with Lisa?'

'I've been out already – Humpy says I'll wear Tinky's legs out. And I've done my maths and English. Maz, let me help you.'

'Oh, all right then.' Lucie can be good company, and I admit I've grown fond of her.

'You need a bigger bowl,' she says, taking over in a very Fox-Gifford-like way. Lucie will go far.

I weigh out butter and sugar on the scales. The recipe says to soften the butter by leaving it out of the fridge for a while, but I didn't plan ahead and it's solid. I try mixing it into the sugar, but it rolls around the bowl. I can't even squash it with a spoon.

'Humpy melts it in the Aga,' says Lucie helpfully. 'We could put it in the microwave.'

'Are you sure?' I'm not sure. 'How long for?'

Lucie shrugs. I put the bowl in for a minute on high. The butter melts to a clear yellow soup and the sugar solidifies.

'I don't think I should have done that.' I prod at the contents. 'Should we start again?'

Lucie is frowning. 'I don't know.'

'We'll keep going.' I can always – I check my watch – make another one.

I add flour and eggs, then check the recipe, remembering I was supposed to add them in stages, not all at once. When I mix it up, the mixture is lumpy. Bubbles of flour burst into the stiff mixture and a couple of pieces of eggshell float to the top. I add some milk, make it too runny, add more flour . . .

'I don't think I'm cut out to be a baker.'

Lucie's giggling.

'You know, Maz,' she says, 'you should do what my mummy does. Go out and buy a cake.'

'I can't do that. I wanted it to be special for George's birthday.'

'You can order a special one. Seb wanted one with a sheep on it, so Mummy had one made.'

'I want to do it myself.' What kind of mother am I, if I can't bake my son a cake? 'What do we have to do next, Lucie?'

'Line the cake tin.'

'With baking parchment?' I revisit the recipe book. 'I don't have any.'

'What about Humpy? She might have some.' Lucie's ahead of me, on her way out of the Barn. I follow across the yard, greeting the dogs en route, before entering the house via the tradesmen's entrance, and continuing into the kitchen where Old Fox-Gifford is barking down his prehistoric mobile, his back turned to us.

'Don't you know who you're talking to? I'm a highly respected member of the profession, and you're treating me like a bloody criminal. It's a disgrace!' Old Fox-Gifford throws the mobile to the floor where it skitters across the flagstones and comes to a stop against a bucket of sugar beet that is gently steeping in water.

I clear my throat, but Lucie's already there, pinging one of his braces.

'Granpa,' she yells, darting away and picking up the mobile for him. 'Maz and I are baking a cake for George.'

Old Fox-Gifford frowns as Lucie starts rummaging through one of the drawers of the dresser.

'I'm sorry,' I say, awkwardly because I'm embarrassed, even if Old Fox-Gifford isn't. 'We came to see if Sophia had any baking parchment for George's cake.'

'Oh, I haven't a clue. Baking cakes – that's women's business.'

There's nothing remotely metrosexual about Old Fox-Gifford, I think, and instead of feeling annoyed as

I usually do when he makes that kind of chauvinistic remark, I feel a little sorry for him for everything he's missed out on by being so determinedly masculine. You see, I'm actually looking forward to making a cake.

'Found some,' Lucie sings out.

'We'll bring the rest back,' I say, and Lucie and I race each other across the yard. Back in the kitchen, Lucie draws around the tin with a purple felt tip pen, and cuts out circles and strips. I worry about the pen marks, but Lucie doesn't think they will matter.

'Maz, I've done it for Humpy before, and no one has ever died eating cake, have they?' she says brightly, while I'm adding cocoa powder to the cake mixture and giving it a final stir before I pour it into the tin. The recipe says 'pour', but this mixture sludges out of the bowl. I put it in the oven, set the timer and wait, chatting to Lucie. She's always chattering. She talks about the wedding.

'I've never seen you wear a dress,' she says.

'Didn't I wear one to the party on New Year's Eve?'

'I can't remember, but you don't wear them to work.'

'Dresses aren't terribly practical when you're on the floor, grappling with a Rottweiler.'

'You have bought a wedding dress?' Lucie asks worriedly. 'You aren't going to the church in trousers?'

'I've got the dress,' I say. 'That was the first item I ticked off on my wedding planner. Emma and I went shopping together.'

'What's it like? Does it make you look beautiful?'

'I hope so.' I smile. 'I need all the help I can get.'

'Dad thinks you're beautiful,' Lucie says.

I'm flattered, I think, and it reminds me that, in spite of our niggles over work and booking the honeymoon,

I am incredibly lucky to be marrying Alex Fox-Gifford.

'When are we going to choose the bridesmaids' dresses?' Lucie goes on.

'The next time you come and stay. Emma's coming with us to make sure we don't go to Hack 'n' Tack instead.' I'm teasing her – Hack 'n' Tack is her favourite shop.

'Maz, you can't wear jodhpurs to a wedding,' she says sternly. 'Or boots.'

'I might have to wear boots,' I say lightly. 'I've had to send the shoes back to the bridal shop. I ordered them in ivory to match the dress but a pink pair turned up instead.'

Lucie chuckles, and I think, I can laugh about it now. At the time, I was not happy about the extra hassle.

Lucie insists on checking on the cake halfway through which I thought was not a good idea.

'You don't want to burn it,' she says.

'I don't want it to sink in the middle either. I've heard you shouldn't open the oven door while it's cooking because it makes the cake collapse.'

As it turns out, it ends up with a well in the centre and blackened around the edges.

'That doesn't look very appetising,' I observe.

'It'll be fine when you've turned it into a tractor and iced it,' Lucie says optimistically. 'I'm sure you can fix it, Maz. You fixed Hal when Granpa shot him.'

'This isn't quite the same.' I smile. 'You know, I'm going to stick with being a vet in future.' Suddenly, I have great admiration for bakers and cake-makers like Jennie of Jennie's Cakes, and thinking of Jennie . . . I've ordered the wedding cake, so . . . 'I've just had the best idea,' I tell Lucie. 'Let's ring Jennie and order a cake. It's a long shot that she'll be able to make it for

George's party tomorrow, but it's worth a try. Quickly.'

Alex whistles in admiration when he sees the cake.

'You didn't make a cake for my birthday,' he says when I'm getting ready for George's party in the Barn the next day. 'That one is a triumph.' It is a sponge cake, iced and decorated with a red tractor and two candles. 'Maz, I didn't realise you could bake like that.'

'That's because she can't.' Giggling, Lucie puts her hand across her mouth. 'She cheated.'

'Thanks for that, Lucie. I think we could have kept your dad fooled a little longer.' I rest my hand on one hip as I arrange pots of fruit jelly (made with a vegetarian alternative to gelatine) on the kitchen table. 'Jennie made the cake last night and iced it this morning. She said she'd charge double because it was out of hours, but she was joking. I saw the wedding cake. She's got it wrapped and maturing in her larder.'

'Won't it go bad?' asks Lucie.

'Jennie uses brandy as a preservative,' I explain.

'I don't think I'll like it,' says Lucie, wrinkling her nose. 'Did you ask how Guinness, the pony, is?'

'Jennie says he's doing fine. He's started to jump again. You'd better watch out – he'll be competition for Tinky Winky.'

'Oh no,' says Lucie. 'Tinky is my games pony. Humpy's looking for a showjumper for me to ride, and when we finish breaking in George's pony' (yes, Sophia bought one for him just after he was born) 'I'll be able to show that one until George is old enough to ride.'

'A pony for every occasion,' I observe.

'That's right,' says Lucie. She's certainly dedicated to

228

her pony pursuits. She spent much of the afternoon running around on foot practising throwing potatoes into various buckets around the yard.

'What about Liberty's foals? Aren't they supposed to be showjumpers?'

'They'll be fine when I'm onto horses,' Lucie says confidently. 'What can I do now?'

'You can put some of those crisps into a bowl.' I glance at the time. People will be arriving soon.

'I'd better get the birthday boy out of bed,' Alex says. We encouraged him to have a nap earlier on, and he's still asleep, but not for long.

The guests turn up. There are the Old Fox-Giffords, Mrs P, Ben and Emma, Izzy, Frances, Lynsey and Fran, and a handful of mums and tots from Toddler Group. I invited my mother, but she couldn't make it. She can't get time off for George's party as well as the wedding. She has a job as manager of a car-valeting company that her current boyfriend has set up.

We eat and chat, and the conversation inevitably turns to weddings.

'I wish you'd let me help, Maz,' Sophia says.

'You should,' Emma says mischievously. 'What about doing the favours and decorations for the tables?'

'Favours? What favours? We didn't have those in my day.'

Emma explains and suggests that Sophia can make up baskets of sugared almonds for the Reception.

'That doesn't sound like much of a contribution,' says Sophia.

'It's most valuable,' says Emma.

'It would be a real help,' I say, joining in.

'Have you got something old?' asks Sophia.

'Alex,' I say, laughing.

'Daddy's pretty ancient,' Lucie agrees.

'Something new?' says Sophia.

'The dress,' says Emma.

'What about something borrowed?' Sophia takes advantage of my hesitation because I'm picturing myself outside the church with that fox fur of hers around my neck, and its eyes staring into mine. 'You can borrow my tiara, the one I wore to my coming-out ball. I was a debutante, you know.'

'Thank you, but I have a headdress.'

'Oh?' Sophia says, disappointed. 'There's always something blue.'

'I'm on the case,' says Emma. 'Don't you worry. Maz will have something blue on the morning of her wedding.'

'A cold nose, I should imagine,' says Sophia.

'We're going to choose the bridesmaids' dresses next time we're down for the weekend,' Lucie says.

'I'm not sure how we're going to deal with Emma's bump – it's going to be much bigger by Christmas,' I say.

'What colour will they be?' says Lucie.

'A dark red or bottle green,' I say.

'Not purple?'

'Not purple,' I confirm. 'You see, they have to match the flowers.'

'Maz, something must have gone wrong with your planning,' Emma points out. 'You're supposed to match the flowers to the dresses, not the other way round.'

'I like to be different,' I say, making excuses for my lapse as Lucie disappears off to find more jelly and ice cream. 'Sophia, have you any news about the potential clash between the wedding and the Mounted Games? I mean, will Lucie be at the wedding, only it seems a shame to buy her a dress if she isn't going to be able to wear it.'

'I'm trying to work it out,' Sophia says. 'Lucie and I may have to miss out, which will be very disappointing for her.'

'On the competition, you mean?' I say curtly.

'The wedding,' Sophia says.

'I'm sorry you feel like that. Doesn't Alex's happiness mean anything to you?'

'Well, of course it does. It's just unfortunate that you picked the wrong date. Maz, nothing's been settled. The other options are that our reserve takes Lucie's place on the team, or if we're lucky, Lucie and I will be able to attend the wedding and miss out on the reception.' Sophia pauses. 'I shall have to see what Alexander thinks about that.'

'So should I buy Lucie a dress, or not?'

'I should. She can always wear it to the New Year party here at the Manor.' Sophia changes the subject, as I'm silently fuming at the thought of splashing out on a special dress when Lucie might not be at our wedding. 'Isn't it almost time to cut the birthday cake?' Sophia changes the subject. 'Only Fox-Gifford will soon be fussing about taking the dogs out for their afternoon constitutional, and I have horses to feed.'

I light the candles on the cake and we sing 'Happy Birthday' to George.

When Alex opens his mouth to join in, George's eyes grow wide with surprise. I smile and George's expression switches from anxious to reassured. He chuckles.

'Are you laughing at my singing?' Alex says at the end.

'You don't sing all that often,' I point out. 'George hasn't heard you do that before.' I've only ever heard Alex singing 'Auld Lang Syne' when seeing the New Year in.

'I used to sing in the school choir,' he says.

'I can't imagine that.'

'I had an ulterior motive – it meant I could meet girls. The girls' school down the road needed some baritones and tenors – even though they had quite a few of their own.'

'Alexander, really,' says Sophia.

'That's my boy,' says Old Fox-Gifford.

I lift George up so he can blow out the candles. He isn't sure what to do at first, but Seb shows him how to do it, spattering the cake with spit. I relight the candles and George blows his cheeks out and sucks air in, and the flames flicker and dance, but don't go out.

'Seb, you'll have to help George again.' Alex picks up a knife, as the two boys huff and puff all over the cake, eventually extinguishing the candles to the applause of our guests.

Alex cuts the cake as practice for cutting the wedding cake.

'That's a neat job,' I say, smiling as he dissects it into equal-sized slices.

'I'm not a bad surgeon.' Alex has time to eat his slice before his mobile rings, and he's called out, leaving me to say goodbye to our guests, and clear up after everyone, and collect up Seb and Lucie's belongings ready for their mother to pick them up and take them back to London tonight, in time for school tomorrow morning. Once that's done, I give George a bath, singing 'Happy Birthday' again, several times, at his request.

232

It's a foul night. The rain is beating against the windows. George is awake, sniffling. As well as being high on sugar, he has a cold. The bedroom smells of eucalyptus oil. George ends up in bed with me and I don't hear Alex when he gets back. In the morning, I find him asleep on the sofa under a horse blanket with his boots on.

'Alex?' I touch his shoulder.

'I didn't want to disturb you. I didn't get in till gone four.'

'Tea?' I ask.

'Coffee, four sugars,' he says. 'Thanks, darling.' When I turn back, he's asleep again. I let him be.

I check with Old Fox-Gifford and Sophia who are eating breakfast in the kitchen at the Manor that reeks of kippers, wet boots and the horses' garlic supplement.

'I've left Alex sleeping,' I say. 'I wondered whether you could postpone his morning visits so he can catch up.'

'I'll do them,' Old Fox-Gifford says, giving me a long stare. 'I wouldn't like anyone to be under the impression that I'm not pulling my weight.'

Chapter Fourteen

For Richer, for Poorer

On a dark and windy night in the middle of September, I go out on a visit to see Sally, the golden retriever. She's recovered from the surgery to remove the lump which turned out to be completely benign, but she can't go for more than a couple of months without seeing either myself or Emma for some minor ailment.

Tonight, Penny, by her own admission, has over-reacted, because Sally has been up to her old tricks, stealing food. Sally almost died when she did this once before with the Christmas dinner. This time, she gobbled up a pheasant that Declan, Penny's husband, had left to hang in the shed.

By the time I arrive, although Sally looks very sheepish, she has no more than a touch of tummy ache. I recommend starving her then giving a bland diet for a couple of days.

'Have you sent out your invitations yet, Maz?' Penny asks when I'm leaving the Old Forge in Talyford.

'Not yet,' I say, a little embarrassed, because I really should have done by now.

'You'd better hurry up.' Penny spins her wheelchair away from the front door to let me out. 'There isn't much time . . .'

'Tell me about it,' I say, amused. 'I've been trying to pin Alex down to do them with me. You and Declan are invited, by the way, in case we don't get around to them.'

'Thank you,' Penny says. 'We accept. It's going to be amazing. Talyton's Wedding of the Year. Everyone's talking about it.'

I return to the Barn at nine, looking forward to checking in with George, wandering into his room to watch him sleeping. At least, I hope he's sleeping, and not giving Alex too much trouble.

I jump out of the car and head across the yard. The lights are off, a good sign, although the stable lights flick on as I walk past. Liberty doesn't whicker at me for once. I reckon she's lying down – unlike George, she loves her bed. I go straight into the house, kicking off my shoes and abandoning my sweater at the bottom of the stairs. On the landing, I hesitate at George's bedroom door, listening for his breathing.

He isn't here. I can tell without checking his cot. Alex must have given in and taken him to bed, but when I reach our room, there's no one there either. In spite of the fact that I know George is perfectly safe with Alex, my heart starts to beat faster. Where are they?

I open a curtain and look out. I don't know how I missed it, but Alex's car isn't in its space on the yard, which can mean only one thing. He's gone out on a call.

He must have taken George with him because Sophia

is out at some Pony Club meeting. Something must have happened. Old Fox-Gifford needed help with a calving, or two urgent calls came in at once. When I take a second glance, I realise Old Fox-Gifford's Range Rover is there on the yard, so I can only assume that he and Alex have gone out together. Not for the first time, I wish our lives weren't so complicated . . .

I'm just about to text Alex, when headlights appear on the drive. He's back. Smiling, I fly downstairs, turn the lights on, and flick the switch on the kettle. Alex ambles in, looking pretty wrecked, his hair messed up, blood and muck on his trousers, and his hands in his pockets.

'Hi,' I say, greeting him.

'Hi, darling.' There's no energy behind his voice. He sounds completely exhausted, but my concern for him vanishes as the blood drains from my body.

'Alex, where's George?'

'George?' Alex frowns.

'Yes, George.' At first it crosses my mind that he's pulling my leg, pretending he's forgotten his son's existence, but the muscle in the side of his cheek tautens, and his eyes widen in pure panic.

My heart beats a tattoo of galloping hooves.

If Alex hasn't got George with him, where is he?

'What have you done with George?' I take a grip on Alex's forearms. 'Come on, Alex, you must remember.'

He groans. 'I forgot. I must have left him behind.'

'Where?' I want to shake him.

'I must have left him at the Pitts'.'

'Oh, Alex, how could you?'

'Maz . . .' Alex tries to put his hands up. 'Lynsey will be looking after him. There's no harm done.'

'No harm done? You could have left him anywhere,

in some bloody cowshed, in the middle of a field . . .' I can't help swearing. Alex tries to hold me, his arms enclosing mine, but I'm not having it. 'How could you forget the most precious—'

'Maz, I didn't mean to, did I? You know I'd never . . .' Alex tries to hold my gaze, but I turn away. 'I'll go back and get him. Right now.'

'No, you won't. I'll get him.' I tear myself away from Alex's grasp. All attempts at being understanding and reasonable have, like the velvet bats that dart among the buildings out in the yard, long deserted me. All I want is to have my son back safe and sound. I grab my keys, slip into my shoes and leave Alex standing there.

I drive like a demon, arriving at Barton Farm to find George in the kitchen with Lynsey. 'George!' My joy at finding him falters when I recall the circumstances of our reunion. George looks at me from the chair at the oak table, where he's sitting perched on a foam cushion so he can see over the top, as if I'm mad. Lynsey's daughter, Fran, who's three years old, is kneeling on another chair beside him, helping him draw on a piece of scrap paper. He's having a lovely time.

Lynsey sits twisting her sandy-coloured hair back into a hairband. Her arms are strong and her wrists thick. She's wearing jeans and what looks like one of her husband's shirts. She has seven children, Fran being the youngest. I don't know how she does it.

'I hope we haven't disrupted Fran's bedtime routine,' I say.

'I'm afraid we don't have much of a routine,' Lynsey says. 'If I put her to bed too early, the boys only wake her up. Coffee, Maz?'

'I'd better not, thanks. I had coffee with Penny not

very long ago. I'll never get to sleep if I have any more. And I ought to get George home – he's supposed to be in bed, not gallivanting around the countryside. I could kill Alex.'

'Oh, don't be too hard on him, Maz. I was always leaving one or other of mine behind. They didn't come to any harm.' Lynsey pauses. 'Fran, don't do that.' She extracts the felt tip pen from her hand where she's been drawing squiggles on George's face. 'He's a guest, not one of your brothers.' She stands up and fetches a couple of yoghurts from the fridge, giving one to Fran and one to George. 'I hope you don't mind,' she says apologetically.

'Not at all. Thank you for taking care of him. I imagined him abandoned in the dark in some filthy old cowshed.' I cover my eyes briefly, trying to dismiss my fears.

'Alex left him here while he and Stewart went down to see one of the cows. We couldn't get her up. Alex did though. He gave her some magnesium and she was up like a shot. It worked like magic.'

'Why did it take two vets to deal with a downer cow?' I ask, confused.

'Two? I know he's got a pushy grandad, but I didn't think George was a qualified vet yet,' Lynsey chuckles.

'Wasn't Old Fox-Gifford here too?'

'No . . .'

'Oh? He's supposed to be on duty, not Alex.' In the homely kitchen far away from the Barn and Otter House, I begin to relax. 'Alex was supposed to be looking after George because I was called out.'

'It all sounds very complicated, Maz.' Lynsey raises one untamed eyebrow. 'Looking after George, organising a wedding and running two practices – I hope you don't mind me asking, but is it getting on top of you both? Do you think you might need to ask for some extra help of some kind?'

'Another vet would be good, but Alex and his father refuse to consider that option.'

George leaves his yoghurt and yawns. I go over and pick him up, sit back down again and let him snuggle against me.

Lynsey clears her throat. 'You don't think Alex is covering for his father, do you? It's just that the gossip among the farmers around here is that Old Fox-Gifford appears to be giving up the reins. There are also rumours flying round, completely unfounded probably.' The way Lynsey qualifies the completely unfounded part makes me wonder how much is rumour and how much fact. 'About whether or not he should still be working at his age.'

'Why? What's he done?' How much has Alex been concealing from me? I feel betrayed. I knew something was up.

'There was the horse he vetted not so long ago for one of the Pony Club mums,' Lynsey says. 'You must have heard about that.'

I don't know whether or not to pretend I have, to save face because I feel like a fool. However, Lynsey goes on to explain anyway, that Old Fox-Gifford passed the horse as sound, missing the fact it was half blind with a cataract in one eye.

My instinct is to defend Talyton Manor Vets.

'Anyone can make a mistake,' I say, my voice sounding shrill.

'Old Fox-Gifford's made a few recently.'

'He's always been prone to making gaffes.' In the next breath, I wonder what I'm defending him for.

'He's been a good vet, but it seems to us that it's time for him to retire gracefully.'

'You'll have to convince him first.'

'Stewart's had a word with Alex.' Lynsey bites her lip. 'We thought you might give Alex a nudge too.'

'Will do,' I say rather stiffly because, if Alex has been keeping his problems to himself, he's hardly likely to listen to me. In fact, he hasn't been listening to me. I shift on my chair. George is asleep now, heavy and warm in my arms. I press my lips to the top of his head. 'Thanks for looking after him, Lynsey, and for the chat.'

'Oh, it's nothing, Maz. I like a bit of drama now and again. It's pretty quiet on the farm sometimes . . . even with Stewart and all the children. And talking of children, I expect you'll be wanting a brother or sister for George soon.'

'I don't think so,' I say, smiling.

'One more doesn't make much difference,' says Lynsey. 'Believe me.'

'I'm not sure that I do.'

'Well, I went on to have six more after Sam to give that theory a proper test, and I'd say it holds true.' She pauses. 'I hear Emma's having twins.'

'Yes, they're due in the New Year, so I can't have another baby yet, even if I wanted one. Lynsey, I have more than enough on my plate already.'

I head for home, wondering how on earth to deal with my stubborn father-in-law to be, and his equally stubborn son.

'Alex, we need to talk,' I tell him when I've arrived home and put a sleepy George straight to bed.

'You do, you mean?' Alex raises one eyebrow. He's still in his dirty clothes. In fact, although he's sitting on

240

the sofa, he's playing with his keys and looks as if he's just about to go out again.

'I'd like us both to talk, Alex. You know, have a conversation like we used to.'

'Is this about the wedding?'

'No, although it would be good to have a chat about the preparations some time. It's about your father. This thing about covering for him – it has to stop.'

Alex frowns. 'What do you mean?'

'You know very well what I mean. Lynsey let it slip – she didn't mean to.'

'And?' Alex picks up his mobile from the arm of the sofa.

'Don't move.'

'Look, Maz. It isn't a big deal.'

'Alex, can't you see – it's a big deal to me. To us,' I say miserably. 'You'll end up doing it all, which is exactly what your father's aiming for. It isn't right. It isn't bloody fair.'

'So, what do you propose I do about it?'

'Speak to him, Alex.' I touch his hand. His skin is cool and slightly roughened by frequent exposure to harsh soap. He refuses to use moisturiser because he's a real man!

'I'll get around to it sometime.'

'That isn't good enough.' I'm angry and frustrated by his response. 'The longer you let it drag on, the more resistant he'll be to the idea of taking on another vet. That's the only way forward, Alex. Unless you dump some of your clients.'

'That's quite an appealing proposition, but it's like committing financial suicide. All right,' he sighs. 'I hate to say it, but you do have a point. I can't go on like this.'

'I don't want to have to take someone else on

honeymoon because you're tied up here,' I say, trying to lighten the mood. 'Unless Johnny Depp or Orlando Bloom are free.' I move around behind Alex and slide my hands down over his chest. I lean down and press my cheek against his, his stubble imprinting my skin.

'I'll see what I can do. I don't know why you're getting so wound up about the wedding. We've booked the reception—'

'Although we never did go out for dinner at the Barnscote.'

'We can do that any time.'

'Elsa has phoned me several times at work to talk about menus,' I point out. 'I had no idea choosing the food and wine was so involved. Sparkling wine or champagne for the speeches and cutting the cake?'

'Champagne, of course,' Alex says.

'Stuffed peppers, or a pasta dish for the vegetarians?'

'I'll leave that decision to you. Come on, Maz. You must be almost there. We've met with the vicar and booked the church. We've got some ideas for the music.'

'Yes, and whatever you say, I'm not having that one that goes, "Here comes the bride, all fat and wide".'

'You say you've bought the dress,' Alex goes on.

I nod. 'And Lucie's.' I smile as I recall her cantering about in the bridal shop in a deep scarlet gown with puff sleeves and a full skirt.

'I've really got to get going, Maz.'

'Going? Where this time?'

'To visit Guy over at Uphill Farm – he's got a cow down now. There must be something in the water.'

He's being ironic. These cases are random and sporadic.

242

'But you will talk to him?' I say, as Alex stands up. 'Promise?'

'I promise. Anything for a quiet life.'

'Thanks, Alex.' I'll be checking up on him, though, to make sure he really does talk to Old Fox-Gifford. Once he's made his father see sense, they can go ahead and employ a locum or assistant and that will be one more task I can tick off the wedding planner: find cover for Alex for honeymoon.

We hold a practice meeting in the staffroom a couple of days later. Everyone is present: Emma, Izzy, Shannon, Will and Frances. Will sits at one end of the sofa, Shannon at the other and Miff between them. Tripod has disappeared – I can't help suspecting that he finds meetings rather dull. Frances, who takes the minutes, has her swivel chair from Reception, while I sit perched on the edge of the worktop and Emma, who sets the agenda, takes the stool. Izzy leans against the worktop, having bought filled rolls from the baker to keep us going over lunchtime.

Today, Cheryl's request to re-register at Otter House is number one on the list of items to be addressed. Of course, I should have been able to deal with it without bothering the rest of the team when she came in two weeks or so ago, but Cheryl isn't one to take no for an answer.

'Should she be allowed back on our books, or not? That is the question,' Emma says. 'On the plus side, Cheryl was once so impressed with Maz that she named a kitten after her.'

'Thanks. I'd forgotten about that.' I'm blushing at the memory. The kitten, delivered by Caesarean, was called Cheriam – that's Cheryl's stud prefix – Maz.

'Aw, sweet,' says Shannon.

'It wasn't because the kitten reminded her of you?' says Izzy.

'Hey, are you trying to tell me something?' I rub my chin, feeling for imaginary (I hope) whiskers.

'The kitten was sweet. Cheryl isn't. She would have had Maz struck off over Blueboy, if she'd had the chance.' Emma glances towards Will who is nodding off, with his eyes half closed and a mug of tea on the verge of tilting into his lap. 'Will. Will!'

He jerks awake. 'Otter House Vets . . .' he garbles as if he's answering the phone. 'Oh no,' he goes on, pulling himself together. 'I'm sorry. I must have fallen asleep.'

'We really must liven these meetings up somehow,' Izzy says lightly.

'What I was saying, Will,' Emma continues, 'is let Maz's experience be a lesson to you. When a client asks you to dematt their cat, make sure you get them to sign for exactly what they want done.'

'Blueboy's coat was so knotted I couldn't possibly have done anything else but clip it all off,' I say in my defence.

'Yes, but you should have made that clear to Cheryl before you went ahead and did it,' says Emma.

'Emma, I know that . . .'

She smiles ruefully.

'It's done now,' I continue. 'I thought we'd seen the back of her.'

'She never was what I'd call a bonded client,' says Emma. 'She came to us from Talyton Manor Vets and she's been to at least two other practices further afield since she left us. I told her we had to have her records for the cats' welfare – that's how I found out.'

'So, she's easily impressed and rapidly dis-illusioned,' says Izzy. 'Do we really want her back?'

There's a long silence. Will utters a low snore, and Frances rescues the mug from his hand, putting it safely on the worktop.

'Let's not all rush in with an opinion at once,' says Emma. 'Maz?'

'You know how I feel. It's a "no" from me.'

'And from me,' says Izzy.

'Me too,' says Shannon. 'I remember those posters she put up in the window at the Copper Kettle, dissing Maz and the practice.'

'What about you, Frances?' says Emma. 'You have to deal with her as well.'

'It's up to Maz,' she says.

'Will?' Emma tries him again, but he's sound asleep with his head tipped back and jaw dropped open.

I smile to myself. I didn't sleep much the first year I was in practice – I was always on tenterhooks, wondering what I was going to see next and whether or not I could handle it.

'About Cheryl,' I say hesitantly. 'My gut instinct is, as I've said, not to let her come back, but, in her defence, she seemed genuinely sorry, and she has quite a few cats which is good for our business.'

'And, you know,' says Emma, 'like Mr Kipling, she does make rather delicious cakes. She might bring some along.'

'I don't think they're as good as Jennie's cakes,' says Izzy.

'That's why Jennie's doing the cake for the wedding,' I say as Izzy continues, 'I love her cider cake. Have you tried it?'

'We're wandering off the subject,' says Emma

sternly. 'We can talk about cake any time. How about we register Cheryl and her cats with conditions?'

'What, like making her sign a code of conduct?' I say.

'Something like that.' Emma pauses. 'Look at it this way. If she's with us, she won't be slagging us off to the other vets in the area.' She checks her watch. Time is ticking by. 'So, are we all in agreement? Cheryl comes back on probation.'

'Agreed,' I say. Izzy nods while Frances scribbles a note in her pad.

'I'll give Cheryl the news,' says Emma.

'Any other business?' I ask.

'Your wedding, and the birth of my babies,' Emma says. 'If by any mishap, these two events coincide, how are we going to manage staffing? Is one vet – i.e. Will – enough?'

'It could be, if he isn't asleep all the time,' Izzy observes.

Chapter Fifteen

Ten Weeks and Counting

Cocky's back. This time though, he's here for a check-up and I don't need to get him out of his cage because his skin is looking better and his feathers are beginning to regrow.

'I thought I was going to have to invest in a feather transplant,' says Peter. 'They can do hair in humans. Can they do feathers in birds?'

'I can't imagine so.'

'Perhaps you should try, Maz. It would be a feather in your cap if you succeeded.'

'Very droll,' I say, amused. Peter's jokes are at about the same standard as Izzy's, but he has brought along a box of fresh fruit and veg as a thank-you – and in lieu of cash. I forgot to charge him last time, and I can't bring myself to backdate payment.

'You were wrong about Cocky needing the company of his own kind. I've been leaving the wildlife documentaries on for him while I'm out and about, and he's totally hooked. I reckon he thinks he's in with a chance with the birds on the telly, so he's looking after himself properly.' Peter puts his face close to the cage. Cocky hops along the perch, tips his head to one side, and says – or more accurately, whistles – the words, 'Hot stuff.'

'Did he just say what I thought he said?' I ask. 'I'm impressed. I haven't met many talking cockatiels.'

'He's talking about me.' Peter grins. 'I've spent a long time teaching him to repeat the odd phrase.'

'Peter, if you want my opinion, I think you need to get out more.' I am aware of the noise level rising outside in Reception. Peter looks at me, one eyebrow raised.

'Mr Fox-Gifford,' Frances shouts in her receptionist's tone of voice, clipped, firm and no-nonsense. 'You will have to wait or make an appointment at a mutually convenient time to see Maz, just like everybody else.'

There's the sound of a scuffle and a yelp.

'That dog must be properly restrained, or you'll have to take him back out to the car,' says Frances. 'There's always one who doesn't read the sign: all dogs must be kept on leads.'

'It's that bloody rabbit winding him up,' Old Fox-Gifford barks.

I have heard enough.

'I'm sorry, Peter. I'm going to have to deal with this.'

I open the door to find Old Fox-Gifford in a deerstalker, blazer and old school tie, standing with the hook of his walking stick through Hal's collar. Hal, the ancient black Labrador, pants and rasps, trying to get to the client who's standing in the corner, her back pressed against the wall beside the pet food stand, and holding a rabbit in a carrier above her head.

'Get that dog outside, Old Fox-Gifford.' I glare at

him, then before he can open his mouth to argue, continue, 'Otherwise I won't agree to see you.' I am not sure why he is here. Is it about Alex? Has he had a word with him, and let on that it was my idea?

Peter carries Cocky out of the consulting room and, having said goodbye to him, I turn to the rabbit's owner. She's one of the newer residents of Talyton – I noticed on the computer that she has an address on the new estate. 'I'm sorry. That shouldn't have happened. Take Bob straight through.' I hope he hasn't suffered a heart attack, I think, feeling somewhat panicky myself.

I check the rabbit over. Fortunately, he's fine. Distracted by the smell of the carrots in the box that Peter has left on one end of the table, he lets me give him his routine vaccinations without flinching. I apologise again.

'Oh, he's just a grumpy old man. He was extremely rude to your receptionist.' Bob's owner smiles. 'He looks like some old tramp, and he smells odd too.'

'Does he?'

'Couldn't you smell it?' Her nose twitches, much like the rabbit's. 'It's like a mixture of eucalyptus and creosote.'

'Mothballs,' I say, not wanting to admit that this old tramp is my future father-in-law.

'I notice these things,' she goes on. 'I love perfumes and essential oils. Some of them can be very soothing.'

Perhaps I should try some, I think.

Once Bob, the rabbit, is safely out of the way, I call Old Fox-Gifford in from where he's standing outside, leaning on his stick and chatting amicably to Frances. I'm surprised. He was livid when she came to work at Otter House.

'Why are you here?' I ask him, as he shuffles stiffly

into the consulting room, with Hal following slowly behind on a borrowed rope lead.

'Hal has met with a bit of an accident.'

'What's he done now?' Hal beats his tail against the table leg and presses his nose into my crotch. There doesn't seem to be much wrong with him.

'I'd rather you didn't say anything to Sophia or Alexander. In fact –' Old Fox-Gifford stoops forwards and touches the side of his nose – 'we must keep this between ourselves . . .'

'That's no problem. I do understand the rules of client confidentiality.'

'I ran the old dog over.'

'You what?'

'I didn't intend to. The silly old bugger was sunning himself. He didn't hear me, and I didn't see him until it was too late. I drove right over him.'

'It doesn't look as if he's suffered any serious damage.' I frown as I stroke the top of Hal's head. Why bring him to me? Old Fox-Gifford's a vet with years of experience. 'He's scraped his nose, that's about all.'

'I can see that.' Old Fox-Gifford sounds slightly exasperated with me for pointing it out. 'I'm worried about his insides. I thought you, being the small animal expert, could make sure there's no internal bleeding.' He falls silent and utters a cough. 'I've checked and I can't feel anything specific, and I would have asked Alexander, but he's out and I wouldn't want to bother him.'

With the fact that he's run the dog over, I muse.

'I'd hate the old boy to drop dead,' he goes on. 'He's the best dog I've ever had, and I've had a few.'

I call Izzy through to help me lift Hal onto the table where he stands, trembling so violently that he makes the table vibrate. I give him a kiss and a biscuit to calm him down, before I check him over – all over – picking up a film of grease on my fingers from his grubby coat. Every now and again, I glance at Old Fox-Gifford who stands in the corner, his hand trembling too, on the end of his stick. For a moment, I feel sorry for him, an old man who's lost confidence in his own judgement, and then I remember he's just admitted to running over his dog.

'That could have been one of your grandchildren,' I say eventually, having ascertained that Hal shows no signs of being about to bleed to death, and decided that I'll keep him in under observation for a few hours to make absolutely sure.

Old Fox-Gifford looks down at the floor.

'Should you be driving at all?' I go on when he doesn't respond. I realise I shouldn't have raised such a sensitive subject in front of Izzy, but then there's no point in being anything but direct with Old Fox-Gifford.

'I've been driving for over fifty years,' he says, rounding on me suddenly. 'This was an accident. If Hal hadn't been lying there, I'd never have run him over. It's the dog's fault. He was in the bloody way.'

'So that will be your excuse in court, will it? It was the other driver's fault that he was on the right side of the road, your Honour. The pedestrian stepped out at the wrong time . . .'

'That's ridiculous. Hal was on private property. My land.' Old Fox-Gifford hesitates. 'What do you think anyway? How is the old bugger?'

'There's nothing obvious, but I'm going to keep him in for observation until tonight to be on the safe side.'

Izzy frowns at me. I know what she's trying to say,

that last time Hal stayed here, he barked the whole time, but I choose to put Hal first. He's a wreck, and I've been itching to get my hands on him to tidy him up. Now I have the perfect excuse.

'While he's here,' I add, 'we'll cut his claws and give him a bath.'

'Dogs shouldn't be bathed. It strips the oils out of their coats, takes away their waterproofing and shine.'

Izzy helps me get Hal back down onto the floor.

'Shall I take him straight through?' she asks.

'Yes, thank you,' I say, and I wait until the door closes behind her and the dog before I continue talking to Old Fox-Gifford. 'I won't charge you, seeing as you're family. All I ask is for you to listen to Alex when he talks to you.'

'About what?' he says suspiciously.

'What we've talked about before, the arrangements for cover for our honeymoon,' I say, not wanting to reveal too much. Old Fox-Gifford's response is a snort of derision, so I don't hold out much hope. Alex is going to have to be completely frank with him.

Once Old Fox-Gifford has left the practice, Izzy and I set to work on Hal. He barks non-stop, sending Tripod skedaddling away, and Miff asking to be let out the back door into the garden. She used to be able to squeeze through the cat flap, but she's recently acquired a middle-aged spread, as if she's coming out in sympathy with Emma and her pregnancy.

We brush, bath and blow-dry Hal. We give him a pedicure, scrape as much of the brown concrete-like tartar from his teeth as we can without having to sedate him, and rinse his mouth out. We clean the wax from his ears and start him on ear drops. We clean his eyes and start him on eye drops. Finally, I run a blood

252

test to check his kidneys and liver are working okay, before starting him on medication for his arthritis.

'That was like a full MOT.' Smiling wryly, Izzy washes her hands afterwards. 'I suppose it's what I should expect with him belonging to a vet. They never practise what they preach. Look at Miff. She's getting fat.' She pauses. 'How is Ginge? Are you taking care of him?'

'When he wants me to,' I say. 'It's all right, Izzy. I give him his tablets every day for his thyroid.'

'Do you brush him now he's too old to look after himself?'

'When he lets me.'

'You see. If a client said that to you, you'd say they shouldn't let that stop them.'

'I know . . . Izzy, now you're making me feel guilty.'

'There's a freebie came with the order today,' she says, smiling. 'It's a detangling comb – take it home and use it on your poor cat.'

'I'll do that, but if I'm off work with cat scratch fever, I'll blame you,' I tease. 'You did get the invite to the wedding, didn't you? I've sent them out at last.'

'Yes, Maz. I thanked you, if you remember.' Izzy reddens. 'I haven't replied formally though yet, have I?'

'You don't have to write to me,' I say. 'A verbal yes or no will do. I'm trying to refine the menu for the reception.'

'It isn't easy when you have all these different diets to cater for,' says Izzy. 'We had a demi-vegetarian, whatever that is, two pescatarians and a vegan to accommodate at our wedding.'

· 'Tell me about it. I asked people to let me know about their preferences and some of Alex's relatives have come back with info like, don't like gravy or mushrooms, and eggs disagree with me, so no egg, thank you.'

'What on earth will you give them then?'

'Oats, hay and water, or a tin of dog food, I reckon. They're part of the horsey set.'

'I see.'

'I'm not sure how to seat them either. I don't know whether to sit them all together, or dilute the Fox-Gifford effect by spreading them out.' I pause. 'I never thought it would be this complicated.'

'Well, you have to think about these things,' Izzy sighs. 'You don't want any fights breaking out.' Suddenly, she chuckles. 'Maz, you should see your face. Lighten up. Your wedding day's supposed to be the best day of your life. And it will be,' she adds firmly.

Old Fox-Gifford comes to collect Hal. I don't offer because I don't want him barking in the car on the way home, blasting George's eardrums and wrecking his hearing, in case he might want to be a musician one day like Russ Jackson. I give Old Fox-Gifford the dog and a bag of treatments. I doubt any of them will end up in or on Hal, but I can pop in now and then to treat him. It isn't great practice, but it's better than nothing.

As Old Fox-Gifford leaves, Izzy offers to help him lift Hal into the back of his Range Rover, but he declines. We watch him from Reception, opening the boot and pulling out a plank that he leans against the bumper before encouraging Hal to walk along it up the gentle slope and into the car.

'That's pretty cool,' says Izzy.

'That isn't,' I observe, as Old Fox-Gifford reverses at speed out of the parking space, slams on the brakes within inches of the wall, and shoots out of the drive across the pavement and straight into one of Talyton's legendary Victorian-style lamp posts. He reverses again, hitting the pillar this time.

'Izzy, did you see that?' I gasp, but Izzy's already off out through the door, running down to the street and waving at Old Fox-Gifford's Range Rover that's disappearing off away along Fore Street and out of town, smoke pouring out of its exhaust. It's been battered, mistreated like a welfare case, and now it looks terminally ill, but it can move.

'He's driven off,' Izzy says somewhat unnecessarily when I join her on the pavement. 'He can't do that. It's like a hit and run.' We turn to examine the lamp post more closely. It's leaning. I give it a shove, but it doesn't move. 'That could have been a pedestrian,' Izzy continues. 'It could have been one of us.'

'Fifi won't be happy when she finds out one of her precious lamp posts has been damaged. The Council will have to pay.'

'We'll have to pay through our taxes,' Izzy corrects me, 'unless Old Fox-Gifford owns up.'

'Let's own up for him. I'm going to call the police.'

'Maz, I admire your public spirit, but are you sure that's wise? He's your future father-in-law. He'll have disowned you before you marry into the family.'

'He isn't all that fond of me anyway. I'll take the risk. He really shouldn't be behind the wheel any longer. He's dangerous.'

'Wouldn't it be better to have a quiet word with him, ask him to think about what he's doing and see if he'll pay up for the repairs?'

'If I report him, he'll be investigated and declared unfit to drive. He won't be able to argue about it. It will be official. Sorted.' If he can't drive, he can't be on call, or go out on his rounds. Old Fox-Gifford will be forced to face up to retirement, which means he'll have to take on another vet to help Alex out. The people of Talyton – and George, of course – will be safe to venture out on the roads. The Range Rover will be allowed to rust in peace.

I head back inside and pick up the phone.

When I get home, there's a police car parked outside the Manor. I don't investigate. Now that I've had time to reflect on the drive back, I'm not sure I've done the right thing.

I park beside Alex's four-by-four, and my spirits lift at the prospect of an evening together. As I pass the stables, Liberty whickers from over her door, and the foal's muzzle and tips of her ears appear over the top. I wander on through the yard to the Barn where, just inside the open door, I pick up a chicken and toss her gently back outside.

'Pesky chook – when will you ever learn that this is not a chicken house?' I say, as she flaps her wings and her ruffled feathers settle. 'Hi, George. Hi, Alex,' I call. 'Where are you?' I hear footsteps – Alex's – upstairs. I catch sight of George toddling towards me around the back of the sofa with a piece of blue tubing from a stethoscope around his neck. He sticks the end in his mouth and bites it.

'George, no.' I squat beside him and try to extricate it from between his teeth. 'That isn't very nice, is it? Yuck.'

He's immensely strong, and it's only with a struggle that I get it away from him, at which he screams and plonks himself down on his bottom, kicking at the floor in his sandals.

'Hasn't Daddy found your slippers?' I hide the prized stethoscope behind my back, edging towards the bookshelves where I sneak it onto one of the higher shelves out of George's reach. 'Where is your Daddy? What are you doing here home alone?'

'He isn't.' I turn at the sound of Alex's voice. He's at the bottom of the stairs, naked apart from a towel wrapped around his middle, his hair dripping. 'Darling, how was your day?'

'Have you been in the shower?'

'Well, yes. I didn't think you appreciated the fragrance of retained placenta with dinner.'

'Why didn't you take George up with you?'

'He didn't want to come. He said no.' Alex shrugs. 'He'd made his mind up.'

'He's two years old, Alex. You're supposed to make his mind up for him.' I pause, noticing the police car disappearing out of the yard. 'Do you know what the police were doing here?' I find that I can't bring myself to admit that they could have been here because of me.

'Father says it's a social call about various parish matters, such as the best way to manage the youths who drink cans on the Green, and set fire to the recycling bins.'

'Have you spoken to him then?'

'About?' Alex raises one eyebrow.

'Are you being deliberately vague?'

'Oh, Maz . . . I saw Father briefly when I collected George after work this evening, that's all.'

'I can't do everything, you know. Alex, I'm babysitting our lovely new assistant—'

'Which is why I really don't need one,' Alex interrupts. 'I haven't the time or the patience for that.'

'You could take on someone who's been qualified

for a few years. You don't have to employ a graduate straight out of vet school. But that's beside the point. As I said, I can't keep doing everything: work, look after George—'

'I look after him too.'

'If you can call what you were doing while he's strangling himself with a stethoscope looking after. Not only that, I'm organising our wedding, and it's supposed to be your responsibility to book the honeymoon and cover for your practice while we're away. I'm still trying to firm up the menu with Elsa, an impossible task when your guests are so finicky about their food.'

'Mine?'

'Yes, yours, although they might as well be mine seeing as you didn't help me out with the invitations in the end.'

'I stuck the address labels onto the envelopes,' Alex says.

'What about the seating plan?'

'I can do that.'

'You say you'll do it, but you won't.'

'I'll get it done in my own time. I'm not going to kill myself trying to keep to the deadlines on your wedding planner. Maz, there can't be much left to do.'

'There's loads. I haven't booked any transport yet, or broken in my shoes, or settled on the music for the church, or the entertainment for the reception.' I move through to the kitchen area, sit down at the table and rest my head in my hands. A wave of exhaustion tinged with frustration washes through me. A tear trickles hot and wet down my cheek. 'Alex, I don't think I can do it all any more.'

He steps up beside me.

'Maz, I didn't realise . . .' His voice cracks as he strokes my hair and the nape of my neck. 'What can I do? Apart from read my father the riot act,' he adds drily. 'I'm not sure what's wrong with him at the moment. He's preoccupied with sorting through the paperwork in the office. He's done the bare minimum for years, yet now he wants it tidy, attended to and filed away. Can we lighten the load any more?' Alex continues. 'I mean, we already have a cleaner.'

'Yes, Mrs P, the woman who does, but unfortunately not very well,' I point out.

'It would be insensitive to ask anyone else,' Alex says gently.

'I'd rather she didn't come in any more because I feel that I have to tidy up before she arrives.'

'That's just ridiculous though.' Alex backtracks quickly, perhaps aware of the way the hairs are bristling at the back of my neck. 'I don't mean that you're ridiculous. I mean that it rather defeats the object of paying her to help.'

'I know.'

'Is there anything else? We can't do much about the work situation now Emma's pregnant, but we could pay for George to have another day or half-day at nursery so you get a break.'

'Alex, I don't like leaving him at nursery as it is.'

He sighs. 'You see, Maz, when I try to offer solutions, all you can do is throw them back in my face.'

'I don't.'

'You do.'

'I don't,' I repeat, sensing another row developing. I don't want to argue with Alex. I don't want to fight all the time.

'What exactly is it that you want? You have to tell

259

me, because I haven't got a bloody clue.' Alex hesitates. 'Why don't we put back the wedding, if it's stressing you out so much?'

'Do you mean that?' I look up at him. He's serious. I feel sick with disappointment. Alex has changed his mind. 'I thought you wanted to be married by Christmas.'

'I do. I did, but not at the expense of everyone's sanity, Maz. If it takes the pressure off . . .' He swears softly. 'I've said the wrong thing, haven't I?'

I bury my head again, and let the tears roll.

'It was a suggestion. An idea. That's all. The last thing I want is to delay the wedding any longer, and you've done so much preparation already . . .' He bends down and whispers in my ear, his breath warm and conciliatory. 'Please don't cry. You do a fantastic job, and I don't show you how much I appreciate it enough –' he pauses, and adds sheepishly – 'if at all.'

I peer through my fingers.

'I'm sorry,' he says.

'I'm sorry too. What's happening to us, Alex?' I mutter, my voice thick and my chest tight.

'We're under pressure,' he says, a faint smile on his lips. 'It happens. We'll get through this. You'll see. In another couple of months – we'll soon be counting down in weeks—'

'I am already,' I cut in.

'All right then. In however many weeks—'

'Ten,' I say, counting down to the wedding in December.

'In ten weeks, I'll have that ring on your finger—'

'Have you bought the ring yet?'

'Maz!' Alex looks hurt. 'Trust me. I'll be ready. You

have to believe me when I say there's nothing I want more than for you to be my wife.'

I reach out and give his hand a squeeze. I believe him.

Chapter Sixteen

Black Dog

It's an ordinary day. I wake up, aware of the musky warmth of Alex's body to one side, and the soft baby smell of George's to the other, and wonder how many life forms you can fit into one king-sized bed. I'm not sure how either of them ended up where they are. The last time I heard Alex, he was going out on a call to see a sick cow, and George was asleep in his cot. Alex snores lightly and George snuffles incessantly, while Ginge lies on my chest, clawing, purring and dribbling onto the duvet.

The light filters through the curtains, cancelling out the glow of the alarm clock, and the sound of a car rolling up in the yard impinges on my consciousness. It has to be Lisa, Sophia's groom, and she starts work at 8.30, which means . . .

'Alex.' I shake his shoulder. 'We've overslept.'

Muttering something unintelligible, Alex sits bolt upright, sending Ginge flying off the bed. George opens his eyes, pauses for a moment to draw breath and bursts into tears.

'What happened to the alarm?'

'We must have slept through it.'

'I'm going to be late.' Alex jumps out of bed, and scrabbles on the floor for a shirt and trousers. 'I'm supposed to be at Headlands Farm by nine.' Alex rubs his cheeks, checking to see if he needs to shave.

'Oh, Alex,' I sigh.

'If I'm late, he'll probably leave the practice and go elsewhere. He's pretty fed up about the vasectomy thing. Father swears Robert didn't point out the ram to him – it was in a separate pen – but Robert insists it was in with the others he wanted doing.' Alex shrugs. 'I don't think anyone knows exactly what happened.'

'I'm certainly none the wiser. Your stories seem to have conflicting punchlines.'

'Father is always right. He's never made a mistake in his life, or admitted to one. I don't suppose he'll break the habit now.' Alex kisses me on the nose. I lie back, holding George in one arm, while stroking Ginge and watching Alex throw his clothes on.

'Don't have any illusions, Maz,' Alex says gruffly. 'That cat doesn't love you. He wants his breakfast.'

'I don't believe it's love. It's more about mutual respect.'

'So that's why he's putting his claws through the duvet cover.' Although he's a vet, Alex struggles to find anything to like about cats. 'Have a good day then. Think of me slogging my guts out.'

'I've got loads to do. You try having George all day.'

I don't mean it. I love being with George. He chatters all morning, helps me unload the dishwasher, and prepare a casserole for the slow-cooker. By midday, he's ready for a nap. I put him in his cot with the baby monitor turned on, so that I'm free to go and find Old Fox-Gifford.

He's summoned me, presumably to give me a rollocking over calling the police, but I see it as an opportunity to raise the subject of his future. I feel bad about it. It isn't really my place to interfere, but someone has to step forward. For the sake of Talyton Manor Vets, Alex, our family, other people's safety and animal welfare, Old Fox-Gifford should not be practising.

I'm pretty sure I know how he'll take it, but to soften the blow, I thought I'd suggest he takes on an advisory role as a consultant perhaps, a position in which he can either be proactive, marketing himself to clients, or take a back seat and let Alex look after the practice. It's time Alex had the chance to shine, as I know he can.

Pulling on a fleece, I cross the yard. It's close to the middle of October and there's a blustery wind that alternately whisks up and deposits fallen leaves across the gravel. There's a slow drip from the eaves of the stable block where a gutter is blocked, and a muddy puddle at the bottom of the steps up to the loft.

Old Fox-Gifford is at the desk in the surgery with paperwork laid out in front of him and his gun lying broken across the top. I notice that Hal is slumped across his master's feet, and his master is wearing slippers.

I stand at the door, ready to dodge any potential missiles, clearing my throat three times before Old Fox-Gifford becomes aware of my presence.

'Hello,' I say.

'Alexander isn't back yet,' he says, looking up.

'I'm not looking for him.' I pause, wondering whether to make my excuses and leave. Why am I so in

264

awe of him? It's ridiculous. 'I've come to see you.'

'It's been a long time since a young filly came looking for me.' Old Fox-Gifford is wearing a shirt under a grey cardigan that's patched at the elbows, and faded pink cords.

'You asked to see me, remember?' I wonder if I should take a seat, except there isn't one. I clear a couple of dirty mugs from the windowsill and perch. 'I wouldn't have chosen to seek you out.'

'That's what I like about you, Maz. You're straight talking –' Old Fox-Gifford stares at me, sending a shiver of antagonism down my spine – 'which is why I find it so disappointing that you went behind my back, making false allegations about my driving.'

I don't deny that I reported him.

'You rammed into that lamp post, then drove away,' I say hotly.

'It was hardly a hit and run,' Old Fox-Gifford counters. 'It's all a fuss over nothing as far as I'm concerned. Yes, I admit I gave the post a bit of a nudge, but there was no damage.'

'How can you say that? The post is bent.'

'They're all bloody bent,' he blusters. 'They're historic – they're bound to have taken a battering over the years. Like me . . .' His voice trails off, almost wistfully, and I wonder if he's thinking back to happier times. I wonder what he's expecting me to do – retract my statement? 'How did you imagine I was going to carry on working if I couldn't drive? Thanks to you, I'm being banned from motoring on medical grounds.'

'That sounds fair enough to me.'

'Fair? How does your pathetic little mind work?'

Relations between us improved when I treated Hal after Old Fox-Gifford shot him by mistake, but they've gone rapidly downhill again. I'm not surprised though. I'd be pretty angry too, if someone reported me, but I'm not a danger to other road users. Old Fox-Gifford most definitely is.

'You'll thank me one day,' I say.

'I don't think so, because now you're going to get your way, which is what you've planned all along – to destroy Talyton Manor Vets. You're like some shark of a banker, waiting to snap it up in some corporate takeover.'

'I don't think so.' My forehead is tight. Is he paranoid? Insane? Emma and I have enough to do without buying into another practice. And yes, I can deal with kidding goats, but I'm no expert when it comes to large animals.

'Alexander will be obliged to take on an assistant now, thanks to you. You'll be able to swan off on that honeymoon you so badly want.' He shakes his head slowly. 'That's the trouble with people nowadays. They're all out for what they can get, celebrity and instant gratification.'

I can't see what that has to do with me.

'One day, you'll be lady of the Manor. All of this –' he spreads his arms – 'all of the estate from the north covert down to the River Taly, from the Farley shingle to Dead Man's Bend, will belong to you and Alexander, along with the mortgages and the myriad hassles that come with it, and I say good luck to you because you are going to damn well need it.'

He pulls a hip flask from the drawer in the side of the desk, unscrews the lid and takes a slug of what I'm guessing is brandy. 'You'll be wondering what it's all about. What it was all for.'

'If you're questioning the meaning of life, it seems a

bit late to me,' I say, confused. I'm apprehensive too. Old Fox-Gifford's always seemed bear-like to me and often rude, but I'm used to that. Today, he sounds aggressive, unhinged even, and I'm beginning to fear for my safety.

'Where's the boy?'

'George?' I say, surprised by this non-sequitur. 'Sleeping.' I have the baby monitor in my hand. 'Was I supposed to bring him along too?'

'I'm glad you haven't. He doesn't have to be party to this.'

This? The emphasis he places on the word is odd. My scalp tenses, the muscles underneath crawling with doubt. The 'telling-orf' over me reporting him to the police was low-key, very un-Fox-Gifford like, as if there's something more sinister going on here. Call it a sixth sense, but I'm on the alert.

'So we can continue.' Old Fox-Gifford touches his half-moon glasses that are thick with dust on the end of his veiny nose. He slides a bill onto the spike he uses to keep them secure, the paper wavering as he does so. He picks up another bill and writes a couple of figures into the ledger with a scratchy fountain pen.

'I can't believe you still do all of that on paper when you have a computer.'

'I have no need of a machine. I have it all up here.' He taps his temple.

'You're still needed here,' I tell him. 'There's work for you to do. Have you thought about setting yourself up in a consultancy role?'

He gazes at me, his expression colder than ice.

'Don't try to pull the wool over my eyes. You mean I can potter about here, doing the admin and giving clients advice over the phone, like a bloody receptionist.'

'Receptionists aren't allowed to give advice.'

'But they do though, don't they?' he says, his mood lightening. 'Frances was always very good at telling people what to do so they didn't have to pay to see a vet. Our services won't be needed soon, what with television and the Internet. Only last week, some idiot came in with a cat with a flea allergy and a book's worth of pages they'd printed off the World Wide Web on how I was to treat it. As if I was going to take any notice . . .'

'What did you do?'

'Sent them away with a flea in the ear.' He hesitates. 'I expect they ended up at Otter House. Did they?'

I nod.

'And you read all that guff?'

'The first page,' I admit. 'I like owners to be well-informed but that amount of information was ridiculous, especially as most of it was wrong.'

'Well, I hate to say it, but that's how it is nowadays. The world's gone mad and I don't wish to be part of it any more, so . . .' Old Fox-Gifford stabs the next bill onto the spike. 'That's it. I'm done here. Apart from chasing the Pitts for the last quarter's money, Alexander won't have to worry about the accounts until the end of the month.'

'So, is that all you wanted to see me for?' I ask, wondering if I should get back to check on George. I don't like the idea of him waking up to find himself alone, although Sophia would probably be of the opinion that it's good for him.

'Not quite, Maz.' Old Fox-Gifford picks up the gun, checks the barrels, then snaps it shut.

'Shouldn't you do that outside?' I say, nervously.

'You sound very much like Sophia. Why would I take this little beauty outside when I want to make use of her indoors?' Old Fox-Gifford turns the muzzle towards his face, resting the stock on a heap of old journals that are on the table, and my heart misses a beat.

'What do you think you're doing?' And then I think, he's winding me up. 'Oh, stop messing about. You haven't loaded it.'

'I loaded her up last night, but I had things to do, affairs to settle.'

'You're serious?'

'Dead-ly.' He smiles. He actually smiles. 'You aren't laughing, Maz.' He shrugs. 'I never was much of a one for jokes, unless they were made at someone else's expense. I apologise for dragging you into this, but I have one last favour to ask—'

'And I shall refuse it,' I cut in quickly.

'You won't because it's about old Hal. The others can look after themselves, but this dear boy, well, he's special.' Hal beats his tail against the floor as if he's in total agreement. 'I want you to take care of him. He likes you.'

'You've called me here to ask me to look after your dog?'

'Indeed. You will, won't you?' His eyes grow wide and beseeching. 'If you decline,' he goes on, as though reading my mind, 'I shall shoot myself anyway.'

'I'd do it for Hal's sake, but you aren't going to kill yourself.' He's bluffing. He has to be bluffing. But he's serious, a voice says in my head. My heart seems to stop altogether. Suddenly, I'm completely focused on the muzzle of that gun, and on where Old Fox-Gifford's hands are, relative to the trigger.

'You have so much to live for.' I don't know what to say, but I have to say something to buy more time, if nothing else. 'The decision to kill oneself shouldn't be made on impulse.'

'Here we go,' he sighs.

'It's never all that bad . . .' I begin, thinking, how can I stop him? I've been in some difficult situations before, but nothing in my experience has prepared me for this.

'Maz, tut tut, that's a platitude. I thought you of all people, an intelligent young woman, could come up with something better than that.'

'What about Sophia? Alex? Your grandchildren?' I can't believe how cold and controlled he is.

'They'll be better orf without me.'

'What about Fifi, and your friends in town?'

'They're always after something: a judge for the show, a donation to Animal Rescue, a contribution to the repairs to the bell tower.' He shakes his head. 'I shan't miss any of them.'

I pull out my mobile and start touching the screen.

'What are you doing? Put that down!'

My thumb hovers over the 'call' icon.

'I said, stop or I might just end it right now.'

'I thought you could have a word with Alex, I mean, Alexander,' I say. 'Your son.'

'Yes, yes, I know very well who he is,' Old Fox-Gifford says, his sideburns seeming to bristle with his characteristic impatience, and I feel encouraged by this spark of fight that's appeared from beneath the layer of defeat that seems to lie over him, like the covering of dust that lies over everything in the surgery. I lay my mobile down on the windowsill beside me.

'You're a coward, you know,' I say, my voice rising uncontrollably.

'It isn't what I would have chosen,' he admits. 'However, one or two of my contemporaries chose suicide as the way out. It's something to do with being a vet, I suppose, having the means and knowledge of how to do it.'

I know about the figures, but I'm not going to feed his compulsion to kill himself.

'Would you mind breaking the gun again?' I say, trying another tack.

Old Fox-Gifford smiles again. 'You're afraid I might aim it at you?'

'Can you blame me? You shot Hal by accident once.' I try turning the conversation around to his dog. If he won't have second thoughts for his family, perhaps he will for Hal.

'I was going to . . . When it came to it though, I couldn't do it . . .'

'What do you mean?'

'Hal. This morning. I took him down to the copse. I couldn't go through with it.' I watch him eye the gun keenly, and I think, this isn't over yet. I take a small step towards the desk. Old Fox-Gifford slams one hand down. 'Get back!'

The softly-softly approach isn't working, and I wish I'd watched a few more detective dramas. I get angry instead.

'If you go through with this, it will only prove that you've never cared about anyone except yourself.'

'There, and I thought I was a member of a caring profession,' he says acerbically. 'I was once. It's all gone now though. The profession no longer looks after its own. They're about to throw me to the lions.' He thrusts a piece of paper, a printed letter, across the table. 'Look at that.'

I duck forward and pick it up, stepping away again when he glares and lifts the muzzle of the gun just enough to be a threat to himself. I read as he continues, 'Nothing can save me now. It'll be all over the veterinary press by tomorrow. I'll be a laughing stock.'

'It isn't the end of the world . . .' The letter's a follow-on from the one I found in the flowerpot. It was sent by the Royal College of Veterinary Surgeons with the date of the preliminary hearing: alleged negligence over the vasectomy of a teaser ram at Headlands Farm. 'Anyone could have made the same mistake.'

'Anyone didn't,' he says more gently. 'I did, and I'm tired. I'm too tired to fight any more. This is my choice. I'm not doing it out of spite to hurt anyone. I'm doing it for the family practice, to save Alexander's reputation being tainted when I'm struck orf the register. I can't live with the shame of it.'

'You won't be struck off. You might be suspended for a few months, and ordered to do some extra CPD.' All vets are obliged to do some Continuing Professional Development, attending courses and reading journals, to keep abreast with current thinking in veterinary practice. Old Fox-Gifford does go to a few local meetings, but it's to meet his cronies, not to learn anything new.

'I've sailed close to the wind, but this time, I'm caught up in a maelstrom and I'm going down.'

I make to move forwards again, but Old Fox-Gifford lifts his hand, leans across the table and stretches his arm towards the trigger of the gun.

'It's too late. Tell Sophia there's a letter for her – it's

tucked behind her jewellery box. And don't talk badly of me in front of the . . . young ones. Let them know that I loved them . . .'

'I'm not going to let you do this,' I say, refusing to give up. 'If you love Lucie, Sebastian and George, you will break that gun, get up and walk out down those stairs. Can you imagine how Lucie will feel if you go ahead with this? She adores you. You're her grand-father. And Sebastian – he looks up to you too. And George – well, you're part of his life . . .' I pause for breath. 'How do you think Alex will feel, having to tell them, having to explain what you did?' I watch Old Fox-Gifford ponder, my heart thudding hard. At last, he picks up the gun and breaks it.

'Happy now?' he mutters. 'All right, sod orf and leave me alone.'

'Wouldn't it be better if you came outside for some fresh air?'

'Don't you trust me?'

I stare back at him.

'Look.' He shows me the gun. I move to take it from him, but he snatches it away and rests it across his lap. 'I'm thinking about the grandchildren,' he confirms.

Reassured that he's changed his mind, I turn and head back down, thinking that I'll go and fetch Sophia from the stables so she can have a word with her husband and decide what to do. He needs help, and I wonder about suggesting that Sophia calls Ben on his behalf. However, Sophia is on her way up to the surgery anyway, and I meet her at the bottom of the steps.

Before I can open my mouth to speak, my eardrums explode with the sound of a single blast. I turn and scream, 'No . . . You bastard. No!'

Sophia pushes past me as we both try to go up the steps at the same time.

'Fox-Gifford,' she calls, 'I'll have your guts for garters. You've gone and spooked all the horses.'

'Sophia, stop!'

'How many times have I told you not to fire that gun indoors? Fox-Gifford?'

'Don't . . . Don't.' I try to pull Sophia back, grabbing at her jacket, but it's too late. Ears ringing, I stand at her side, gazing at the terrible scene. A tiny wisp of smoke rises from the barrel of the gun, and what's left slumped across the desk doesn't look like Old Fox-Gifford any more. There's blood everywhere.

I feel as if I'm watching from outside and he's in a film. I don't know why I move past Sophia to check his pulse. Force of habit, I expect. I don't know what drives me, but I reach out for his hand, the one that's fallen from the trigger to lie warm and claw-like across the paperwork on the desk. I give it a squeeze, but there is no answering pressure.

From the state of him, there's no chance he's alive. He's gone. Old Fox-Gifford is dead.

'I can't believe it,' I mutter to myself, as I stroke his fingers. 'Why? Nothing can be so awful that you had to end it like that, surely?'

I'm trembling with shock and guilt for not being able to stop him. I step back, keeping my eyes on the body. Hal, who's probably too deaf to have heard the shot, remains at his master's feet, settling himself back across them, and resting his head on his paws. I choke up with grief for Hal, and Alex, and Sophia and the children.

Will I mourn Old Fox-Gifford's passing? I don't know.

I don't feel anything except a hollow sensation in my belly and rising anger at this pathetic old man for putting me through this, because he'd made the decision way before I walked in through that door. What was it? Some kind of revenge? Some way of convincing himself that he was in control right up to the end?

Did he ever think of anyone apart from himself? He was selfish and self-obsessed.

I bite my lip until I can taste blood and I'm not sure if it's mine or his, and a wave of nausea rises through my gullet, acid hitting the back of my throat. I throw up in the wastepaper bin, and then I stand there, my fingers all thumbs as I try to wake up my phone.

I also try to entice the dog over, but Hal, faithful to the end, remains with his master as the warmth of his body begins to ebb away. I turn back to Sophia who is standing, staring at her husband, her face drained of colour and her fingers pressed to her mouth as if she's stifling a scream.

'Sophia.' I reach out and slide my hand around her back. 'We should go and wait outside. Come on.'

She lets me guide her down the steps, and across to the bench alongside the side wall of the Manor, where I snap a few twigs of vegetation that have overgrown the woodwork, so she can sit down.

I call the emergency services, then Alex.

'Alex, you need to come home.' My voice wavers, and it's only now that I start to cry.

'Are you all right, Maz?'

'Yes . . . No, not really. It's your father.'

'What's he done now?'

'Come home, Alex,' I plead. I don't want to have to

275

tell him over the phone. I'm used to breaking bad news, but not this.

'Maz, you have to tell me why,' he says, although from the flat tone of his voice, I suspect he's guessed.

'Your father is dead,' I say quietly. 'I'm sorry.'

'I'm on my way.'

'Take care,' I add, but he's cut the call already. 'Alex is on his way,' I tell Sophia, but I doubt that she hears me. I call Ben who's walking Miff down by the river. He promises to come straight away.

Soon, the yard is filled with flashing blue lights, a couple of police cars and an ambulance. I can't understand why they've sent two police cars – I thought Talyton St George merited only one. Ben arrives too. Mrs P and Lisa set up a point for making restorative mugs of tea, resting a tray on the mounting block outside the stables. Fifi Green turns up as well, offering support from the local community. I don't understand how she found out, but I'm grateful because she offers to sit with Sophia while I go and check on George.

I call Otter House on my mobile, as I make my way back to the Barn. The baby monitor in my other hand starts to flash and snuffle.

'Otter House Vets. How can I help?' It's Frances.

'It's Maz. Can I speak to Emma, please?' My hands are shaking so violently I feel as if I'm about to drop everything. 'It's urgent.'

'I'll get her, dear,' Frances says, and I wonder if she already has some inkling of the terrible event that has just occurred at Talyton Manor. 'Emma, it's Maz for you.'

'Hi,' I say, when Emma comes on the line, 'something's happened and I wanted to ask for the day off tomorrow, if we could swap.'

'Is it true about Old Fox-Gifford?' she says. 'Alex was at Chris's when he got the call. Chris called Izzy.'

I find I can't answer.

'I take it that's a yes then. Oh, Maz, I'm sorry. What was it? A stroke?'

'Emma, it was . . .' I can hardly speak. 'He shot himself, in the surgery. He threatened to do it in front of me, but I thought . . . I thought I'd convinced him not to. I went down to find Sophia and then . . . he was gone.'

'Maz, no! Why? Why did he do it, and why did he inflict it on you, of all people? Or did you just happen to be in the wrong place at the wrong time? I'm sorry,' she repeats. 'All these questions . . .'

'He asked me to look after Hal when he'd gone. I tried to stop him,' I repeat, 'but you know what he's like . . . He wouldn't take any notice, and he had the gun . . . and . . .'

'You don't have to go into detail,' Emma says gently. 'Maz, stay where you are. I'm coming straight up to the Manor. I'll have George while you and Alex do whatever you need to do.'

'You don't have to drop everything,' I say, but I don't mean it. I need Emma here. I need someone I can trust to look after my son, while I support Alex.

'Of course I do. What else are friends for? You're in shock. I can hear it in your voice. Listen, I've got three waiting. I'll ask Will to see them. I'll be right over.'

Not knowing what else I can do until Alex gets here, I get George up.

'Hi, George.' I lift him out of the cot and sit him on my hip to carry him to the bathroom before we go downstairs.

'Mumma,' George says, wide-eyed as he traces the

277

tracks of my tears with his fingers. I touch my forehead to his, and strangle the cry that starts in my throat. I don't want George to be sad because I am, but life is going to be strange for a while.

I take George outside, handing him over to Lisa when I notice Alex's car turning up. Although I'm shocked and sickened by what's happened, and know he'll be utterly devastated, my spirits lift slightly at the thought of seeing him. I rush to his side as he gets out, and throw my arms around him to comfort him, and be comforted.

'Alex,' I breathe as he holds me tight. 'Oh, Alex . . . I'm so sorry.'

'Maz, what happened?' he says, his voice gruff as he looks into my eyes.

'There's no easy way of saying this. He shot himself.'

'He what?' Alex's brow furrows. 'He wouldn't . . .'

'He threatened to do it and I thought I'd talked him out of it, but when I left him, he went ahead anyway . . .'

Alex is silent, his eyes dark with emotion, shock and disbelief.

'So you were there? Oh, Maz, that's horrendous. What was he thinking of?' Alex shakes his head. 'Why?' He pulls me closer, running his fingers through my hair as I sob into his shirt. 'I don't understand. What was so bad? Why did he have to drag you into it? My poor darling.'

'He said he wanted to have a word with me.' I raise my head as Alex takes half a step back and gazes at my face.

'With you? Why would he pick on you?' Alex releases me. 'I need to see him.'

'Are you sure?' I say doubtfully.

'It's something I have to do.'

'I'll be with you then.' I take hold of his hand, but when I reach the bottom of the steps to the surgery where Ben meets us, I can't go any further. I can't face going up there again. It's too much. 'I'll have to wait here for you.'

'Go back to the Barn, Maz. You've had more than enough trauma for one day. I'll catch up with you later.' Alex squeezes my fingers and he's gone.

When Emma arrives a couple of minutes later, she's looking larger than ever, still in her maternity tunic top and with her stethoscope around her neck. She throws her arms around me as far as she can.

'I have never been more pleased to see you,' I say, hugging her back.

'I didn't stop to change.'

'I can see.' I retrieve George from Lisa. He is pleased to see Emma, holding his toy tractor up to show her. It helps somehow. It's a small gesture that hints of normality.

'Tea?' I ask, walking across the yard to the Barn with her and George.

'I thought you might need something stronger. I stopped by Lacey's Fine Wines and bought you a bottle of vodka. Have you got any orange juice or tonic?'

'There's some tropical fruit drink in the fridge. That'll do.' Once we're inside the Barn, Emma pours me a large one with a splash of juice and hands me the glass.

I take it, swirl it around as though it's medicine that requires mixing, and knock it back.

'I can't believe he's gone,' I say, as Emma pours me another, and juice for George and herself. 'He said he wanted to have a word with me, so I went to see him, assuming it was about the accident yesterday – when he ran into the lamp post and I reported him to the police because he drove off. Em, I couldn't bear to think of him carrying on driving, causing an accident and wrecking lives, because he was too stubborn to admit he couldn't do it any more. I feel so bad.' I want to curl up into a ball and hide. 'This is all my fault.'

'Of course it isn't. Old Fox-Gifford made his choice.' Emma frowns. 'It couldn't have been an accident?'

I shake my head slowly. 'It was no accident. He threatened to kill himself. I thought I'd talked him out of it, so I left the surgery to find help. I thought Sophia should be with him. Then there was this huge bang . . .' I shudder. 'Why did they let him keep that bloody thing? You would have thought, after what he did to Hal, someone would have made him give it up.'

'I 'ungry,' says George.

'Again? You're always hungry.'

He nods, his expression serious, and I allow myself a small smile. Life goes on . . .

'Where's Alex?' Emma asks when we're watching George devouring pasta and tomato sauce. 'I don't want to intrude, Maz.'

'I think he's up in the surgery.' I want to be with him at a time like this, but he's saying goodbye to his father, and then, I guess, he'll have to talk to Ben and the police, and be there to comfort Sophia. I'm part of the family. I shall be a Fox-Gifford by Christmas. Unless. A tiny doubt springs into my mind. It spreads like strands of cancerous tissue throughout my brain. How can there possibly be a wedding so soon with Old Fox-Gifford dead?

I am guilt-ridden for even thinking about it, gutted at the thought that all that work and planning might go to waste, and devastated that we might have to delay our marriage. And then I'm more angry than ever at Old Fox-Gifford for wrecking everything. The shot might have lodged in his brain, but the consequences of his death will ricochet through the family, his friends and the Talyton Manor practice for a long time to come.

'There'll have to be a funeral first,' I say aloud.

'First?' says Emma.

'Before the wedding . . . it doesn't seem right.'

Emma reaches out and holds my hand. It's comforting.

'I held his hand,' I say, remembering.

'It's a human instinct,' says Emma, and I recall that she's seen more human death than I have, with her dad dying suddenly when she was in her teens, her mum dying from cancer, then the miscarriages and the loss of baby Heather . . . 'Maz, would you like me to ask Ben to prescribe you something to help you sleep tonight?'

I shake my head. 'He's already asked me. I'd rather not. I need to be compos mentis for George.'

'What about arranging a meeting with a counsellor? Maz, you have just been through the most harrowing experience.' Emma talks about post-traumatic stress while the memory of Old Fox-Gifford's demise replays in front of my eyes over and over again.

'Maz. Maz? Have you heard a word of what I've been saying?'

'I'm sorry, Em.'

'Why don't you go up and have a warm bath?'

'Why?'

'Because you're shivering. I'll look after George.' Emma smiles. 'I need the practice. In fact, I need all the practice I can get. Come on, George, let's go and run Mummy a bath.'

'It's all right,' I say. 'I'll do it.'

I go upstairs to the bathroom. Having undressed, I glance at the mirror. I look haggard. In the bath, I scrub myself clean with soap and hot water until my skin stings.

'Shall I stay?' Emma asks when I return downstairs. 'I know, I'll stay until Alex is back. I don't think you should be alone tonight.'

'I'm not alone.' I wave towards where George is sleeping on one end of the sofa, and Ginge the other. 'I'm never alone.'

'You know what I mean.' Emma makes my mind up for me, saying she'll sleep in Lucie's bed.

'I sleep in Loose' bed,' says George cheerfully. Loose is his name for Lucie.

'I don't mind,' says Emma, looking at me.

'There won't be room for you, the babies and George,' I say, afraid that George will accidentally kick her in the stomach. 'He isn't a good sleeper.' It occurs to me that he might not sleep at all because he had an unusually long nap today, as if he understood something bad was happening and chose to sleep through it. It also occurs to me that, if I'd taken George to see his grandfather this morning, Old Fox-Gifford might still be alive.

When I tell Emma of this theory over another small vodka, she dismisses it.

'Don't torture yourself, Maz. He would have done the deed eventually.'

'Yes, but I'm sure he wouldn't have done it if George had been with me. I would have had time to get him some help.'

'Do you really believe he would have accepted it? Of course he wouldn't. The fact that you said he was tidying up the paperwork, and that he asked you to go and see him so he could talk about Hal, suggests he had this planned.' Emma strokes her bump. 'He could have had it planned for years.'

'He always said he wanted to die in harness. He didn't want to be turned out to grass.'

'He wasn't the retiring kind, in more ways than one,' Emma sighs.

'I can imagine he always wanted to go out with a bang, and he succeeded there,' I say blackly. Whenever my conversation with Emma falters, I can hear the ringing of the shot in my ears.

'Where is George?' Alex's voice cuts into my consciousness. It's strident and harsh, but my heart lifts. I stand up from the stool in the kitchen and walk across towards him, holding out my arms, but he bypasses me without even glancing in my direction. He bends down and whispers in George's ear to wake him before sweeping him up from the sofa.

'Dada, Dada, Dada.' George clasps his hands around Alex's neck and kisses his cheek.

'Hello, Son,' Alex says quietly, while I look for clues as to how he is feeling. His face is impassive, unreadable when he turns to me. I recognise that look, yet I don't recognise my fiancé. I begin to shiver again. He's brought the evening chill in with him.

'Emma.' He acknowledges her with a nod of his head.

'I came as soon as I heard the news,' she says, getting up to greet him with a brief hug. 'I'm so sorry, Alex. How is Sophia?'

'She's in shock,' says Alex gruffly. He lowers George to the floor.

'If there's anything Ben and I can do, just say.' Emma takes George by the hand.

'Thanks.' Alex bites his lip.

'I'll take George up to bed and read him his favourite bedtime story,' Emma says. 'What do you like best, George?'

'Poteman Pah,' says George, sticking his fingers into his mouth.

'Postman Pat,' I say, translating. 'I'll be up to kiss him goodnight.' I turn back to Alex.

'Will you take the phone, Maz?' he says. 'It won't stop ringing. It's upsetting Mother no end.'

'Of course. What if someone wants a visit?'

'Then you can hand it over to me.' Alex makes to move away, but I stop him, my hand on his arm.

'How about you, Alex? How are you?'

His eyes are dry, his mouth set in a grim straight line.

'All right, I suppose.' He shrugs, and reconsiders. The barrier between us lifts briefly when he adds, 'Numb,' and falls again.

My chest tightens with the agony of feeling that I can't reach him. He isn't going to let me.

'Would you like me to come back over to the Manor with you?'

He shakes his head.

'How is Hal? Is he with you?'

'My father has just died and all you can ask after is the dog?' Alex swears.

'That isn't fair, Alex,' I say, hurt.

'Isn't it?'

'I asked because your father asked me to take care of Hal.'

'He did, did he?' The muscle in Alex's cheek tautens.

'Was this before or after he found out that you reported him for driving away from a major accident? I know all about it. He rolled into a lamp post at what, two miles an hour, when he was turning out of the car park at Otter House. Kevin – PC Phillips – told me.'

'He shouldn't have done—'

'It was good of him to let me know, seeing you were too cowardly to mention it yourself. What were you thinking of?'

'Alex, you're upset.' I'm crying again.

'Of course I'm bloody upset.' Alex hesitates.

'Alex, will you hold me? Please . . .' I sob, clutching blindly at his clothes. I sense he is torn. He lifts my hand and plants a cool kiss on my skin, making me feel more hopeful. He wants to go through everything again, as I have done with the police and Emma, because I was the last person to speak to Old Fox-Gifford. And I don't really want to relive the scene, but I do it for him.

'So what else did you say to him, exactly?' Alex's breath smells sour. 'He was my father. I need to know what happened, Maz.'

'I don't know, Alex. He killed himself.'

'Bloody hell, Maz. You were there.' Alex steps back, his eyes dark with anger. 'What did he say?'

'He asked me to meet him at the surgery. I assumed he was going to have a go at me about reporting him to the police, which he did.'

'And?'

'He was going through the bills. He had the gun on the desk and Hal at his feet.'

'Go on.'

'He closed the gun and rested it on the journals so the muzzle was pointing towards him. Then he asked me to look after Hal. He'd tried to put Hal down himself – whether with the gun, or by injection, he didn't say.'

'Did he say why?' Alex says. 'Why did he decide to . . .?'

'He didn't explain, apart from showing me a letter from the Royal College with a date for a preliminary hearing over the ram vasectomy he missed. He said he couldn't live with the shame of being struck off the register. I told him it wouldn't come to that.' I sigh deeply. 'I tried to stop him, but when has he ever listened to me? When has he ever listened to anyone?'

I feel slightly drunk, my mouth furry and my tongue not moving with its usual synchronicity.

'We talked about him having to give up his job, about the possibility of him adopting more of a consultancy position, rather than being hands on. It was my idea – I thought it would help.'

'You what?' Alex says. 'You said what? What business is that of yours?'

'You wouldn't speak to him. What else could I do? Carry on watching you being ground down, losing clients, possibly losing the practice altogether because you couldn't talk to him about giving up? You're the coward, Alex.'

I wish I hadn't said that. I wish I could take it back, but it's too late.

'Alex, I didn't mean it,' I say, in desperation. 'I'm so sorry.'

'I've got to get back to Mother,' he says curtly, turning on his heels.

'Oh, Alex . . . Don't go. I'll come with you. Let me be there for you, please.'

'Goodnight,' he says, cutting me short.

286

I watch him leave. He's in control. He's bolted, chained and padlocked his emotions in a metaphorical chest at the bottom of the ocean, and thrown away the key. I wonder how long it will be before he releases them, before he can start getting back to normal, whatever the new normal will be now that Old Fox-Gifford is gone.

Emma returns downstairs and pours me another vodka. We sit on the sofa until Emma is nodding off and I send her off to bed. I remain, not caring about the cold or the dark. I am numb like Alex, but not comfortably so.

Chapter Seventeen

All Creatures Great and Small

'Alex didn't come home last night,' I say to Emma when we're in the staffroom at Otter House, during a break. I had a few days off before I came back to work. I could have taken longer, but Alex doesn't need me – it seems as if he can't bear me anywhere near him – and I'd rather keep busy. 'He hasn't slept at the Barn with me and George for three days. He says he doesn't think his mother should be in the old house alone.'

'I can understand that,' Emma says.

'I don't mind, but . . .'

'It's early days, Maz.'

I know that Emma is right. I can't help feeling hurt though that Alex hasn't been over to spend an hour or so here and there with George, at least. George is a toddler. He doesn't understand that his grandfather has died. For myself, I guess I'm yearning for some reassurance that everything will work out in the end, because our relationship hasn't felt all that strong recently. Alex even made it clear that my presence wasn't welcome when Old Fox-Gifford's will was read.

'I'd almost prefer it if Sophia stayed with us, in Lucie's room.'

'I expect she wants to be in her own home, with her memories of Old Fox-Gifford,' Emma says. 'How is she?'

'Wretched.'

'And the funeral arrangements?' Emma lowers her voice. 'Everyone's expecting a fitting send-off.'

'I've offered to help, but Alex and Sophia are making plans together. I believe Fifi has a hand in them as well. She's been up to the Manor with quiches and salads, and jars of coffee. Ben has visited again, and it seems that the vicar can hardly keep away.' I sit back on the sofa with Tripod on my lap. 'Actually, everyone's been really helpful and supportive.'

'As they should be,' Frances says, entering the staffroom with the phone. 'Old Fox-Gifford was quite a character.'

I smile to myself at some of the double-edged tributes Old Fox-Gifford has received. For 'character', read 'difficult old bugger'.

'Frances, have you been eavesdropping?' Emma says, amused.

'You two, you speak so loudly . . .' Frances hands me the phone and a note. 'It's Robert at Headlands Farm – he wants Alex to visit.'

'I'll call him.' We've been fielding all the calls for Talyton Manor Vets during the day, and I've managed to provide advice for a couple of Alex's clients, but Robert is definitely a special. I contact Alex on his mobile.

'Hello, darling,' I say. 'How are you?'

'How do you think?' he says brusquely, making me wish I had been more tactful and not asked. I'm not sure where I stand with him at the moment. 'What's up?'

'Robert wants a visit. I wondered if you wanted me to hand it over?' When I say hand it over, I mean to the nearest large animal practice which has helped Alex and his father out in a crisis before.

'I'll go.'

'But—'

'I have to go. It's what Father would have expected.'

'Alex—'

'I'd appreciate it if you came up to sit with Mother. Mrs P has gone out. It's bridge night.'

'I'll have to get George from nursery on the way.'

'Whatever,' he says. 'Is there anything else?'

'I wondered if it would help if Emma took your calls while she's on duty tonight. She offered.'

'Maz, leave it.' Alex swears.

'I'm only trying to help.'

'I don't need it. I can manage perfectly well myself. In fact, I'll take the phones back now, thank you very much,' he adds, dismissing me and cutting the call.

I stare at the phone, my eyes pricking with tears. Emma reaches over and takes it from me, resting it on the arm of the sofa. She pats my shoulder.

'Don't take it personally, Maz,' she says. 'Alex must be devastated. He's been going out and about with his father since he was a boy, and he's worked with him for years.'

'It feels like he blames me.'

'He's taking it out on you because you're the person he's closest to. It's no excuse, but it's understandable.' Emma pauses. The patting stops. I shift away from Emma's touch. 'You see, you're pushing me away now,' she goes on. 'It's a natural reaction.'

'I suppose so.'

'Alex might have reacted very differently, if Old Fox-Gifford had had a stroke, or cancer. His father chose to die. I can't imagine how Alex must be feeling.'

'I know,' I say quietly. I'm trying to be strong and hold it all together for George, but, like a sandcastle on the tideline, I'm preparing for the waves to overwhelm and wash me away, because I'm grieving too, for Alex.

Thanks to Old Fox-Gifford, I'm not sure that anything will be the same again.

'I'd better go,' I tell Emma.

I take George to the Manor. His presence does help, I think, because he's someone to care for. He picks up on our sorrow, but it doesn't impinge on him in the same way. Life goes on, I guess.

Sophia holds him, carries him to the window of the drawing room, and looks out into the darkness that is falling over the sweep of parkland beyond.

'I'd better let the dogs out,' she says out of the blue, her voice constrained. 'He always let the dogs out at seven. And nine,' she goes on. 'He loved those dogs. They were his life. That's why I don't understand.'

Sophia doesn't understand, and she was the person who was closest to him. I don't say anything. I don't know why he did it, although I am beginning to take comfort in the realisation that it wasn't my fault. Old Fox-Gifford had many issues that could have triggered his decision to end it all.

'You know, Maz,' Sophia begins again, 'I truly believe that he put those dogs before me. I'm not sure he ever loved me. He never said as much.'

'He did say to me once when he was talking about the attributes of a good wife, that he couldn't have

291

chosen better . . . Yes, those were his words. "I couldn't have chosen better."'

Sophia turns towards me, touching her throat.

'Did he really? That doesn't sound like my husband.'

'That's what he said.'

Sophia raises one fist and shakes it. 'Damn you, Fox-Gifford! If only the silly old man could have brought himself to tell me face to face. He never confided in me. Still, thank you, Maz. It's a small comfort to me.'

'That's okay,' I say.

'It's the way he was brought up. His mother –' Sophia manages a smile – 'well, Maz, you think you're going to have trouble with the mother-in-law. Mine was the one from hell, and his father was a tartar. And then Old Fox-Gifford had years of public school education to teach him how to behave like an Englishman with a stiff upper lip.'

'I'm sorry.' I don't know what to say.

'I'm glad you've taken a stand over George's schooling, Maz. Don't let Alexander change your mind. A mother always knows best.'

I'm surprised at her stance. I don't think she would have given me that opinion while her husband was alive.

Sophia glances towards the clock on the mantelpiece. 'The dogs.'

'Sophia, I'll do it. I'll let the dogs out.' I haul Hal up by the collar from where he's been lying in front of the fire, making the most of the meagre warmth from the smoking logs of damp apple-wood, and take the dogs outside, half expecting to meet Old Fox-Gifford, gun in hand, in the corridor to the kitchen.

*

Two weeks after Old Fox-Gifford's passing, and immediately following the inquest into his death, we bury him in the churchyard on a wet October day. Apparently, there was no room in the family crypt, and, in spite of his sense of tradition, he left instructions that he wished to be interred outdoors because he didn't want his grandchildren to suffer nightmares as he had when, as a small boy, his father had forced him to visit his dead grandfather underground. Sophia showed me part of the letter he'd left for her.

'This had a profound effect on me,' it read. 'From those days forth, I discovered that, although I could control everything else, I could not exorcise the skeletons of my forebears from my mind. You cannot shoot a ghost, once raised.'

Talyton's church is like a cathedral in miniature, built from local sandstone. The bells in the tower are tolling. The gargoyles' mouths are pouring rainwater, creating dark stains down the stonework, and the churchyard is bordered by deep-green yews, adding to the sombre atmosphere.

The coffin arrives in a carriage drawn by a pair of black horses with plumes on their heads. Sophia waits with me and Fifi Green, as the bearers – Alex, Stewart, Chris, Guy, and two distant uncles of Alex's who don't appear tall enough or strong enough to share the weight – remove the coffin that's made from oak with brass attachments.

The horses paw the ground, their iron shoes sparking against the metalled road outside the church. Sophia stands proud, cool and pale, dressed in black with her ghastly, moth-eaten fox fur around her neck.

'I thought he would be the death of me,' she mutters. 'I thought he was indestructible.'

Fifi holds Sophia's arm. 'He lives on in your lovely son. How is Alexander?'

'You can ask him yourself, not that you'll get a satisfactory answer. He says he's bearing up, that life goes on, but I can't tell how he's really feeling. Like his father before him, he keeps it to himself – unless he's angry. You soon know about that, don't you, Maz?' Sophia turns to me. 'Where are the children?'

'They're inside the church. Lynsey thought they'd get cold.' There was some debate about whether or not the children should attend the funeral, but, in the end, we let them decide for themselves. Well, Lucie and Seb did, although I suspect their decision had something to do with them having to have a couple of days off school. George didn't have any say in the matter.

'You will walk with me,' Sophia says.

'Of course,' I say. Fifi walks one side. I walk the other, and we follow Old Fox-Gifford's coffin slowly into the church, where the organist is playing Mendelssohn's 'Wedding March' at speed. I notice how the vicar crosses the aisle to have a word. By the time we're halfway to the altar, the organist has swapped to a more appropriate fugue by Bach.

The church is packed. I cannot sit beside Sophia and Alex in the Fox-Gifford family pew because there isn't room. I end up with Lynsey and Emma, and the children. While we wait for the service to begin, Emma whispers to me.

'How is Alex? Maz, I know you don't want to talk about it, but you need to.'

'He's well, he's still carrying on as if nothing's happened. It's weird.'

'He's a strong character.'

'I think it's a weakness being so tough.'

'It's just the way he deals with things,' Emma suggests.

'I don't know if he is dealing with it, because he won't talk to me. When I ask, he clams up. It's so difficult. I want to be there for him, but all the time he's pushing me away. I think I must be doing something wrong . . .'

'It must have hit him hard, losing his father like that. They spent a lot of time together.'

'Yes, but I'm not sure you could describe them as having been close. They didn't have an easy relationship.'

'Alex probably feels guilty.'

'What for?'

Emma shrugs. 'I don't know. When Mum died, I went through a lot of guilt. I kept thinking, could I have saved her if I'd noticed sooner that she was ill? Alex must question whether he should have recognised his father's depression and at least tried to prevent him doing what he did?'

'You're saying all this as if he cares. Em, Alex is going around almost as if there's nothing wrong. He isn't cheerful. He's very cold.' Shivering, I pull my coat tight around me. 'He'll talk to his horse.'

'Maz, he must be very depressed,' Emma says.

'To be honest, Em, it's shown me a different side of him. I know it hasn't been very long, but the way he is, is making me question whether I want to marry him at all.' I rub the corner of my eye, pretending there is a hair in it.

'You could make him an appointment with Ben.'

'He wouldn't go. Alex would perceive it as a sign of weakness.'

Emma changes the subject. 'Did you hear the organist's mistake?'

'He's drunk, I expect,' I say. 'Apparently, you have to watch him, otherwise he's off to the Dog and Duck for a swift pint. I'm going to organise someone to keep an eye on the morning of the wedding.'

'How long is it now? Just under eight weeks?' Emma smiles. 'I should know. The twins are due three weeks after that.'

I smile back.

'Once this is over,' says Emma, 'and we've said our farewells to Old Fox-Gifford, you and Alex will be able to move on. It shouldn't be as hard as you think. After the dispatching, we have a matching and double hatching to look forward to.'

The organist changes tune, announcing the beginning of the service, and we fall silent, apart from George who chatters to his toy tractor, running it up and down the side of the pew. Alex pays tribute to his father, and we sing the hymn 'All Creatures Great and Small'.

'Aren't you going to have this one at the wedding?' Emma whispers.

'We were. I'm not sure now . . .' I wonder if it will remind us too much of Old Fox-Gifford's funeral.

After the service, I stand at the grave under an umbrella with George strapped into his buggy, so he can't go and investigate the hole, or play in the mound of wet earth at the side. As we wait for Old Fox-Gifford's coffin, surrounded by Alex's family, friends and clients, my umbrella becomes snagged on someone else's.

'I'm sorry,' I say, turning to find Fifi Green with Frances. I unsnag the brollies, and they carry on with their not-so-hushed conversation.

'Talyton will never be the same again.' Fifi wears a black hat, jacket and pleated skirt with heels. 'He was a one-off.'

'Indeed,' says Frances, who's dressed almost exactly the same. 'He was a singular man.'

Fifi dabs her eyes with a handkerchief.

'I was very fond of him. He was a great ally when those dreadful people wanted to develop the land by the Green.'

'I remember,' sighs Frances.

'And he was a wonderful judge at the show. He never stood for any nonsense, yet he was charming with it.'

'You're wearing your rose-coloured spectacles. He was a difficult man. Not that I like to speak ill of the dead.' Frances raises a gloved hand. 'I worked for him for years, so you see, I probably know him better than you do, Fifi.' Do I detect a note of triumph in Frances's voice? I smile to myself.

'I don't think so,' says Fifi. 'There was a time when Old Fox-Gifford and I were very close.'

'I'm surprised you should mention that,' says Frances. 'I don't understand when you have a lovely husband of your own. You have that little goldmine of a business –' Fifi and her husband own the local garden centre where they sell everything from solar-powered, light-up gnomes to Christmas decorations – 'yet you risked it all for a fling with—'

I'm aware of Sophia watching the pair of them across the grave, an odd expression on her face. I clear my throat.

'Ladies,' I say, aside to the pair of witches. 'Not now.'

Fifi and Frances are not easily silenced. They lower their voices and change the subject.

'The next time we're met together here, Maz, it will be for a happier occasion,' says Frances.

'I hope so,' I say quietly, unsure that anyone else, Alex included, will be in the mood for a wedding.

'Old Fox-Gifford would be furious. There was nothing he enjoyed more than a free lunch,' Fifi says.

'And a good knees-up,' says Frances, apparently determined not to be outdone.

'He offered to pay for the cake and champagne at the wedding reception,' I say. 'He could be generous when he wanted to be.'

Sophia holds the wake at the Manor. She has brought in a team of caterers, led by Elsa from the Barnscote Hotel. Shannon is doing some waitressing to earn some extra cash. Clive runs the free bar, and Jennie supplies cake.

'He left instructions for a good send-orf,' I overhear Sophia telling Fifi in the drawing room. Skye, the Shetland pony, is bumping his muzzle against the long window, asking to be let in. The dogs, for once, are locked out in the lobby at the back of the house – Old Fox-Gifford would never have allowed it, and I have to confess that I'm not entirely happy that Hal is among them. He's looking pretty wobbly on his back legs now, and I don't think he's going to last much longer. He'd be better off in his usual place in front of the fire. 'That was one burden he didn't leave me to bear,' Sophia continues.

'You've done very well, Sophia,' Fifi says. 'It's just what he would have wanted.'

'Which you would know, better than anyone else,' Sophia says acidly. 'Fifi, you can stay for the wake – I don't want to make a scene – but from now on, you are not welcome here in my house.'

I have never seen Fifi Green lost for words before. Her glass of Buck's Fizz drops to the floor, her face blanches and her lips form a painted O. Several people, including Shannon, go running in to help her. I go in to rescue Sophia. She's had one shock too many, if she really didn't know about Fifi's dalliance or affair, or whatever it was, with Old Fox-Gifford.

'Thank you, Maz,' she says stiffly, when I hand her a brandy. 'You have been a brick.'

I believe that's a compliment. A brick though?

I look around for Alex. He appears to be coping with the attention, everyone slapping him on the back and telling him he's great for handling his father's death as his father did with his father before him. Yet for me, at home, it's a different story.

Much later, the children are asleep – you see, miracles do happen – and I find Alex outside in the semi-darkness, leaning over Liberty's stable door, watching her and her foal. I join him, hugging my chest, because in spite of wearing a coat and hat, I'm freezing.

'Alex, aren't you coming inside?'

'When I'm ready.' He keeps his face turned away from me.

'I know you're hurting,' I begin.

'How can you know how I'm feeling?' he says snappily. 'You haven't just lost your father.'

'You forget. I lost mine too, a long time ago.'

'I'm sorry.'

'Yes, I was devastated, and angry with him for walking out on us, and leaving us in limbo.' I pause to take a breath past the constriction in my throat. 'Alex, you are allowed to grieve for him. If you don't, I can't see how you'll be able to move on.'

Alex doesn't respond.

'It was such a shock.'

'Stop saying that, Maz. You're like a broken record. On and on and on . . .'

'You're bound to be angry.' I'm floundering.

'Yes, with people around here, telling me what to do, what to think, what to feel.'

I feel as if I've been slapped. I'm your fiancée, I want to say, but the words won't come.

'I've been prepared for years,' Alex says. 'I thought he was gone when the bull got him. I've done all the grieving stuff. I have no intention of going through it again.'

He's in denial, I think, and being bloody-minded, just the same as his father.

'Alex, let's go inside . . .'

He shakes his head.

'At the wake today, people were asking about the wedding,' I begin, 'only it seems that if we go ahead, it might look insensitive to your father's memory. We could postpone it, but Christmas was the only date we could settle on.'

'Maz, I can't think about weddings now.'

'You mean, you'd prefer to postpone it?'

'I didn't say that.' Alex runs his hands through his hair. 'I wish you wouldn't reinterpret everything I say, because you never get it right. I said I can't think about something so –' Alex appears to be searching for the right word – 'trivial.'

'Trivial?' My blood could hardly run any colder, but it does. 'Are you saying our marriage is trivial?'

'There you go again.' Alex kicks the bottom of the stable door. 'I mean that it isn't that important compared with Father topping himself, stopping Mother having a nervous breakdown – especially with that woman, Fifi's, revelation today – and keeping the business going.'

'Alex!'

He starts to walk away, stopping after a couple of steps where the shadows start to swallow him up. 'I've had a long and difficult day. I've had enough of being nice to people, and more than enough of wedding talk, because they all bloody well asked me too.'

'All right. We'll postpone it,' I say. 'Let's take our time. There's no hurry.'

'I wasn't thinking about postponing it . . .' Alex's eyes glint in the darkness, but I don't think he's crying. 'I think we should cancel.'

'Cancel?'

'Yes, let's forget it.'

'Run that past me again.' I need to be sure.

'Cancel it, Maz. Call the whole thing off.'

I can feel the tears rolling hot down my cheeks.

'I mean it. I'll pay any outstanding deposits.'

I don't care about the money. 'Alex, just answer me one thing,' I say. His words are like clamps on my heart, squeezing it until it cannot beat any more. 'Do you still . . . love me?'

Alex walks away across the yard in the direction of his car. Too much pressure. I shouldn't have asked. I gaze up at the stars, blurry specks in the navy sky, thinking of the engagement ring locked away because I haven't been wearing it recently. I should have had it on my finger so I could take it off and make some dramatic gesture to show Alex that I really don't care, which would be a lie, of course. I care about Alex and our future more than anything else in the world, George excepted. The wedding that I've looked forward to, that I've spent months planning for, is off. I hear the sound of Alex's car driving away, and I'm devastated.

I try to hold it together. I have to – for George's sake. It isn't his fault. He didn't choose his parents. It would be all too easy for me to hide myself away in the Barn, call Emma and tell her I'm not coming in to work, but I don't. It's more important than ever that our business thrives because, whatever Alex decides to contribute, I want to be able to support myself and my son. I have my pride, and that's what's going to make it doubly difficult for me to face up to people like Elsa at the Barnscote, and the vicar, to tell them the wedding is off. Having given George his breakfast, I detach the wedding planner from the fridge, throw the fridge magnet – the one Emma gave me in the shape of a horseshoe for luck – in the bin, and start ripping the pages into tiny pieces.

'I wan',' George says, holding out his hand. 'I wan'!'

'There you are, darling. You help Mummy.' I give him a sheet, and watch him tearing at it with his teeth and spitting the soggy bits out. He thinks it's hilarious, and I can't help smiling as he giggles his way through the task, destroying what remains of the dreaded list. I wash his face and pick the paper off his T-shirt so he's tidy when I drop him at nursery on the way to Otter House. When I get there I grab a mug of tea with Emma.

'It was an impressive funeral,' Emma says, rinsing out the mugs in the staffroom before we head off for the morning ward round together. It's the day after Old Fox-Gifford's send-off – and Alex's brush-off, except it was more than that. I bite my lip. It might as well be the end of the world.

'Rather appropriate I think for a man who was larger than life. Everyone's talking about it,' Emma goes on.

'I'm sure,' I say. 'I wish it hadn't happened like this though. I shouldn't feel guilty, but I do.'

'You did the right thing, reporting him. Old Fox-Gifford should have given up driving and retired ages ago.'

'I'm sorry though. His work was what kept him going. It gave him a purpose. People looked up to him, and he had that great camaraderie with his farming clients. He felt needed, I suppose.' And that's partly why I feel so devastated – because Alex appears to have decided that he doesn't need me in his life any more. That's what he's saying, isn't it, that there's no point in him marrying me because he's realised that he can't see a future for us as a family; him, me and George.

'Talyton Manor Vets has always been a real family affair. There can't be many of those left.' Emma gives me an affectionate nudge. 'It's the end of Old Fox-Gifford's reign, but the dynasty continues.'

'Alex is hoping that at least one of his children will inherit from him . . .' Mentioning Alex's name, having been thinking about him and what he said, all last night, I find I can't continue.

'Are you all right, Maz?' Emma says gently.

'I'm fine. I couldn't sleep.' I hold up one hand. 'Please don't be nice to me, otherwise I'll get . . . upset.'

'What's wrong?' Emma touches my shoulder. 'You can tell me.'

I start to cry. 'Alex has cancelled the wedding.'

'Oh, Maz, I'm sorry. After all that effort you've put in.' I notice through my tears that Emma has a small smile on her lips. 'Maybe it's for the best.'

'How do you work that one out?' I sob.

'Christmas isn't a great time for a wedding. Hey, you'll be able to rearrange it for late spring or early summer.'

I shake my head.

Emma frowns. 'Maz, didn't you say postponed?'

'No, cancelled. The wedding's off.'

'I don't believe it. Why?' When I don't answer, Emma goes on, 'He shouldn't have made that decision now – he's in mourning, it's probably the most stressful time of his life . . . Shall I talk to him?'

'That's where I went wrong, Em. I tried talking to him and he—'

'Broke down,' Emma finishes for me.

'No, he didn't. He was . . . I've never seen him like it before. I feel as if I don't know him.'

'Give him time. He'll change his mind.' Emma tries, and fails, to reassure me.

'It's too late for that. He texted me this morning to confirm that it was up to me to cancel the reception and everything else. He's too busy.' It's going to be a painful and humiliating experience. 'All that other stuff about not wanting to employ an assistant, or a locum for the honeymoon. I can't help thinking that he had cold feet and couldn't bring himself to tell me the wedding was off. His father dying . . . it's given him the perfect excuse.'

'Oh, Maz.' Emma's eyes glitter, and her upper lip trembles, and knowing she's sad for me, upsets me more. I end up blubbering into her scrub top, her arms around me and her bump between us.

'Why don't you take the day off?' Emma asks gently, when I eventually extricate myself.

'I'd rather stay here.' I grab a paper towel from the dispenser and blow my nose. 'It might stop me from going mad. And anyway, I'm going to meet the family at the church at lunchtime.'

'Maz, poor you,' says Emma.

In Kennels, I glance along the cages. There are three inpatients: a cat, a dog and a custard-coloured rat. I start with the rat, taking its own cage and record card across to the prep bench.

'This is Bella,' says Emma. 'The owner's a Twilight fan. She has Robert at home – in separate accommodation, I hasten to add. Anyway, Will did a lumpectomy yesterday and Bella took a while to come round so he decided to keep her in for observation.'

'It says a "mastectomy" here,' I say, reading the card.

'That's the technical term, I believe.' Emma is being sarcastic.

'Did he send it off for histology?'

'The client's coming back to him on that one. She doesn't think she'll be able to afford it from her paper round.'

'I see.'

'It's all right. I told him to do his best to talk her out of it today and he seemed to see the logic in that. If the lump returns, it'll be the end of the rat anyway. If it doesn't, then great . . . Either way, we've saved the client an awful lot of pocket money.' Emma pauses as I open the front of the cage. 'By the way, she nipped Will.'

'She isn't going to nip me.' I dive in quickly to catch the rat by her shoulders, making sure she can't twist her head round. I take a look at her wound

305

underneath. It's clean and dry, and there are no stitches. 'That's a neat job.'

'Will used subcuticular sutures,' says Emma, by which she means ones under the skin. 'There's no need for a collar or body stocking to stop Bella chewing them out.'

'I'm impressed.' I put Bella back inside her cage and slip the catch shut while Emma writes up the notes. We make a good team. I used to think Alex and I were good together too . . . I bite back a tear. I can remember feeling absolutely gutted when my previous boyfriend, my ex-boss, dumped me to return to his ex-wife, but it had nothing on this sensation of devastation and loss.

I'm aware that Emma is staring at me.

'I'm fine,' I insist.

'Yeah, right,' she says.

I fetch the cat next, picking up the drip bag from the hook outside his cage.

'Is this Blueboy?'

'He came in yesterday. He was a bit slow to come round, so we decided to hang on to him overnight too.'

'You've shaved him.' He looks ridiculous, as he did before, with a fluffy face, paws and bottlebrush tail, and the rest of his coat short and smooth.

'Cheryl gave us express permission, in writing and in triplicate. She's decided not to use him any more. She's retiring him from both showing and stud duties.'

'What was the result of his blood test?'

'He's negative for the PKD gene, so it must have been Cassie's mother who was affected, and she's dead, so that's it.'

'The best possible outcome then.'

'Not quite. Cheryl's looking for a new stud cat.'

Emma smiles. 'It isn't great for the cat population, but it's good for our business, I suppose. Anyway, I reckon Blueboy's good to go, which leaves us with Tolstoy here, a dog with literary aspirations.'

'Isn't he another one of Saba's puppies?' I ask, taking him out of the big kennel where he stands wagging his tail in rather a subdued manner. 'He looks just like Seven, apart from not having the harelip.'

'This is an odd one,' says Emma, taking the record card when I hand it over to her. I pick Tolstoy up and lift him onto the bench, where he stands trembling and looking quite pathetic. 'He's been off-colour, nothing spectacular, just less keen than usual on his food, and not wanting to play.' She sticks a thermometer under his tail, at which he promptly sits down. 'That isn't very helpful, is it?' Tolstoy turns his head and licks her on the nose.

After a minute or so, she checks the thermometer.

'Thirty-eight degrees. A marked improvement on yesterday.' Emma takes charge of the patient, and checks the rest of him over, while I draw up a dose of antibiotic.

'Is Tolstoy going home?' I ask.

'With an appointment to see one of us on Friday,' Emma confirms.

'That will be Will . . . Is that okay?'

'We have to start trusting him with more at some stage soon.' Emma touches her belly. 'Very soon. What's he on? The dog, I mean, not Will.'

'Amoxicillin.' I hand her the syringe. It feels like the old days. 'Here's one I prepared earlier.'

'You're ultra-efficient today.'

'I have to be.' With Alex returning this morning only to shower and change, it's been down to me to keep life as normal as possible for our son. 'I've had to pack all the paraphernalia George needs and drop him at nursery on the way here,' I go on, 'and get myself ready, although that comes last now. Just you wait, Em.'

'I'm waiting,' she says, amused.

I carry on consulting, while Will operates and Emma does some paperwork in the office.

At lunchtime, I leave Otter House, walking briskly to the church and hurrying up the path to join Alex, Sophia, George, Lucie and Seb in the churchyard to see the new memorial for Old Fox-Gifford. The wind is whistling around the graves and blowing Lucie's red umbrella inside out.

When I see Alex, his hands in the pockets of his waxed coat, my heart misses a beat. Is he going to tell me it's all been a mistake? He destroys the faint surge of hope that rises in my breast, acknowledging me with a nod and a curt, 'You made it then. I thought you might have been tied up at work.'

'You hoped, you mean,' I say bitterly, taking him aside until we're close to the high wall under the canopy of one of the yews. 'You would have preferred me to stay away.'

Alex shrugs. I notice that he hasn't shaved.

'Perhaps you should move out of the Barn for a while,' I say, because, having seen him again, I don't know how I'm going to cope with living under the same roof at the moment.

'That's ridiculous, and you know it.'

'If you don't like me enough to commit to marrying me, I can't see the point in staying together,' I say miserably. To my regret, because I didn't want to give Alex any satisfaction in seeing what he's done to me,

308

tears like acid pour down my cheeks. The idea of marriage was not all that important to me until Alex proposed, when it suddenly seemed a great idea. We were living together, we had a baby and marriage made perfect sense. The idea of cohabiting seems worthless now.

'Alex, I don't understand what's happened, what I've done—'

'I've had enough of inquests,' he says sharply. 'I don't want to talk about it.'

I follow him back to the grave, arms folded across my chest, my feet dragging. I feel as if I want to hit him, to get some kind of reaction, any reaction, instead of his long cold stare.

Lucie is stroking the black granite headstone that has been erected on Old Fox-Gifford's grave. It is of fitting proportions, engraved with his name, qualifications and dates. There is no tribute. Sophia points out that this is because what he requested was far too long-winded to fit.

'So, I decided to leave room for me instead,' she says.

'Humpy, you're not going to die,' says Lucie. 'Are you?' she adds doubtfully.

'We all have to die one day,' says Sophia.

'But you will wait until after the National Horse Show,' Lucie says.

'Lucie, I plan to be here for a very long time. Until Scheherazade has grown up and had foals of her own, and those foals have had foals.'

'And those foals have had foals,' adds Seb for good measure.

I can understand why the children are feeling insecure. It's hard enough when your grandfather dies, but for him to have chosen death himself . . . It must make them question how much he valued them, if he could do that. It seems the ultimate act of selfishness to me.

Perhaps he didn't want them to see him failing though.

Lucie places a bowl of flowers on the grave. Seb leaves a picture of Hal, one he's drawn. All serious, George drops a toy tractor onto the ground beside it, and we stand for a moment in silence. I glance towards Alex. His mother is holding his arm while he stands there, impassive, apart from the muscle twitching in his cheek. He appears to be fine, while I'm in pieces. I gaze up at the clouds, at the rain sweeping in, and wonder when – and if – Alex will break.

Chapter Eighteen

For Better, for Worse

A few days later, I take advantage of a break at work to cancel the wedding reception at the Barnscote. I should have done it before, but I've only just been able to bring myself to phone Elsa, partly because I'm afraid I'll break down and be unable to speak, partly because I'd hoped against hope that Alex would say he'd made a mistake, a rash decision as a result of losing his father, and change his mind.

'Are you sure, Maz, only . . .?' says Elsa.

'Quite sure,' I say sharply to cover up my distress. This is the last thing I'd planned, the last thing I ever wanted. 'You have our deposit. If there's anything outstanding, let me know.'

'I'm very sorry.' There's a moment's silence. 'Are you looking for another venue?'

'No. I'm sorry too, but I'd rather not talk about it.'

'I understand,' she says, but I don't think she has any idea. 'If you want to book up for a Christmas lunch or dinner, do let us know in plenty of time. Our tables are filling up fast.'

'Goodbye.' I have no intention of celebrating Christmas this year, any year, although I'll have to put on a brave face for George's sake. Following on from speaking to Elsa, I contact Jennie about the wedding cake. She tells me not to worry about it, considering the circumstances, and says she'll have no problem selling the tiers on as individual Christmas cakes.

I slip my mobile into my pocket and wander back to Reception, hoping to find something to distract me.

'Hey, Maz, look at this,' says Frances, waving me over.

There's one of those gift bags containing a bottle of some kind on the desk at Reception, the pattern on the bag competing with Frances's tunic top for the accolade of most garish. Frances slips her Dame Edna specs onto her nose and peers at the label.

'Oh, it's for Will,' she says, surprised. 'Fancy that.'

'He has a fan,' I say. 'Who is it from?'

'It says, "From Jack Pike, with thanks and lots of licks." Look, he's signed it with a paw print.'

'A muddy one?'

'No, dipped in paint, I should imagine. Oh, how sweet.'

Jack Pike is a liver and white English springer spaniel. His owner, Ed, is a huntin', shootin', fishin' kind of man.

'He's the one Will referred for an MRI,' I say.

'Indeed,' says Frances. 'Didn't you hear? They found a tumour on the brain scan. He's had treatment and he's in remission.'

Frances looks at me, smiling. 'I believe you'll have to eat your words, Maz. Didn't you say it was excessive referring Jack to the specialist?'

'Expensive.' Unnecessary too, or so I thought. I was

wrong. Obviously. A prompt referral has saved Jack's life. I wonder how Ed, who's married with two children, managed to afford it.

'There's a present for you, Will,' I say, taking it through to Kennels. Shannon is holding Cleo, the tortie and white 'care' cat on the prep bench while Will looks down its ear.

I hesitate, unable to believe what I'm seeing.

'Will, don't you realise you'll end up having to knock her out?'

'She's fine,' Will mutters.

'Can't you see anything yet?' Shannon says impatiently.

'No . . . No, it's pretty dark down here.'

'You haven't got some wax or something blocking the end?' With one hand, Shannon reaches for the pot of cotton buds on the shelf and removes the lid, keeping hold of Cleo who is becoming increasingly annoyed, twitching the end of her tail and making small, but threatening, noises in her throat. Izzy's been training Shannon well. It never ceases to amaze me how nurses are so proficient at multitasking.

Will examines the otoscope and pokes a cotton bud into the cone that he's taken out of Cleo's ear. 'It's no different.'

Shannon starts to giggle.

'I know what you've done – you haven't turned the brightness up on the light.'

Will fiddles for a moment.

'Oh, yes,' he says.

'Has the light dawned at last?' Shannon says, and I wonder if I should have a word with her about her sharp tongue. She's beginning to sound remarkably like Izzy. She's judging Will too harshly. He's the vet

313

whereas Shannon is an, as yet, unqualified nurse.

I wonder if this situation has more to do with Shannon and what happened – or didn't happen – between her and Drew, our former locum, than Will himself. She's over Drew – it happened over two years ago now, but maybe . . . She hasn't had a boyfriend, as far as I know, although she's often out and about with her girlfriends.

'Eureka,' says Will.

'What is it?' says Shannon. 'Don't keep me in suspense any longer. Any second now and Cleo's going to loop the loop.'

'Ear mites,' Will says triumphantly, at which Shannon picks up one of the bottles from the shelf and hands it over to him.

'I assume you'll want this then.'

'Well, yes. Thank you.'

'Do you want to flush first?' she asks.

'Um . . .' Will deliberates for a minute or so. 'No, I don't think so.'

'All right then, if you're sure.'

'I think so . . . Yes, I am sure.' I think he's forgotten I'm here. I clear my throat.

'There's a present for you, Will,' I repeat. 'I'll leave it here while you finish off. I don't want to be witness to a bloodbath.' I don't know why I say that – a picture of Old Fox-Gifford reaching for the trigger of his gun flicks into my head. I take a breath and stay, deciding that I need the distraction. It's been three weeks since it happened and the memory is as fresh as ever.

'Thank you, Maz.' Will turns his attention back to Cleo, squeezing the drops into one ear, while Shannon rolls her eyes at me. She really must stop doing that. Will massages the first ear, Cleo mewing and scratching with her back leg. He lets go and the cat immediately shakes her head, spattering ear drops everywhere.

'Ugh,' says Shannon, grabbing a piece of paper towel to wipe her face. 'Why didn't you cover the ear with cotton wool like Maz does, so when they shake their heads, the drops stay in?'

'I didn't think,' Will stammers, gazing ruefully at the greasy spatters down his top.

'I'd even got the cotton wool ready for you. Honestly, now I'm going to smell of ear wax all day.'

'I'm sorry, Shannon. I'll make it up to you.'

'Don't bother, Will. You'll only make a mess of that too.'

'I'm impressed, anyway,' I join in. 'Will's managed to tame the cat with the worst reputation in the practice. How did you do it?'

'Ah, tact and patience,' he says, grinning. 'I've learned a lot from Izzy. I've been respectful and treated Cleo as an individual. As a result, we have an understanding.'

'You're winding me up.'

'I don't know, to be honest. When I first met Cleo, I missed the "care" warning on her notes.'

'I don't know how,' says Shannon. 'It's in red with stars and exclamation marks all over it.'

'You know me,' Will says. 'Anyway, I stroked her and gave her a treat. I think she quite likes me.'

'My theory is that she prefers male vets,' says Shannon.

'So she's a misogynist, as well as being prone to violence,' I say lightly.

'It's a misandrist,' Will chips in. 'You're referring to a man who hates women.'

315

'Thank you for that,' I say, passing him the bag. 'You're doing well today. There's a present here from Jack Pike.'

'It looks like wine,' Shannon says as Will pulls the bottle halfway out of the bag.

'It's whisky, a single malt. That's kind of Ed. He shouldn't have though – I was only doing my job.'

'Enjoy it,' I say. 'You deserve it. I'm sorry I doubted your judgement. You saved Jack's life.'

Will blushes. 'At least I managed to get something right.'

He takes the present upstairs to the flat, leaving me with Shannon.

'You were a bit sharp with Will just then.'

'Was I?' Shannon says blithely as she returns Cleo to her cage, straightening the Vetbed inside first.

'You know you were.'

'Well, he is a bit of a—'

'Respect, Shannon,' I cut in. 'You have to show him some respect and cut him a little slack. He's fairly new to all this. You remember what it was like when you started work here, you didn't get everything right first time.'

It seems that my words have hit home.

'I still get things wrong,' she confesses. 'Like the order for the vaccines. Oh, I'll try to be nice to him. It's just that he's so boring when he goes on about his spiders and lizardy things, and then it takes him half an hour to examine each inpatient in the mornings when it takes you and Emma five minutes max, and he can never make a decision about anything.'

It's true that Will finds it difficult to make decisions. He asks me through to the consulting room during afternoon surgery. It's a reasonable call because it's

Cassie, and, as Will says, she's definitely one of my specials.

'One more time,' says Clive. 'I know, Maz. I'd rather not, but Edie isn't ready to let her go.'

I admit her and, with Will's help, put her on a drip to get some fluids into her. She hasn't been eating or drinking. Her mouth is dry and, when I tweak the skin over her neck, it forms a tent that takes much longer than it should to collapse back down. She's weak, hardly able to stand, and her breath smells of ammonia.

Within a couple of hours, her condition is worse. She's throwing up and crying, and I can't bear to see her like that. I call Clive. Within fifteen minutes, he's back with Edie. Frances buzzes through to me to let me know they're here.

'I thought you should also know, Maz,' Frances says, 'that Edie is very drunk. She can hardly stand.'

'Show them into the staffroom,' I decide. 'Kick Miff and Tripod out. Not literally,' I add blackly. 'We are supposed to be caring.'

'Oh, Maz,' Frances sighs. 'You don't have to joke about it. I know you're upset.'

I don't say anything. I have to. It's my way of coping.

Shannon and I take Cassie through to the staffroom where Edie and Clive are sitting side by side on the sofa. Shannon spreads a towel across Edie's lap and I rest Cassie on top of it. I draw up some of the final injection from the bottle I've brought with me.

'My poor baby,' Edie sobs.

'It's all right, love,' says Clive, when it's clearly far from all right. I can smell alcohol on Edie's breath. Her long hair – dark with a silver streak – is flat and greasy, her purple top is stained and hangs from her bony frame, revealing a grubby bra strap. She's a wreck.

317

'I wish we hadn't left her this long,' Clive goes on, stroking Cassie's head.

'We gave her a chance,' Edie mumbles. 'She came back to us last time.'

'She's been a true fighter.' I don't understand how Cassie survived this long with the amount of urea she had in her blood. It just goes to show how you shouldn't rely on lab tests alone. 'Are you ready, or would you like more time with her?'

'Put her out of her misery,' Clive says gruffly.

I slip the needle into the plug on the drip tubing, kinking the tube so the drug goes into the cat and not into the bag. Slowly, I push the plunger, sending the blue fluid swirling through the tubing. Within seconds, Cassie rests her chin on Edie's hand and utters a low sigh as her body relaxes and her breathing stops. I know before I check for a pulse that she's gone. I nod towards Clive as Edie is hugging Cassie to her chest, tears running down her face.

'We'd like her cremated. I don't like to think of her left outside with the dogs.' Clive means the ones he's buried before in the garden at the Talymill Inn. 'And I'm going to make an appointment to have the kittens tested. I don't want to see them suffer in the same way. I don't want Edie to have to worry about them each time they're off colour for any reason.' Shannon extricates the cat's body from Edie's grasp, then Clive helps his wife up, an arm around her waist. 'It'll give us some peace of mind, at least.'

I watch them go, Edie stumbling along the corridor and Clive holding her up.

Shannon looks at me, eyebrows raised.

'It's very sad to see her like that,' I say. It reminds me that some people have problems far worse than mine.

Will Clive's problems be compounded by the kittens' lab results?

When their results come in after another week, I call Clive straight away.

'Don't keep me in suspense,' he says.

'It's good news. They're both clear.'

'Thank goodness for that. I'll tell Edie . . .'

There's a long pause and I'm not sure what to say.

'Actually, Maz, I don't think she'll care,' Clive begins again. 'She's at rock bottom.'

'I'm sorry, Clive. If there's anything I can do . . .'

'There's nothing anyone can do now. Edie has to decide for herself . . .' Clive clears his throat. 'I'm very sorry too, Maz. I heard about you and Alex. Elsa mentioned it – we buy our sausages from her.'

'It's one of those things,' I say glibly. 'Clive, I've got to go . . .' I'm not in a great hurry, but I don't want to talk. I go home early to spend some time with George.

Alex is in the surgery, tidying up. I offer to help, but he makes excuses. He says it's something he has to do on his own. He doesn't seem to be getting very far, I notice, because he's in the office at midnight with the light on, asleep with his head on the desk. When I check up on him, all he appears to have done is take down his father's ancient veterinary textbooks off the shelves and stack them up on the floor.

I reach out to touch his shoulder and change my mind.

'Alex,' I say quietly, thinking that this is much like waking George. You're never quite sure how he'll react. 'Alex, come to bed.'

He sits up and yawns.

'I've too much to do,' he says, his voice like shattering ice. 'Leave me alone.'

319

'Can we talk? I could stay and chat while you're sorting the books out. Shall I go and find a couple of boxes? I'll bring drinks, and something to eat. You didn't have any dinner.'

'Maz, stop trying to mollycoddle me.'

Mollycoddle? What kind of a word is that? It sounds like his father speaking.

'It's suffocating,' Alex goes on. 'Please go, before I say something I regret.'

'Alex . . .' His name catches in my throat. I take a breath, telling myself to calm down. He's lost his father, he's depressed and overworked . . . He's a man and he's retreated to his cave to lick his wounds. Well, he can't stay in there any longer. I've had enough of keeping it all together, and taking sole charge of George, and walking on eggshells because I don't know where I stand. 'Alex, I need you to make a decision about . . .' My heart hammers so loudly, I can hear it echoing around in my head. '. . . us. I need to know if we have any kind of future, because I can't carry on like this. It's the not knowing . . .' I turn and walk away, stumbling down the steps. I can't continue. It's too painful.

Alex doesn't follow, and I spend another night alone in our big bed. Sometime in the early hours I can bear it no longer and I fetch George from his cot and bring him into bed with me. His warm body and snuffling comfort me slightly and eventually I doze off.

Chapter Nineteen

Dearly Beloved

I wish I knew what was going on between me and Alex. Sometimes, he seems happier, playing with George and talking to me about life in general, nothing deep and meaningful. Sometimes, he retreats and refuses to talk at all. He sleeps on the sofa, or in Lucie's room, a matter of great sadness to me, because it suggests that, eventually, one or the other of us will be moving out.

'It's time for the old dog to go,' I say at breakfast on a chilly mid-November morning. Hal was lying on the Axminster in front of the fireplace in the Manor house, incontinent and confused, when I checked on him earlier. (The pony has been banned from the drawing room out of respect for Hal's feelings.) Sophia asked me my opinion on the dog, although she knew already what it would be.

'Tell Alexander,' she said quietly.

'Your mother wants us to do the deed today,' I say, watching Alex eating Coco Pops. I bought them for George, but he prefers Cornflakes. 'Alex, are you listening?'

'What was that, Maz?' He looks up from the bowl.

'About Hal.' I decide it would be best if Alex comes to his own conclusion – maybe he'll be more comfortable with the decision to put him to sleep if he thinks it's his idea. 'Will you have a look at him on your way out this morning? He doesn't look too good.'

'Does he ever? He's always looked pretty manky, at least for as long as I can remember.'

'Alex . . .' Oh, what's the point, I think. I might as well save my breath. But then I think of Hal when I kissed him on the top of his smelly old head. He wagged his tail once. That's all he could manage. 'Alex, it has to be done. No matter how you feel, whether you're keeping him going because you can't face up to making the decision at the moment, or because you can't bear to lose that link with your father, it isn't fair on the dog. He's a poor old thing.'

'He's old,' Alex says snappily. 'He's a bit rickety, that's all. He isn't suffering.' He stares at me. 'But if you think it's the right thing to do, I suppose I'll have to bow to your superior opinion, since Father asked *you* to look after Hal.'

My heart hammering painfully fast, I pick up my mug and walk away. I am furious with Alex for not putting Hal first for some reason known only to himself, but I realise that I can't push him just yet. I'd hate him to regret the decision afterwards. It isn't just the patient who has to be ready.

It's the weekend and I'm off duty, but I find that I don't want to hang around at home with Alex in this strange, oppressive mood. I stick my wellies on and set out with George in the cross-country buggy. We head for the river valley, singing in the rain. It's showery and we're well wrapped up against the cold.

As we reach the footpath at the bottom of the hill, I catch sight of a big black dog. At first, I wonder if it's Poppy, one of the black Labs who's followed us from the Manor, but when I call it over, it disappears among the brambles and dogwood. I don't worry about it – there's bound to be a dog-walker somewhere nearby.

'Which song next, George?' I ask, leaning over to look over the hood of the buggy.

'Bus,' he says, grinning in anticipation.

'We've already had that one. Twice. And Mummy made up extra verses.'

'Bus,' George insists, so 'The Wheels on the Bus' it is.

Several more verses later, we reach the path alongside the river which is in full flow, snaking through the green fields where a flock of sheep are grazing beneath the trees along the edge of the old railway line. You can't see the bottom today. The water is muddy and stained with iron.

'Out,' says George. 'I. Out.'

I debate for a moment, considering the risks. George. Water.

'If you hold Mummy's hand,' I say rashly. I unstrap him from the buggy and hang on to him by his coat as he toddles across the path to launch himself towards the river. 'No, George.' I pull him back just in time. He stamps one foot in the mud.

'Look at the bird over there.'

'No derd,' he says, shaking his head, and I'm thinking, where is a bird when you need one, because I could do with one to distract him? As if in answer, a pair of ducks come flying down, slapping into the water and bobbing away on the current. George claps them. He's happy now, but the rain that is coming down harder, interspersed with hailstones, as though the man in the clouds – yes, that's what we call him – is throwing them down in odd handfuls, is seeping through my coat.

As the sky darkens further, a sense of gloom descends over me. It isn't just about Hal. It's about me and Alex. What am I going to do if we can't get talking and turn our relationship around? Hanging on to George, I gaze up at the hills beyond the old railway line. I can't imagine staying here if we split up. I couldn't bear it. Everything would remind me of Alex. We first met down here by the river . . .

Maz, you are not going to cry, I tell myself, but I do squat down in the mud and give my son a hug.

'Shall we go home?' I say, pressing my lips to his cheek.

'No,' he says.

'We could have milkshake and a biscuit.'

'No,' George repeats, but he pulls away and starts trying to clamber into the buggy. I take him back to the Barn. It's an uphill slog.

I'd hoped, by going out, to have given Alex the space to work out what he was supposed to do about Hal. In the end though, I have to take the initiative. By lunchtime, I'm not giving Alex the option to ignore Hal's plight any longer. I hand George over to Sophia who decides to take him out to Talyton to pick up some shopping. She appears to be coping reasonably well – she's started riding again since the funeral – but she prefers not to be in the house when Hal is put down.

Having helped Sophia persuade George into his car seat and sent them on their way, I fetch the visit case and ask Alex to come and look at the dog who hasn't budged from the drawing room.

I sit down at Hal's head and look up at Alex.

'Do you want to do it here?' I ask, opening up the visit case beside me.

Remaining silent, Alex holds out his hand for the syringe that's resting in the lid. I pick it up.

'I'll do it, if you want,' I say gently, noticing how Alex's hands are trembling. He looks rough around the edges, as if he hasn't slept for a week.

'I'll do it.' He snatches the syringe from me, and my chest grows tight, my heart is breaking for Alex and for Hal. Where is the cool, devil-may-care attitude Alex used to have? I watch him spray surgical spirit vaguely in the direction of Hal's front leg. It gets up Hal's nostrils and makes him sneeze.

'Aren't you going to clip a bit of hair off?' I ask tentatively.

I sensed Alex was upset, but he's angry now.

'You mean I'm going to miss the bloody vein.'

'He is pretty flat,' I say, referring to Hal's circulation. It isn't always easy to find a vein in this situation.

I bite my lip, and a metallic taste seeps across my tongue, as I watch Alex unsheath the needle. Remaining silent, I take a grip on Hal's leg and raise the vein with my thumb. Alex peers at Hal's leg, his brow furrowed and I wonder if he can see. It's a gloomy, overcast day outside. I shift slightly so as not to block the meagre light falling in through the long windows.

'Hey, don't move,' Alex says snappily, and I feel Hal now shifting alongside me, and I worry that he's getting stressed because he knows Alex is stressed and it's making me stressed worrying that this isn't going to go well.

'Raise it again,' Alex says.

'I am.'

'Start again. I can't see it.'

I wrap my hand around Hal's elbow and press. I try pumping his paw to increase the blood in the vein, but the result is not impressive.

'I said he was pretty—'

'I know what you said,' Alex cuts in. 'I know. Just raise it again.'

I want to say, don't speak to me like that. I know why he and his father never had nurses to help. No one would stay if they treated them like that. And I am – or was – supposed to be his fiancée, the love of his life . . . Comforting Hal, I gaze at Alex, at the curve of his cheekbone and the stubble on his face.

I fight the instinct to touch him, to tell him, no matter how he feels, that I feel the same way as I have ever done, and, no matter what happens, whether or not he has fallen out of love with me, I still love him, and always will . . .

Aching with uncertainty over how he feels about me, I try to concentrate on the job in hand. My legs begin to cramp as I wait, watching Alex staring at Hal's leg and occasionally giving it a prod. Poor Hal gazes at me with his clouded eyes, his expression saying, let me go . . .

'Alex . . .' I say quietly. 'It has to be done.'

Alex seems to make his mind up and stabs the needle into Hal's skin. Hal winces as Alex draws back on the syringe. To my alarm, there is no blood. He's missed the vein. Cursing quietly under his breath, Alex withdraws the needle, then takes a second stab. Still no blood. Hal utters a whine of protest. It hurts. I can feel his pain and I can't stand it.

'Alex, stop right there. This isn't right, and you know it.'

He hesitates, and looks me right in the eyes, and to my horror, I find he's crying.

'Nothing's right, is it?' He swears and throws the syringe onto the floor, the needle sticking into the Axminster and staying there. Alex gets up and goes to the window, standing there, facing out with his head in his hands. I listen to the clock on the mantelpiece ticking.

'You do it, Maz,' Alex mutters eventually, and he stays where he is while I fetch a fresh needle and a piece of bandage to use as a tourniquet to raise the vein. When I return, Hal beats his tail once against the carpet.

'Good boy. Let's get this over with, shall we?' I clip the hair from his leg to give myself a better view of the vein, raise it, and, having planted a kiss on the top of Hal's head, I slide the needle into the vein. I'm in, and Hal has hardly noticed. I release the tourniquet and inject the drug into his system. Within a heartbeat, his head slumps onto my arm, he utters a sigh and falls into unconsciousness. I watch the side of his chest, the dying flutter of his heart, feel the tears roll hot down my cheeks.

'Goodbye, old chap,' I murmur, stroking his crumpled ear before getting up and moving away. 'He's gone,' I tell Alex, at which he walks back over and sits down, lifts Hal's head onto his lap and howls, crying for him in a way he never did when his father died that day, and I'm crying too, and I want to comfort him, but something holds me back.

I sit down opposite Alex with the dead dog between us, symbolic of our relationship perhaps. I don't know how long we stay there, the three of us growing cold as the other dogs come in and out, milling around to sniff Hal's body as if they are trying to make sense of what has happened, and say their farewells. Poppy, the young Labrador, spends ages with her nose pressed to Hal's mouth.

The damp wood in the grate in the fireplace sends up a curling wisp of blue smoke. It needs a good stir up with the poker, as Old Fox-Gifford used to do, but no one has bothered.

I am choked up, but it was the best result for old Hal. I can console myself with the fact that he led a charmed life with Old Fox-Gifford looking out for him, fathering those puppies of Saba's, the Labradoodles, and a good death, but Alex is distraught.

'Aren't you going to move him?' I ask eventually, but Alex doesn't reply.

'We could move him together?'

Alex doesn't want me here, I can feel it. He doesn't want anything more to do with me.

I wonder about moving the dog alone. I don't want Sophia or the children coming across Hal's body.

'What about the arrangements for Hal? I assume you'll want him cremated and his ashes back.'

Alex shakes his head. 'Of course I bloody well don't. I'm not soft. And even at cost, it's too damned expensive.'

'Alex! Your father wanted his ashes back so they can be buried with him.' I pause. 'If you're so worried about money, I'll pay.' I lean towards him slightly. 'And don't you dare tell me you're too bloody proud to accept.'

'Maz, just shut up, will you? I've made my mind up. I don't need to analyse every bloody decision I make. I don't want to talk to anyone. I don't require counselling. What I want is for everyone to shut up nagging me.'

I stand, my heart aching for him. For us.

'Alex,' I say quietly. 'I can see that my presence in your life is causing you grief. If you want me and George to move out, let me know. But,' I add, 'if that's what you choose, I'm making it clear that I won't be coming back. I've made mistakes. I know I'm not the perfect fiancée, or the perfect mother for that matter, but I've been doing my best to hold everything together, and, if my best isn't good enough for you . . . I love you . . . Always will . . .' I can no longer speak. It doesn't matter though, because I have nothing left to say. It's over.

I watch him kneel and stagger up with Hal's body in his arms. As he heads towards the double doors out to the garden, he trips on the curling edge of the carpet, and struggles to keep his balance and his hold on Hal. I duck forwards to grab Hal's front end with one hand, and open the doors with the other.

'Where do we put him, Alex?'

'In the freezer here?' Alex's eyes are puffy, and his nose is red.

'What, and you'll call the crematorium? Wouldn't it be better to put him in the back of my car so I can run him down to Otter House? We have a regular collection, and our freezer isn't full. There's room for one more.'

'All right. Back up then. We'll go through the house.'

'Are you sure?'

'It's a long way round otherwise.'

'Do you think we should cover him up?'

'There's an old throw on the chair. Use that,' Alex says. 'You can let go now. I've got him.'

Eventually, after some manoeuvring, we get Hal into the back of my car on a plastic sheet, with a throw over the top. It's rumpled, and both of us reach out at the same time to smooth it down. Our fingers touch. Neither of us moves.

'Maz?' I hear Alex's breath catch and feel the lightest pressure of his skin as he slides his hand over mine. I look up. For the first time in weeks he seems to have lost his cold, buttoned-up look. His eyes look moist. Is he crying again? A pulse beats erratically at my throat. 'I'm sorry . . .' he says. 'I've been a complete and utter bastard. I was angry with you for interfering when you were doing it for all the right reasons. You had to go through my father killing himself and me rejecting you because I was jealous that he chose to talk to you, not me, before he died and that he asked you, not me, to look after the dog.'

I shrug my shoulders. 'You shut me out,' I point out. 'You made me feel as if you didn't care. You haven't confided in me, or talked about what happened with your father's will. You told me before that the estate was mortgaged to the hilt and I can only assume from your reticence that the situation is now much worse. Alex, I wish you didn't bottle things up.'

'Oh, Maz, this isn't about money. Mine and my mother's financial state is about the same.'

'Why couldn't you say that before? It wasn't that difficult, was it?'

It's Alex's turn to shrug. 'As I said, I'm sorry . . . I mean it.' He slides his fingers between mine. 'Where's your ring?' he says suddenly. 'I noticed you'd stopped wearing it. Ages ago.'

'I know. I kept forgetting to take it off at work, so I put it away, and then I was so busy . . .' I hesitate, realising how this must have looked. 'Alex, did you think I was deliberately choosing not to wear it?'

'I began to think you'd changed your mind about marrying me. The ring disappeared. You were complaining about how hard it was to plan a wedding . . . Maz, what's a man supposed to think?'

'You could have just come straight out with it and asked me where it was.'

'I was afraid of what you were going to say. I know you came into this with your eyes wide open, or so you said – I thought with George, the parents and the daily grind, that you'd changed your mind about . . . about us.'

'It isn't always easy,' I admit. 'Alex, what happened?'

'You didn't put up much resistance over cancelling it.'

'The wedding. I was gutted, but you were adamant. I couldn't see any prospect of changing your mind. You can't force someone to marry you. You can't make someone love you. Anyway, the ring's in the safe at Otter House. I didn't know what to do with it.'

'So you've kept it? I thought you might have pawned it, or thrown it in the river,' Alex says, with a tiny flash of humour. 'I wouldn't have blamed you.'

I turn to look at his face.

'But you do blame me,' I say.

'I know.' Alex lifts my hand from the dead dog, and without letting go, we step away and Alex shuts the boot. We stand side by side, hand in hand, looking towards the fields and naked trees. I don't know what to say. I don't know how I feel. I resent the way he's hurt me, yet I'm also hopeful that this is the beginning of a reconciliation because, no matter how he's behaved, I want him back. I've been lost without him.

Eventually, I squeeze Alex's fingers. He squeezes back – hard, and the gobstopper of doubt in my throat begins to dissolve.

'Maz, do you think . . . can you ever find a way to forgive me?'

I catch sight of a pair of seagulls swooping across the grey sky.

'I realise how much I've hurt you,' Alex goes on. 'I can't take it back, but I can promise you it will never happen again.'

'Now you're blaming yourself. We've both done things wrong. I could have – no, should have – been more supportive. I should have trusted you. You're big enough and –' I was going to say ugly enough, but when I look into his eyes, I am reminded of how beautiful he is, how he can still take my breath away. His fingers tighten around mine, and he leans towards me until I can feel the warmth of his lips against mine. 'Oh, Alex . . .'

'I've missed you,' he murmurs.

I've missed being close to you, I echo silently. It will take time for us both to forgive and forget what has passed, but for now I live in the moment, taking comfort in his embrace. It's as if I've been dead, and with each kiss, he's gradually bringing me back to life.

We're together, but I have no expectations beyond that. Hope, yes, but it's fragile, waxing and waning over the next few days, as Alex begins to come to terms with his father's death.

One evening I return home from work in the dark with George to find Alex waiting for us in the Barn.

'You're early,' I say.

'I postponed my last call to vaccinate a couple of

ponies out in a field.' Alex turns to George. 'They might have eaten their carrots, but I'm not stumbling around in the dark and the mud. Besides, I have other plans for tonight.' He looks at me, and his lips curve into a smile that hints of mystery and anticipation. My heart lurches. 'First though, Mother's asked us to get the mare and foal in. Lisa had to go home early, and Mother's going along with Mrs P to play bridge. You don't mind, Maz?'

I don't have much to do with the horses, if I can avoid it, but I'm happy to help out occasionally. Alex persuades George to wear a coat and hat, and straps him into the buggy, giving him a toy tractor to keep him occupied for a few minutes.

'Shouldn't he have his snowsuit on?' I say. 'It's freezing.'

'He'll be fine,' Alex grins. 'Let's get this done.' He parks George outside Liberty's stable and fetches a head collar and foal slip, and together, we head out to the paddock where the horses are waiting at the gate. Liberty whickers, recognising Alex. He catches her, while I try to get hold of Shezza, who appears to have changed her mind about coming in.

'Stand still and let her come to you,' Alex says. 'That's it,' he goes on, as I slide the slip over her head. Alex opens the gate and leads Liberty through, while Shezza prances about beside me all the way to the stable. We let them go and watch them settle, Liberty pulling at the hay in her net, the foal lying down in the bed of shavings.

'She's grown, hasn't she?' I observe. 'Look at those legs.'

'I'd rather look at yours,' Alex says, nudging me.

Is that his rather clumsy way of saying the old Alex

is back, I wonder? I'm not sure. I turn my attention back to the foal.

'When will you start her?' I ask.

'I'll begin with some long-reining when she's two, then I can back her lightly at three, turn her away and bring her into proper work at four. That's the plan anyway.'

'It seems such a long time . . .'

'Some things are worth waiting for,' he says gruffly. 'Maz, I meant to wait until George was in bed, but . . .' He turns to me, goes down on one knee on the concrete and takes my hand. With the other hand, he fumbles around in his coat pocket, pulling out a ring, my engagement ring.

'Maz, I thought, after what happened, that I shouldn't take anything for granted, so here we go.' A pulse of joy throbs at my throat as he continues, 'Will you marry me?'

'Alex, of course I will.'

'Really?' he says. 'I thought you might have changed your mind.'

'There were times when I was all for walking away,' I say quietly, 'but my feelings for you haven't changed. So yes, Alex, I will marry you.' Trembling, I stretch out my left hand. Alex slides the ring onto my finger where it glints in the light above the stable door.

Standing up, he wraps his arms around me and presses his lips to my hair, my cheek, my ear . . . I interlink my fingers around the back of his neck, and breathe his warm, musky scent.

'Let's set the date,' he murmurs. 'For the wedding,' he adds, as if I don't know what he's talking about.

'I suppose it will have to be sometime next year now.'

'I don't want to wait,' Alex says abruptly. 'I thought we'd revert to the original date in December.'

'That's next month, Alex.'

'So? We can do it. I'll do my share of the organising this time. Please?'

'If you're certain.' It makes sense, I think. We can still have our Christmas wedding.

'I'll advertise for an assistant and book the honeymoon. Maz, I want to make it up to you. I'm here for you now, and always will be, I promise. For better, for worse.'

Eventually, he releases me and we walk back across the yard with George.

'So,' Alex says later, 'how did you find the perfect assistant?'

'You mean Will?' I smile. I'm sitting on the sofa. Alex is lying down on his back with his legs crossed over the arm, and his head in my lap. George is tucked up in bed. The fire is burning in the grate, the guard clipped across, and Alex's faint aroma of antibiotic and mints mingles with the fragrance of pinewood. 'He isn't perfect yet, but he's getting there. He's worked out a real-life approach to cases and charging for them at last, and he's learned to speak what I suppose you'd call clientese, so they actually understand what he's talking about. Emma and I put an ad in the *Vet News*. I thought I showed it to you.'

'You may well have done, but I would have ignored it back then, thinking you had an ulterior motive, trying to convince me I needed an assistant when I didn't want one.' He adds, 'When I didn't think I wanted one . . . I've been a stubborn bastard, haven't I?'

'Alex!' I bash him lightly over the chest with a cushion.

335

'What did you put?'

' "Keen new graduate wanted for friendly country practice. Small animals only." '

'That was wrong.'

'Only by one goat,' I point out.

'Will could have you for misrepresentation,' Alex teases. 'What else?'

' "One in three rota", although that's going to change when Em has her babies . . .'

'Cluck, cluck,' says Alex. 'You sound broody, Maz.'

'No more,' I say quickly. 'Not yet anyway.' I return to the subject of the advert. 'The real hook was the mention of doughnuts. I'm sure that's why we had so many enquiries. Several applied, we had a shortlist of three and Will was the best candidate for the job. Except, funnily enough, he isn't that keen on doughnuts. He only plucked up the courage to tell Emma the other day that he preferred flapjacks.

'Seriously though, Alex,' I continue, 'you have to decide what you're offering and what kind of person you want for the job. Do you want to train up a new graduate, or take on someone with experience?'

'Considering what you've gone through with Will, I'd have to choose an experienced vet – as long as they're not too set in their ways. Maz, you mustn't let me talk myself out of it.'

'I shan't, don't you worry. I'll write the ad for you, if I have to.' I stroke the side of Alex's face, feeling the prickle of his stubble and the heat of his skin against my fingertips.

'You haven't got time to write the ad,' Alex says eventually. He takes my hand and kisses it. 'You'll be too tied up with reorganising the wedding.' He hesitates. 'Chill, Maz. As I said, I'm going to help this time, and I'm sure Mother will want to contribute. It would keep her occupied and her mind off, well, you know . . .'

I smile wryly.

'Alex, we'll never be ready. It's too short a time. I struggled to plan everything when I had five or six months, let alone less than five weeks.'

'We'll do it,' Alex says. 'Stop looking at me as if I'm mad. I know I've been useless recently.'

'With good reason,' I cut in.

'Maybe. Losing my father was a massive blow. I didn't know how to deal with it. I'm back on track now though. I'll still have dark moments when I feel like I'm in a tunnel with no end in sight . . .' He clears his throat. 'We didn't always get on. In fact, there were many times . . . Oh, it doesn't matter now.' Alex sits up and shifts around to embrace me. 'What does matter is . . . you, me and George . . . and the wedding.' He kisses me on the tip of my nose, and fresh flames flare from the fireplace. 'I love you, Maz.'

'I love you too . . .'

What is the first thing I do? I call Emma the next morning to let her know that Alex and I are back on track and the wedding is on. After that, I call the vicar to re-book the church – which isn't a problem – and Elsa at the Barnscote to talk about the reception – which is. I contact Clive.

'Clive, I have a favour to ask.'

'Go ahead,' he says.

'I'm planning a wedding. It's back on.'

'That's great. I couldn't understand why it was off in the first place. You two are made for each other. Congratulations.'

'Thanks, Clive. Anyway, we were going to have the reception at the Barnscote, but it's too close to Christmas and they're fully booked. And then I remembered that Izzy and Chris held their reception at the Talymill Inn.'

'Yes, we don't normally do wedding receptions. They're all right in the summer when you can put a gazebo up on the lawn, but in winter, the venue is – well, snug,' Clive says. 'I suppose what I'm saying in a rather long-winded way, Maz, is that yes, we'd love to host your reception, but it depends on how many guests you're expecting.'

I give him a rough idea of numbers.

'I think we could squeeze them in, if we used the bar and the dining room. And, if push comes to shove, there's always our living area. We could tidy that up a bit.'

'I don't want to make life difficult for you, Clive. What about Edie? Will she be happy with that arrangement?'

'Ah, Edie isn't at home,' Clive says. 'She's visiting her sister, back in East London. She's going to be staying there for a while.'

'Oh, dear.'

'I'm missing her, but it's good news. When Cassie was put down, she hit the bottle with a vengeance. A couple of days later, she was admitted to hospital, they ran some blood tests and told her, if she carried on as she was, she'd be dead within a year or so.' I hear him sigh ruefully. 'I kept telling her that, but she wouldn't listen to me. Anyway, she's gone to spend some time with her sister where there's no bar, and no vodka to tempt her. She's going to AA up there, and having help with her addiction.'

'How long will she be away?'

'I couldn't tell you. What I do know is, I'm going to have to make a decision about the pub, because Edie can't live here as a recovering alcoholic.'

'So you're going to quit? Will you go back to London?'

'I don't know yet,' Clive says. 'I don't want to. I love it down here. I love the pace of life, the countryside, the people . . .' His voice trails off. 'I've got to go. Would you like to drop in sometime and let me know exactly what you want for the reception in the way of food and drinks? We'll have the Christmas decorations up by then. There'll be a tree, lights and candles. The pub always looks at its best at that time of year.'

I'm happy that I've got the reception booked, but I'll miss Clive, should he decide to return to London. I recall the stress of having to see forty patients all before lunchtime, the constant traffic snarl-ups, and the throngs of grey commuters, chasing the clock. It isn't what I'd choose.

I'm getting married now and settling down. Talyton St George has turned out to be my forever, happily-ever-after home. I couldn't go back.

Chapter Twenty

It's Me or a Dog

Alex and I employ a professional company to clear out the surgery, decorate and refit it. It takes a couple of weeks, that's all. Alex is keeping it minimalist, because he has plans to convert one of the modern barns.

He has several applications for the post of assistant, and interviews three potential new vets. I meet all three. The woman he offers the job to turns it down because she has a better offer at a practice elsewhere that has more toys to play with, as she puts it. Alex is quite put out, but it means that he employs the person I preferred.

'He's perfect, Alex,' I tell him over breakfast, when Alex is fretting over whether he's chosen the right vet.

'He has an earring,' Alex says, getting up to put his cereal bowl in the dishwasher. 'I'm not sure my clients are ready for that.'

'Oh, don't be silly. There'll be a few of the old guard who are suspicious of him, and the women of Talyton St George could feel a tad let down if he does turn out to be gay.'

'What makes you think he's gay?'

'The way he acts. He seems quite camp.'

Alex rests one arm around the back of my neck. 'I don't care,' he chuckles. 'As long as he knows his lungworm from his lumpy jaw, and he's organised, confident and can use both a sat nav and a map, I'll be happy. I have to admit, I've been back through the other applications and this one, he's like cream, he keeps floating up to the top.'

'Those things matter, but the most important criterion is, will you get on with him? You have to work together. You have to be able to disagree without falling out completely.'

'Like in a marriage, you mean?' Alex smiles again. 'Is there anything else I'm supposed to have done?'

'Your suit. You said you were going to buy a new one. And I'd really appreciate it if you picked up the presents for the bridesmaids and pages.' Amused by his expression of alarm at the thought of having to choose something suitable for Emma, I go on, 'It's all right. I've made a list. All you have to do is take it into the shops – I've even written down which ones.'

'Thanks, Maz. I'd better be off. Kiss?'

I turn my head and kiss him on the lips.

'See you later,' Alex says. 'Have fun with George.'

It's my day off, but George has been up with the lark at five thirty. Will and Emma are working together, Will on ops, visits and evening surgery, and Emma on minimal consulting and admin, because she wants to postpone going on maternity leave for as long as possible. That's the plan, but at eight thirty, not long after Alex has gone, I receive a call from Emma.

'Maz, don't worry, everything's fine. I'm at the hospital for a few tests which means Will's on his own at the practice. I know you have George, but is there any way—?'

'I'll get down there as soon as I can. Em, when you say you're fine, what do you mean? Fine as in perfectly well, thank you, or fine as in not great really, but I don't want to worry anyone?'

'Let's say I'm a little under the weather,' Emma says after a telling pause. 'My blood pressure's up and my ankles are slightly swollen. I look as if I have cankles.' She's trying to make light of it, but I can tell she's concerned. I'm apprehensive for her too. I hope the babies are okay. 'Ben says I've got signs of pre-eclampsia.'

'Oh?' That isn't so good, is it, I think?

'If it is, it means monitoring and rest.' Emma's tone lightens. 'I could do with an excuse for a break – I feel heavy and slow, like a walrus out of water.'

'You can have a break any time,' I say. 'You don't have to come in to work. You know that.'

'I do, but I'd get bored at home. There are only so many times you can rearrange the furniture in the nursery.'

'Well, if there's anything else I can do . . . If you have to stay in, I can take Miff off Ben's hands.'

'Thanks, Maz.'

'All the best, Em. I'll be thinking about you, so make sure you let me know immediately you have any news.'

'Maz, this doesn't mean I won't be able to help with the last of your wedding preparations. I can make calls to chase up Jennie about the cake, as long as you're happy about the cupcake idea.'

'Yes. Yes, I am.' I wouldn't be able to look at a traditional wedding cake without thinking of Old Fox-Gifford and that would make me sad.

'And I can have a word with the guy at the garage about hiring the cars.'

'Thanks, Em. I really must go now. Call me later.'

I tip Ginge out of the buggy where he's been curled up sleeping. He's looking well – his coat is glossy and he's put on some weight. I'm optimistic that he's going to make a few more months yet.

'Cat's gone now, George,' I say. 'You can have your buggy back.'

'Cat. Gone,' he repeats. There are no discussions about sitting in the buggy today. It's George's buggy, and he doesn't want Ginge getting back in it.

Having strapped George in, I take him out into the yard to find Sophia who intercepts us, coming out of the tack room at the end of the row of stables with Liberty's purple hoodie in her arms. Yes, I know it's hard to believe but Alex's horse wears an insulated rug with a hoodie during the winter.

'George, Humpy's here,' Sophia calls. She bends down stiffly to greet him before looking up at me. 'Aren't you going to Toddler Group this morning?'

'Emma's having a few tests at the hospital today, so I've got to go into work, which means –' I hesitate. It's a bit of a cheek, isn't it? 'I could try asking Flick at the nursery . . .'

'You'd like me to have the boy for the day.' Sophia's eyes light up with pleasure. 'I'd love to, as long as you don't mind me taking him out and about. The farrier's coming this morning, and I'm taking Lucie's pony, Tinky, to see the physio this afternoon.'

I smile to myself as I thank her. Tinky Winky gets his

own physiotherapist, whereas Sophia, who's clearly in more need of one than the pony, doesn't. Sophia goes around the stables in long thermal yard boots stuck over with duct tape, while the horses have new shoes every seven or eight weeks. That's typical Fox-Gifford logic for you.

'Is Emma all right?' Sophia asks.

'She says she's fine, but I'm not sure. We'll know more later. Sophia,' I say, a thought occurring to me. 'I'm redoing the invitations for the wedding, and I wondered if you would prefer it if I didn't invite Fifi. I know you had a bit of a falling-out and you told her she wasn't welcome at the manor any more.' I'm trying to be tactful out of respect for Sophia's feelings.

She looks at me, and for a moment I wonder if I've offended her by even suggesting that Fifi should be invited.

'I didn't want her causing a scene,' I go on.

'Invite her,' says Sophia. 'What's done is done, and I don't want people to have to start choosing sides. No, Maz, Fox-Gifford was right about one thing. You should keep your friends close, and your enemies closer.'

I leave George in the buggy, watching her, worrying he'll get kicked by a horse, and worse, that Sophia will decide he's ready to ride one.

'I thought we'd have liver and onions later – they're your favourite, George.'

'I've packed him some lunch,' I say, thinking of the cheese and wholemeal sandwich, carrot and hummus, that will end up languishing in the box.

'It'll save you cooking him a dinner tonight, Maz,' says Sophia, knowing that I can't argue with that. At the moment, our fridge contains a bar of chocolate and a few of those pots of good bacteria that have been there so long that they've turned bad.

'Sophia, how would I manage without you?'

'I like looking after George. He's my ray of sunshine. He reminds me more of his grandad every day.'

I let that one go. I drive to work, with the radio on, catching my breath as I wonder what to expect. Some of the clients are bound to be Emma specials, as I call them.

I am pleasantly surprised though. Bridget brings Daisy in for a check-up.

'She's looking great,' I say, when we're encouraging Daisy to walk onto the scales. 'And so are you, Bridget.'

'I've lost over a stone.' She rests her hand on one hip to show off her figure. She's no longer wearing her baggy Petals sweatshirt, but a slim-fitting layered look. 'I'm on a very low dose of insulin now, and I feel fantastic.'

'You'll have to do the diet and exercise DVD,' I say lightly.

'I could do one for dog owners: how you and your pet can lose weight, the fun way.' She smiles. 'There are two flaws here. One is that I haven't got any "before" photos because I couldn't bear to see pictures of myself in that state. You knew I was in denial, didn't you, Maz? Two,' she goes on, 'it wasn't exactly fun getting to this stage. I miss my chocolate fix, and I am no more fond of exercise than I was before.'

'So, no DVD then,' I say, grinning.

'I think not.' Bridget looks at the display on the scales. 'I forgot to check with you where you want the flowers delivered and at what time? I'm happy to drop the bouquet and posies to the church on my way to set up the arrangements at the reception.'

'That would be wonderful, Bridget. It would mean I have one less thing to worry about on the day.'

'Are you nervous?'

'A little,' I admit, turning my attention back to the patient. 'Daisy weighs exactly the same as she did the last time.' I note it down in her diabetes chart. 'That's brilliant. Now she's lost the weight, she needs to maintain it.'

I take her through to the consulting room to give her a thorough check-up, then when I've finished, I kiss the wrinkle on the top of her head. Daisy turns and licks me on the face. She's happy. I'm happy. Her diabetes is under control, she isn't panting or struggling to move, and she smells so much sweeter now her skin infection has cleared.

The next appointment is Allie Jackson. I haven't seen her for a while, not since Harry the hamster met his demise. I check her information on the monitor when I call her up from the waiting list, but Frances has not inputted the animal's details yet.

Frances has been what I'd describe as a bit dippy recently, as if she has other, more important, concerns on her mind. I suspect they have something to do with her burgeoning romance with Lenny. Shannon helped her choose a mobile phone the other day, and she's been teaching her how to text during their breaks. I can't imagine how they're getting on – by her own admission, Frances has always been technophobic. She used to stab the computer keyboard with the end of a pen because she was scared of it.

Back to Allie though. It crosses my mind that she could be here to ask me to health-check a couple of stick insects, or a gecko, but when I call her through, she's carrying the tiniest blond puppy with the biggest brown eyes.

'All right, Maz. I know what I said,' Allie says, her voice high with excitement. 'But I saw these chihuahuas advertised in the *Chronicle* – I couldn't resist. Meet Blondie.' She places the puppy on the table. Blondie is wearing a pink harness and lead. Allie is looking smart too, and younger somehow. Instead of her usual sweaty work suit, she's wearing a cool, acid green mac and cream trousers.

I scratch my forehead. 'I thought you wanted something you couldn't grow fond of? That's adorable.'

'She is cute, isn't she?' Allie hesitates. 'I swapped the husband for her.'

'I'm sorry?'

'He hated Harry, and when I said I was having a dog, he told me I couldn't. If I brought one into the house, he would walk out.' She smiles wryly. 'I called his bluff.'

'Are you and the children going to be all right?' I ask.

'It will be tough. I'm under no illusion, but I'm glad I stood my ground this time. It was a case of "It's me or a dog". The dog won out.'

It seems strange to me, wishing Allie well for the end of her marriage, when I am about to embark on married life. I return the conversation to Blondie.

'She's nine weeks old and she's had her first vaccination at the breeder's,' says Allie. 'I just wanted you to check her over. And I was worried about her diet – I'm not sure I'm feeding her the right food. And she has a sore on her back – it's very small, but I wondered if it could be infected.'

Allie's relationship with Blondie is going to be just

the same as her relationship with Harry: obsessive and overly fond. Blondie will want for nothing. I smile to myself as I run my fingers through her silken coat. I hesitate, part the hair and catch one of the black-brown creatures that are whizzing about across Blondie's pale skin, between my thumb and fingernail.

'Here's the cause of the sore on her back,' I say, showing Allie. 'Blondie has fleas. Don't worry,' I add quickly as Allie opens her mouth, 'we can get rid of them and they won't have caused any lasting harm.'

'Oh, my poor little puppy-dog,' Allie wails. 'No wonder you've been itchy-witchy.'

I treat Blondie for fleas and book her in for a second vaccination and Izzy's next series of Puppy Parties.

'Allie, I don't know if you can help,' I say before she leaves the consulting room.

'Try me,' she says.

'I'm trying to find a wedding photographer for the third Saturday in December. It's proving impossible. Does the *Chronicle* have any freelance contacts who might be willing to do it? I don't want any action pictures, like the one of me hanging from that cliff . . . I'm not asking for perfection either.'

'There's Simon,' she says. 'I can give you his number.'

'Thanks. I hope he can do it. I'm running out of time.'

When Allie has gone, and I've seen the rest of the appointments, I call Allie's contact. At first, he thinks he's already booked for another event, but on checking his diary, he finds that he's free. Result! The more I get done from the list, the more I look forward to the wedding. I can hardly wait.

I catch up with Will towards the end of the afternoon. He asks me to help him with a post-mortem on a young cat that died unexpectedly.

'I thought you should do it, Maz, otherwise the client will think I'm hiding something,' he says. He looks exhausted.

'Of course I can. Will, are you all right? It happens, you know, you can't save them all,' I continue when he doesn't respond. 'Sometimes it's impossible not to become emotionally involved.'

'I'm not,' he says curtly. 'It's more . . . well, I feel as if I've let everyone down.'

I think we're talking about the same thing, but if Will finds it easier to define his reaction as feelings rather than emotions, I shan't argue the point. I follow him out to Kennels where Izzy's laid the cat out on the prep bench ready for one of us to open it up.

'It was a young cat,' Will says, as we throw on gowns, gloves and aprons. 'I didn't expect it to die. I can't believe I didn't spot something was wrong when it came in for a vaccination the day before.'

'Cats are good at hiding the fact that they're ill.'

'I did a full clinical exam. I checked the pulse, listened to the chest, nothing.'

Apart from the obvious, that it's lifeless, there isn't anything externally that suggests what might have gone wrong, so I open the cat's chest and belly, parting the skin and muscle and snipping through the ribs. The lungs are filled with fluid and the heart is three times the size it should be. I point it out to Will.

'So it's heart failure, damage to the muscle,' he says.

'Sadly, yes.' I check for any other possible cause of death before I start to close up the chest and belly. It's pretty soul-destroying having to sew up a dead patient, but it has to be done because the client wants the body back to bury at home.

'I'll do it,' Will offers.

'I'm nearly there now.'

'I can't just stand here. I feel I need to be doing something.'

'I know. Would it help if I talked to the client? I can give them the outcome of the PM.'

'Maz —' Will looks at me abjectly — 'I don't think this is right for me. I'm not in the right job.'

'You mean you want to move on to another practice already?' I say, shocked and a little hurt that he doesn't feel as if he's settled well into our team. 'If you want to change your shifts, or if you'd be happier living out, rather than over the shop, so to speak, I'm sure we can make some changes that would suit you better. You should have said something before.' I didn't think I made a bad boss. I thought I was fairly approachable at least.

'I mean, I don't want to be a vet. I got it wrong. I can't do this any more.'

For a moment, I think he's going to burst into tears. Izzy moves in to wrap the cat in a towel and pop it into its carrier, before she leaves us.

'It's happened to us all. It's the pressure of the work, the unpredictability, the irregular hours, the sad times. You're stressed out. You need a few days off, that's all.'

Will shakes his head. 'For me, it's mainly the frustration of not being able to do the job properly.'

'When clients can't afford the best treatment, you mean,' I cut in. 'What we believe to be the correct approach to a case isn't always the right one for them.' I'm thinking of a dog that we had on chemotherapy for a while – the drugs prolonged his life, but also extended his suffering. 'Welcome to the real world, Will. You have to do your best within the constraints. It's the way it is.' I look on the bright side. 'The clients like you.'

'Do they?' he retorts glumly. 'It doesn't feel like it. Mrs Dyer hates me.'

'Mrs Dyer is one client out of hundreds, and she has good reason to be funny about male vets. What about Mr Brown and Pippin? And Clive.'

'Each time Mr Brown comes in, I dish out Pippin's steroids while he's going on about how wonderful homeopathy is. Clive's a good guy, but I feel obliged to gush and create an illusion of fondness for Persian cats, or rather their crosses since Cassie's gone.'

'Clive isn't like that. He's quite straight,' I say, smiling. 'It's all part of the art of veterinary medicine. It's all very well knowing the science, but the greatest asset is the art of handling people.'

'It doesn't feel right. It's rather false. Oh, I don't know,' he sighs. 'I don't know what to do.'

'Sleep on it.'

'I can't. I'm on call. I can't sleep when I'm on call.'

'I'll do it then. Take tomorrow off, have a lie-in, go for a walk by the sea, put everything in perspective.'

'Thanks, Maz, but no thanks. You're already having to cover for Emma on your day off. I'll soldier on.'

'Are you sure?'

'I'm sure,' Will says.

'If you weren't a vet, what would you do instead anyway?' I ask him.

'Go and work in the City? Get an internship at a referral centre. Go back to uni and do a PhD.'

'Will, you have to do whatever makes you happy.

As long as you don't leave Otter House before the middle of January – I'd like to be able to enjoy my honeymoon.'

'Oh, I'll give you notice. I wouldn't leave you in the lurch,' Will says. 'How do you stick it, Maz?'

'I love my job and having George has made me change my priorities. My career is no longer the be-all and end-all. I like our clients, most of them anyway.' I spray the prep bench with disinfectant and wipe it down. 'Ultimately, the good bits outweigh the bad.'

'Maz, Lynsey's on her way,' Frances interrupts. 'Raffles is sick. He's vomiting blood. I didn't think it should wait.'

'Thanks, Frances. Will, would you see her, please? I've got to pick George up from nursery before I meet Clive to go through last-minute details for the reception. I don't want Flick and her staff locking the door on me like they did last week. I'm beginning to worry that he'll be taken off the register, and have nowhere to go.'

Much later, when I'm sprawled on the sofa, cuddled up with George because I'm too exhausted to put him to bed, Alex turns up.

'How was your day?' I ask him. 'How was the new boy? Justin?'

'He overslept and turned up just in time, so to speak. He had a few drinks with Stewart last night.'

I'm not surprised. He's staying at the farm with the Pitts until he finds more permanent accommodation.

'And then he struggled to get blood out of a cow, which is pretty impressive considering the size of their veins,' Alex goes on. 'Eventually, he settled down and got on with it. I sent him over to Guy's while I went over to Robert's.' Alex grabs a glass of wine from the bottle in the fridge. 'You know, I could get used to this. Do you want one?'

'Please . . . A small one, though. Will's on duty tonight.'

'How did it go with Clive?' Alex asks.

'I never thought I'd hear myself say this, but everything's under control. I made the final choices for the food and Clive's arranged the music. The best news, though, is that Clive isn't moving back to London. He and Edie are putting the pub on the market in the New Year, and buying a new business. He says he isn't ready to retire just yet.'

'How is Edie?'

'It's early days, but apparently she's determined to beat her addiction because she wants to be around for Cassie's kittens – and Clive, presumably. Clive seemed pretty optimistic, but he says she'll have to stay with her sister until the pub's sold.' I admire Clive's loyalty, I muse, thinking of the vows Alex and I will soon be making: in sickness and in health.

While Alex is dishing up some casserole from the slow-cooker, Emma calls me. She's been admitted to hospital for a couple more days.

'They're a bit like Will. They're doing every test possible. I wouldn't be surprised if they carry me off on a trolley for a brain scan. Mind you, I am going mad cooped up in here.'

'I'll come and visit,' I offer.

'Tomorrow, maybe. Ben's here now. You need to concentrate on those wedding plans. Just call me now and again.'

As soon as I put the phone down, Lynsey gets in touch.

'Hello, Maz. How are the wedding arrangements going?'

'I feel much better, having booked the reception. I thought I'd never find anywhere this close to Christmas.'

'Is there anything I can do?'

'I'll let you know . . .' George tries to swipe the phone from me. 'No, George.' I kneel up on the sofa so that George, even at full stretch, cannot quite reach it.

'To be honest, I rang because I wanted to talk to you about Raffles. Will's admitted him as an inpatient, and I'm really worried.'

'I'm sure you are,' I say, 'but he's in the best place.'

'You couldn't – I know this is a bit cheeky –' Lynsey rephrases her request. 'Would you have a word with him?'

'Because?' I wonder how to respond. Lynsey's a friend as well as a client, so I'm happy to do her a favour, but it seems disrespectful to Will, as if I don't value his judgement. 'You want me to check up on him.'

'Well, yes. He hasn't had much experience, and he admitted he didn't have a clue what's wrong with Raffles. You can see why I'm concerned. In fact, I'm worried sick.'

'Why don't you call him direct?' I suggest. 'He won't mind. He's on duty. He can give you an update on how Raffles is getting on.'

'Oh, I don't know . . .'

'Lynsey, Will is a professional. He's done five years' training to do this job. He'll let me know if he needs support.'

'Are you sure?' she says doubtfully.

'Absolutely. Trust me, Lynsey, I'm a vet.'

I confess my thoughts do turn to Raffles a couple of times during the night, and it is a relief when, arriving at the practice the next morning, I find him alive. I would never admit that to Lynsey or Will, though.

Will is in Isolation with Raffles, the area under the stairs where we keep patients that might be a source of infection away from the others.

'What's up?' I ask, scanning the inpatient details on the record card pinned to the front of the cage: 'Raffles Pitt. Barton Farm. Heinz 57. Male. Entire. About four years old. Collapsed.'

'I don't know, Maz. I told you I was bloody useless.'

'Hey, stop that. Did you have a bad night?'

'I was called out four times, and then I couldn't sleep because I was worrying about this little chap.' Will hangs his stethoscope around his neck. 'I admitted him because he had tummy ache. He's been vomiting blood, he's restless, and now he's started panting and his muscles are twitching. His heart rate is so fast, I can barely count it.

'He's dehydrated, but why? It's a mystery to me. He's been vaccinated – it's in his notes that you did it.' Will scratches his head like a dog with lice. 'He was a healthy young dog. I don't understand it. Is it a virus, something he's eaten or some obscure metabolic disorder?'

'I wouldn't jump straight for the metabolic thingy,' I say. 'Let's go with first principles. What do you suggest you do next?'

'I've taken some blood – Izzy's putting it through the machine right now. I've got him on a second drip, given him some antibiotics as cover in case there's an infection there, drugs to stop him throwing up and I'm debating giving him something to slow his heart. What do you think?'

'I think you can forget about possible side effects and go ahead. If we don't know what's going on, we'll have to treat the symptoms as they arise. Will, that's all we can do. Let me know as soon as the bloods come through. I can call Lynsey if you like – she's a good friend of mine.'

'No pressure then,' Will says, anguished.

'You've done a good job so far. I wouldn't have done anything differently.'

Will is frustrated because he doesn't know what's wrong with Raffles, but he's going to have to learn to accept that you can't know everything.

'Lynsey won't think any less of you. We treat lots of patients that get better without us ever having a clue why they were sick in the first place. It's life, Will. It's a vet's life.'

As soon as the results of the bloods come through, I call Lynsey and ask her to come and see Raffles. There's usually a recognisable pattern of changes in the blood that suggests one condition over another, but Raffles's results are baffling. What's more, his health is declining, and I would hate for Lynsey and her family not to have the chance to say goodbye . . .

Raffles is very quiet – in human terms he looks as if he has a headache. He has a long body, short bowed legs, a curly tail and a wavy strawberry blond coat, an altogether comical appearance, as if he's several different dogs put together. I remember him with a smile on his face, muscular and energetic, but not now.

Lynsey comes in with Sam, her oldest boy who's

about twelve now. He's wearing a hoodie, jeans and wellies. Blond-haired and tall for his age, he walks in holding a squeaky ball.

'It's Raffles's favourite toy.' He hands it to me. 'Can he have it in hospital to remind him of home?'

'Of course.' I show them through to Isolation where Will and Izzy are changing the bag on the drip.

'I've given him some diazepam,' says Will.

I don't have to ask what it was for. Raffles must have had a fit, not a good sign. I decide to go into that with Lynsey later. First of all, we need to try to find out why Raffles is sick so we can target his treatment.

I start at the beginning, following the maxim that common things occur commonly.

'Does he eat out?' I ask.

'He is a bit of a scavenger. He'll eat anything.'

'He stole the butter off of the table.'

'Does Stewart put rat poison down on the farm?'

'No, we don't. Not with the other animals, and the children. Do you think he's been poisoned?'

'It's a strong possibility.' It would help to know what he's eaten, then we could give him the antidote, if there is one, but it isn't going to be that easy.

'I've been thinking,' says Will, joining in, 'what about chocolate toxicity? Could Raffles have had access to chocolate?'

'We do have chocolate at home, but I can't imagine Raffles could have got hold of it,' Lynsey says, half smiling. 'The kids wouldn't have let him, would you, Sam?'

Sam looks down at his wellies.

'Sam?'

'Mum, I didn't mean to,' he mumbles.

'Sam, look at me.' Lynsey lifts his chin. 'Please tell us

what Raffles ate. Maz and Will won't be able to save him otherwise.'

'You know the tree chocolates you bought . . .' Sam's eyes are filled with tears.

'The ones I hid on top of the dresser for Christmas?' Sam nods.

'I took them, Mum,' he confesses miserably. 'I left them on the floor and Raffles snaffled them up.'

'Oh, Sam,' Lynsey wails. 'How could you?'

'I didn't know. I didn't know they would hurt him, did I?' He looks towards Raffles. 'He's very still – is he dead already?'

'No,' I say. 'He's on some medicine to keep him asleep.'

'He's going to die, isn't he, and it's all my fault?'

'Sh,' says Lynsey, putting her arms around Sam's shoulders. 'Let's not go blaming anyone. It's one of those things. C'est la vie.'

'Can we bury him next to Cads?'

'Sam, that's enough. I can't bear to see him like this, but Raffles isn't going to give up yet. Do what you can for him,' Lynsey says, choking up.

'We'll do our best,' I say, trying not to choke up myself.

The Pitts lost a dog, Cadbury, a chocolate Lab, ironically enough, and I can't blame them for being afraid they're about to lose another one.

Suddenly, Will sees that having the precise diagnosis isn't the holy grail of veterinary medicine, because, although there's the personal satisfaction of making the link between the dog's symptoms and him snaffling the tree chocolates in advance of Christmas, it isn't going to make any difference to Raffles. It's too late to flush out his stomach, there's no antidote, and judging by the amount he's eaten, it's still touch and go. Some of them make it. Some don't.

Towards the end of the week, I'm first in to the practice – because I've left George with Sophia for the day. I switch on the lights and monitors on my way through the practice, grabbing a clean scrub top from the pile in the laundry, on my way into Kennels.

As I round the corner past the prep bench, I catch sight of a pair of bare feet sticking out across the floor in front of the bank of cages.

'Will?' I dart across to where our assistant is lying down, his head on a rolled-up Vetbed and his torso wrapped in a duvet. 'Will, are you all right?'

He groans and rolls over, sending an empty mug clattering across the floor. Raffles, who's in the cage above him, having been moved out of Isolation, whines. I notice that he's thrown up again, not a good sign.

'Will?' I lean down and give him a gentle shake. 'It's eight o'clock.'

He utters another groan and opens his eyes, squinting in the daylight. Suddenly, he sits up.

'What the –' he mutters thickly. 'I came down to sit with the dog. I must have fallen asleep. What a prat!' He staggers up, keeping the duvet tight around his body, and failing to conceal his knobbly knees and skinny calves. 'You must think I'm a complete idiot. You won't mention this to the others, will you?'

'No one will know if you hurry up and get yourself upstairs. Izzy will be here any minute.'

'Thanks, Maz.'

'If you want to know what I think,' I call after him as he makes a quick exit, 'it shows great devotion to duty,

Will. I'm impressed.' I lean down and pick up the paperwork he's left – he's made a graph of Raffles's heart rate over time, and notes for a case report of theobromine toxicity. I smile to myself. I used to consider myself completely devoted to my work, but Will has taken it one stage further.

I read through Will's notes and look at Raffles, who is about the same.

'Oh, Raffles.' I ruffle his coat. He groans and rolls his uppermost eye. 'Stupid dog,' I tell him fondly. 'You've been through enough. Don't give up.'

I call Lynsey.

'How is he now?' she asks.

'About the same, I'm afraid.' I give Lynsey time for the implication of that statement to sink in.

'How long do we let him go on suffering?' Her voice sounds unusually small.

'I don't like the idea of giving up just yet. Why don't we reassess the situation at the end of the day? I'll take some more blood. If there's no improvement, then . . .'

'I'll have him put down,' Lynsey says. 'There's nothing else you can do, is there?'

'All we can do is continue giving him supportive treatment. It's up to Raffles now.'

'Thanks, Maz. I'll call later.'

I cut the call and give Raffles another dose of antibiotic before I join Izzy and Frances in Reception. Frances is reorganising the display of dog and cat toys to incorporate the Christmas range. I notice how she makes herself start every now and then, squeezing the squeaky plastic crackers and puddings by mistake. Izzy is on a chair, putting up loops of tinsel and foil bells. The Christmas tree, a real one from the farm she shares with Chris, lies on its side on top of the scales.

'Um, health and safety, Izzy,' I observe. 'Emma will have a fit if she sees you on that chair.'

'I'll be fine. I've done this for years, before I came here. I've always been in charge of decorating the practice.' She grins down at me. 'I love Christmas.'

'Could you at least move the tree before one of our clients falls over it?'

'Give me five minutes. Maz, look in the box. There's a snowman.'

I peer into the cardboard box that's overflowing with beads and baubles. There's the ugliest snowman I've ever seen with blue eyes and red lips, about as tall as Daisy the Bulldog, and much broader.

'It sings and dances on the spot,' Izzy says happily.

'Where did you get that from?' I ask.

'The garden centre. Fifi gave me a discount.'

'I'm not surprised. It's hideous.'

'I'm going to put it on the top of the filing cabinet. Frances, you'll have to find another home for some of the cards. Alternatively, I can string them up and hang them down the wall.'

I leave Izzy to it. She wants to put the decorations up earlier every year, and at this rate, it won't be long before she's putting them up in June.

At the end of the day, filled with trepidation, I take another look at Raffles. Will is there with him, adding notes to the draft of his case report.

'How is he?' I ask.

'There are definite signs of improvement.' Will hugs his paperwork to his chest. 'It's all good.'

'Why are you so intent on writing this up when you're planning to leave the profession?' I challenge him. He's been very quiet about his intentions since our chat about his frustrations with the job.

361

'Ah, I've had time to think,' he says, smiling wryly. 'You were right – I was tired and at a low point, but Raffles has shown me that I'm not completely useless and that I can make a difference.'

'That's fantastic, Will. I thought you might be about to quit without giving yourself a chance.' To be honest, in spite of his assurance that he'd give us notice, I was afraid he might crack up and walk out on us before the wedding. 'You know, I wouldn't want anyone else as our assistant. You're an asset to the practice.'

Blushing, Will thanks me. 'I'll go and type this up – unless you need me for anything else.'

'No, I can finish off here. You go.' I'm confident now that he'll cope with running the practice single-handed while Emma and I are off work; I decide this while watching him stride out through the double doors into the corridor before I turn my attention back to Raffles.

Izzy has left the radio on in Kennels. Slade is playing 'Merry Christmas Everybody', and as Raffles lies there, wagging the tip of his tail, I think, just maybe, it will be a very merry Christmas, after all.

Chapter Twenty-one

Something Blue

'It's to thank you and the team at Otter House for saving Raffles's life,' says Lynsey, when she drops in with fruit cake on the Friday afternoon before the wedding. Raffles went home on Monday. In the end, he was in with us for two weeks. 'We didn't think chocolate would be appropriate. What are you doing at work anyway, Maz? It's your wedding day tomorrow.'

'I've got some last-minute sorting out to do.'

'When I got married, I was panicking right up to the last moment.'

'I am panicking – inwardly – but I figure that if I've missed anything, it's too late to do anything about it now.'

'Well, I'm glad you're all so dedicated. We're over the moon that Raffles is home. I didn't realise how much I'd miss him.' Lynsey touches the corner of her eye. 'I love him like he's one of the children. Silly, isn't it? Stewart thinks I'm soft in the head.'

Stewart's wrong, I think. Lynsey is one of those

people who's soft in the heart, friendly and generous to a fault.

'I hope Will's staying,' she goes on. 'He's a gem.'

'We're very lucky to have him,' I agree.

'I hope Alex's new assistant is half as good.'

'He'll have to be twice as good to get the approval of the farming community,' I point out lightly. 'I'll bet they test him out. There'll be a few jokes at his expense, I'm sure.'

'He seems . . . charming.' Lynsey checks her watch. 'I must get going soon. How is George?'

'He's fine, thanks. He's at nursery today.'

'Is he looking forward to the wedding?'

I smile at the memory of Alex picking George out of the cot when the alarm went off today, swinging him around, and singing, 'Mummy's getting married in the morning.' George was chuckling, while my heart melted at the sight of my two boys together.

'George knows he's going to dress up and walk behind me with Emma, Lucie and Seb, but he doesn't really understand why. I hope he doesn't decide to say no and sit on his bottom halfway down the aisle. I wouldn't put it past him.'

'You've watched too many Wedding Day Disaster programmes,' Lynsey says.

'I haven't watched any,' I smile. 'It's my overactive imagination.'

'Oh, everyone has last-minute nerves. It's perfectly normal.'

'I wonder if Alex is feeling the same.'

'I expect so. He has more to be nervous about than you. Stewart's spent the last few days writing his speech.'

Stewart is best man. Tact is not his strongest point.

'It's all right, Maz. I've told him to tone it down, or else he'll have me to deal with.'

A scary thought. I imagine Lynsey is a formidable woman when roused. I remember her ire when she gave birth in the practice, having discovered that her husband had been having an affair. Yes, really. It's a long story.

'The forecast is for snow here tomorrow.'

'Snow! Really?' I feel like a child again, filled with excitement at the thought of snowmen and snowballs, and, best of all, snow swirling down from the sky like Nature's confetti for my wedding.

'Light snow, but it rarely settles here in Talyton. I can't recall a white Christmas and I've lived here all my life.' Lynsey checks her watch again, and I think, I really must be getting on too. 'Have you heard about the weather further north? It's been on the news.'

'I haven't been paying much attention recently,' I have to admit. 'I've been too busy.'

'It was on this morning. There have been several inches of snow in the Midlands – the motorway's closed at Bristol.'

'Izzy did mention a weather warning this morning, but I didn't take any notice,' I say, remembering. 'I hope all our guests can make it.' Most of them are local, but a few, including my mother, are travelling longer distances. 'I guess this means the Pony Club Mounted Games will be cancelled. Sophia was still planning to drive Lucie and the pony there after the wedding tomorrow, so they were ready for the competition on Sunday.'

'Every cloud has a silver lining,' Lynsey says. 'Alex told Stewart he wasn't happy about it. Won't Lucie be disappointed?'

'A little, I suspect, but she didn't want to miss out on the reception.'

'Where's Emma?' Lynsey begins again. 'I haven't seen her for a while.'

'She's taking it easy, I hope. Doctor's orders – proper ones from the consultant at the hospital, not Ben's. The babies are due in three weeks' time, or thereabouts.'

Lynsey checks her watch for a third time. Her eyebrows fly up, disappearing under her windswept hair.

'I have to dash. I was meant to collect the boys from school five minutes ago. I'll be hauled into the head's office for another talking to. See you tomorrow, Maz.'

'Tomorrow . . .' I echo, as she leaves. I feel sick with anticipation and the proverbial nerves. What have I forgotten? Will the organist stay out of the pub? Will the cupcakes arrive at the venue in one piece? I dismiss my worries. They are ridiculous. This is between me and Alex, a public celebration and confirmation of our love for each other. As for the rest, they're merely the trappings of tradition, and yes, although they're lovely and special, they are trivial.

As long as the people turn up – they are what matters.

We aren't busy, so I spend time chatting with Frances in Reception.

'How long are Lucie and Sebastian staying with you?' she asks.

'Until Boxing Day. Their mother's going to take them back to London when Alex and I fly out on our honeymoon.' I pause.

'Shouldn't you be having your hair done, or something, Maz?' Frances goes on.

'It's all organised for tomorrow. Don't worry. Everything is under control. I have my planner printed off and I'm gradually ticking the boxes.' I pause, optimistic now. 'Nothing can possibly go wrong.'

'I admire you for how you've coped. There was more than one occasion when I thought this wedding wasn't going to go ahead.' Frances pulls a tissue from the sleeve and dabs at her eyes. 'Oh, I always cry at weddings . . . You and Alex. It's soooo romantic.'

'You know, I think we should close up early.' I move to the window and look outside. It's gone four and the town is beginning to close up too. The Christmas lights are on, twinkling between the lamp posts. The odd flake of snow drifts down from the leaden sky. Peter, the greengrocer, waves as he walks past, pushing his bike with an enormous turkey-shaped package perched on the handlebars. A family strolls the other way, one of the children clinging on to a Santa balloon. A gust of wind snatches it out of his hand and it flies upwards, spinning away across the roofs of the houses.

Although I feel sorry for the child, my heart soars too. By this time tomorrow, I shall be married.

'When is Will due back?' Frances asks.

'He's taking the phones from ten.'

'I can't believe you, Maz. It's the night before your wedding and you're on call.'

'Only till ten,' I say lightly, 'and it's really quiet. People are going home for the night, lighting fires and wrapping presents. The forecast is for snow. They won't want to turn out later.'

'Shannon says that Will's gone out with one of her friends.'

'Oh, it isn't serious. Shannon told me that her friend,

one of the trainee vet nurses on her course, is merely saying she has a special interest in geckos because she wants to say she's going out with a vet.'

'That's a bit mean, isn't it?' says Frances.

'Yes, but it could be a double bluff, couldn't it? This friend might not want Shannon to know how she really feels.'

'Maz, I'm sure you're making it more complicated than it is.'

'Relationships are complicated,' I say, thinking about mine and Alex's, the ups and the downs over the past few months, and now . . .

'You'd better get going. You need your beauty sleep,' says Frances.

'Thanks for that. Go on. Go and dust down your hat for tomorrow.'

'Thank you, Maz. I can't wait. I adore a good wedding. It reminds me of mine . . .' She picks up her coat. 'It'll be pretty chilly in church, and you don't want everyone to freeze to death, so don't be late, dear.'

'I don't intend to be. Now, go home, Frances. I'll lock up before I collect George.'

'Don't forget him now.'

'As if.'

Frances pauses at the door, tying a scarf around her head. 'By tomorrow night, you and Young Mr Fox-Gifford will be husband and wife.'

'Less of the young,' I say with mock sternness. 'My husband is becoming quite the old man at times.'

'As he should be. That is the way of the world.'

'Goodnight, Frances.' I start to close the door behind her, then remember. 'Oh, you didn't say. Are you bringing company tomorrow? I need to let Clive know final numbers.' I don't really. I'm being nosy. 'You are bringing Lenny?'

'No, Maz.'

'Oh, that's a shame . . .'

'Lenny will be bringing me, if you don't mind. He is a gentleman.'

'You're both very welcome.' I kiss Frances on the cheek. 'Thanks.'

'What for?' she says, surprised.

'For . . . being you,' I say. 'Goodnight.'

'Goodnight, Maz.'

I watch Frances walk to her car and drive away. I slide the top bolt across, followed by the bottom one, at which Emma's Saab comes careering up to the path leading to the entrance, the front bumper stopping just short of the planter of evergreen shrubs. Emma gets out, holding a bundle of towels to her chest. She stumbles to the door. I unlock as quickly as I can, open up and take the bundle that she presses into my arms.

'Maz, it's Miff. Help me. I think she's dying.'

My heart beating so fast that it aches, I carry the bundle through to Kennels, throw on all the lights and lay it on the prep bench. It's a dog-sized bundle, bloodstained, and panting.

'What happened?' I ask, carefully unwrapping what is left of Miff, uncertain and scared of what I'm going to find.

'I was walking her on the Green. She was attacked. A big black dog. At least, I think it was a dog. It all happened so quickly. It went for her, snapping at her chest and legs. She tried to get away, but it grabbed her by the neck and shook her. Oh, God, it was awful.' Emma presses her hand to her mouth. 'I had to hit it over the head before it would let go, then it ran off, yelping. Oh, poor Miff. Look at her eyes . . . Her colour's terrible.'

I can't disagree. It's shocking. Miff's lying on her side, gasping for air, her tongue pale and blue, her beautiful brown eyes bulging out of their sockets, reminding me of a goitrous frog. In fact, they are out of their sockets, popped out by the attacker when whatever it was picked her up by the scruff of her neck. It isn't a good look, but I'll deal with them later, if I can stabilise her. If . . .

I grab a stethoscope, the first one that comes to hand, and listen to Miff's chest, assessing the wounds over her ribcage that are leaking blood into her wiry coat at the same time. There are no breath sounds on her left lung, and much gurgling on the right.

'Shall I call Izzy?' I ask.

'No time.' Emma fetches a couple of bags of fluid from the cupboard, and rips the wrapping from a giving set, ready to set up an intravenous drip. My partner is huge now, her bump barely covered by an outsized mac. Her ankles are swollen, and her complexion pale.

'Emma,' I say, concerned, 'you shouldn't be doing this.'

'Miff's my dog, and this is an emergency and there isn't time to get anyone else.'

'All right,' I say, trying to calm her. 'Let's get on with it, but you monitor and I'll operate.' I get onto my mobile while helping Emma set up the drip. I call Alex.

'Two things. Can you pick George up from nursery and take him home to give him his tea? And will you ring the dog warden to see if they can trace that black dog, the one that's been on the loose for a while? It was on the Green not long ago – it might be a good time to catch it. I'm going to be tied up here for some time. It's Emma's dog. I haven't got time . . . I'll explain later. Thanks, darling.'

We get Miff lightly anaesthetised and tubed, and Emma takes over ventilating her, effectively breathing for her using the bag on the anaesthetic circuit, while I make an untidy job of clipping the hair away from Miff's wounds and spraying them liberally with surgical spirit. We hardly speak – we don't need to, we're so used to working together.

'How's she doing?' I ask, as I scrub up and throw a gown on.

'Not good,' Emma mutters. 'Hang in there, Miffy. Please.' A tear drops onto the drape that covers Miff's neck, and I remember how Miff is extra precious because she was Emma's mother's dog. 'Shouldn't we X-ray first?' I detect a note of self-doubt in Emma's voice.

'Better not to waste any time,' I say shortly. 'Let's see if we can stabilise her breathing first.' Because I'm thinking, if we can't, we can't ventilate her forever, although Emma will want to try, and how much brain damage will Miff have already suffered, and is it really worth going on with this? I'm fond of Miff too, though. I've looked after her several times while Emma's been away. While there's life there's hope . . .

'Maz, she's on her way out . . .' Emma's voice breaks with grief.

'Don't give up on her just yet. Keep going with that bag.' I pick up forceps and scissors and enlarge one of the wounds on Miff's chest. It doesn't look much, about the size of a dog's tooth across, but it's deep. I follow its track through the layers of muscle between the ribs, and pssst, there's the sound of air leaking out of Miff's chest and the tiniest draught. I can see Miff's uppermost lung, salmon pink in colour, collapsing away into the depths of her ribcage. Emma squeezes the bag and the lung comes up again.

'Her colour's looking better.' I glance at Miff's tongue that lolls out of her mouth, past the tube that carries the lifesaving oxygen into her windpipe. 'She's still with us.'

'In body, if not in spirit,' Emma says stiffly. She opens a pack of sterile suture material and drops it onto the instrument tray for me. I use it to close the different layers of the wound one by one, then hold my breath, listening for the pssst sound.

It doesn't come. My hopes rise ever so slightly. Emma stops squeezing the bag. Miff's chest rises, quivers and falls again, then after what seems like minutes, not seconds, rises again, falls and settles into a jerky, but constant, rhythm. Her colour, though pale, turns gradually from blue to pink. Emma glances at me. I know what she means, that this looks more promising.

'Chest drain?' I ask.

'What do you think?'

'We'd have to keep her sedated for a while. I'm not sure that's such a good idea.'

'Let's try without. We can put one in later, if we need to.'

I check the other wounds which turn out to have penetrated the skin, not the chest, and leave them open so as not to trap any infection from the other creature's teeth.

'Eyes next then, before I give those wounds a good flush,' I say, but Emma's already on the case, soaking them in warm saline. The longer they are outside the sockets, the more they swell, the more difficult they become to put back in place, and the more likely it will be that Miff loses her sight. I watch Emma trying to push the first eye back, but it won't go.

'I'll do it,' I offer, noticing how her fingers tremble as she holds the eyeball carefully in a wet swab.

'Thanks, Maz. I don't seem to be able to do it.'

'Will you grab a stool and sit down, Em? I'd feel better if you weren't on your feet.' She does as I ask, and I take over on eyeball duty. Luckily, I'm not squeamish, but it still unnerves me.

I try to push each one back into its socket, but I have no more luck than Emma did. I don't like doing it, but there's only one way to go, and that's to snip the eyelids to give more room for manoeuvre. It works and the eyes slide back in. A wave of relief washes through me. Chest sorted, and eyes back where they belong. We're getting there. I'll flush the open wounds while Miff's still asleep, then all we need to know is how Miff's brain has been affected by the trauma and what sight she has left, both of which will take some time to discover.

'So, tell me,' I begin. 'Why were you out walking on the Green in this freezing weather when it was almost dark? I thought you were supposed to be resting.'

'I've had enough of not doing anything, Maz. It's so boring all this hanging around. Miff asked for a walk, as usual, and Ben's travelling back from a seminar in Plymouth.'

'Miff could have missed a walk or two. She'll have to get used to it when the twins arrive.'

'I know, but I was feeling uncomfortable. I thought it might help.'

I hesitate. 'How uncomfortable? On a scale of one to ten,' I add, when she doesn't answer. 'Emma?'

'Don't panic, Maz. I've been having some of those practice contractions, that's all.'

'Are you sure?'

'Absolutely.' She dismisses any concerns I might have that she's about to go into labour by changing the subject. 'You should be looking forward to your wedding tomorrow. I'm sorry I've got you into this. I should have stayed at home.' She smiles wryly. 'You are ready?'

'Maybe,' I say, teasing. 'If I'm not ready, it's not for want of you and Frances and everyone else trying. I've got lists up all over the house – on the fridge, everywhere.'

'You did order some extra buttonholes from Bridget, didn't you?'

'Yes. I knew you'd be after me otherwise.'

'Someone has to be. You're a great vet, but you don't show any of the qualities of a good wedding planner.'

'I don't think I'll be changing career any time soon.'

I sew the eyelids closed over Miff's eyes so they can't pop straight back out again, and fit a lampshade collar, one of the soft ones – only the best for our patients – which will stay on for a full week while the stitches are in. It will be disorientating for Miff to wake up temporarily blind, but it's essential. By the time I've finished flushing the open wounds on Miff's chest, we must have been working on her for over three hours.

As Emma allows Miff to come round on oxygen for a few minutes, there's a gasp.

'Was that you or the dog?' I ask her.

Emma gazes back at me, eyes glittering.

'Those aren't practice contractions, Em. They're the real thing. Trust me, I know these things. I made the same mistake myself when I was going into labour with George.' I monitor the tension in Miff's jaw to assess when I can remove the tube from her windpipe. 'Have you called Ben?'

'I left a message on his voicemail.' Emma relaxes again. 'I'm okay now. Don't worry about me, Maz. Miff should have some more pain relief. What do you think would be best for her?'

'I'll get it,' I say, 'then I'll make the tea while we watch her coming round.' We can try to get hold of Ben again then, I think.

'I hope she's okay,' Emma says quietly, as I inject the painkiller.

'We haven't lost her yet. She's a tough little madam. She won't give up without a fight, and neither will I.'

'Thanks.' Emma touches my arm as I remove my gown.

'Let's take her to the staffroom.' It's against protocol, but I'd prefer Emma to be sat securely on the sofa than perched on a stool with that enormous bump stuck out in front of her. 'I'll carry her.' I hesitate. 'Are you sure you're all right?'

Emma nods, one hand touching her stomach that looks taut like an overinflated football, the other gripping the edge of the operating table.

I pick Miff up carefully. 'I'll follow you. You can do the doors.'

'What's that, Maz? Where are we going?' Emma stops, catching her breath.

'The staffroom,' I say lightly. 'Can you remember the way?'

'I'm not sure . . .'

'Come on then.' I move ahead of her and reverse into the doors so I can shove them open with my back, Miff in my arms and the bag of fluid between my teeth. Okay, that's against protocol too, and health and safety, but Emma seems distant, hardly concentrating on what I'm saying. I'm not sure if it's a delayed reaction to what's happened to Miff, or she's worried about how Miff will be when she comes round, or she's distracted by the babies.

On the way to the staffroom, Emma stoops forward, holding her bump. There's an audible pop. 'My waters,' she gasps. 'They've broken.'

I don't know whether to attend to Emma or Miff first. I decide on the latter, lowering Miff onto a Vetbed beside the sofa and balancing a drip bag on a stool before returning to rescue Emma who's leaning with her back against the wall, beads of sweat rolling down her forehead, and crying out.

'My babies – they're on their way,' she groans. 'This feels wrong . . .'

'Hey, everything will be fine. Come and sit with Miff.' I hold Emma's arm and help her into the staffroom before grabbing a towel and spreading it across the sofa. 'Sit down, Em,' I say. I don't know how Miff's managed it, still drunk from the anaesthetic and with her eyes sewn shut, possible brain damage and the hindrance of a lampshade collar, but she's on her end of the sofa with her head resting on the arm.

I grab my mobile from my bag where I left it on the side when I came in, and dial for an ambulance. We've had one baby born at the practice, Lynsey's last one – named after Frances. It isn't a maternity unit, and I don't want any more, especially vulnerable and premature twins.

'The ambulance is on its way,' I say, holding Emma's hand. She gives my fingers a squeeze, forcing the blood out of them, then won't let go as a contraction takes hold of her in a pythonesque grip. As I dial Ben's mobile number one-handed, I count the minutes before the next contraction. They are too close together for comfort. I think these babies could arrive very soon, possibly before the ambulance if there's much traffic. I console myself with the thought that there shouldn't be very much at this time of night, or day. I've lost track of time . . .

Ben's mobile is switched off. I leave two messages on his voicemail in the hope he'll pick them up.

'Emma, where did you say Ben was?'

'I don't know.' Emma bites her lip as if trying to remember. 'He's in Plymouth. He's probably in the car. He doesn't always hear his mobile over the radio.'

'He should be home soon then?' I cross my fingers, hoping Ben will call back, as I contact Shannon to ask her to come in and look after Miff, because I can't leave her as she is. She needs to be monitored. If her breathing deteriorates, she'll need urgent attention. I'm beginning to regret not putting that chest drain in.

Shannon arrives within minutes, wrapped up in not one, but two, hoodies, fingerless gloves, a scarf and faux Ugg boots.

'Is it snowing?' I ask her.

'It's stopped. What we have had hasn't settled.' Shannon turns to Emma, but Emma appears to be in a world of her own.

'Don't worry, Shan,' I say. 'The ambulance should be here at any moment.'

Shannon goes over to Miff and squats down in front of her.

'Miff, your poor eyes. Where are they? Maz, have you taken them out?'

'They're safely tucked up behind her eyelids. She was attacked on the Green. Another dog grabbed her by the scruff of the neck and shook her, making her eyes pop out of the sockets. Hopefully, she'll be fine. Are you happy to stay here? You aren't supposed to be keeping an eye on your mum?'

'Yes, and no. Everything's cool with her diabetes now. She hasn't had a hypo for at least three months.'

'She was looking pretty trim when I last saw her.' I check my watch. Where is the ambulance? Emma needs help.

'Maz, I'm bleeding,' she mutters. Her face has no colour. Her lips are pale. I don't like it. She's shivering and going into shock. If Emma was one of my patients, I would be preparing to go in.

Shannon looks at me, her eyes wide with concern.

'It's all right. You look after Miff. I'll see to Emma.' I've never been so happy to hear a siren as I am now, or to see the lights flashing up from the car park outside, but it isn't over yet. I won't be able to relax until Emma is in hospital with her babies safely delivered. I hold that image in my head: Emma with her twins. The alternatives are too painful to bear.

'I haven't got my bag,' Emma says, when we're in the ambulance at last.

'You don't need a bag.'

'It has all my things in it, music and a sponge.'

'Is the sponge for mopping your brow, or Ben's?'

'It might have to be yours, if he doesn't arrive in time,' she says, in a moment of lucidity.

'Don't worry about it, Emma. I'll fetch it later.'

Emma is worrying about her bag. I find myself

378

beginning to worry about the wedding. It is as if it is fated, as if it isn't meant to be . . .

'Where is Ben? Something must have happened to him.'

'Emma, stop worrying about Ben. He'll catch up with us in time. And anyway, he can look after himself. You have to concentrate on you and the babies.'

'Don't leave me, Maz.'

'As if,' I say, forcing a smile.

When we arrive at the hospital, we are whisked away to the maternity unit. Emma lies on a trolley, a drip in her hand, blood taken for crossmatching for a transfusion. She's been scanned and the babies' heartbeats are being monitored on a machine at her side. One of the heartbeats is steady. The other is gradually rising.

There is talk of haemorrhage and foetal distress with the consultant, and discussion over who is Emma's next of kin, and all the time I'm watching the twins' heartbeats and thinking, it's time to go in and get those babies out.

'She needs a Caesarean,' I cut in, while the consultant in his dicky bow and short-sleeved shirt procrastinates.

He gives me a weary, what-the-hell-do-you-know look.

'I'm a vet,' I say. 'So is Emma. We all know that if those babies aren't born very soon . . . Well, I don't have to tell you what the outcome will be.'

'Let's get her into theatre,' he says smoothly. 'GA. There's not time for an epidural.'

'Don't leave me,' Emma repeats, and I walk briskly alongside the trolley.

'I'll be here.' She's my best, my dearest friend. My chest is tight. I feel completely helpless, especially when the hospital staff refuse to let me stay with her until she's had her anaesthetic. I'm not afraid of losing the twins any more. What I'm deeply afraid of, is that I'm losing Emma.

I watch the doors close behind her, and pace the corridor.

'Maz, where is she?'

I turn to find Ben right beside me, his suit creased and his tie undone.

'In theatre,' I say. 'An emergency Caesarean.'

'There was an accident. The traffic . . . How long's she been in there?'

'A while.' I wish I could be more exact.

'I'm going to find someone to speak to.' Ben pushes through the doors that are marked 'No Entry', and I remember that he's a doctor as well as Emma's husband and has contacts within the hospital.

I have to wait alone, and it's the longest wait of my life.

I go outside to call Alex.

'Where are you?' he says.

'At the hospital. Emma's gone in for an emergency Caesarean.'

'Oh no . . . Maz, that's . . . I don't know what to say, except she's in good hands.'

'She was haemorrhaging and one of the babies was in distress. Alex, this is hideous.' I start to cry.

'Shall I come over and wait with you? I can leave the children with Mother.'

I think for a moment. I'd love to have Alex here. I could do with a hug, but I'd forgotten he'd got all three children with him tonight.

'They're all up,' Alex says ruefully. 'They're too excited . . .' His voice trails off. I know what he's thinking. The wedding. What does that matter now?

'Stay with them,' I decide.

'Are you sure?'

'I'm sure.'

'Keep in touch then, Maz. If you need me, you know I'll be straight over.'

'Alex,' I begin. 'Do you think . . .?'

'I won't do anything about the wedding,' he says, on the same wavelength as me. 'It isn't until eleven tomorrow morning. It's only nine now. A lot could happen before then.'

'Thanks, darling.'

'Emma and the babies will be fine.' Alex is trying to reassure me, but I pick up on the catch in his voice. 'Call me as soon as you have any news. Call me whenever you like.'

When I return to the corridor, scenes of good and bad times with Emma flash into my brain, like a series of YouTube clips. How we met over a dead greyhound in the dissection room at vet school. Endless nights talking over glasses of cheap wine about life, the universe and boyfriends, past, present and future. Long hot summer days on the Backs, one garden party after another. Punting on the river and losing the picnic, Pimm's and pole to an ambush of fellow vet students on another punt.

Our graduation ceremony in the marquee on the lawns in front of the vet school, fooling about in our formal gowns. The day we sat in the Copper Kettle in Talyton and Emma persuaded me to locum at Otter House. The day she lost baby Heather, and how I wasn't able to support her in the way I should have done, because I was scared to tell her I was pregnant with George.

I cross my fingers and my toes for luck. It's a ridiculous superstition, but it is all I have left.

Chapter Twenty-two

White Wedding

'Ben!' Everything stops when I see him emerge into the corridor in a gown that's slipped off one shoulder, like a green toga. His expression is serious. 'Any news?'

He walks up to me, his eyes light up and he smiles, and my body seems to fold with relief.

'Emma's all right,' I say, 'and the twins . . .?'

'They're all out of immediate danger.' Ben steps into my outstretched arms for a hug.

'That's fantastic. I've been so worried.' I can't leave until not only has Ben told me that Emma is safe, but I have seen her with my own eyes. 'Can I see her? Ben, please.' When he hesitates, I continue, 'You're the doctor – you can let me in to see them just for a minute.'

'It'll be a while yet, three to four hours – Emma's in Recovery. She had a general anaesthetic.'

'I don't mind. I'll wait for as long as it takes.' I wipe my eyes with a tissue. 'Well? Aren't you going to tell me about the babies?'

'Emma and I are the proud parents of two wonderful little girls. I'm a dad at last.'

'Have they got names? How much do they weigh?'

'I'll let Emma tell you.' Ben grins. 'She'll be furious if I let on first.'

'Congratulations, Ben.'

'I'll be back,' he says.

I call Alex to give him the update. I'm relieved, excited and over the moon.

'I'll come and pick you up,' he says.

'I'm going to stay until Emma's recovered from the anaesthetic. I need to see her and the babies.'

'Maz, you're sounding broody,' Alex says lightly.

'Anyway, I'm not supposed to see you now until the wedding.'

'We're going ahead then?' It's the middle of the night, yet I hear Alex talking to his daughter. 'We're good to go, Lucie.'

'The wedding is on!' I hear her exclaim. 'We thought we were going to be very disappointed, didn't we? I'll go and tell Humpy.'

'No, not now. Let Humpy have her beauty sleep.'

'But, but, but—'

I picture Lucie springing up and down on the balls of her feet.

'No buts,' Alex says. 'If you aren't in bed in five minutes, I'll have your dress made into a rug for Shezza.'

'You haven't seen Lucie's dress, have you?' I say.

'No,' Alex says, but I can tell from the tone of his voice that he's fibbing. Smiling to myself, I let it go.

Three hours later, at half past one in the morning, Ben returns to show me to the maternity ward where Emma is in bed in a side room. The babies are lying on their backs in plastic cots, swaddled in white blankets, just the tops of their heads, that are barely covered by

384

a fuzz of brown hair, and their closed eyes and noses, visible.

'Em, how are you?' I walk to the bed and take the hand she offers. She's on a drip, a blood transfusion.

'I'd like to say I feel fab,' she says quietly, 'but I feel like . . . rubbish, to be truthful.' Her eyes glitter, her face with little more colour than the sheets. She looks longingly towards her babies. 'I'm scared to hold them just yet. I'm still under the influence . . . How's Miff?'

'Shannon's looking after her. Don't worry about Miff. You must concentrate on yourself and those beautiful babies.' It's strange, but a wave of maternal yearning and a touch of envy washes through me. 'Can I have a cuddle?'

'Of course,' Emma says. I glance towards Ben.

'I'm not sure we should wake them,' he says, and I realise he's speaking as a dad, not a doctor now. I recognise the uncertainty in his voice. It's all very well knowing the theory of how to bring up a baby, but when it comes to the practical . . .

I pick one baby out of her cot. Ben lifts the other into his arms. I have the briefest hold of the baby, smelling her eggy, newborn scent as I touch my nose to the soft new skin on her forehead. I place her into Emma's arms as she lies on the bed.

'I don't know what to do, how to hold her,' she says, but she's smiling now.

'Practice makes perfect,' I say. 'Have you chosen their names yet?'

'Lydia and Elena,' she says.

'Which one is which?'

'I'm not sure . . .' Emma unwraps the baby she's holding and examines her neck. 'This is Lydia – she has a birthmark.'

'Are they identical then, apart from the birthmark, I mean?'

'They aren't, but they're pretty similar,' says Ben.

Lydia stretches out one tiny arm with an even tinier hand and fingers, and yawns.

'She is gorgeous,' I say. 'They both are.'

'Mum would have loved to have met them,' Emma begins.

'She would have been very proud of you.'

'Sometimes I think I can hear her voice, telling me what to do.' Emma smiles tearfully. 'And what she's telling me now, Maz, is that you have to get yourself out of here. Go home and get some sleep so you're ready for the big day.'

'But what about you? Will you be all right?'

'Ben's here now. Go on,' she repeats. 'It's the bride's prerogative to be late, but don't keep everyone in suspense any longer. Especially Alex.' She hesitates. 'There was a time when I disapproved of you two getting together, but he's a good guy, in his own way, and he makes you happy. You make each other happy. So, Maz, go. I'll be here when you get back from your honeymoon. Well, hopefully not here exactly, but at home with Ben and my babies.'

'Thanks, Em. I'll see you soon though. We aren't flying until Boxing Day.'

'I almost forgot,' she says. 'I bought you a present for the wedding, something blue. It should be with the dress, in a bag from Aurora's shop.'

'Thank you.' I kiss her cheek before I leave. 'Make sure you look after yourself and those babies of yours. Don't worry about anything else.'

'What about Will?' Emma says, half teasing.

'Forget about Will. He knows what he's doing at last. He's found his feet. I'll see you soon.'

'You bet. Make sure you bring the piccies as soon as you can.'

Ben walks me to the exit of the maternity ward. 'Thank you, Maz,' he says quietly. 'I don't know what would have happened if—'

'Sh. You can always rely on a vet. They're better than any doctor.'

'I have to say I'm pretty glad you didn't decide to operate.'

'I would have done if I'd had to.'

'I have no doubt that you would. Go on, Maz. All the best for the wedding, and I'm sorry Emma and I can't make it.'

'I'll save you a cupcake.'

'Go!' Ben says, almost pushing me out into the corridor. 'Hurry, or we won't be the only ones to miss out on the wedding.'

It's half past two. I text Alex to say that all's well, then call a taxi to take me back to Talyton St George, deciding to head for Otter House. I don't want to disturb Sophia at the Manor – the dogs would go wild if I turned up in the middle of the night. I don't want to see Alex either. Well, I do. There's nothing I'd like more, but it's supposed to be unlucky for the groom to see his bride on the night before the wedding, so I restrain myself. By going to the practice, I can check on Miff and let Emma know how she is.

When I arrive, Miff is up on her feet, sniffing around for breakfast, apparently unfazed that she can't see with her eyelids sewn shut. Someone – Shannon, I assume – has decorated the front of her cage with tinsel. I text Emma an update before I retire for a quick snooze on the sofa in the staffroom. I don't know about Sophia, but I need some beauty sleep. My face in the rear-view mirror of the taxi reminded me of the Bride of Godzilla.

I'd set the alarm on my mobile for seven so I could be at the Manor for the wedding breakfast Sophia's planned for me and the children at eight, but it's eight fifteen before I wake up. I check my phone. There are several voicemail messages from Sophia.

I call her back.

'Maz, where are you? I've been frantic.'

'I'm sorry. I didn't realise what the time was.'

'Just tell me,' Sophia goes on, 'is there going to be a wedding today, or not? Only it could be that you're backing orf.'

I am getting cold feet, but not in the way Sophia believes. It's chilly in the staffroom without a blanket or duvet. 'Sophia, I'm getting married. Today.' My life is about to change for ever: Ms Harwood to Mrs Fox-Gifford the Younger.

'You shouldn't have worried.'

'But I do. You do make rather a habit of getting yourself lost. I'll never forget the day you went missing in the flood.'

'Alex knows where I am. Roughly, anyway,' I say. 'I've been in touch with him.'

'You haven't seen him, have you? Really, Maz. I thought the idea was to keep you apart until you meet at the altar. It's traditional.'

If she's such a stickler for tradition, I dread to think what Sophia will make of the cake.

'So where have you been?'

'I would have contacted you to let you know, but I assumed Alex would have been in touch.' It occurs to me that Sophia could just as easily have walked across from the Manor to the Barn to see Alex herself.

'Alexander sent the children over first thing, and went off to Stewart's to get ready. I didn't get to speak to him – I was finishing orf the horses.' Sophia sighs. 'In a way, it's a blessing that the National was cancelled. It might have been too much.'

'There's always next year,' I say. 'I've been at the hospital with Emma. We had a few anxious moments. The twins arrived early and in rather a rush.'

'Oh? Are they all well?'

'Emma's lost a lot of blood and the twins are small, but out of danger.'

'That's good news then. Where was Dr Mackie?'

'He was delayed getting back to Talyton. He's with them now, though. Sophia, the wedding is on.'

'Maz, let's think this through.'

'There's nothing to think about. I said, the wedding is on.'

'Logistics, dear Maz. It's like organising Pony Club camp. Have you got time to get back to the Manor, or should I bring everything into town? You can shower and change at Otter House, and Maria can come and do your hair there. It would save half an hour or so. You're way behind, according to your schedule.'

I printed out copies of the wedding planner and gave one to Sophia.

'Eight a.m. The bride's breakfast – champagne and scrambled eggs. You've missed out on that. I know, I'll ask Lucie to bring a basket of eggs. We'll meet you at Otter House. Don't move!' Eventually, Sophia turns up at Otter House with the children and Maria in tow. In the process of texting Alex to let him know that everything is back on track for the wedding, I discover an update from Jennie with a photo of the cake set up ready for the reception.

I show it to Sophia who, as I predicted, wrinkles her nose.

'That isn't a cake, Maz. They're ordinary, everyday buns.'

'They're cupcakes, and Jennie's decorated them with our initials, A and M, in red, green and gold. I had to cancel the order for the fruit cake. When I reordered, I had a change of heart.'

'Well,' Sophia sighs resignedly, 'you've always been a bit of a one for rebelling.'

Will lets me shower in the flat before we congregate in the staffroom where Sophia cooks chewy scrambled eggs in the microwave and burns the toast. I end up drinking champagne on an empty stomach while Maria does my hair. I don't mind. I'm not hungry.

I admire Sophia, how she's found the strength to carry on after losing Old Fox-Gifford and find some joy in her life. She has kept it together somehow. I look at her now, dressed in a polo-neck and slacks, her hair stiffly set.

She's brought the dress and all the accessories, and umbrellas in case it should snow, or rain, for the photographs. She's also brought the three children and their clothes. I hope she's remembered to bring her own.

To think I didn't want her anywhere near my wedding at the beginning. As it's turned out, I couldn't have done without her.

'Thank you, Sophia,' I say.

'It's nothing. It's good to be needed.' She sorts through the pageboy outfits – they are very simple, trousers, waistcoat and tie and a sweater if they need one. 'Come on, Sebastian. You have to wear the tie – Daddy will be wearing one.' She makes sure Seb is dressing himself before returning to me.

'There's a present here from Emma.' She hands me a tiny bag. I open it up.

'It's a blue garter,' I say, laughing. 'Izzy and Shannon bought me one too.'

'You'd better put them both on, before I help you into the dress. And then I have something borrowed for you . . . My fox fur. I've watched how you covet it.'

'Er no, Sophia. You've got it wrong—' I begin.

Sophia's eyes sparkle with amusement, and I realise, with relief, that she's joking. She has her reflective moments, but she's becoming quite the merry widow.

'If you could accept a loan from me, I have a ring – it was my mother's and I wore it on my wedding day. Don't worry, it's very discreet. I'll show it to you.' She takes a small box from her handbag and opens it in front of me. Inside, glitters a simple gold ring set with three rubies.

I remove it carefully and slip it onto my right hand.

'It's lovely, Sophia,' I say. 'Thank you.'

To my surprise, Sophia kisses my cheek. 'I hope you and Alexander will be as happy as Fox-Gifford and I were. Happier, in fact,' she goes on, with a wry smile.

At last we are ready, or as ready as we ever will be, and I prepare to leave the practice as a single woman for the very last time. Sophia and the boys take the first turn in the car, a cream Bentley decorated with white ribbons. Lucie and I take the second trip, agreeing on the way that the journey which should have been from the Manor to the church is way too short. I know I'm running late now, but I need time to collect myself. It's all been too much of a rush, and I'm ridiculously nervous.

The driver drops us at the gate of the churchyard. Lucie fetches my bouquet and her posy from where Bridget has left the flowers in the porch of the church, while I straighten the dress and tweak the veil.

'How do I look?' I say, taking a step back.

'Very pretty, Maz.'

'So do you, Lucie.' The evergreen leaves, roses and berries in her headdress and posy complement her scarlet dress. For warmth, she wears a fluffy bolero cardigan. She hands the bouquet, a cascade of evergreen and red roses, back to me, and we walk along the path together, between the gravestones inscribed with the history of the families of Talyton St George. The sky above us is dark with cloud, as if it might snow at any minute, but I don't care about the weather. I can't wait to get inside the church.

Sophia is waiting inside the porch with the boys. Frances and Lenny are here too.

'I'm sorry to interrupt on your big day,' Frances says, looking flustered, 'but I have to know what the news is about Emma. I've heard she's in hospital.'

'She's a little fragile,' I say, happy to put Frances out of her misery, 'but she's going to be fine.'

'And the twins?'

'They're doing well too. Ben texted me to give me an update. They're very small, but not unexpectedly so.'

'Thank goodness.' Frances touches her throat.

'They've called them Lydia and Elena. They look like Emma.'

'I should think so. They'd be funny little mites if they took after their dad,' Frances says fondly.

'Well, neither of them have all that much hair yet,' I say, with a smile.

'Frances, we mustn't keep the groom waiting any longer,' Lenny says, taking her hand. 'All the best, Maz.'

'Thank you.'

The church is packed – even the extra seats set up at the back are occupied. There are arrangements of Christmas foliage and flowers, holly with scarlet berries, ivy, lilies and roses along the nave and at the altar. I notice, too, that there are lots of hats.

The organist strikes up the wedding march. It's a hurried version, more of a run than a march, but I'm tempted to speed down the aisle anyway, because I'm so late. Lucie, to my right, keeps me to a snail's pace as she imagines befits the occasion. Sebastian walks along in front, breaking into a trot at the end when he sees his daddy.

'Daddy, she's here – your runaway bride,' he calls, at which there is a ripple of laughter from the congregation. 'You thought she wasn't coming.'

George, holding on to my left hand, stops to smile at one of the mums and tots from Toddler Group halfway along, and I realise that I'm going to miss Emma being here in more ways than one.

Luckily, Sophia and Lynsey rescue me, collecting up the three children and taking them aside.

'Thanks,' I whisper, before stepping aside for a moment to greet my mother and brother with a hug. Fifi, who is standing beside her, looks more like the mother-of-the-bride than the mother-of-the-bride does. My mother is wearing a black mini-dress with a tight-fitting red jacket that reminds me of the gear a biker would wear. I'm pleased to see her, though.

I'm glad she could make it, in spite of the bad weather.

'You look wonderful,' she says quietly. 'I'm so relieved you turned up – I thought you were going to miss out on the opportunity of a lifetime.' I can't help wondering if she's about to embarrass me in front of everyone – she's always been good at that. I frown as she goes on, 'One day, you'll be lady of the manor. Think of that, Amanda. You've done very well for yourself. I'm so proud of you.'

'I'll catch up with you later, Mum.' I kiss her on the cheek and make my way to where Alex is waiting for me, his eyes apparently fixed on the angels in the stained-glass window in the wall beyond the altar and choir stalls.

'Alex?' I say quietly. 'I made it.'

He turns and the world seems to stand still. I lift my veil – against protocol perhaps – but I find I prefer not to look at my bridegroom through a haze of tulle. Alex looks me up and down, before gazing into my eyes and mouthing, 'Maz, you are beautiful . . .'

'So are you,' I murmur. Dressed in a suit and tie, Alex looks more handsome than ever.

'I love you.' He takes my hand and leads me to the altar where the vicar is waiting. Stewart moves up behind us.

I think I can hear the words, 'unconventional' and 'not in my day', being uttered among the assembled crowd, our friends and family, but I'm glad I chose not to be given away.

The vicar welcomes us and introduces the wedding service, before making the declaration, 'First, I am required to ask anyone present who knows a reason why these persons may not lawfully marry . . .'

'Did he say "awfully"?' I hear Lucie pipe up.

'Sh, darling,' says Sophia.

'Hurry up and get married, Daddy,' Seb joins in. 'I'm hungry.'

'Where my Iss–?' says George, apparently missing his toy tractor.

'Decorum, children,' Sophia says. 'One more squeak out of any of you, I'll take you outside and you will miss it.'

'Thank you,' the vicar says kindly. 'Can I go on now and get these people married before Christmas Eve, before Santa starts out on his rounds?'

'Yes,' Seb says, 'otherwise we won't have any presents.'

I glance behind me to find three children with Sophia, mouths firmly shut.

The vicar completes the first part of the declaration, and in spite of the fact that I know there is no impediment to our marriage, I hold my breath until the vicar continues.

'Alexander Abelard Fox-Gifford, will you take Amanda Harwood to be your wife? Will you love her, comfort her, honour and protect her, and forsaking all others, be faithful to her as long as you both shall live?'

There's a long pause. Lucie, caught up in the excitement of the day, can't help herself. 'Say yes, Daddy,' she calls out. 'You have to say yes, right now.'

'All right, Lucie.' Alex turns back to me, and gives me a small, apologetic smile.

'As long as you both shall live . . .' the vicar repeats to help him out.

'I will,' Alex says, his voice gruff with emotion.

When it's my turn, I can hardly speak. 'I will . . .'

After the collect and sermon, we sing a hymn, 'All Creatures Great and Small'. I glance at Alex as he sings

395

out loud and clear, and wonder if he is remembering how we sang the same hymn at his father's funeral. It's one of the reasons we chose it for our wedding – as well as the obvious link to us being vets, and the fact that we were confident that the organist could play it – to honour Old Fox-Gifford's memory.

'Is it finished now?' Seb says, as the final chords fade away.

'Sh!' says Sophia. 'They have to say their vows and Daddy must give Maz the ring.'

Alex and I repeat our vows after the vicar.

'I, Maz, take you, Alex, to be my husband, to have and to hold from this day forward; for better, for worse, for richer, for poorer . . .' My chest aches with joy.

'The ring,' the vicar says. 'Stewart, you do have the ring?'

I'm aware that Stewart is patting the pockets of his suit.

'You haven't lost it?' Alex says worriedly.

'Course not,' Stewart smiles. He places the ring on the vicar's prayer book. The vicar says a few words, then passes the ring to Alex.

'Maz,' he whispers. 'Your hand. The other one.'

I hold out my left hand, and Alex slides the ring partway onto my finger.

'Maz, I give you this ring as a sign of our marriage. With my body I honour you, all that I am I give to you, and all that I have I share with you.' Alex slides the ring the rest of the way, and my eyes fill with tears.

I promised myself I wouldn't cry, not in front of everyone, but it's too late. I can't hold back.

'Oh, Maz,' Alex says, anxiety behind his smile. 'Don't cry. I thought I was making you happy.'

'You are. You do . . .' I am the happiest person in the universe.

'A tissue for the bride.' Lucie darts between us. 'It's from Humpy.'

'Thank you,' I say, embarrassed. 'That's very kind.'

'Are you all right to continue, Maz?' the vicar asks.

I nod as I wipe my eyes. Alex takes the mascara-smudged tissue from me and sticks it in Stewart's pocket.

The vicar addresses the congregation, finishing with, 'I therefore proclaim them to be husband and wife. Alex, you may kiss the bride.'

Alex leans towards me.

'They're gonna k—'

'Sh, Sebastian.'

Alex wraps his arms around me and presses his lips to mine, at which the congregation erupts into applause. It's a chaste kiss with the promise of more to come . . .

When Alex and I step outside the church some time later, hand in hand, and having signed the register, I assume that there are rose petals swirling down from the dark sky. The assembled crowd are clapping again, though, not throwing confetti.

'It's snow,' someone shouts.

'It's a white wedding, after all,' Stewart says drily.

'Hey, stop casting aspersions on my lovely wife,' Alex teases.

'Thank you for upholding my honour, my husband,' I smile. It's going to take a while to get used to calling him that. My husband. My darling husband. I glance towards our son who is copying Seb, trying to catch the snowflakes in his mouth.

The snowflakes gleam in George's hair.

''No,' he says, pointing at it.

'No,' says Lucie. 'It's snow.'

'No!' George yells. 'It 'no.'

'Can we make a snowman?' says Seb.

'Not yet. Faster, faster, faster,' Lucie shouts up at the clouds.

'Sh, Lucie,' says Sophia.

'Do you think Granpa's watching us?' she says.

Sophia touches Lucie's shoulder. 'He'll be up there, keeping us company on Maz and your daddy's special day.'

'It was very sad when he died,' says Lucie.

'He was not a well man,' Sophia says. 'I told him he'd go before I did.' Though sad, she appears to find a sense of satisfaction in being right – unsurprisingly perhaps, when Old Fox-Gifford never let her have that opportunity when he was alive.

'Daddy,' Lucie says, changing the subject, 'did you know, by the way, you still have the labels on the bottom of your shoes?'

Stewart bows his head, shoulders quivering. It was him, I know it. Alex's shoes are an old pair, polished up to look brand new. Stewart must have added the labels for a prank. I'm dreading the best man's speech – in the nicest possible way.

'I hate to wreck the schedule,' Stewart says, as the photographer appears with his camera, 'but these good people are going to get wet and cold, waiting here for hundreds of photos. I suggest we do them all, apart from the ones of the bride and groom and close family, at the reception. Is that all right with you, Maz?'

The snow is coming down harder, swirling around the streetlights outside the churchyard that have switched on early due to the overcast conditions.

Although the paths are clear, there is a thin covering of snow across the grass and the gravestones, enough for the children who are running around to leave footprints.

'One more change in the wedding plans will make no difference at all. It's fine with me.' I glance at Alex. I'm not cold.

On the way to the Talymill Inn, I sit beside Alex in the back of the Bentley with his arm around my shoulder, watching the snow sweeping past, blanketing the hedgerows and verges along the lane to the pub.

'I reckon we're going to get snowed in,' I say.

'It doesn't matter. I've booked a room so we can stay and spend our wedding night alone together.' Alex chuckles. 'The best laid plans of mice and men . . . It looks as if we could be spending it with the majority of the population of Talyton.'

'We'll have to make the most of it then. An all-night party could be a lot of fun.'

'As long as we're home in time for Christmas.'

'Before then. I haven't actually had time to do any shopping yet. The only present I've bought is George's. I haven't got you anything, Alex.'

'Mrs Fox-Gifford, I don't care. I don't need anything new.' Alex kisses my cheek. 'All my Christmases have come at once.'

As I lean in to him, my husband and happily-ever-after, a mobile vibrates in his jacket pocket. I raise an eyebrow. 'Who on earth is that? On our wedding day!'

Alex checks the caller's number and looks at me sheepishly. 'I said Justin could call me if he wasn't sure about anything.'

'Go on then,' I sigh. 'You'd better take it.'

It turns out that Alex's new assistant has locked himself out of the surgery up at the Manor. Alex tells him how to break in without a key.

'Sorted,' he says. 'I'm sorry, Maz . . . but you know how it is.'

'I do,' I murmur, tilting my face to kiss him back very gently on the lips. 'It's a vet's life and I love it. I wouldn't have it any other way.'

Acknowledgements

I would like to thank my agent, Laura Longrigg at MBA, my editor, Gillian Holmes, and the rest of the wonderful team at Arrow Books for their enthusiasm and support.

Thanks, too, to Tamsin and Will, my family and friends for their insight.

ALSO AVAILABLE IN ARROW

Trust Me I'm a Vet

Cathy Woodman

City vet Maz Harwood has learned the hard way that love and work don't mix. So when an old friend asks her to look after her Devonshire practice for six months, Maz decides running away from London is her only option.

But country life is trickier than she feared. It's bad enough she has to deal with comatose hamsters, bowel-troubled dogs and precious prize-winning cats, without having to contend with the disgruntled competition and a stubborn neighbour who's threatening to sue over an overzealous fur cut!

Worse still, she discovers Otter House Veterinary Clinic needs mending as much as her broken heart. Thank goodness there's an unsuitable distraction, even if he is the competition's deliciously dashing son . . .

Praise for Cathy Woodman's previous novels:

'Funny, truthful and original . . . I loved this book'
Jill Mansell

'Her style has a lightness of touch that can bring a smile, but also poignant moments that can bring a tear to the eyes'
Writing Magazine

arrow books

ALSO AVAILABLE IN ARROW

Must Be Love

Cathy Woodman

It must be love. What other reason could there be for city vet Maz's contentment with her new country life? The vet's practice where she's a partner with her best friend Emma is thriving, and so is her relationship with the gorgeous Alex Fox-Gifford.

But then circumstances force Emma to take a break from the practice, and Maz's life spirals out of control. What with working all hours trying to keep things going, fending off insults from Alex's parents, keeping one eye on the lusty locum – who's causing havoc amongst the village girls – and dealing with Emma's precarious mental state, it won't take much to upset the apple cart. So when she gets some unwelcome news, only time will tell whether Maz and Alex's love can withstand the fallout.

Praise for Cathy Woodman:

'Funny, truthful and original . . . I loved this book' Jill Mansell

'Woodman's warmth and wit are set to make her the next big thing in rural romance.' *Daily Record*

arrow books

The Sweetest Thing

Cathy Woodman

If only everything was as simple as baking a cake . . .

Jennie Copeland thought she knew the recipe for a happy life: marriage to her university sweetheart, a nice house in the suburbs and three beautiful children. But when her husband leaves her, she is forced to find a different recipe. And she thinks she's found just what she needs: a ramshackle house on the outskirts of Talyton St George, a new cake-baking business, a dog, a horse, chickens . . .

But life in the country is not quite as idyllic as she'd hoped, and Jennie can't help wondering whether neighbouring farmer Guy Barnes was right when he told her she wouldn't last the year.

Or perhaps the problem is that she's missing one vital ingredient to make her new life a success. Could Guy be the person to provide it?

Praise for Cathy Woodman:

'Funny, truthful and original . . . I loved this book' Jill Mansell

'Woodman's warmth and wit are set to make her the next big thing in rural romance.' *Daily Record*

arrow books

All I Want for Christmas

Amy Silver

Twelve days and counting . . .

It is Bea's first Christmas with her baby son, and this year she's determined to do *everything* right. But there is still so much to do: presents need to be bought; the Christmas menu needs refining; her café, The Honey Pot, needs decorating; and she's invited the whole neighbourhood to a party on Christmas Day. She really doesn't have time to get involved in two new people's lives, let alone fall in love . . .

When Olivia gets knocked over in the street, however, Bea can't help bringing her into The Honey Pot and getting to know her. Olivia's life is even more hectic than her own, and with her fiancé's entire family over from Ireland for Christmas, she shouldn't be lingering in the cosy warmth of Bea's café. Chloe, on the other hand, has nowhere else to go. Her affair with a married man has alienated her friends, and left her lonelier than ever.

But Christmas is a magical time, and in the fragrant atmosphere of The Honey Pot, anything can happen: new friends can be made, hearts can heal, and romance can finally blossom . . .

arrow books

One Minute to Midnight

Amy Silver

Nicole Blake's New Year Resolutions, 1990:
1 Start keeping a journal;
2. Lose half a stone;
3. Kiss Julian Symonds

If there are two things Nicole can guarantee about New Years Eve it's that there are *always* fireworks and Julian Symonds is *always* there.

Since she was thirteen, no New Year has been complete without Jules. Through school, university and beyond, as friends come and go, Nic and Jules are at the centre of every party.

Until one year everything changes.

Now, as another New Year approaches, Nicole has bridges to build – with her husband Dom, with her best friend Alex, and with Aidan, the man who broke her heart.

Life is about to change again, and once the fireworks are over and the dust has settled, this time Nicole is determined it will be for the better.

arrow books

Summer of Love

Katie Fforde

Sian Bishop has only ever experienced one moment of recklessness – a moment that resulted in her beloved son Rory. It's not that she doesn't love the outcome of that wild night, but since then she has always taken the safe route. So when dependable, devoted Richard suggests a move to the beautiful English countryside, she leaves the hustle and bustle of the city behind, and throws herself into the picture-postcard cottage garden, her furniture restoration business and a new life in the country.

Until, one glorious summer's evening, Gus Berresford arrives in the village. One-time explorer and full-time heartbreaker, Gus is ridiculously exciting, wonderfully glamorous and completely inappropriate . . .

But anything can happen in a summer of love.

'A funny, fresh and lively read' *heat*

arrow books

A Perfect Proposal

Katie Fforde

It's time to live a little . . .

Sophie Apperly has spent her whole life pleasing others – but when she realises her family see her less as indispensable treasure and more as general dogsbody, she decides she's had enough. So when an old friend offers her the chance of a lifetime, she decides to swap Little England for the Big Apple, and heads off to the land of opportunity.

From the moment Sophie hits the bright lights of Manhattan she's determined to enjoy every minute of her big adventure. And when fate throws her together with Matilda, a spirited *grande dame* of New York society who invites her to Connecticut for Thanksgiving, she willingly accepts. English-born Matilda is delighted with her new friend – though her grandson Luke, undeniably attractive but infuriatingly arrogant, is anything but welcoming.

When Luke arrives in England a few weeks later, Sophie hardly expects him to seek her out. But Matilda has hatched some complicated plans of her own – and so Luke has a proposal to make . . .

Praise for Katie Fforde

'Great fun ... had me hooked to the end' *Daily Mail*

'A funny, fresh and lively read' *heat*

arrow books

Wedding Season

Katie Fforde

All you need is love . . .?

Sarah Stratford is a wedding planner hiding a rather inconvenient truth – she doesn't believe in love. Or not for herself, anyway. But as the confetti flutters away on the June breeze of yet another successful wedding she somehow finds herself agreeing to organise two more, on the same day and only two months away. And whilst her celebrity bride is all sweetness and light, her own sister soon starts driving her mad with her high expectations but very limited budget.

Luckily Sarah has two tried and tested friends on hand to help her. Elsa, an accomplished dress designer who likes to keep a very low profile, and Bron, a multi-talented hairdresser who lives with her unreconstructed boyfriend and who'd like to go solo in more ways than one. They may be very good at their work but romance doesn't feature very highly in any of their lives.

As the big day draws near all three women find that patience is definitely a virtue in the marriage game. And as all their working hours are spent preparing for the wedding of the year plus one, they certainly haven't got any time to even thinka bout love. Or have they?

'A funny, fresh and lively read' *heat*

arrow books

THE POWER OF READING

Visit the Random House website and get connected with information on all our books and authors

EXTRACTS from our recently published books and selected backlist titles

COMPETITIONS AND PRIZE DRAWS Win signed books, audiobooks and more

AUTHOR EVENTS Find out which of our authors are on tour and where you can meet them

LATEST NEWS on bestsellers, awards and new publications

MINISITES with exclusive special features dedicated to our authors and their titles

READING GROUPS Reading guides, special features and all the information you need for your reading group

LISTEN to extracts from the latest audiobook publications

WATCH video clips of interviews and readings with our authors

RANDOM HOUSE INFORMATION including advice for writers, job vacancies and all your general queries answered

Come home to Random House

www.randomhouse.co.uk